Forever Wild

By Jillian Neal

Forever Wild
Written by Jillian Neal
Cover Design by The Killion Group, Inc.
Edited by Chasity Jenkins-Patrick

This book is a work of fiction. Names, characters, places, and incidents
either are products of the author's imagination or are used fictitiously.
Any resemblance to actual persons, living or dead, events, or locales is
entirely coincident

Published by Realm Press
36 South Court Square
Suite 300
Newnan GA 30263
http://realmpress.net/

ISBN 978-1-940174-35-8
Library of Congress Control Number: 2016941567

First Edition

First Printing – July 2016

For Chasity

For believing in me then and helping me become who I am now.
For being there every step of the way.
Listening to me laugh and cry.
Talking me off ledges.
Putting up with my insanity.
And loving me through it all.

Not many authors are blessed with someone like you to hold their hand through the ups and downs. Not sure what I did right to end up with you, but I'd do it a thousand times over again. Thank you for all you do. I couldn't have done any of this without you.

Other Books by Jillian Neal

Camden Ranch
Coincidental Cowgirl
Rodeo Summer

Gypsy Beach
Gypsy Beach
Gypsy Love
Gypsy Heat
Gypsy Hope

The Gifted Realm
Within the Realm
Lessons Learned
Every Action
Rock Bottom
An Angel All His Own
All but Lost
The Quelling Tide

Table Of Contents

Chapter One

"She's a wild one, with an angel's face. She's a woman-child in a state of grace," sang loudly from Indie Harper as she flew up I-80 in her '68 Camaro Z28 in toreador red. Faith Hill sang on, so did Indie. *"She's a wild one, running free."* Her long, dark auburn hair whipped out the open windows. "Woohoo!" she chanted as she flew past the Nebraska state line. Oklahoma and Kansas were now behind her.

She was going home, and for all of the complications and shit sure to come from seeing her mother she couldn't wait to get there. At least that's what she kept telling herself. Nerves tingled up her spine, but she made a valiant effort to ignore them. This would be good. She hadn't been home since the Christmas before, over a year ago.

Her baby sister was getting married. She could endure her mother long enough to get her fix of Pleasant Glen, see her daddy, love on her sisters, and ride her horses. After that, she'd head back to Oklahoma City and get back to wrenching cars.

In a matter of moments, the scents of sweet corn and hay coupled with manure. The breathy memories filled her lungs. Her grin expanded. Had to be a Nebraskan cowgirl to get off on the smell of home.

Slowing as she came up behind a ranch truck hauling cattle, she listened to the radio DJ. "We're throwing it way, way back this Memorial Day weekend. That was Faith Hill's 'Wild One' from 1993. Up next we've got your farming report. You're listening to Husker's Radio KXNP."

Switching off the farming report, Indie frowned. "It's not way, way back. It wasn't *that* long ago." Okay so, maybe she wasn't exactly a woman-child anymore. Staring down 33 decidedly made her more woman than child. Glancing in the passenger seat, where she'd slung her duffle bags since her tool boxes and spare tires were in the trunk, the corner of that damned reunion invitation taunted her.

How the hell had she been out of high school for fifteen years? She could've sworn she was eighteen like two weeks ago. Leave it to Melony to follow their mother's orders and plan her wedding one weekend before the reunion, leaving Indie without a good reason not to attend. Indie adored her little sisters, but Melony's endless desire to make their mother happy galled her to no end.

Their daddy always said Indie got the portions of rebelliousness that were meant for her twin sisters, plus an extra shot. Grinning again, she floored the accelerator and shot around the truck, over the double-yellow line. An oncoming Pontiac laid on their horn. She whipped her Camaro back and flipped them off for good measure. God, it was good to be home.

Fifteen miles outside of Pleasant Glen, her car began its customary lurching clunk. She should've replaced the tires before she left, but she'd figured she had a few hundred miles left on them, and she'd switch them for the Hoosier CO6 radials she'd been eyeing when she got to her father's shop. The Goodyear E70's weren't a great match since she'd cut the quarter panels. Flats were something she was growing quite accustomed to. "Just couldn't wait 'til I made it to Daddy's, could you?" Sighing, she pulled off on the shoulder and hopped out.

Not in any way surprised that a truck pulled in behind her, she tried to hide her eye roll. She *was* in the land of well-bred cowboys, after all. Hauling her jack and wrench set out of her trunk, she didn't stop until her eyes landed on Grant Camden climbing out of his F-250.

Shit.

"Can I give you a hand, ma'am?" Concern thrummed in his tone. She lifted her head, and a broad grin spread across his face. "Indieanna Harper, is that really you, darlin'? My God, it's been a day or two since you showed up back here in the Glen, hadn't it? We missed you, girl. It's good to see ya." He scooped her up into an all-encompassing hug.

"More than a day or two. How are you?" Tension tightened in her throat as she hugged him back. So, maybe there was one other ginormous reason besides her daddy and her horses that Indie was looking forward to being back home.

"I'm good. I'm guessing you don't need my help with that tire, though."

Forcing a chuckle, she grinned. "I know it ain't in the Camden way of doing things to leave me here, so stand back and watch me work, cowboy."

"You got it." Grant held his hands up in surrender, a hearty laugh accompanying his broad grin.

When she rolled one of the spares she carried to the flat, she waggled her eyebrows. "Time me."

Still laughing, Grant checked his watch. "All right, go."

Letting the timer drive her, she whipped off the lug nuts, had the car jacked up, and the tire replaced in minutes. She lowered the car and tightened the nuts before standing. "How'd I do?"

"Seven minutes, fourteen seconds. Damn, girl, if Luke wouldn't lay me out flat when he beat the shit outta me, I'd propose." He winked at her.

And there it was. *Luke.* Her heart sped frantically. Luke Camden. She'd never been more than a friend to Grant, but his big brother Luke, well, there was enough history there to fill every textbook back at Pleasant Glen High. "You admitting your big brother could knock you on your ass, Grant Camden?"

"Don't tell him I said that out loud. He'd get way too much pleasure outta that."

The words *pleasure* and *Luke* rolled through her mind and sent a flash fire of heat spiraling down to her breasts. It didn't stop its collision course until it had taken up residence between her thighs. She'd been back home at least two-dozen times since she and Luke had ended their five-year relationship, when they were freshman at Nebraska-Lincoln. Every single time they were within a hundred miles of one another they sought each other like moths to a flame. She'd knock on his door late the last night of her typical weekend visit and spend several long, delicious hours allowing her body to be worshipped by his. God, it was like nothing else she'd ever experienced.

They never really talked about anything of any importance, never did much more than set his bed sheets on fire, reminisced a little, and promised to call and text more often. She'd wait on him to go to sleep, spend a few hours absorbing the heavenly contentment he offered just holding her in his arms, remind herself why she could never stay there with him, and then she'd run away again.

"Deal." Indie grinned. "How is Luke?" *Geez, anxious much, Indie?* She'd gone far too long without a tryst with him, and it was clearly getting to her.

"He's good. I'm guessing you're in for the wedding. You staying for the reunion, too?"

"Not sure yet. We'll see how long I go without wanting to pulling my mama's hair out and fileting the mayor."

Laughing again, Grant nodded his understanding. "Carolyn's got the whole damn state coming to this wedding. She's in her element, I'm assuming."

"Oh, I'm sure." Indie rolled her eyes. "Speaking of Nebraska's pearl-clutcher-in-chief, I better get to the mansion and get this over with. Tell Luke I can't wait to see him."

Grant smirked. "Sure thing. See ya 'round, Indie."

Climbing back in her car, she was left with nothing but memories that scalded her throat with regret. She'd followed Luke to college. Okay, so that had been his dream, not hers, but the way it had ended, God, what she wouldn't give to go back and … *And what, Indie? Luke Camden is too good for you, too stable, too secure, too … rancher.* He was tied to the land that was tied to the Glen, and that was far too many ties for Indie. She'd always be in love with Luke, but sometimes love wasn't enough. She couldn't stand Pleasant Glen, couldn't stand her own mother — who was married to the freaking mayor of the town she despised — and couldn't erase the past any more than she could ever settle down and become a rancher's wife.

***

"So, Indie's due back in town for Tuck and Melony's wedding. I'm figuring that's why you're dancin' around here like you gotta gnat in your sac. You change the sheets on your bed and clean up your shit or you figure it'll take her a day or two to come knocking on your door?" Austin Camden, Luke's little brother, laughed.

Luke rolled his eyes. "Fuck off, Austin."

"Oh, come on. Don't even act like you aren't playing the part of the three-balled tomcat in this situation. You two get so loud we all have a cigarette afterwards."

Even Luke's father, Ev, joined in the laughter over that. Luke slung another hay bale in the back of his truck. When Grant's truck pulled up, he knew things were only going to get worse. No one but his family and Indie's father knew of their late night trysts whenever she came back to the Glen. Since he shared his family's ranch with his parents, cousin, brothers, and sisters, it was next to impossible to have someone in his home without everyone knowing. The ranch was massive, yet somehow his family always knew when Indie's Camaro headed through the front gates.

Grant's shit-covered boots hit the dirt. Something had clearly happened. Grant looked far too pleased for Luke's liking.

"Never guess who I just ran into," he chuckled.

"Oh, I bet I can," Luke sighed. Every one of the 198 people that lived in Pleasant Glen had inquired as to the possibility of him and

4

Indie getting back together permanently, since everyone assumed she'd be in town longer this trip than she ever had before.

"Indie Harper had a flat out on Route 410. She was heading into town. I pulled over to see if she needed any help," Grant explained.

Luke grunted at the very idea of his Indie needing any help with a flat tire. It was preposterous.

"Yeah, yeah, I know, but I didn't know it was her at first. Anyway, girl changed that tire in under eight minutes. She's something else. When she was leaving, she said to tell you she couldn't *wait* to see you." He stuck the tip of his tongue between his teeth and laughed.

Luke stared his brother down. Grant was lucky they were related. Two days ago when Sloane and Ashley Patrick had droned on for the better part of a half-hour about how Indie was surely coming back to the Glen for Melony's wedding *and* their high school reunion, and how *great* it would be if Luke and Indie got back together in time for the reunion and she stayed this time, Luke had decided to place a well-aimed fist in the mouth of the next person that spoke Indie's name to him. Seeing as this was his brother, he only ground his teeth.

"I ain't pulling your chain, man. Those were her words. All I'm saying is you ain't over her, and apparently she can't *wait* to see you."

"I ain't deaf. I heard you the first time." Luke let that information tumble around in his head. At one time he'd known Indie the way the stacked lightning knew the mid-western storms, the way the ocean knew the shoreline's kiss, the way the Cottonwood trees sought the silt banks of Nebraskan streams — because they knew how to survive.

Awareness of her always sank in long before anyone had to tell him she was back in town. He could sense her presence long before he laid eyes on her beautiful body. His mouth watered as he considered every single thing he knew about Indieanna Harper. The taste of her musk, wild and ripe, the sweet spun sugar of her lips, the way she gasped on his first thrust, the raspberry heat of her nipples when he swirled his hungry tongue around their stiff peaks, the dark fire in her eyes when she wanted more. The way she came with a whimpered cry of his name.

"All right, both of ya. Leave him be," Luke's father commanded. "Austin, if you're taking your newest little one into Lincoln for that doctor's appointment, you need to get a shower. Grant, we still got a dozen heifers that ain't calved yet, and I'm getting worried. You and Brock go check 'em."

Luke was well aware that his brothers and cousin were being sent away so his father could join the throngs of people who had an opinion on how he should handle Indie's return. He made no effort to hide his eye roll. Clearly, no one in the Glen thought he had a brain. The fact that he'd graduated with a master's degree in veterinary medicine and took care of every animal in the local area clearly meant very little.

"Quit rolling your eyes and let me say my piece. You're nearly 33, son, and God knows I ain't gonna fuss about anything you and Indieanna Harper want to do, but I will say this: you've been in love with her since the first day of ninth grade. There hadn't ever been anyone else. You knew she was the one from the moment you saw her. That's how the Camden men work. You know that, too. So, it seems to me she's gonna be here for a few weeks. You're both gonna be in Tucker and Melony's wedding. Maybe you ought to take the opportunity the good Lord's seen fit to provide ya, and see if you can't make her amenable to staying this time."

"You really think I haven't thought of that?"

His father, his brothers, and the entire town of Pleasant Glen needed to butt the hell out. Yeah, he had a plan. Indie wasn't running away from him this time. He'd make her see that he could be everything she needed. He'd make up for her mother's constant disdain and the affair that had torn his baby completely apart. He'd make up for the hell this town had put her through, and most importantly he'd make up for being an idiot when he was nineteen. *'You keep me sane, Luke Camden, and I'll keep you wild'*. That was how they'd always worked until he'd dragged her to college with him. Somewhere she had no interest in being, while her life here fell completely apart. And then, to ice the cake of stupidity he'd baked, he'd begged his mother for his grandmother's engagement ring and had proposed. He'd put their entire relationship in a pressure cooker and had turned up the heat. Trying to tie Indie Harper down was the very last thing in the world she'd needed at nineteen years old. So much for keeping her sane. He'd done nothing but make her run. There was one thing it had taken him years to understand: without her wild soul, he had no sanity.

This time he'd show her how they were two sides of the same coin that couldn't exist apart. He'd keep his normally calm head on his shoulders and see if he couldn't bring a little sanity back into both of their lives, and then he'd show her just how wild she always made him. She always brought out his most primitive instincts, his savage soul, when she took him to bed. He'd prove to her that he never wanted to tame her wild being. He wanted to sate her in every possible way. There'd be no more caging her in. He knew better now. If she wanted to run this time, he'd fly with her.

As it stood, every single time she came knocking on his door, he inhaled her like a junkie too long without a fix. His body took over his brain. He rushed, desperate to absorb the seductive heat that clung to her curves like nothing he'd ever experienced before. This time he was going to take his time and show her that he'd learned a thing or two since they were a permanent fixture in the Glen. He'd drowned his sorrows in dozens of other women in the last fifteen years; none of them had any hopes of measuring up to Indie. Now he had to show her that he knew precisely how stoke her fires in a slow burn that would last forever.

"I figured you had. I just wanted you to know if your mama or I can help, we want to."

Guilt quelled a little of his ire. Tucker Kilroy, Luke's best friend and the guy marrying Indie's sister, had already offered his help, and so had his brothers and sisters. Hell, even Indie's daddy had vowed to do anything he could to help Luke talk Indie into moving back home. He begrudgingly admitted that everyone that had inquired about Indie's return to the Glen had, in one intrusive way or another, offered their assistance as well. That was the thing about living in a tiny ranching town. Everyone knew everything about everyone else. That was the part Indie hated most, but generally they did all mean well.

"She hates this town, Dad. Not sure what I can do about that."

"I 'spect it's her mama she don't care for, and it's the memories of the town that keep her away, son. Given what all of them put her through growing up, and when her mama up and made off with Mayor Jenkins, I can't say as I blame her. Maybe you could show her that most everyone's over the affair and that all those kids that were so cruel to her have grown up as well."

Chapter Two

"Indie!" squealed from her sisters as soon as she exited her car in the driveway of her mother's home. They rushed to her, sweeping her up in an odd dance of hugs and excitement. Indie squeezed Melony and Miranda for all she was worth. Yep. Coming home was definitely a good idea.

"I'm so excited you're here!" Melony continued to gush.

"Yeah, well, I still can't believe you're actually gonna up and marry Tucker Kilroy." Indie grabbed her sister's hand to inspect the engagement ring sparkling on Melony's finger. "If he does to you what he did to most every girl in our graduating class, I'll kill him, and I plan to let him know that."

"He's not like that anymore. I swear. He's amazing." Her sister's gushing hit Indie squarely in the chest as soon as her eyes focused in on the largest house in Pleasant Glen.

"Let's just go get this over with." She drew a deep breath and reminded herself that as soon as she made an appearance here she could escape to her daddy's house and everything would be fine.

"Maybe Mom's kind of trying to come around. She even got you a present," Miranda stated hopefully.

"She did?"

"Yeah, come on." Melony grabbed her hand and attempted to jerk her towards the front door. Indie was almost a foot taller than her sisters. Pulling or pushing her to do anything she wasn't ready to do wasn't really a fathomable scenario.

Indie begrudgingly advanced letting the phrase *'you don't have to stay long'* become her mantra.

"Mama, Indie's here," Melony's call echoed off of the ostentatious marble flooring her mother had demanded be added not long after she'd moved in.

The mayor lifted his head from some newspaper Indie didn't recognize. It wasn't the Glen Gazette, but she couldn't quite make out the title line. "Carolyn," he bellowed, "she isn't staying for supper, is she?"

"Nice to see you too, *Dad*," Indie sneered.

"No, Ernie, we're having supper in Lincoln tonight. I told you we'd been invited over to the Swanson's this evening." Disapproval broadcast from every cell of Carolyn Jenkin's body as she made her way down the stairs. It always did. "Derrick Swanson is the mayor of Comstock over in Custer county," was her only greeting.

"How thrilling." Indie rolled her eyes.

"I picked up something for you at the store the other day. It's in the kitchen."

Indie and her sisters followed after their mother. Indie tried her damnedest not to be excited, or even hopeful. When it came to Carolyn, hope was never a good idea. Her mother had never gotten her a gift outside of the required gift-giving holidays. She thrust a bag from the big bookstore in Lincoln at Indie.

Furrowing her brow, Indie extracted her gift.

"Mother, are serious with this? Oh my God," she spat out her indignation. The clock on the oven alerted her to the fact that she'd been in the mayor's house approximately four minutes and she already wanted to shoot something. She flung the book her mother had gifted her onto the kitchen counter. *The High School Reunion Diet: Lose 20 years in 2 weeks* spun on the granite. Indie fought the desire to vomit. Ire and rage, the inevitable reactions to dashed hope, shot through her veins.

"Anna, mind your tone with your mother," the mayor had the audacity to address her as he entered the kitchen.

"Do not call me Anna!" she shrieked. "My name is Indie, and while we're on that subject, don't address me at all. I feel certain we figured this all out when I was sixteen. You may be married to my mother, but you get no say over anything I do. You got that, *Mayor*?"

"Indieanna Jane, you mind your language and apologize to your stepfather right this very minute," her mother demanded.

"Oh, Mama, I'm pretty sure you already know that we'll be having a snowball fight in hell long before that'll happen."

"I'm sure they'll be fighting no matter where they end up," Miranda sighed as Melony nodded her agreement.

"Mama, Indie looks as gorgeous as always. Why on earth would you give her that book?" Miranda demanded.

"It never matters what I do, it's always wrong. I thought you might actually put forth a little effort for your sister's wedding and your reunion. Luke Camden will be walking you down the aisle next weekend. It might be nice if you didn't look like that." Her mother's eyes ran the length of Indie's long, curvy body, dressed in her typical ripped Wranglers and vintage Ford t-shirt.

If her mother had actually paddled her ass with a wooden spoon like she used to threaten to when they were kids, it would have shocked her less. "What?!" Wait. Had her mother or sisters figured out that at some point during every single one of her trips home she ended up back in Luke's bed?

Melony gnawed on her bottom lip until Indie was certain she was going to draw blood. "Well, I was gonna take you out and get you tipsy before I told you this, but Luke is one of Tuck's best friends, and it just works out height-wise for him to walk you down. Since, you know … you're really tall." She cringed.

Indie's head whirled with the insanity of it all. Her feet longed to sprint back to her car and blaze her way long way past Oklahoma City. Hell, she wouldn't stop until she'd crossed the Grande and was downing margaritas in Monterrey. Walking down an aisle with Luke was way, way more than she could possibly endure. It spoke to places in her soul she'd long since locked away permanently. No way. She couldn't go there. She couldn't ask him to go there. It just wasn't fair. That was way too close to the life she could have lived, she *should* have lived, if everything hadn't gotten so screwed up.

At that moment, Tucker Kilroy himself made his appearance in the kitchen. "Uh, hey, Indie," he offered sheepishly.

She narrowed her eyes and made good on her promise to warn Tucker. "You ever hurt my little sister, Tuck, I'll hang your shriveled sac from my review-mirror, you got that?"

"Indi-anna," gasped from her mother as she clutched her heart.

"Anna, that is inappropriate," the mayor clucked. Indie spun on him. The rage in her own eyes reflected off of the perfectly polished stainless steel appliances as she lunged at the man that had ruined her entire life.

"What did you just call me?" she seethed. Suddenly, Tucker's arms were around her, holding her back.

"I got it, Indie. Just calm down, okay?"

"Oh God, Tuck, no," Melony squeaked. "Never tell her to calm down."

Indie whirled, letting her right fist fly until she connected with Tuck's broad chest. He ground his teeth and backed up. "Dammit, Indie. Luke clearly *is* the only guy who could put up with you. Sure as hell the only one that ever had a prayer of getting you to simmer down."

"Indie, please," Melony begged. Her little sister's plea cooled a little of her burn. "Come on, we haven't seen you in forever. Just please."

10

Rolling her eyes, she cocked her jaw to the side and shot a livid glare to the mayor. "Think I'll head on to Daddy's."

"No, wait. Mel and I want us to go out for drinks tonight. We'll try on our dresses real quick, then we'll go get supper at Saddlebacks." Miranda eased closer cautiously, like Indie was a ticking time bomb set to detonate at any moment. She'd always been the smartest of the three of them.

An involuntary shudder worked through Indie's body. "What dresses?"

"Indie, I want my bridesmaids to wear dresses, but I swear they're cute."

"Mel, I do not *do* dresses. And you most certainly know why I do not do dresses. You were there that night."

"I know, I know, but for me, just this once, please, please, please."

"Say *please* to me one more time."

"Indieanna, stop acting this way. This is not some ridiculous auto shop in Oklahoma. You are a guest in the mayor of Pleasant Glen's home, and you shall act as such," Carolyn ordered.

And there it was. The constant reminder that Indie was the unwanted child, the guest who'd gotten in the way, and the ever-growing thorn in her mother's side. She'd been the one that had walked in on the mayor and her mother going at it in her parent's bedroom the summer between her sophomore and junior years of high school. Indie had never meant to cause all of the trouble. Lost in a sea of confusion and horror, she'd told her father. Her mother had never cared for Indie in the first place. After that, the battle lines were clearly drawn.

Indie's temper had always gotten the best of her, and damn it all if Tucker Kilroy wasn't right. Luke was the only man that knew how to cool her off as well as he knew how to set her ablaze. The steady sanity to her fire. But Luke wasn't here. She'd been trying for years to forgive her mother for what she'd done, for the ways she'd treated Indie her entire life. Her attempts had been about as successful as shoveling sand in the desert with a slotted spoon.

"Come on." Melony grabbed her hand and tugged. Not a brilliant move, but Indie let it go as she begrudgingly followed her sisters up the winding staircase.

"I'm wearing my boots, not heels, just for your information," she informed her sisters. She would look completely ridiculous in heels. Even Luke Camden didn't stand taller than her in heels.

"We all are. It's going to be adorable," Melony squealed.

Adorable was not something Indie would ever achieve. She ground her teeth while her mother's maid adjusted the waist on the short, sleeveless, hunter-green and ivy-colored dress, with a matching ribbon belt that made Indie's five feet eleven-inch, thickly curved body look like the Jolly Green Giant, in her opinion.

"Indie, you look amazing," Melony gushed.

"God, what I wouldn't give for those legs," Miranda sighed.

Indie stared at her perfect, petite, blonde, thin sisters. The DoubleMint twins had nothing on them.

She glanced at the old wooden vanity table in the guest bedroom that held her sister's wedding gown and the bridesmaid's dresses. The vanity used to contain her mother's Avon samples and demos back before she'd had an affair with the mayor, had left her father running a garage on the poor end of town, and had effectively ruined Indie's life.

She recalled the way her mother would splash Sweet Honesty perfume samples and Peachy Keen lip gloss on the twins when they were in middle school. They served as her own personal sales force. When Indie inquired about some lip gloss her freshman year in high school, she was told by her own mother that she just didn't *look* like an Avon girl. Her mother's excuse had been there was no point in Indie wearing makeup since she spent all of her time either under cars in her daddy's shop or galloping hard and fast on her horses. She was generally smeared with either grease or dirt. Makeup wasn't for cowgirls, it seemed.

At some point in her adolescence, the taunting jeers from her school peers about her height and the size of her breasts, that were far too large for her frame, joined her mother's constant derision over her tomboy ways and her weight, and had become the gospel that raised Indie. She checked the mirror again, half expecting it to reflect the powerless feelings she hid with her temper. At least the scars from her breast reduction surgery weren't visible. If only the dress had any chance of covering the scars on her soul, they'd be in business.

"We got to go all the way to Lincoln for the check-up, and Hank has to get his shots. You sure you don't mind watchin' him?" Austin handed Luke his stepson, J.J.

"Nah, I got him. You go on. Tell Hank to give them nurses hell over those shots."

"Oh, don't worry he'll give 'em hell, then he'll give me and Summer hell for the next two days. Makes him feel sick. Kinda kills me every freaking time."

"He'll be all right." Luke couldn't help but chuckle at his little brother, rodeo bull-rider, professional bachelor, turned loving, devoted husband and doting father.

"Unka Wuke!" J.J. trilled. "Slide!"

Smiling at his nephew, Luke was well aware that the little guy had him wrapped around his finger. "Yeah, okay, we'll go slide."

"Big twuck."

"Yep, we'll go ride in Uncle Luke's new truck." Luke winked at his nephew as he applauded excitedly.

Austin shook his head. "Spoilt so bad he stinks." He razzed J.J.'s hair. "You be good for Uncle Luke, J. Promise Daddy."

"No." J.J. shook his head combatively. Since that was his response to most every question, Luke wasn't too concerned.

"He'll be fine." Luke was looking forward to spending the last of the afternoon with his nephew. Maybe he'd be able to come up with some way to execute the plan he'd been crafting ever since Tuck and Melony had announced their upcoming nuptials.

He needed to prove to Indie that he never wanted her to stop being a mechanic. They could be married, and she could help run her father's shop. Next on the list was getting Indie to fall in love with the ranch again. That seemed a much easier goal to obtain than working on getting her to love the whole town all at once.

At one time, Camden Ranch had been her favorite place to be, a solid, steady home she could always run to when things in her own home got ugly. He glanced around the rolling grasslands dotted with cattle surrounding him for miles on every side. The sun was just beginning its descent behind the corn fields in the distance. The splendor and serenity of it all shouldn't be a hard sell.

After that he'd work on showing her that the Glen had its issues, but what town didn't? If he was insanely lucky, he might even be able to negotiate a treaty between Mayor Jenkins, Indie's mother, and Indie.

Only two problems that he could see stood in the way of his plans. He had to get Indie to agree to giving him the next two weeks to try to convince her of all of that, and to prove that his bedroom skills were vastly better than the way he'd been taking her with all the frustrated fervor being away from her for so long always brought on. He needed to seek her out as soon as possible. And the fact that trying to negotiate anything at all with Indieanna Harper generally worked about as well as trying to baptize a cat.

When Summer and Austin headed out, Luke buckled J.J. into his car seat. More than happy to take his nephew to the elementary school playground, he didn't feel like being home alone anymore anyway. Being in the vicinity of Pleasant Glen High, which backed up to Pleasant Glen Elementary, might help him think. He was effectively asking Indie to help him resurrect their past so they could create a future together. Might as well go back to the original scene of the crime.

J.J. babbled as Luke drove them to the playground. He took off running as soon as he was released from his seat. He was already wearing through his third set of cowboy boots since he'd moved to the ranch with his mama almost a year ago. Luke hated to admit he was a little envious of Austin. Until that damned reunion invitation had shown up in the mailbox, he hadn't considered how much he'd wanted to have kids of his own one day. How the hell had fifteen years gone by, anyway?

J.J. wanted to run around the swings for a few minutes. Luke kept a close eye on him while he let his mind wander. The hometown bleachers backed up to the playground. God, he could almost see her standing there, giving him that sexy-as-sin smirk that always spoke directly to his groin.

When his cousin Brock's parents had up and moved him to some tiny beach town in North Carolina, Luke had been concerned. Brock had always played receiver to his quarterback. They were a team unto themselves. Even without his counterpart, Luke decided to try out for the Pleasant Glen football team anyway, but never expected to become the starting quarterback. Their high school was the only one in the county. Kids from ranches up to sixty miles away were bused in, but there were still only 75 kids in their graduating class. Young Rodeo had far more hopefuls than the football team. Luke was never really sure if he was any good or if it was just that he could throw a ball and there wasn't much competition.

He'd fly down that field on those cool, crisp autumn nights under the scoreboard lights, ignoring every single cheerleader that flirted shamelessly with him because of his uniform, not because of who he was, and pull Indie into his arms and let the entire school know she held his heart forever. It had been that way since Freshman year.

The regret still ate at him. The whole town finding out her mother was keeping the mayor's bed warm. The snide remarks, haughty

14

glances, and downright cruelty kids and adults alike had shown Indie had broken her thoroughly. He'd done everything he could think of to be there for her while the world tried its damnedest to dismantle her very soul.

She'd always been picked on for being so tall and for the size of her chest. Her mother's indiscretion poured lighter fluid on an already blazing fire. His little hellcat had proven how tough she could be, never letting on that it bothered her, but he knew better. How was he the only one that understood that when she shouted at her mother, their teachers — hell, even the preachers, and Sunday school teachers at the church — it was so she wouldn't cry? If she screamed loud enough and fought hard enough, maybe it would fill the empty voids, mend the invisible bruises her childhood had left behind. She was a beautiful storm that scarred the very earth surrounding her. All she'd ever really needed was someone to mend her own wounds. She needed his sanity, not his pressure.

He'd known it all those years ago. He just hadn't known then how to fill the abyss with his love. Now, he knew. He could be everything she'd ever need, show her how much she meant to him, prove that he loved her just the way she was. When she wanted to storm, he'd love her in her rage and be her steady anchor. When she wanted to be quiet, he'd hold her close in his arms and be the ease that would make her want to stay. And when she wanted to burn, when she needed to blaze in her passion, he would provide the constant friction and heat that would reduce them both to embers, until like a phoenix they could fly again.

Another memory flashed through his mind. Standing at the doorway to his dorm room holding that damned ring, both crying while she tried to explain why she couldn't stay, why she had to leave, how she never wanted to hurt him, but couldn't marry him because she wasn't good enough, and that he just wasn't wild enough for her in a confusing jumble of words that had robbed the breath from his lungs.

He should've been the man she needed, the lover that made her every wild fantasy come true, the arms that would be her strength when she just couldn't fight the whole damn world alone any longer. The thing was, at that time, he was only a boy. Nothing more than a ploughboy thinking he knew how to be a real man, a real cowboy. Thinking what she needed was stability that he'd stupidly believed a ring would somehow provide. Back then, he was full of shit.

Now, he could prove himself, show her exactly how she needed to be loved, keep her sated, show her badly he wanted her, how fucking beautiful she is, and that he'd fight with her, *for* her. Whatever it took, he'd prove what they could be together.

He'd show her he was all man, all vestiges of the boy she'd left long gone. He knew what he wanted, knew how he wanted it, and how to go about getting it. If she'd give him half a chance, he'd sure as hell make up for the way he'd been before and show her that he knew exactly how to keep a woman begging for more of him. Come hell or high water, he was going to prove himself now.

"Slide!" J.J. pointed to the long metal slide all of the Camden kids had flown down at one time or another. Chuckling, Luke lifted him up to the top and guided him down to keep him from landing on his head at the bottom.

Ten minutes into the sliding and begging Luke to chase him around the playground, the hair on the back of Luke's neck stood. His spine stiffened and his cock stirred. His eyes frantically tracked the crimson red Camaro Z28 she'd restored a couple of years ago as it pulled into view, and there she was … his Indie.

Having sworn on her custom hex keys and her ratchets that she'd meet her sisters at Saddleback's at sundown, she'd flown out of her mother's fancy-ass house and took to the road.

Indie's mouth hung open. The car seemed to slow of its own accord. Her heart refused her another beat and the breeze whipping through the windows took her breath away. There he was. She'd had no idea why she'd driven this way. She was heading away from her daddy's farm. The ghosts of her past had escorted her down the winding road that ran parallel to the train tracks in her hometown.

Luke Camden was holding a little boy. They were playing on the old elementary school playground. The same one she'd played on as a little girl. Her chin trembled. She swallowed back liquid emotion. Grant's expression when she'd stupidly admitted that she wanted to see Luke flashed in the few tears she trapped on her long eyelashes. Someone else clearly held his heart now. Someone that wasn't her. Someone that would never be *her*.

"Unka Wuke," the little boy bellowed loudly. Her heart jerked back to a sprint in a second flat. "Unka Wuke, slide," he repeated.

Uncle Luke. Wow. So that was one of his brother's or sister's little boys. She tried to wonder which one of his siblings had finally settled down. She tried to care, but a heated tidal wave of thankfulness

16

overwhelmed her. It wasn't his kid. The way her heart had stalled when she thought it was terrified her.

Her eyes keenly traced down his muscular physique to those well-worn Wranglers that always made her entire body long to strip him naked. For one split second, she tried to convince herself she could run fast enough down the hill to him to make the past fifteen years disappear. She could fly into his arms. He could make it all go away. She could tell him how sorry she was that she kept running away and about the book her mother had the audacity to give her. He could tell her how beautiful he thought she was and make every insecurity disappear with one of his sizzling glances laced with pure unadulterated intention. She swallowed down raw regret.

His hand lifted from the little boy's, and he waved. She shook herself. Clearly, he'd seen her. She should get out and go talk to him, but instead she called herself a chicken, forced her gaze back to the road, returned the wave, and got the hell out of there. What was wrong with her? Why couldn't she talk to him in the daylight? Tell him how she'd been feeling? There was so much more to them than late night trysts once, maybe twice a year. Wasn't there?

Haunted memories rose up from the dusty dirt under her tires.

'Heard what your whore of a mama has been doing with the mayor, Indie. Bet that makes you proud.' Cindy Spann's sneering taunt ricocheted through her mind. *'Better watch out Luke. Like mama, like daughter, you know. When Indie starts cheating on you like the fat ho she is, give me a call.'* That bitch, Megan Morgan, the captain of the cheerleading squad, had shoved her number into Luke's hand right in front of Indie. He'd crumpled it and tossed it in the trash, but that didn't change anything about what had happened.

Since her eleventh birthday, she'd been harassed mercilessly for the size of her breasts. She'd begged her parents to let her have the reduction surgery. At eighteen, just a month after graduation, they'd finally allowed it. Her father had worked endlessly to afford the elective surgery. The entire town thought the mayor had paid for it. She'd been on the cover of the gazette, still bound in wrapping and gauze, under the headline, 'Is this what our taxes are paying for?'

Luke had held her hand as she sat in the surgery prep room and swore that he loved all of her no matter what bra size she was, that he'd loved her right then, and he'd love her the very same when she got out of the operating room. What eighteen-year-old kid makes vows like that? Luke Camden.

Her mind continued to review her painful childhood. She recalled the terrorizing pain in her father's eyes when the story of the affair had broken in the paper. His tearful gaze as he'd pulled her into his arms and held her tight stabbed through her gut all over again. Bile-soaked remembrances singed her throat.

"Since you're over fifteen you get to choose which parent you'd like to live with, Indieanna." The stupid judge's question dripped with disdain over the entire thing. The whole fucking town knew, and most of them loved nothing more than to offer her pity while they talked about her family out the other side of their mouths.

"I'm living with my daddy. I never want to see my mother again," she'd vowed readily to anyone who'd listen. Luke had been right there, right beside her the entire time. He'd skipped school and waited outside the courthouse on her. They'd taken off in his truck and hadn't looked back. He'd held her for hours when she finally broke down in hysterical sobs. She'd spent the week at his parent's house on the ranch. She was certain the entire Camden family knew she hadn't stayed in the guest bedroom where his sweet mama had put her things.

Her daddy never said a word about it. She'd finally bolted out of Chemistry class that Friday when she realized she'd left her father, her hero, all alone on what had to be the worst week of his life, too.

Her mother had been the mayor's secretary. Indie had been too young and too stupid to wonder why her mother seemed to be working longer and longer hours. God, the clichés ate at her soul. Back then, all she'd cared about was spending every waking moment with Luke, riding her horses, and helping her daddy work on cars. If her mother wasn't around, she had free rein to do all of that.

"I was such an idiot." That fact added to her gall. She rolled her eyes as she turned the car around a few miles outside of town and headed back to her daddy's.

It was so incredibly thoughtful of her mother to wait four whole weeks before she up and married the mayor. From that moment on, Indie had slowly but surely lost every single thing she'd ever believed in. Everything she'd ever understood had dissolved around her.

It had taken her two additional years to finally push Luke away, too. She'd existed in a hazy reality caught somewhere between the girl she'd known her whole life and a haunted replica of herself that couldn't see her way out of the confusion that consumed her. He'd given her a ring and the only thing that had made sense to her was to run away. She'd been trying to save him — and them — from the pain she'd seen in her father's eyes. Nothing lasted forever. She couldn't hurt Luke the way her mother had wounded her father.

Passing back by the school yard, Luke and his nephew had left. Her heart faltered again. It had been fifteen years, and she couldn't let it go. Couldn't forgive the hateful comments she'd endured, the pitying stares cast in her direction every place she went. Couldn't forgive her mother for making her father feel unloved and incapable of keeping a woman happy. Couldn't find it in herself to let it all go because it had cost her everything.

Unable to believe in love at all if her own mother couldn't love someone as good as her daddy, Indie had lost the only man that had ever had a chance of taming her wild heart.

And until her dying day, she would continue to punish her mother and the mayor for what they'd done. The vengeance was necessary to her very survival. She knew no other way to exist. The vengeance had driven her out of his dorm room where she'd spewed forth pure lies about him not being wild enough for her, right into her car, and had her flying down the road until she was far enough away no one had ever heard her mother's name and she'd located a mechanic shop with a help wanted sign.

Why the hell had she wanted to come back here in the first place? She should have known the whole thing would never give her peace. Not even Luke could make this place bearable. This entire tiny town would never be anything more than an effigy of horrifying recollections. Coming home was always a bad idea. How could she actually have been excited about this? Apparently, she was *still* an idiot.

Chapter Three

By the time Indie pulled into her father's gravel driveway it was a little easier to remember why she'd been anxious to arrive in Pleasant Glen a few hours before. The small, red-brick, one-story home that had raised her stood steady and safe in the distance, painted in the endless colors of the setting sun.

The lights in her father's three bay garage near the road were all on, beckoning her home, and there he was: her daddy, Ben Harper, the absolute salt of the earth. Dressed in his dirty coveralls, leaning against a late model Mercury he must've been fixing for someone and wiping his hands on a shop rag, he beamed at Indie like she was the very thing he'd been waiting to arrive his entire life.

She leapt from her car and raced towards him.

"Well, if it ain't my beautiful baby girl finally coming to see her daddy. Thought you'd forgotten your old man." He winked at her as he reached and pulled her into his solid and substantial embrace. She buried her face against the warm cotton coveralls and inhaled the scent of oil, gasoline, brake fluid, and Old Spice. Contentment flowed through her veins, immediately soothing the insanity of her day. She was safe. She was home.

"Let me look at'cha, Indie Jane. Lord knows I don't get to see you near enough." Keeping his strong hands on her shoulders he stepped back and grinned. "Prettier every single time. You didn't bring some guy I'm gonna hate home with ya, did you?"

Indie laughed. "No, Daddy. Every man in Oklahoma City gets mad when I can out-wrench them and they get bitchy about it. I can't deal with 'em. All they ever want to do is play X-Box all day anyway. Drives me crazy."

Chuckling, her father grinned. "There's my girl. Always knew it was gonna take a real cowboy to ever keep up with you." He studied her hazel eyes long enough for her to blink and glance away, uncomfortable by what he might find there. "Been to see your mama I'm guessing, and might'a run into someone else that upset my baby girl. There somebody out in town that I need to go speak with?"

"How the hell do you do that?" she sighed.

Laughing again, he shook his head. "I know my girls like I know the back of my own hands, darlin'. Tell me what pissed you off then tell me what made you cry."

"I didn't cry, but Mama pissed me off. We're like gasoline and a match. You know that. She gave me a book about losing weight before the reunion. Pissed me off something good. Why does she do that?"

Sighing, her father bent back over the Mercury. "Your mama's always worrying about what she looks like. Never saw her own beauty. You get that from her. Speaking of needing a cowboy, I can think of only one man that ever had you convinced you were beautiful, and you didn't let that ride for very long. Your mama probably called herself trying to be helpful. She can't ever just let you girls be yourselves. Always wanting to spit and polish you clean. She gets everything so damn screwed up." He shrugged. "If she realized how little other people think about her, she'd be a helluva lot happier. Reminds me of someone else I know."

He shot her a pointed glance and then grabbed a QuikSteel epoxy to repair the cracked manifold.

"I don't give a damn what other people think about me, and you're gonna have to sand that first." Indie pointed to the visible crack.

Her father smirked. "You don't say." With a quick eye roll he added, "You ain't out-wrenched your daddy yet, so why don't you grab some sandpaper and take out your irritation with your mama on that manifold. For now, I'll let you keep feeding yourself that line of pure shit about not caring what other people think. God knows you ain't gonna tell anyone else they might've been right, even me. But when you start choking on it, I'll try not to laugh at'cha outright."

Rolling her eyes, Indie scoured the crack with a small piece of sandpaper she located on top of her daddy's rolling toolkits. Being back in the shop with her father almost made up for the hell she'd endured at her mother's house, but he was awfully keen to bring up Luke at every available opportunity. What was that all about?

"You left out half of the story, Indie Jane."

"No, I didn't. She gave me that book. I threw it on the counter. Oh, I also tried to scalp the mayor, got into it with Tucker Kilroy, who I cannot believe Mel is marrying, and had to put on a dress. That alone should earn me my bad mood."

"Well, alrighty then, you go right on and be in a bad mood. I love ya anyway, but I also want to know what made my little girl cry."

"Nothing made me cry. I wouldn't give Mama the satisfaction. Dust must've gotten in my eyes or something. But you know how I get coming back here. I think I hate it, but then I'm here with you in the shop and I love it again. Maybe I have multiple personalities or something. I should probably see a shrink."

"If I know my girl, and I do, I'd say you *saw* ... Mr. Camden, maybe?"

Indie scrubbed the sandpaper over the engine with more vigor.

"Mmm hmm, wondered when the two of you would run into one another."

"I didn't *see* him, see him. I saw him on the elementary school playground. He was with a little boy."

Her father's face fell. Empathy warmed his hazel eyes. "Oh baby girl, that what got you upset? I 'spect that was Austin's stepson, J.J. Austin got married last December after he won the PBR buckle. His wife had another baby back in March."

"It wouldn't matter if Luke is his daddy. None of my business. I don't care."

"You are good at a helluva lot of things, Indie Jane. Lying sure as heck ain't one of 'um."

She felt her face heat as she worked her jaw. Her daddy had always been able to see right through her anyway. No use in arguing. That thought struck her as odd. She loved to argue with most anyone, her mother being her favorite target. Maybe she wanted to argue until she felt like her mother understood her, accepted her ... loved her the way her daddy did.

"So, it *does* matter. Matters to my girl. Matters to Luke, and you care a mighty lot. What I can't quite figure is why the two of you fight so hard to stay apart 'til you just can't stand it anymore, and then you go flying into his bed, but you won't admit to the other that it still matters more than anything else."

Tossing the sandpaper away, she dusted off her hands. "How do you know it still matters to him?"

"Same way I know sun's gonna rise early tomorrow mornin'. Same way I know Nebraskan winds gonna keep right on blowin'. Way I know when a storm's riding in on that same wind. Same way I know you're gonna have no fewer than a half dozen blow-ups with your mama and the mayor 'bout this blessed wedding. Same way I know you're pissed about Melony taking up with Tuck Kilroy because of the way he acted in high school, and you can't quite admit to yourself that all of ya have grown up a little bit between now and then. And the very same way I know some things are meant to be and that me saying that is gonna make you huffy."

"I ain't huffy, and why are Mama and I gonna keep fighting about the wedding?"

22

"Your mother thinks Melony ought to ask me if it'd be okay if the mayor walked her down the aisle."

"What?! She's crazy. You're her daddy."

"Melony's already informed her of that. Apparently she's gonna give the mayor some special flower-thing that goes on your tux, but your mama ain't happy with that."

"It's called a boutonnière, and I swear I have no idea how you put up with her as long as you did."

"I've never regretted the years I spent with your mama, Indie. It gave me my girls and that's a gift no one else could'a given me. I do resent the fact that she wants to pretend all those years away. I resent that a whole lot."

"And I'm guessing I'm gonna go to bat for you when she brings up this ridiculous idea to me and that's why we're gonna fight."

"You know, Indie you don't have to fight my battles for me, but that fact hadn't ever stopped you from trying."

"She makes me crazy."

"I know that, too, baby girl."

"She's making Luke walk me down the aisle." Indie cringed.

Her father's hearty laughter simultaneously warmed her soul and caught her off guard. "What's so funny?"

"Oh, just tickles me when fate shows her hand. Looks like maybe, just maybe, she's holding all the aces this time."

"Mama or Fate?"

"The fates, baby girl. Never stand in their way."

"There's no such thing as fate, Daddy. Life sucks and then you die."

"Well, ain't that a sunshiny forecast from my Indie? Fate's there, whether you want to give her a nod or not. Tickles me that you swear she ain't there while your mama's playing the part of the lightning rod. One way or another, sweetheart, you're gonna figure out that what you're running *from* is what you should be running *to*. If that weren't the case, why is my girl still running?"

Before Indie could argue, the soft neighs and snorts of the horses traveled on the wind to her ears. A broad grin replaced her father's correctly predicted scowl on her face.

He chuckled. "Sounds like someone realized you're home. You better go on and see 'em."

"Come with me."

"Let me get this sealant on, and I'll meet you at the barn."

Indie took off to see her horses. Okay, so maybe there were a few good reasons to keep coming home. Romeo met her at the fence. He nuzzled her chest and then turned back towards the paddock, restless. His ears twitched and his tail was in constant motion. Something was wrong.

"Where's Juliet, boy?"

He snorted. Worry troubled his coal black eyes. Indie could read horses almost as good as she could read cars, and infinitely better than she'd ever be able to understand her own mother.

Stroking down Romeo's side, she headed towards the paddock. Juliet was standing near the barn with her right front hoof off of the ground.

"What's wrong, girl?" Indie rushed to pull the chain attached to a single light bulb hung from the center of the barn. She checked Juliet's leg and hoof, but didn't see anything wrong. Her stomach churned as she searched for anything that might've caused her horse harm. It was a little early in the year for rattlers and there was nothing on Juliet's leg to indicate a bite.

Her father joined her in the paddock.

"She won't put her hoof on the ground." Panic rose in her tone.

Furrowing his brow, Ben performed the same check Indie had already gone through. "She was fine this morning. All right, baby girl, you're gonna have to tell me how you want to handle this. Seems fate ain't messing around this time. You know who the local vet is. He's the only one who's gonna come all the way out here. We can load her up in the morning and take her into Ogallala to see Dr. Carrion if you really don't want to call Luke."

Indie considered. Luke played vet for all of the local farms around the Glen. He hadn't finished his doctorate degree but made it all the way through his masters before he went back to ranching. He was darn good at it, too. He'd know what was wrong immediately and be able to fix it. His cool, steady hands put the animals at ease. She'd seen him work with his own cattle and the Camden Ranch horses long before he had any kind of degree. She didn't want Juliet to have to go through being trailered and driven almost an hour away.

"It's getting late. Might need to wait 'til tomorrow morning either way. She don't seem to agitated and is loving up on you." Her father pointed out. Indie nuzzled Juliet's mane and gave her a rubdown. She neighed happily, but still wouldn't settle on her right hoof.

"Let's see how she is tomorrow, then we'll decide," her father negotiated.

24

"No, I'll find Luke. It's fine. I want him to look at her tonight."

"You do whatever you want, sweetheart. Tell him I said she was perfectly fine this morning. I rode her. No problems."

Pleased to hear that, Indie begrudgingly checked the time on her phone. "I swore on my hex set that I'd meet Mel and Miranda for drinks. I'll go out to the ranch if I don't see Luke in town."

"That sounds like a plan, but never swear on your hex set, Indie Jane. You know better, but since that's the case, you better get. I'll check Juliet again before I head in for the night."

"Call me if she gets worse, or if you get lonely, or if you just wanna show me how much you love me and rescue me from my little sisters' girl talk."

"Get out of here, sunshine. You know your sisters love you."

Chapter Four

Luke continued to call himself an idiot. Every time the door to Saddleback's opened his heart leapt and hopeful expectation coupled with the liquor swirling in his stomach. He should have just gotten off of his ass and driven out to her daddy's place. He knew that's where she'd run to, and they had plenty to talk about.

Saddlebacks, the liquor-infused honky-tonk of Pleasant Glen, was full of cowboys and cowgirls looking to blow off a little steam that evening. The waitresses were pulling double-duty with the bartenders. An endless supply of food was being served up constantly, and there was a local band playing covers fast and furiously. Seemed everyone in a forty-mile radius sought out companionship that night.

Summer had come into town, picked up J.J., and dropped off Austin. Luke, Grant, Austin, and their cousin Brock were now seated at a table front and center.

Luke tried to keep up with conversation, but seeing Indie drive off yet again had scrambled his head. Why had she stopped, waved, and then left? She'd told Grant she wanted to see him. Well, he'd been standing right there.

A gnawing concern continued to eat at him. She had to have seen J.J. What if she thought he was his kid? What if she'd assumed he was married with a family now? He had to find her and tell her J.J. wasn't his, but that she was. Regret continued to weight his every thought when it came to him and Indie. So many things he'd fucked up. So many things he desperately wanted the chance to fix.

"Can't believe Summer let you out for the night," Brock teased Austin.

"I think she's sick of all of the testosterone she's living in, plus she's freaking exhausted. She took the boys to Mama and Daddy's so she can get some sleep before Hank cries all damn night from them shots. I ain't staying long. Plan on making a trip to my house before I pick up my kids, seein' if maybe Summer might like to try and fail at making another one," Austin laughed.

Luke shook his head, but before he could call his brother a dumbass, Melony and Miranda Harper entered the bar — and right behind them was none other than Indie.

Grant, Austin, and Brock's laughter ended abruptly. Every Camden eye slid to Luke. A half-second later every single pair of eyes in the whole damn bar were on him. He swallowed down another sip of Crown and considered. She was there with her sisters. He had no claim as of yet, and that fact burned through him like a kerosene soaked fuse. He didn't give a shit how long it had been. She was his.

He scooted his chair back, but remembered that it was high time he showed her a little patience. No more taking her like a man possessed. She needed a steady hand and they hadn't exactly announced to the town that they'd been together more than a few times in the last decade or so. He was the sanity, even if seeing her drove him insane with need.

She leaned into a nearby booth. The tight vintage Ford t-shirt she was wearing cradled her cleavage perfectly. The hem pulled upwards and her low-slung Wranglers revealed the small of her back. Red satin panties played peek-a-boo with him for a split second. Damn, damn, damn if that sexy little peek didn't have him so hard up he'd be aching for days.

Nothing more beautiful than his Indie in red lingerie, her favorite kind to wear, his favorite kind to see her in. She never had any time for makeup or the other ridiculous fussing that so many women insisted upon. No, his baby was naturally beautiful with long auburn hair the precise shade of the Maple leaves in the late fall, cool green eyes, and the most beautiful pink lips he'd ever seen.

As soon as the bandages had come off of her chest, she'd taken to wearing the fieriest red lingerie she could get her hands on. Femininity redefined. Screw the make-up, perfume, and pearls. His girl knew precisely how to make him ache, red satin and lace. His mouth watered. His palms burned to hold her against him, to cup her ample breasts in his hands, and brand her entire body until she remembered exactly who she was and who she belonged to.

"Ain't Indieanna Harper lookin' some kind'a gorgeous to-night," Grant goaded.

Luke shot him a warning glare. He felt his biceps flex and his nostrils flare.

Austin smirked, getting in on the game. "Got them legs that go on for ten country miles."

"And fuck me runnin' if them curves weren't built for speed. Look at 'dat azz. Keep a man nice and warm all night long." Grant waggled his eyebrows.

Luke's eyes flared. "Don't," he commanded.

"She always was the whole damn bucket of chicken, wasn't she?" Austin pitched.

"Hell yeah, all legs, thighs, and breasts." Grant knocked the ball out of the park.

"I ain't kidding. Shut the fuck up," Luke snarled.

"Something's gotta make one of you move. If it has to be me making you so jealous you can't see to beat the shit outta me, so be it," Grant continued to challenge. "Maybe I'll ask her to dance."

"Maybe I'll beat the shit outta you just before I feed you your sac for breakfast."

A low whistle slid between Grant's teeth. "But you're just gonna wait 'til she comes running back to your bed instead of going after her this time, making this thing official, and convincing her with either the head on your shoulders or the one in your dirty blue jeans that she needs to stick around this time, right?"

"Uh, am I in danger of getting my ass whupped if I ask how she got less developed up top than the last time I seen her back in eighth grade?" Brock looked genuinely concerned he might be overstepping his bounds.

Luke tried to rein in his temper for his cousin's sake, but the outrage over the very idea of Grant spinning Indie around the dance floor of Saddleback's continued to sizzle through his veins.

Luke's eyes sought hers with heated magnetism. This time she offered him a quick sweet grin and a half-wave. His heart swelled. She never smiled at anyone like that. She'd smirk, or scowl, or flip someone off if they were stupid enough to mess with her, but a sweet grin, she reserved those for people she cared about deeply.

Sighing, he supposed he should answer Brock's question. "Everyone at school and practically everyone in this whole damn town were so awful to her about them, and her back and shoulders hurt all the time, so she had them reduced right after we graduated."

It still killed him that what people thought affected her badly enough to make her go through surgery. It was yet another failing on his part. He'd obviously didn't tell her or show her how stunningly beautiful she was often enough.

He watched her thank Aaron, one of the bartenders, for the Fireball he sat in front of her. Before he could make his way over to her, Adam Gentry, slimy fuck-whistle if ever there was one, asked her to dance.

Grant, Austin, and Brock all cringed. Luke stood, determination and gall armored in his drive. Indie shook her head and pushed Gentry back. *Asswipe.* His eyes still hadn't raised above her tits, and he was effectively drooling in the shit sloshing out of his cup. *Drunk bastard.*

Indie leapt from her seat. Luke almost grinned. There was his fire. "Get the hell away from me, Adam! You're drunk."

"I just wanted a hug. Haven't seen you … in like … long time," Adam stumbled over his words. Luke shoved two other cowboys he didn't know out of his way. Indie caught his eye and fury rocketed through every muscle in his body. Her fight was fierce. She appeared unaffected to everyone but him. He saw the fear playing in the depths of her eyes.

"Get the hell away from her, Gentry," Luke's low baritone voice thundered off the wood paneled walls of the bar.

Melony and Miranda turned to see him. Their mouths hung open stupidly for a half-second before they beamed and started dancing in their seats like sparklers on the Fourth of July.

"You heard him, Gentry. Get before you get gotten," Austin sneered. He, Grant, and Brock were right behind Luke, ready to fight if it came to that. Family through and through.

Before Luke could process any of that, Gentry, in all of his drunken stupidity, leaned in. He kept his right hand reaching undeniably for Indie's breasts. Luke dove for him, but Indie's back hand reached him first and was equally effective in knocking Adam Gentry for several loops. He stumbled backwards, and Luke slid to the side to let him fall on his ass. He had someone far more important to catch. His arms wrapped around her, blocking her from view of the entire bar, cradling her in his strength and his love.

"I've got you, darlin'."

"Geez, bitch, what the hell?" Adam started spewing as soon as he managed to get himself upright. Rage ignited in Luke. He turned and stared Adam down. Grant shoved Adam back in a booth as Brock and Austin bared down on him.

"You got exactly what you deserved. Now get the hell away from her. She ain't fighting by herself anymore," Luke snarled.

Luke's vow somehow spoke directly to Indie's soul. She clung to him fiercely, terrified to let go. Her heartbeat drummed in her ears. What was going to happen next? His chiseled jaw flexed against the top of her head. My God, the way he was holding her in a warm sanctuary of solid muscle was … perfect. Where had the sweet, gentle, boy she'd known gone? She tried to remember when his boyish charm had turned into this man that looked like he'd been dipped in pure sex appeal and carved with a chiseled blade. When had this fierce, dogged grit appeared? Somewhere in the last fifteen years when she'd been running away, he'd turned into a full-fledged cowboy. She'd been viewing him under the cover of darkness. Clearly, she'd been missing out.

Her pulse quickened as he ran his hands up and down her back, steadying her. Indie lifted her eyes to his. A storm of fire consumed their icy blue depths. The black t-shirt he was wearing clung to the chiseled muscles of his arms and chest, and the worn Wranglers covering his long legs had her licking her lips involuntarily as her gaze landed on his zipper line.

Suddenly, he captured her quick breaths with his mouth as he layered her body to his own. She tensed and then her body melted in to his. God, she'd needed this for so long. This sure as hell wasn't a *nice to see you* kiss or even a *wanna go get busy in my truck and never see each other again* kiss. No, this was a declaration. He took her lips with more intensity than he'd ever packed in a kiss before. *Before.* She tried to remember the last time she'd been kissed. Never like this. Never with enough fire to brand her soul, not even with him.

Her entire body responded like a slot machine that had just rolled three cherries. His lips demanded her compliance. She moaned softly in his greedy mouth. Those hands of his, those massive hands, one braided in her long hair, the other cupped her ass.

Angling his head to take more of her, he nipped her bottom lip and then sucked away the pain that left her breathless and aching for more. What the hell was he doing to her? The initial intensity waned slightly, and he softened his claim, making her needy.

His tongue coaxed the seam of her lips until she opened for him. The red-hot cinnamon of the fireball she'd been drinking mixed with the heat of his whiskey in a combustible explosion in her mouth.

Her hands fisted his t-shirt, worked up over his pecs, and then circled around his neck. She pulled him closer, running her fingers through his dark brown hair. God, this was so good. This … *this* was why she'd come home.

Her hips bumped readily into his, so anxious she was almost embarrassed by her own desperation. A low growl of approval vibrated against her tongue. When the entire bar broke out in wolf-whistles and applause, she pulled away, gasping for breath.

"Pretty sure you just announced to the whole damn town that we might've seen each other a time or two in the last fifteen years." She couldn't quite decide if that irritated her or not. She knew perfectly well that her pleading eyes, her nipples standing at attention and giving him a full salute, and the fact that she couldn't take her hands

30

off of him probably spoke much louder than her words anyway. "Just what exactly are you doing?" she finally demanded.

"What I should have done fifteen years ago. That wasn't my kid you saw me with today. That's Austin's little boy. Let's go. We need to talk." Luke grabbed her hand and half-dragged her towards the door. She turned back to see her sisters, who she was effectively abandoning.

Melony gave her two-thumbs up and was grinning like she'd just won the lottery. Miranda raised her glass to Indie with an identical beaming grin. A lot of help they were.

Luke's gait increased in speed, pulling Indie along. Her entire world tilted off its axis. She had never let anyone, even Luke, order her around like this. The fact that it turned her on more than anything she'd ever experienced in her thirty-two years of life only irritated her more.

"How much have you had to drink?" She finally landed on a plausible reason for why calm, steady, steadfast Luke was suddenly acting like a berserk caveman.

He spun when they reached a brand new F-450 Lariat Diesel Dually. *Damn, that's a nice ass truck* was her only coherent thought as he caged her between his hardened body and the doors. "Not enough for all of that to have only been the whiskey talking, but enough to sure as hell want to do it again."

She tried to work her way through that explanation. "Wait, so you're saying ... what are you saying?"

He continued to chase his breath as he stared up at the star-strewn night like the answer to her question might be written in the darkened sky. "I'm saying ...." He edged closer. Intensity rolled off every chiseled plane of his body. "I don't know what I'm saying." His fire lost just a little of its white hot heat.

Something inside of her snapped, freeing her of the lies she'd been living for too damn long. "I don't think that's true. I think we both know what we'd like to say to the other, and we're too damn chicken to say it."

"Fine, you want to know what I'm thinking, I'll tell you." Apparently he'd seen her proclamation as a challenge. A quick swallow tensed his neck. Her eyes watched his Adam's apple contract. Her nipples gave another tightening pulse. "I miss you every fucking day, Indie. Every woman I've been with since you left me all those years ago only makes it worse. I compare them all to you, and dammit, none of them will ever measure up. I have no fucking clue where this will end us, but for some idiotic reason I want to find out. You and I

… I mean … you haven't been home one single time that we haven't ended up in my bed, darlin'. Don't you think that means something? Because I think it does, and I'm more afraid of not taking the chance than I am of ordering you to my bed for the next few weeks and figuring out if I can't convince you to stay there permanently. I'm a moron. There, I said what I've been thinkin'. Now, you go."

Wow. Well, okay then. Being ordered to spend two weeks in his bed sounded very, very appealing, but what exactly was he wanting to chance? "Uh," *brilliant Indie. Uh is utter brilliance. They should give you some kind of medal for speaking.* She rolled her eyes at her own lack of ability to verbalize what she wanted to say.

"Uh, what?" he demanded. Damn, the boy had lost all of that endless patience that used to get on her nerves. So far she'd have to say she liked Luke the man even more than she'd liked Luke as a boy.

"I miss you like that, too. I kept talking myself out of calling you or coming back and seeing you more often, staying longer. I was scared. There, I said it, too." She stared down at the compacted, light-brown Nebraskan dirt that was making a valiant effort to keep her upright, even if she was fairly certain she was going to keel over at any moment. "I just hate this town, and I hate my mother, and I hate … everything except Daddy … and … and there's something wrong with Juliet. And what exactly are you wanting to take a chance on?" She clamped her mouth shut before anymore stupidity could pour out of her lips.

"Look at me, Indieanna."

She lifted her eyes to his.

"Don't sound to me like too much has changed, 'cept there being something wrong with your horse. How long you staying in town this time?"

"For the wedding, so at least a week. I might survive another week and go to that stupid reunion. God only knows why I'd do that. Apparently, I've become a sadist in my thirties."

A sexy smirk formed on those lips of his. "Yeah, I thought the same thing when the invite came. If I haven't talked to you in the last fifteen years, there's probably a real good reason, so why the hell would I want to see you now?"

Laughter escaped the tight lock she'd put on her lips as she nodded her agreement.

"Give me a shot." His right hand reached and cradled her face. His thumb gently stroked her cheekbone. Her eyes closed and a soft sigh escaped her. Where the hell had that come from?

32

"Give you a shot to do what?" She tried for her normal irritated tenor, but sounded a great deal more like a purring kitten.

"Give me a shot to show you that I should never have let you walk out all those years ago. To show you that I'm not a douchebag that just kept trying to pressure you into a marriage you weren't ready for. Be my date to your sister's wedding and the reunion. And every night between now and that reunion you're mine. Make this whole fucking town so happy they might shut the hell up and leave me alone, which would be a merciful blessing if ever there was one. Every night for the next two weeks, let me prove to you that I can be just as wild in bed as you wanted me to be back then, that I can be the man you need, that you don't have to give up anything to stay here with me."

"Luke ... I," she shook her head. Again he captured her protest with another whiskey-laced, heat-emboldened kiss. Just outside the neon glow of Saddleback's, he pinned her in the space between the cab of his truck and the bed. His tongue explored her mouth and his hands traced slowly up her waistline.

A breathy gasp accompanied the shudder of her body as his thumbs gently circled around her nipples, cupping the heavy weight of her breasts, giving her sweet relief. "Mmm, Indie, honey, you're making me think all kinda things. How you always come so sweet for me, trembling against me, with your juices dripping down the back of my throat, them fingernails clawing at my back. Damn, I need some more of that. There's so much I want to do with you that you've never given me the chance to do."

"Oh God," she groaned. His hands tracked under her t-shirt, caressing her waistline.

"Still so creamy and soft. They sensitive tonight, baby? Need me to be careful?" His right hand folded the large cup of her bra back, and heaven help her, his callused fingertips traced over her breasts, teasing her and setting her on fire. She trembled in his arms. "I can be gentle if that's what you want, but I know how badly you need to be taken. I can tell, sugar. I always know. So many things I need to prove to you. I'll show you who you belong to. Make your sweet little pussy ache with every step you take. Fuck you so hard you can't ride a horse for a week. Open you up wide, remind you how good my cock feels deep inside of you. Make you want it every single night."

Several rather disjointed thoughts whirled through Indie's head as she worked her hand to his jeans and palmed the fierce bulge he was now sporting. Damn, but he was hung like a horse.

First of all, he remembered how sensitive her breasts were after her surgery, and seemed to remember that the scar tissue was still occasionally tender. Secondly, when the hell had Luke Camden learned to dirty talk like that? She tried to remember if that had been a part of their trysts before, but couldn't recall him ever igniting her the way he continually did that night.

Okay, get it together Indie. She jerked her head back and tried to breathe in more than the musk of Luke aroused. The scent of aftershave, hay, leather, and sex filled her lungs. It was an intoxicating combination. She yearned to lean over the bed of his truck and order him to show off every skill he'd acquired.

Pushing him back so she could think, she licked her lips. Her tongue indulged in the delectable taste of cinnamon, bourbon, and the hungry masculinity of Luke. She forced herself to go on with the only inevitable conclusion that would come of spending the next two weeks curled up in his bed. "And what happens when I fall right back in love with you, but I still can't stand this fucking town? I ain't lookin' to break my own heart again, Luke."

Fury stormed in his pale blue eyes. "Dammit, Indie, why is it every time we're together all you can think about is getting away? I said two weeks. We'll deal with after that *later*."

Her stubborn resolve made a rapid reappearance. "What makes you so sure I want to get back in your bed when you're bossing me around, dragging me out here, manhandling me, and feeling me up whenever the hell you want to?"

He cocked his left eyebrow and that damned stubborn smirk appeared on his face. "Oh, sugar, you never was any good at lying, either to me or to yourself. You loved every moment of this just as much as I did. You know what you want, and so do I."

Where had all of this confidence come from and why was it so fucking appealing? Letting her heart and her pussy overrun her mind was going to bring back all the pain she'd already endured, but at that moment, with Luke Camden offering her two weeks of nothing but panty-melting sex, hanging out with him, having a date both to her sister's wedding and her reunion, and maybe … just maybe not having to run away this time soothed her wild soul. Maybe she *could* deal with afterwards later. Maybe she should. Maybe it was time to throw all sense of caution to the wind and really live again.

"What's it gonna be, Indie Jane? Come be my girl again. If you still want to run back to Oklahoma City in two weeks, maybe this time I'll go with you. All I know is this walking around on eggshells shit until we just can't stand it anymore and then fucking you like a man just released from prison whenever we're in the same town is over. If you don't want to stay, there's gotta be some way to see each other still, and if there's not, you can be damned sure I'll make the next two weeks tide me over for the next decade."

"You mean like some kind of long distance thing that we both know will never work? You'd actually leave the ranch occasionally? And where would that get us? Nowhere."

"You ain't agreed to this yet, darlin'. I'm still waiting to hear if you're too scared to see just what we might discover."

Oh, he *was* good. She had to give him that. Banking it all on the fact that she'd never turn down a direct challenge. "I don't know where this cocky bastard routine came from, Luke Camden, but you're damned good at it."

A half-grunt of amusement sounded from him. "I ain't the boy you left, sugar. I'm a grown man. I know what I want, and she's standing right in front of me. If I only get you for two weeks that's better than nothing."

"I never really thought you weren't wild enough. I just said that," she defied.

With one long stride, he'd erased the slight distance she'd put between them. He narrowed his eyes in on her. "Getting real, real tired of you lying to me. That wasn't the only reason you left, but it sure as hell was one of 'um. That, and you were afraid to tell me and show me what you desperately needed from me, which was for me to back the fuck up and let you breathe. I was too young and too stupid to figure it out then. That ain't the case anymore. I'm gonna learn you all over again, beautiful. Learn you inside and out. There won't be one thing you desire that I don't see to. This time, I'll be the one showing you what you need and what I crave from you."

"I ain't staying in the godforsaken town, Luke. Long as we're both fully aware of that, then fine, let's do this. You and me back together again, setting our sheets and the whole damn town on fire, gettin' every tongue in the Glen wagging about how loud I make you howl, and how thoroughly fucked I look when we show up at church together Sunday morning and sit beside my mama and the mayor."

Carnal hunger radiated from the fire in his eyes. It sizzled in the humid air between them. His muscles flexed. Her breaths quickened as he edged closer still. He leaned in and brushed a suckled kiss over the tender patch of skin just under her earlobe. "You want the whole town to know you're shaking that sexy ass in my bed again, darlin'? We'll take care of that right now."

Threading his fingers through her hair, he tugged gently, pulling her head to the side and exposing the tender skin of her neck. Realization of what she'd just agreed to and of what he was about to do spiked her blood. Luke Camden was hers again. Wild rebellion fed her soul. "Yes," she urged him on.

He flicked her earlobe with his tongue then ran his teeth over the sensitive skin, making her quake. His lips blazed a soft, seductive trail laced with heated breath and pure intention straight to her neck. Releasing her hair, his fingertips traced from her throat to the hollow of her collarbone as he began to suck.

A low groan hummed from her. His teeth and his tongue worked in accord, nipping and then sucking away the delectable pain he left behind. His right hand cupped her breasts again. She swayed against him until he pulled away, leaving her with a visible claim of ownership.

"All mine." His thumb tended the skin he'd marked. By tomorrow morning, everyone would know they were back together. A deep purple brand was now burned on her neck, and it might as well have spelled out Camden.

"Get in the truck," he ordered.

"Where are we going? I'm not leaving my car here."

"Get in the damn truck, Indie, we're going to see about Juliet. I'll bring you back to your car on our way to my bed. I intend to own every single scream I make you give up for me tonight, but I ain't fucking you hard and dirty, slapping your ass, and making you beg with your daddy in the room next door."

Indie's mouth hung open. Holy fucking hell, Luke Camden had somehow morphed into the man straight out of her every fantasy. Extremely aware that she'd just effectively launched herself right out of the hot skillet and into the fire, she saw no other choice than to let herself be consumed by the raging heat that had always existed between them.

Two weeks from then, she was going to be more miserable than she'd ever been before. He was insane if he thought he'd be able to convince her to stay in this stupid town, but the idea of being his again, even for a little while, just wasn't one she had any hopes of denying herself.

Chapter Five

All right, Camden, you have two weeks, better make the most of every moment. Luke opened the truck door for Indie and helped her step up. "You're gorgeous, you know that?" he vowed. His eyes tracked the curvature of her spine and landed on her ample backside as she stood on his running boards and slid into his truck.

"You're full of shit, you know that?" she came right back.

Huffing, he slammed the door and climbed in the driver's seat. "Seeing as how you're mine again, I think every time you don't take a compliment from me, which are always sincere, I might just turn you over my knee."

She tried with all of her might to look unaffected by his suggested plan, but a luscious grin formed on her beautiful pink lips despite her efforts.

"You are absolutely beautiful. You have always been beautiful, and you will always be beautiful. You got *that*?"

An eye roll was her only response this time. It wouldn't have driven him as crazy as it did if she was one of those women that postured at compliments, pretending they didn't know they were true, but she wasn't. She really couldn't see her rampant sex appeal. He added that to the list of things he needed to accomplish in the next two weeks if he was going to get her to stay.

"What's that look for?" he inquired.

"What look?"

"Indie, honey, I've been in love with you for most of my life. I know your looks. You got that *I'm freaking out but I'm gonna play it cool* thing going on."

"You remember that time after the first ice of winter when we all decided to be idiots and go out and spin the trucks in your back fields?"

Luke turned to stare at her for a long moment before he cranked the truck. "Uh, hell yeah, I remember that. Scared the shit out of me." Luke, Austin, Grant, Tucker, Matt Seaton, and the rest of their crew all went out in the Camden fields after school, thinking it'd be cool to spin the trucks on the ice instead of the dirt like they did in the summer and fall. Being a show off, Luke had locked up the brakes of his old Dodge Ram so they could keep spinning. Indie was loving every minute of it. That had driven him on. It always did. She got him going with nothing more than the fire in her eyes and a broad grin on her face. He'd been thinking life couldn't get much better right up until the CV axle on the rear tire had snapped. The steering wheel seized and they were headed straight towards the old salt house, which was constructed of solid concrete bricks. He shook his head still angry at himself. "All I could think was I was about to get my girl killed. I'll never forgive myself for being so stupid."

"Yeah, but remember how we'd been having a ball right up until then."

"Yeah, I remember that, too. Also remember skipping school the next day so you could fix the joint, and my tire, and the alignment so my parents never found out."

Chuckling at that, she nodded. "I just kind of wonder if this whole two-week thing is gonna end up the same way that did. Time of our life until it all has to end."

"Do me a favor."

"Beyond fucking you senseless for two weeks, being your date to my sister's wedding, and our dumbass reunion? It's a good thing you're so freaking good looking. Seems like I'm making all of the concessions in this plan of yours."

"You know when you get sassy and stubborn with me it just makes me want to fuck you harder, so hush up. I'm on ragged edge just having you in my truck. I've been thinkin' about what I want to do to you since the last time you were home, but I need to take care of Juliet before I take care of you. I just don't want you to go into this thinking it has to end. At least give me a chance to prove to you that life here ain't half as bad as you remember it."

"Luke," she set to argue again.

"Please."

"Fine, but you make me a deal. Don't be so sure this is going to work out that I feel like a Grade-A heartless bitch when I go back to Oklahoma in two weeks. It don't matter how much I love you. I cannot live in this ridiculous town."

"Fine." He tried to hide his grin. All he needed was a chance, and she'd just admitted she still loved him. He'd sure as hell take that. She'd rarely let that admittance slip, even before they'd broken up.

He laced their fingers together, holding her hand on top of her thigh just the way they used to always drive together. "Tell me what's going on with Juliet."

"She won't put her right front hoof down. Dad says he rode her this morning and she seemed fine. I checked her leg and hoof and couldn't see anything wrong. I'm worried about her."

"I've got all my bags in the tool box, honey. I'll get her taken care of. Trust me."

"I do. That's what scares the shit out of me," she mumbled as she jerked her hand out of his and folded them across her cleavage. Still defensive and still blocking what she used to be teased about so cruelly.

"Hey," he held his now empty hand out. "Come on, it's me. Don't shut me out. Scream, cry, curse, throw things, be mad as hell, be stubborn, be happy, feel anything you wanna feel, sugar. I'll still be right here."

Begrudgingly, she rejoined their hands. "I know you will. Don't you ever get sick of my insanity?"

"You're not insane, Indie. I love how there are things you're willing to fight for, and you know I get a kick outta you letting that temper fly. Turns me on something fierce. Can't wait to see that fire in my bed for the next two weeks. Tuck called me and said you all but beat the shit out of him for telling you to calm down. Rookie mistake. I told him he was a dumbass for ya."

That seductive heat that whipped and whirled through her veins bloomed across her cheeks. She smacked his shoulder. He feigned injury just to hear her giggle.

"Did he tell you what my *mother* got for me?"

Now they were getting somewhere.

"Said something about a book. He was in awe of the power you pack in a punch, so he missed the title."

She laughed, but whatever that book had been about had gotten to her. "It was something about losing twenty years in two weeks. Might as well have been pounds, not years." She strangled on the harrowing confession.

Luke pulled in to the gravel driveway of her father's farm and hit the brakes. "Look at me."

The pain of it all darkened her pine green eyes to a deep jade. "You're beautiful, baby. You know it. I sure as hell know it, and your mama's an idiot. Always has been. Always will be. What's that saying, you can't fix stupid you can only sedate it."

"I'd prefer to beat it back with a 2x4."

Laughing, he nodded his agreement. "Point is, you can't change her, Indie, bad as you've always wanted to, so why let her bother you so much? Long as I've known her she's basically been a miserable cow. So, let her be."

"You of all people should know that not being able to leave her be and get over it makes me almost as crazy as what actually comes out of her mouth."

"Let's go see about Juliet, but we're not finished talking about your mother," Luke ordered.

"I ain't really in the mood to be psychoanalyzed, Luke Camden," she huffed.

"Oh yeah?" He caught her as she leapt out of his truck. "Just what *are* you in the mood for, sugar? I have several plans for you, but I might be willing to negotiate if there's something specific you're needing."

Her eyes narrowed, and their customary stubborn fire blazed on. Those full pink lips pursed and images of them wrapped around his cock filled his mind. He longed to order her to suck him off right then and there.

"Let's get something straight. This two-week thing you've decided we're having is about you and me in bed making up for the last fifteen years and getting our fill. It ain't about therapy sessions over my mother, or about who was mean to me in high school. It's about wild sex, the dirtier the better. You got that?"

Luke ran his hand over has mouth to keep from laughing. Her father, who'd walked up behind her in time to hear her diatribe, cleared his throat.

"Daddy!" Indie spun into her father. Luke lost his battle and cracked up.

Her father's smirk said he wasn't upset with her plans. "Does all that mean you won't be able to help me run the shop while you're home?"

"Are you serious? You really want me to run the shop?"

"I've always wanted to work with you, Indie. You know that. I can't afford to have the shop closed, but I sure could use a day or two off. I was hoping you'd like it, maybe decide to stay more than a few weeks."

Indie whirled around and glared at Luke. "You two think you're so smart, don'tcha? I should have known you'd be in on this together. I ain't moving back, so you can both get that little idea right out of your heads."

"Hey, we can hope though, right? I miss you like crazy, baby," Luke vowed. He reached for her, reveling in the way the tense set of her body eased at his touch.

"He ain't the only one that misses you every day either," her father added. "Can't blame us for trying."

40

"Long as you're okay trying and failing. And hell yes, I'll run the shop for you. I'd love to."

"Let's go see about Miss Juliet," Luke urged. This was perfect. If she thought her daddy needed her to come home to help with the shop, maybe that would convince her to stay if Luke couldn't.

"I checked her a few minutes ago. Still won't put any weight on that hoof."

"I'll take care of her, Mr. Harper." Luke knew Ben was aware that he wasn't only referring to the horse.

"I have no doubt." He offered Luke a kind grin as they headed towards the paddock on his small farm.

Juliet had settled on her belly in some hay. Romeo, Indie's solid copper Quarter and Juliet's mate, stood over her, protecting her constantly.

Concern and empathy filled Luke's soul. It always broke his heart to see any animal in pain. The way he saw it most humans fucked everything up. Animals knew what they were put here to do, knew how to love, knew when to mate, and didn't need anyone telling them much of anything.

"All right, boy, it's okay. I'm gonna take care of her," Luke assured softly. He let Romeo sniff his hand and gently petted his muzzle. A moment later, Romeo eased away. The trust in his eyes levied another round of responsibility on Luke. He wouldn't let any of them down.

Settling in the hay beside Juliet, Luke stroked down her side a few times. Indie and her father looked on. Another one of those sweet grins formed on Indie's features. Luke offered her a quick, reassuring wink.

Juliet was hurting badly enough that she didn't put up too much of a fight when Luke tenderly lifted her hoof. "Can you hand me my flashlight, darlin'? It's right there in my bag."

Indie had the light in his hand a second later. She sat on Juliet's other side, loving her and telling her that it would be all right.

"I've got you, girl, just let me find it." He kept his voice soft and soothing. Juliet gave a slight sigh of impatience. "I know it hurts. I'm gonna get it taken care of." Reaching in his pocket he pulled out a pack of sunflower seeds he always kept on him. He fed her a handful and accepted her nuzzle of appreciation.

Luke began to hum, and Juliet laid her head in Indie's lap and relaxed. A minute later he'd located what he'd been looking for. "Okay, she's got an abscess. It's right here. Hard to see, which is good, means the infection is localized."

"What do we do?" Panic crept into Indie's voice.

"I'm gonna take care of it, sweetheart. Just need a good-sized, clean bucket. I've got some Epsom salts in my truck. Need to soften up her hoof, so I can get it to drain. She'll be good as new as soon as we get it cleaned out, and I'll give her an antibiotic. See if you can't get her to stand up again. I'm gonna go get everything I need. Might be a long night."

"Buckets are in the tack room," Ben explained.

A few minutes later, Luke had Juliet's hoof soaking in warm salt water and the horse seemed very appreciative.

"Poor baby. I hate I didn't see it earlier," Indie lamented.

"She'll be fine. They take a little while to get big enough for us to see 'em."

"It's my fault," Ben sighed. "I just can't seem to keep up with everything lately. I should have had her re-shoed weeks ago."

Concern darkened Indie's features. "I'm sure she'll be fine, Daddy. Don't worry."

"She just needs a little TLC. I'll check on her for the next few weeks 'til her sole's stronger and she's good to go again," Luke vowed.

"Thank you," Indie threw her arms around him. He held her to him, reveling in the feel of those luscious curves clinging to him. His cock stirred anxiously, but he shut it down for the tenth time that night. He had to get the horse back to rights before he could bed her. Impatience surged through his veins.

Ben offered Luke a conspiratorial grin behind Indie's back. They were definitely in this together.

"If you two've got this, I think I'll head on in. I'm beat." Ben brushed a kiss on the top of Indie's head before he made his exit.

Three hours later, Luke gently eased Juliet's hoof out of the water. It was improving, but wasn't soft enough to drain as of yet. He settled her back and rubbed her side.

Indie was half asleep against the wall of the barn opposite him. A round of old hemp rope hung on a hook several feet over her head. If that wasn't temptation, he didn't know what was. Leaving Juliet to soak for a few minutes, he slid down the wall and seated himself beside her. He brushed a tender kiss over her lips, deeply appreciative of her responding grin. "Go on to bed, baby doll. I'll stay up with her. It's gonna be nearing morning before I get it all cleaned up and wrapped."

"No, I don't want you to be up with her by yourself." A deep yawn almost stole the words from her lips.

"Indie, darlin', go on to bed. I'll come inside and tuck you in then I'll come back out here. I need to know my girl's warm and comfortable."

"No." She seemed to be regaining her typical reaction to being told to do something. Shaking his head, he chuckled.

"Fine." He stood and quickly located a clean horse blanket before reseating himself beside Juliet. "Come here, then."

She debated arguing for the sake of arguing. She always did, and that stubborn spite always spiked his blood.

"Now," he pointed to the spot in the hay beside him.

Her mouth twisted in consideration, but she could barely hold her eyes open.

"You used to like sleeping in my arms, darlin'. That changed in the last year?"

Sighing, she stretched her arms over her head and popped the crick out of her neck. "Definitely not." With that, she crawled on all fours across the slight space, making him moan. The delighted smirk on her face said she knew she was pushing every button on his body with her luscious ass up in the air, slinking to him like a sex kitten that needed his satisfaction. She settled her head on his lap and traced her index finger up the bulge against his zipper line, grinning over the effect she'd had on him. "It wasn't that I didn't want to come over here. It's that I know if I lay down on you, I'll go to sleep and I wanted to stay up with you."

Luke settled the blanket over her and began gently easing his fingers through her long auburn hair. "How about you let me take care of Juliet *and* my girl. Lookin' after you was always my favorite job. You promised me two weeks. That starts right now."

Her blinks extended in length as he played with her hair. She'd always loved that, a surefire way to soothe her day no matter what it might've held. "Pretty sure it started when you kissed me like you owned me back at Saddleback's in front of the whole damn town."

Chuckling softly, Luke nodded his agreement. "I do like the sound of owning you," he goaded. "Rolls right off my tongue, real sweet like."

She eased to her back so she could stare up at him. "Don't get ahead of yourself, cowboy. We both know I ain't a tamable kind of girl. Nobody's gonna *own* me."

"Oh sugar, I have no desire to tame you. I want you wild. Dirtier the better, just like you so eloquently told your daddy," he laughed.

She covered her face with her hands. "I cannot believe he heard me say that."

"He didn't seem too surprised. I got the distinct impression he don't really care what we do as long as you might think about moving back. 'Sides, there's a difference in being tamed and being owned." He carefully lifted Juliet's hoof again and pressed along the abscess. It was getting closer.

"I'm going to indulge you in this line of ridiculous conversation because I'm sleepy, and I want you to get back to playing with my hair. What's the difference?"

Luke considered for a minute as he returned his fingers to her hair. "Being tamed ain't all that bad if you like the person doing the taming, I 'spose. Since trying to tame you would work 'bout as well as lighting a bottle rocket in a Dixie cup, I got no interest in that. To me, *owning* you would mean it's my job to see to everything you need in my bed and out. Anything you want or need is my top priority. Means you're willing to give me total control of what happens between us in my bedroom. Means you'll let me explore, let me show you what I've longed to share with you for the past decade, let me own your pleasure, take it all for myself, give you everything I know you've needed, and everything I sure as hell want from you."

Intrigue lit the fire in her eyes. She stared up at him for a long drawn minute before she settled on giving him her sexy smirk. "My God, Luke Camden, have you gone and gotten kinky on me?"

Never dropping her gaze, he traced his fingers over the soft curve of her cheek and gently teased the mark he'd left on her neck in the parking lot of Saddlebacks. The first of many he intended to leave on her body. My God, the things she did to him, the way the mere mention of her name could shoot fire through his veins until he was nothing more than a savage, wild and demanding. He never would've had his hands up some woman's shirt or marked them all for himself in a damn gravel parking lot. That wasn't him — until he was with her.

He tempted the top swells of her breasts and loved that her breathing changed with nothing more than a gentle caress from his fingertips. "So many things I crave to do with you, honey. So many things I want. Every time you came to me in the past few years, and I was so needy for you I never took my time, I hated myself. I owe you better. I owe *us* better. You're so damn beautiful, Indie, and I have always loved you. I want to know you again, really know you. Know all the things you've never shared with anyone else. Know things you won't even admit to yourself, things you don't think anyone should know. You never have to say them out loud, sugar, I'll figure 'em all out and guard them with my life, but I want you to know me that way, too. You still drive me wild. You always will. But I want to be your sanity again. I let you down on my end of our deal. I want to make you feel things you've never felt before. Let me show you, honey. Let me show you how it could be between us."

She sat up, chasing her breath. Her bottom lip slipped through her teeth. "I take it the answer to my question is yes, then."

Chuckling, he brushed a few strands of her hair behind her right ear, watching her eyes close in an extended blink as he caressed her cheek with his thumb. "Okay, yes. The things I want to share with you would probably be qualified as kinky. That okay with you?"

"Oh, hell yeah, cowboy, but fair warning, there's been a kinky Luke Camden in my dreams for years now. Gonna take a helluva lot of skill to out-do my fantasies."

Certain that he was going to combust in his Wranglers, Luke let that information travel on the blood flowing rapidly from his brain to his cock. His entire body was honed in on nothing but her scent and the need that darkened her eyes. His muscles tensed, desperate to hold her, to share more with her than kisses and a quick feel-up. His cock ached. He needed the relief that could only come with burying himself inside that tight, silky channel that always felt like it had been sculpted for him alone. He wasn't a horny teenager anymore. He needed more. "Just so you know, Indie Jane, I'm taking that as a direct challenge."

"Good."

Ticking his left eyebrow upward, he decided to see just how much she might let him get away with. "That means I'm in control. You do what I say when I say it."

She laughed at him outright. "In bed, hell yeah. You think I'm going for that out of bed? You've clearly lost a large portion of all of those brain cells you had up there back when we were in school. I wouldn't make that deal with you or anyone else, and you know it."

His customary grunt of annoyance was louder than he'd intended. "Can't blame a guy for trying," he allowed.

"Can't blame a girl for telling him he's crazier than a shithouse rat."

"What is it you're so afraid of? Surely it ain't me. Somewhere in all of that stubbornness you know good and well I'd never do one single thing that didn't bring you pleasure."

"I ain't doing your laundry, cooking your dinner, or cleaning your house. I ain't playing your wife."

"And you're really gonna sit there and tell me that you thought I'd ask you to do those things? I'm a grown man. I do my own laundry, clean my own house, take care of my own shit, and mostly cook my own meals. I do eat up at Mama and Daddy's occasionally to keep Mama happy."

"Oh my gosh, your mama's cookin'. Now, that's something I might consider moving back for."

"Well, then I sure as hell will make sure you get it on the regular, darlin'. But take back all of that insanity about me getting you to do chores for me."

"Fine, but you still only get your say *in* the bedroom."

Indie wasn't certain how much longer she was going to be able to pretend she was unaffected by his confession and his plans. The red satin panties she loved were soaked thoroughly. So wet she longed to beg him to lay her out on the blanket he'd covered her in, remove them entirely, and bathe her swollen skin with his tongue until he soothed the liquid fire flowing readily from her pussy. Her nipples throbbed anxiously against the lace of her bra. *Suck me.* The words formed on the tip of her tongue, but she ordered herself not to beg … yet. She felt fevered and raw, in need of relief. She had no idea that his sexual preferences had darkened dramatically with age, but she intended to fulfill his every fantasy, just as long as he did the same for her. Two weeks wasn't nearly long enough. Her dirty dreams of him came by the dozens. Hell, her favorite vibrator might as well have been named Luke. She'd figure something out. Maybe coming back to the Glen more often wasn't such a terrible idea.

For the moment, she forgot all about her mother, the mayor, the book, the affair, the town, and every other shadow of her past that always darkened her trips home. Every cell in her body needed to feel his touch. She scooted closer, letting everything go. Nuzzling her head on his shoulder she grinned as he wrapped his arms around her.

"That's it. There's my girl. I've got you, honey."

She wished she could take back that shithouse rat comment. God, why did she have to be so bitchy all the time? What was wrong with her? He was offering her every single thing she'd ever wanted. She just couldn't bring herself to apologize.

"You okay?" he soothed.

"Yeah." She swallowed down the raw regret that had been housed in her soul since she'd left him standing in his dorm room holding an engagement ring so many years ago. "Maybe better than I've been in

46

a long time. This is crazy though, Luke. We're just gonna get hurt all over again."

"Hey," he cradled her face in his hands. "You promised me you'd give me a chance. You said you wouldn't go into this damned and determined to leave again."

And that, right there, was the scariest thing she could ever have agreed to. If she waved the white flag, if she didn't constantly harness her stubborn resolve throughout all of this, she'd lose herself all over again. It was inevitable.

"I have an amendment to our bedroom agreement, actually." The low smooth gravel of his voice sent a hot flash of lightning through her veins, kindling the fire between her legs.

"What's that?" She felt her face pull into a grin, the one she only ever gave to him.

"Me being in control doesn't only exist in my bedroom. If I tell you to get nekkid for me, say, in the mayor's mansion, a barn, Saddlebacks, my truck, hell, in the church bathroom, you do it. You drive me crazy with wantin' you, honey. Your sexy body, the way you smell, the way you argue with me, the way you look at me like you're lookin' at me right now like you want me to fuck the life out of you and then you want to argue with me, it all drives me nuts. There's sure to be a time or two over the next few weeks that I ain't gonna make it back to my house. I'm gonna need you right then and there, up against a wall, over a fence, back of my truck, wherever. I've never had any patience when it came to you. That fact hadn't changed."

Delight surged through Indie as she laughed. "Well, I did swear to always keep you wild, but I'm curious. Just what does the tiny, sleepy town of Pleasant Glen think of *this* side of calm, cool, and collected Luke Camden, town vet, ever-reliable cowboy, eldest son of the highly respected Camden family, and partial owner of the legendary Camden Ranch?"

His dark chuckle sizzled across her skin. "Not too sure anyone could ever be legendary in the Glen, and truthfully, I don't give a damn. I got the impression shocking people was on top of your list of desires."

"Well, yeah, it is. I just didn't know you'd be up for it."

"Oh honey, you have so many surprises in store, but know this, I don't share this side of myself with anyone else. Only you. You've always brought out my more basic nature. When you're around, I can't help myself. I believe you're currently wearing my mark in a real apparent locale. That won't be the only way I let everyone know you're mine again."

The anxious shiver that worked through her had nothing to do with the cool Nebraskan temperature that night. "I suddenly have a deep desire to get nekkid for you in the mayor's house, but seeing as we're in my daddy's barn, that horse stall is available."

"Anxious, sugar?"

Indie swore the wicked grin he gave her should be illegal. Every reproductive organ in her body was damn near line dancing.

"First time I have you won't be in your daddy's barn, but don't worry, I ain't opposed to it in the future. Been thinking about making good use of that rope and the hay bale pulley up there."

"Oh, okay, I get it. I'm dreaming, right? In a minute, I'm gonna appear in the school cafeteria nekkid, or my teeth are gonna fall out, or some other bizarre thing will happen, and I'll wake up."

Humored skepticism formed on the chiseled lines of his face. "If this were a dream, would me wanting to tie you up and have my way with you be good or bad?"

A surge of heated blood scalded her cheeks. She still wasn't totally convinced she was actually awake. "Good," she admitted cautiously.

His rumbled groan as he caged her body against the wall of the barn and affixed his lips to hers with enough heat to melt away any hesitation she might ever have had awoke Romeo, who came to check on Juliet. Luke's hands raced over her body like he couldn't decide where to touch her first.

"Oh God, yes," she gasped as they settled on her tits, stroking softly, cupping their heavy weight in his strength, and soothing their need. Before she could process anything beyond how badly she'd wanted this and how good it felt, her shirt was up over her bra and she was helping him pull her arms out of the sleeves. Wasting no time in doing away with the red, lacey undergarment, he circled his tongue around her left nipple and gave several soft suckles before he nipped, drawing a gasp from her lungs.

"You let me know when you figure out that you're awake, darlin'." His teeth slipped along her wet nipple, and she writhed. Her hips thrust, so anxious to feel his weight on hers. Another hickey was branded between her breasts before he jerked away. "Dammit, I'm so fucking weak when it comes to you. We're not doing this tonight." Skipping the bra that had landed nearby in a pile of hay, he eased her shirt back down. Beyond frustrated, she begrudgingly shoved her arms back in the shirtsleeves.

48

"Why?" she all but whimpered. "It ain't like we haven't done it in a barn before."

The memories of their wild youth painted themselves on the canvas of his ice blue eyes, but he shook his head. "Because you deserve better, Indie. You deserve my best. You deserve hours of extended foreplay, me making you so wet you drip down your thighs and soak my bed sheets. Me making you beg for all I can give you. Me worshipping you, kissing every single spot on your body, several of them more than once, a few I'm betting haven't ever been kissed before. Me awakening sides of yourself you aren't even aware exist, darlin'. That's what you deserve, and for the next two weeks that's the only kind of love we'll be making."

Her entire body vibrated in anticipation. Her breath continued elude her. The undiluted desire in his eyes was intoxicating. Her brain and her pussy went to war. Her brain said the scenario he'd just described would definitely be worth waiting for. Her clit had no patience, however. Before she could formulate either a demand to get on with it or an agreement which didn't come easily to her in the first place, Luke knelt beside Juliet and eased her hoof from the bucket once more.

"Okay, girl. Let's see if we can't get this fixed up."

"Let me help." Indie ordered her lascivious side away for the moment.

"This shouldn't hurt much, but try to keep her calm. I'll try to be quick."

An hour later, Luke had drained the abscess, doctored it, bandaged Juliet's hoof, and had given her a shot of antibiotics to stop the chance of it spreading. Juliet was almost as good as new. Indie grinned when her horse nuzzled Luke's chest in appreciation as she stood on all four of her hooves and then walked gingerly to her stall while he cleaned his hands with an antiseptic medical grade wipe.

"Thank you." Indie threw her arms around Luke. "I can pay you." That felt odd, but she was certain her father paid him when he saw to the horses in her absence.

Offense tensed the hard line of his jaw. "You ain't paying me. Why would you even say that?"

"I just figured Daddy would've offered, and I'm not used to us being *us* again. Plus, I'm tired and cranky, so don't get all huffy on me."

"Yeah, I'm beat, too, I guess. I gotta be up in a little while for chores. I'm sorry, darlin'. I don't think I'd be up for much tonight.

Come home with me though. I love wakin' up with you in my arms. When I get back from chores, we'll get started on our reconnecting." He laced their fingers together and guided her out of the barn.

Delighted with that idea, Indie considered, but one glance towards her father's house had her shaking her head. "I need to visit some with Daddy. I was at Mama's longer than I was here this afternoon, and I know he gets his feelings hurt."

The hot breath from his irritated sigh whispered through her hair and she almost gave in. "Fine, but I'll be back to pick you up after chores tomorrow mornin', so be ready for me, and I get a little something before I go."

The heat that had been searing through her veins all damn night ignited in a blaze of yearning. The darkened need in his eyes emboldened. "And what is it you might like, cowboy?"

"It ain't what I'd like, sugar, it's what I won't survive without. I want to put you to bed tonight, strip you down, tuck you in, make sure you remember how good we are together. I'm about to go home and get off in the shower imagining it's your hands wrapped around me instead of my own, but I don't want you touching yourself unless I'm watching. There's my first bedroom rule, but I figured I ought to give you a little something to tide you over. Like I said, I'll be taking good care of you from now on."

Indie's mouth hung open in stupefied shock. Her mind raced through a thousand other bedroom rules she longed to hear him make. Her pussy tightened and throbbed at the very idea of allowing him total control of her pleasure. Her lungs begged for air it took far too long to provide. Fantasies swamped her brain. Tied up to his bed, or on her knees before his cock, arms bound behind her, him instructing her. Luke Camden watching her get herself off under his command. It took her typical stubborn irritation a full minute to re-engage. "Are you actually standing there telling me I can't masturbate whenever the hell I want to, because ...." Suddenly, his index finger pressed over her lips and he narrowed his eyes. She opened her mouth again, but he shook his head.

"Do not bite me, and you just willingly said I could have total control in the bedroom, and don't get ornery and tell me you'll just do it in the shower. You can make yourself come as often as you'd like, long as it's me you're thinkin' of and I'm right there watching. You got that, Indie Jane?"

"I *will* do whatever the hell I want to do whenever the hell I want to do it, whether you're watchin' or not, you got *that* Luke Camden?" *Indie, shut the fuck up. This is precisely what you want.*

The firm smack of his right hand against her ample ass brought another rush of wet heat to her pussy and added to the extreme confusion she was currently living. She tried to chase her breath simply so she could beg for more.

Before she could process beyond that, he consumed her mouth like a man possessed. Compliance. She understood. Her mind scrambled and she was unable to resist opening under the urging of his tongue. When he turned his head to extend the kiss, "You need another one, darlin', or can you behave?" murmured against her lips.

Giving up any ability to reason through this new side to their relationship, she trembled in his arms. Some part of her mind longed to argue, but curiosity overrode her brain. Giving him compliance amped the desperate need consuming her entire body. What would it be like to let him own her like this? She had challenged him to be kinky, after all. She supposed she got what she'd deserved. And just then, this side of Luke Camden felt like a drug she longed to consume for as long as it was available, one she'd fantasized about more times than she could count. She had no idea where this was going, but she sure as hell wanted to find out. A soft, throaty moan escaped from deep in her chest.

He pulled away with that cocky smirk affixed to his face. "I'm gonna take that sexy little noise to mean you're gonna behave."

"Guess you'll just have to wait and see, won't you? I honestly can't wait to find out just how far you'll go for me." She channeled her sexiest coo, watching the fire in his eyes roar to a blaze.

"Don't push me, Indie, honey. I know precisely what you need, and I ain't afraid to give it to you." With that, he leaned and lifted her up into his arms. The move effectively ripped her out of the lusty haze filling her brain.

"Put me down. I'm too heavy to carry like this."

"You're testing my patience something fierce, Indieanna. You trying to earn another one? Next one I'm pulling your jeans down, and I'll turn your sexy little ass as pink as your pussy. Now hush, or I *am* gonna take you in that barn and show you how fucking gorgeous you are. I'm putting you to bed, and I don't want to be interrupted by your daddy. I'm flat out of patience. If I need to put something in your mouth to keep you quiet, believe me, honey, I will."

Silently, he opened the back door to the home that had raised her, settled her on her feet, and closed it back. Taking her hand in his, he led her to her childhood bedroom and sealed them inside. Indie could just make out her father's rhythmic snoring from the other side of the house.

"Now, I want you to sleep naked for me tonight, baby. I want to think about your sexy curves tangled up in them sheets needing me. Lift your arms." His smooth, whispered gravel elicited another quick moan from her as she obeyed without hesitation this time.

He tossed her shirt away and tenderly ran his fingertips down her breasts, tracing her soft midsection until he landed on the snap of her jeans. Her body swayed anxiously.

"Lord Almighty, you are so damn beautiful. You make me hurt," he grunted as he popped the snap and slid the soft denim down her long legs. "I fucking burn for you, you know that?" Desperate to have some part of him in her hands, she slid her fingers over the rock hard bulge in his Wranglers. His eyes closed in an extended blink as air hissed through his teeth. Indie palmed him, wishing his clothes away but far too caught up in the low intonation of his voice to strip him. Her body was limp with need. "That's right, beautiful. You feel what you do to me. It's all for you. Step out of them boots." When he called her beautiful, somehow she always believed him. His vows erased the taunts she'd endured for much of her life.

When she was bare save her red satin panties, he stepped back and licked his bottom lip like he couldn't believe he was the guy lucky enough to see her this way. The fire in his gaze heated her flesh. His desire coursed through her veins taking residence between her legs. She shifted, sliding her thighs together back and forth, desperate for the friction she required to get relief.

His low growl summoned her gaze. "That's my job, honey. I told you. You're so damn needy aren't you? Need me to touch you? Need me to make it feel better?"

"Now," she whimpered. "Dammit, I'll do what you say. I'll let you be in control or whatever, just please get on with this. God, I need you."

"Fuck, I like you like this, sugar. Needy and beggin'. Them panties so wet I can see how bad you're cravin' me."

Luke stared unabashedly at the damp crotch of her pretty little panties. God, he wanted to tear them away from her, throw her on the bed, and take her hard and fast until he bathed her walls in his cum, made a claim she'd never forget. But not this time. He was playing this hand with deliberate, methodic design. There was only one way to get her to stay. He had to tap into that well of rebellion that housed all of the pain she'd endured long ago, silence those demons with his love, banish them completely, until he'd freed her so thoroughly she had no hope of recalling the cages that had once existed in her soul.

Bringing fresh air to her lungs to calm her rage had always been his job. He had a plan, and he was sticking to it this time. The prize was more than worth his patience. He wasn't stopping until he was waiting on her at the end of an aisle. He'd existed without her long enough.

Stepping to her, he traced his fingertips over the wet satin, making her writhe. He tracked his hands back up her silky skin as he nibbled at her neck, listening to her impatient gasps of breath. "So fucking gorgeous. So wet. That all for me, sugar?"

"You know it is," she whimpered.

"God, I can't wait to kiss and lick every square inch of your skin. Can't wait to feel you against me while I take you slow and gentle and then hard and fast over and over again. I dream, Indie, I dream of the way your beautiful tits feel against my thighs when I make you suck me." He spun his thumbs around her diamond hard nipples. "Every single time I jack off, it's your pussy and your ass I dream of filling so full of my cum you're overflowing, dripping down your lips, coating your thighs. Want me to take your panties off, doll baby? I need to see that pretty snatch all pink and wet for me."

"God, yes," she groaned as her body leaned into him.

"Put arms hands around me. Hold onto me."

She complied willingly. Docile and sweet when he had her like this. Working the panties over the lush curves of her ass, he helped himself to handfuls of her ample backside. He shoved the panties to the floor and cupped her mound, pressing his palm against her clit. Her fingernails dug into his shoulders. Perfection.

He pressed his middle and ring finger deep in her channel. His own eyes closed in pleasure as the heated liquid silk consumed him. Her body cinched, pulling him deeper, and his low groan filled the air around them. Ordering himself to keep it quiet lest her daddy know what they were up to, he slicked his thumb with her honey and teased at the hood of her clitoris.

"Yes, yes." She began to ride his hand. He knew precisely where he was going. Knew how to give her what she wanted, but he wasn't in any hurry. "More," she pled.

"Not yet, darlin'. You're gonna get used to coming when I tell you to. Been thinking about having my hands in you for so damn long, I intend to enjoy this."

She ground harder against him, her body desperate and demanding. "That's it. Let it feel good for me." Curling his fingers, he stroked her g-spot, tentatively at first, making her quake in desperation. The spicy heat of her arousal filled his nostrils, thick, warm, and ripe with her rebellion. His mouth watered, so hungry to taste her juices. "You smell so damn good, baby. Make me crazy with wantin' to taste your sweet cream."

"Then taste me. I know you want to. I can see it in your eyes. God, you love it don't you. You love that you were the first guy to ever touch me like this, love that you know how to make me come all over your face when you lick me, love that you were the first to taste me. Do it. I'll take everything you've got and then some."

His cock burned so fiercely he was concerned his Wranglers might catch fire. He did love that he'd been her first, the first guy to ever touch her tender virgin skin, the man who'd opened her, giving her everything he was, the first to ever see her come completely undone at his touch. If he had any say at all, he'd also be the last.

Closing his eyes, commanding himself not to give in, he clenched his jaw until he was certain if he opened his mouth the next thing he said wouldn't be lay back and spread your legs for me. "Not tonight, darlin'. Later. This is it for tonight. I'll get my taste. I'll suck what I get from you off my fingers, gorge myself on them until I decide it's time to have my fill of it from your pussy. Right now, I want these." He leaned and swirled his tongue around her left nipple. His name hissed from her lips. She was so close. He eased up, extending his delectable torture.

He drowned her nipple with his kisses until he finally drew it into the fiery heat of his mouth and began to suck. Gently, he eased his thumb under the hood of her clitoris and gave her what she required to come.

The throbs of her sweet clit were timed to her racing pulse. His own heart thundered in his chest. He sucked harder. He was going to have a dozen half-moon fingernail marks on his shoulders. The pain registered instantly as undeniable pleasure and racked readily in his balls. "So good, isn't it, baby?" He released her breast and whispered in her ear as she panted for breath. "Feels so good right there. I know."

"Oh God," she purred.

"Breathe for me, sugar. Have to remember to breathe." Another stroke deep inside of her and another rotation of his thumb and she came with a racked gasp of breath. He eased his hand away and wrapped her up in his arms as she collapsed against him in a storm of aftershocks that he swore shook his soul as well.

"I love you, Indie," he vowed readily as he lifted her back into his arms and settled her in the bed. He grinned at the ancient cowhide-patterned sheets she'd had since they were in high school.

"Stay with me." The yearning in her eyes made him consider doing just that, but he refused to have sex with her that night, and if he crawled in the bed there'd be no stopping himself. He just wasn't that strong, and the line between keeping her sated but constantly begging for more was razor thin. There was too much at stake for him to give in because she made him weak. Luke doubted her father would be too thrilled to wake up to them naked in her adolescent bed together anyway.

He leaned down and brushed a tender kiss on her temple. "Not tonight, darlin'. I gotta get up and do chores in an hour. I'll be right back to pick you up. I promise."

She leaned up on her elbow and gave him a kiss that made leaving her room feel like he was being asked to stand barefoot in a hot oven. He settled the sheets around her gently. "Sweet dreams, doll baby." Locating the jeans he'd stripped off of her, he stole those red satin panties that had all but driven him right over the edge. He made a show of inhaling her scent from the fabric before he shoved them in his pocket.

"Those gonna be covered in jizz when I get them back?" A deep yawn contorted her beautiful face before she achieved a sleepy smirk.

"Who says you're getting them back, sugar? I'll see you in the morning. Sleep good."

When Luke passed Saddleback's, he cringed. Her Camaro was the only car in the empty lot. *Dammit*. He'd completely forgotten they were supposed to pick it back up on the way to the ranch. Whole town would surely be talking by morning. Half the residents of Pleasant Glen had watched him drag her out of the bar. No doubt what everyone would suspect now. That was sure to go over like a lead balloon. Rubbing his eyes, he pressed the accelerator harder. There was no way to get the car now, and he was beyond exhausted.

He headed in his front door, stripped, grinned at the peek of red satin in the pocket of his discarded jeans, and collapsed into bed. So far his plan was on track. She'd given him the two weeks and agreed to his bedroom conditions. He just needed a little help from fate and he'd have his girl right back in their hometown where she belonged permanently.

Chapter Six

Less than two hours from the time his head had flattened his pillow, a knock sounded on Luke's front door. A long, largely incoherent string of expletives flew from his mouth as he stumbled to answer it. Normally, his brothers and sisters would get started on the chores without him if he had a long night out with a sick animal.

Just enough of his brain cells were still functioning to remember that no one knew he'd been doctoring Juliet. Everyone was under the impression he'd driven off into the sunset with Indie to kindle the old flames and no one was going to cut him any slack for that.

He jerked the door open, rubbing his hand over his stubble and through his hair.

A glint of sunlight floated low over the pastures near Luke's home, turning the navy blue sky a deep indigo.

Brock offered him an apologetic gaze. "Sorry, man. I, uh, assume last night went well. I'd let you sleep, but I got a heifer in trouble. Sacs been showin' for too long without anything else. She started last night when I got back from town. Nothing's happening. I'm worried we're gonna lose her and the calf."

Luke managed a nod. Damn, this was gonna be one long day. "Let me grab a cup of coffee. I'll be right there. Can you get her in a headgate?" Brock followed Luke into his kitchen where he made a quick cup of coffee using the fancy coffee maker that made one cup servings his parents had given him for Christmas.

"I'll try. Can't get her up at all currently. I've got the chains out there though."

While the cup filled, he pulled on his jeans and a clean shirt. He tossed Indie's panties on his dresser. Brock pretended not to notice, but the smirk on his face said otherwise. Luke offered no explanation. Wasn't anybody's business but his.

He cringed when they reached the heifer. Poor thing was laying on the ground, damn near groaning out her agony. Luke's stomach clenched. Holly and Natalie were trying to help. Grant was pulling on shoulder gloves. The ones Brock had been wearing were laying nearby.

"I've got her." Luke scrubbed up and grabbed his own set of gloves before he coaxed his way past the visible sac and worked his way to the canal. *Dammit.* "Got four hooves already in the canal. I don't think I can reposition it. Get her in that head gate."

"You gonna do a cesarean?" Grant patted the cow's side gently. "It's all right, girl."

"Don't know another way to save 'um both. Get her left side scrubbed and shaved. I gotta get my kit."

By the time he got back, Natalie and Brock had the cow secured, and Brock was easing a razor down her side. Holly was scrubbing her hands and arms to help him. His youngest sister's determination rolled off of her waves. You never told Holly she wasn't going to do something. She was almost as stubborn as Indie, but not quite. If she was as hellbent as Luke on saving the mama and the calf, he was fine with her help. They'd certainly done this before.

He drew up the anesthesia and set to begin.

A few minutes later, Luke's cell phone rang in his pocket. "Get that." He leaned his hip outward while he made the final incision. Grant grabbed the phone.

"If it ain't Indie Jane calling," he goaded as he answered her call.

Luke hated he couldn't talk to her and explain why he wasn't on his way to pick her up. He could just make out her greeting.

"Yeah, hang on, he's right here."

Luke stared at his brother, certain he'd lost his mind. "I'm a little busy." He gestured to the small hoof he was currently easing out of the cow.

"You birth. I'll hold the phone." Grant held the phone to his ear.

"Hey, doll baby, sorry I'm late. I'm in the middle of a c-section."

"Oh my God. Why are you talking to me?"

"Grant has the phone to my ear. I can multitask." Gently, he paired the calves back hooves and gestured for Holly to rupture the amniotic sac.

"I'll let you go. I'm gonna go have breakfast with Daddy then I'll come out there."

"Your car's still at Saddlebacks." He glared at his siblings as they all snickered.

"Shit. Forgot about that. Oh, and just for your information, I'm wearing nothing but the smile you left me with and ... socks."

Luke couldn't help but chuckle. Her slight rebellion and the impish tone of her voice sent a flashflood of blood to his cock. "That ain't *exactly* what I told you to do."

Holly rolled her eyes and shook her head at him.

"My feet got cold, and I haven't ever been too good at doing *exactly* what anyone tells me to do."

58

A grunt escaped Luke's lips as he attached the chain to the calf's hind legs. Ornery little vixen. They sure as hell could play this game. In fact, he'd love nothing more. "I need to go, sugar. We'll continue this conversation later, because believe me, I've got plenty to say about that."

"Mmm, can't wait."

Grant ended the call for him. Before his siblings and cousin could begin their teasing and harassment, Luke frowned. "It's twins. That's what was wrong. Pull now." He and Grant took hold of the chains and pulled the first calf free. "Get her breathing." He handed the calf to Brock, who had the baby breathing a second later. He cleaned her up while Luke eased the second towards his incision.

Indie set her phone aside, rubbed her hands over her face, and blinked several times as she took in the bedroom that had been the backdrop for her entire childhood. It took her a moment to process that she was not sixteen, she had not been messing around with a teenage Luke Camden in her childhood bedroom the night before, and she really had no reason to feel like she'd done anything wrong. The heady excitement that always came from a healthy dose of rebellion still brought a grin to her face, however.

Sitting up in bed, she let the feeling of Luke's instructions for her to sleep naked work through her. She still needed to figure out how exactly he'd turned into the personification of her every dirty fantasy, but just then she didn't care. Kicking the sheets off of her feet, she grinned at the socks she'd added, partly for warmth but mostly for spite. *Bring it on, Luke Camden. Let's see how far you'll really go playing a surly dom.* The ancient alarm clock on the bedside table announced it was nearing nine. She hadn't meant to sleep so late.

Her father knocked on her bedroom door. "Indie Jane, you want some coffee? I made breakfast."

Instinctively, she jerked the sheets back over her chest. Time seemed oddly variable. She couldn't quite place the current version of herself correctly on the timeline of her life. "I'll be up in a minute, Daddy," she called. "And hell yes on the coffee."

She heard the customary pops of the old parquet flooring as her father shuffled back to the kitchen.

Indie dressed and padded down the hallway towards the smell of coffee. Her father's smirk greeted her as he handed her a mug. "Found Juliet messing with this when I went to check her this morning. Might not want to leave them in the barn." He picked up her bra from the counter and placed it in her other hand.

Certain her face was now the color of the bra in question, Indie returned to her room and tossed it in the hamper. She took a long, drawn minute to regain her composure before she rejoined her father at the breakfast table. He was still chuckling. "I'm guessing you might also like a ride to town to retrieve your car."

Indie ground her teeth. The first sip of her coffee eased a little of her annoyance however. "Yeah, if you don't mind. Luke's doing a C-section on one of their cows this morning. I thought I might go out to the ranch and see if I can help."

"Boy's better than any vet with an actual degree. He really ought to go back and finish just so he can get the prescriptions easier. The vets in Ogallala gives him a hard time when he orders meds, but they won't come out here and take care of the animals so they always fill 'em. They just like to remind him that they have degrees hanging on their office walls and he don't. He's the one that does all the work, though. This town wouldn't make it without him."

Irritation ticked in Indie's blood. She hadn't known any of that, but when she considered someone making Luke feel less than, the desire to forcefully remove their heads from their bodies welled in her soul. Who the hell did they think they were anyway? She dared one guy with some fancy-ass degree to say to her face that Luke wasn't the best vet and the best man in the entire Midwest. *You have the best, Indie. So, why the hell do you keep running from him?* Whoa. Her brain pulled that one right out of left field. She drowned the thought in more coffee and her father's slightly overcooked eggs and bacon.

"I'll kill him," Indie huffed an hour later when her father pulled into the gravel parking lot of Saddlebacks. Blue flashing lights alerted everyone on Main Street that morning to the fact that her Camaro was still in the lot. Clarke Newsome, the illustrious sheriff's deputy of the Glen, and the pipsqueak who'd ratted Luke and Indie out to the principal one day when they were making out under the bleachers a good fifteen years ago was leaning against her car. Indie's blood boiled. She still hadn't forgiven him for tattling, and now he was leaning against her prized possession. Clarke had always been jealous of Luke and looked for any opportunity in school to make his life miserable. It appeared nothing had changed in that department. Nothing in this stupid town ever did, she reminded herself.

60

"Don't scalp him," her father sighed. "I ain't got time to bail you out today, and it sounds like Luke's busy, too."

Indie narrowed her eyes. Eliza Olsen was dressed in her waitressing uniform and had her finger wagging in Clarke's face. As soon as Indie's father had the truck in park, she leapt out.

"Get your ass off my car right this minute, Clarke, or I'll recover my seats with your skinny hide."

Eliza laughed. "He ain't got enough fat on him to fry his ears, Indie, much less make seats out of. Now *get* Clarke. I ain't kidding. Me 'n Ed don't give two hollers that her car's here. It ain't hurtin' nothing."

Indie couldn't help but grin. Eliza and Ed had owned Saddlebacks for as long as she could remember. She'd always adored Eliza. A warm contentment washed through her, an odd sensation given how irritated she'd been just a moment before.

"This vehicle was parked in a private lot all night, Miss Harper. I'm writing you a ticket. You keep up with that disrespectfulness to an officer of the law, and I'll add trespassing, loitering, and threatening an officer to the charges."

Ben's hand landed on Indie's shoulder a moment before she lunged at Clarke. "Don't do it, baby girl. He sure as hell ain't worth it."

Eliza's hand moved from her hip to jabbing Clarke in the shoulder. "You got one thing right, Clarke. This is a private lot, a private lot owned by me and mine, and if I say Indie can park her car here for as long as she likes, she can. I'm glad it's here. Makes me happier than a pig in mud she and Luke might me workin' things out. Now get, 'fore I go find me a skillet."

Indie took a half second to wonder just how many people were already aware she'd agreed to being Luke's for the next two weeks. She ran her fingertips over the rather large purple hickey on the right side of her neck. She'd let him brand her like a billboard, so she supposed she really couldn't complain. Her father hadn't commented on the mark, though he'd most certainly seen it. She'd have to wear four scarves to cover the thing, and she was definitely not a scarf-wearing kind of girl.

Clarke turned his frustrated glare on Eliza. "You start letting just anyone park here all night, won't be long before we up and have street gangs right here in Pleasant Glen. Is that what you want?"

"Oh, dear Lord in Heaven." Ben rolled his eyes. "Clarke, son, ain't there somebody jay-walking down by the drugstore, or maybe Aunt Bea's jarring up some kerosene pickles or some'um? Indie's takin' her car on to Camden Ranch now. Ain't no harm done. Let everyone be."

"Every single man in this town, save your pansy-ass and maybe Mayor Jenkins owns pitchforks and pistols, and sure as heck knows how to use 'em both. They also got enough strength to haul hay, cattle, horses, and just about anything else. Let some street gang try out the Glen, you mo-ron, they ain't gonna get far," Eliza retorted. She cringed a moment later. "Oh, I'm sorry to speak ill of the mayor like that, Indie. He's been in here every day this week, prattling on about one thing or another. On my nerves something fierce."

Indie beamed at her. "Believe me, no offense taken. I got about as much use for the mayor as I do for Clarke."

"Both 'bout as good for our town," Eliza agreed. "You know, that's what I oughta do. I oughta march right inside and call up Luke. He'd bury you in the ground like a daisy then run you over with his tractor. Now, 'fore I call up to Camden Ranch, *get.*"

It irked Indie that Eliza thought she needed Luke to fight her battles for her, but the image of Luke running over a half-buried Clarke with a tractor was rather humorous.

"Fine. If the Olsen's aren't going to press charges there's not much I can do, but when them street gangs from Omaha take up here, don't say I didn't warn you." With that, he flung himself back in his squad car and drove out of the lot.

"That boy is just eat up with the dumbass." Eliza shook her head. Indie and her father cracked up. "I am sorry 'bout all of that, Indie. I was so excited when I saw Luke up and kiss you like that last night and then he dragged you out here and mmm, mmm, mmm, just like a scene outta a movie, so romantic. I wish Ed'd take some lessons. You know, you oughta let Luke take a lick or two at Clarke. Serve him right, and there ain't nothin' sexier than when men fight over ya."

Indie fought not to gag and settled for rolling her eyes instead. "I don't need Luke fightin' for me, and that wouldn't be much of a fight anyway, Eliza. Thanks for letting me leave the car here." She opened the door to her Camaro before she leaned to brush a kiss on her father's cheek. "I'll be back later tonight."

"Uh huh, I'll believe that when I see it." He turned to Eliza and smirked. "Indie ain't gonna make Luke fight Clarke for her. She much prefers to make him fight her stubbornness instead, and trust me, 'Liza, that *will* be one hell of a fight."

Before Indie could argue or make a retort, her father waved and headed back to his truck. His chuckle was drowned out by the crunch of the gravel under his tires.

Eliza's lips were pressed together to keep from laughing. When she managed to unhinge them, she smirked. "I'd say your daddy's right about that, Indie, and if it were me, a strong hunk-a-man like Luke Camden wouldn't have to ask me twice to be his. I'd have my suitcases unpacked in his house and supper on the stove 'fore he had a chance to change his mind."

Simpering, Indie slammed the car door and drove away. "Have supper on the stove 'fore he had a chance to change his mind," she mocked indignantly. Rolling her eyes, she pressed the pedal harder. She wasn't cut out to be a rancher's wife. She was a mechanic, for crying out loud, and a darn good one. Besides, this wasn't 1955.

In less than 24 hours half the town already knew they were back together. In Oklahoma City no one cared what the hell she did, and she liked it that way. As she turned onto the long dirt road that would ultimately lead her to the ranch, she tried to drown out the rest of her thoughts with the radio. No one in Oklahoma City cared what she did because no one cared ... at all.

Chapter Seven

Indie slowly guided her Camaro through the rusty gates of Camden Ranch. A million memories rushed through her, stealing her breath. Miles of pasture land extended in front of her car. Everything was the same, but somehow different than she recalled. The seasons had passed, leaving nothing entirely unchanged. Improvements had been made. Part of her had wished right up until the moment she'd passed through the first set of gates that the ranch would be precisely the way it had existed for her entire teenage life.

As she passed his parent's home, the large, clapboard two-story with chimneys on all sides and a wide front porch, she longed to race up the front steps and not stop until she'd made it to Luke's old bedroom, top floor, second door on the right. She wanted to see the old football trophies that used to sit on top of his chest of drawers, making shapes in the dust left behind.

She wanted to inhale the aroma of Luke mixed in with Lava soap, saddle oil, and his mama's cooking wafting up the stairs from the kitchen. She wanted to watch him turn the knob on the door before he eased it closed so his parents wouldn't hear it shut and wouldn't know they were up there alone together.

For a moment, she wished she could erase the last fifteen years the way his mama used to wipe away the hearts Indie would draw in the dust with her fingertip, right beside her name, when poor Ms. Camden finally understood that the dust didn't bother Luke at all. He spent his days kicking up dust and mud, generally mixed with manure. A little dust on his furniture didn't concern him. She'd always loved that about Luke. He was never afraid to get dirty. And based on what he'd shared with her the evening before, he was more than willing to get down and dirty with her over the next few weeks. A broad grin spread across her face as she turned down the well-worn path towards the largest barn in the center of Camden Ranch. She couldn't wait to get started.

She parked her car along a barbed wire fence beside a few trucks she didn't recognize. Her eyes scanned the horizon. Luke was seated on the ground with something in his hands. Grant and Holly were hunched over him. The thought that he might be injured had Indie sprinting from the car. He was cradling a calf. Grant had a bottle to its mouth and hungry slurps filled the relative quiet of the morning. Indie's heart sank. "Did her mama not make it?"

Luke lifted his head. His sexy grin filled her with something dangerously akin to a depth of love she already knew would pull her under. "Hey, sugar. Sorry, I meant to meet you at the gates."

"I just let myself in. I figured your daddy wouldn't mind. If you want to keep people out, you might want to change the keycodes on the locks once a decade or something." She tried for a joke, but she really hadn't even considered that time had built a distance between herself and the Camdens all its own.

"No one minds, Indie Jane. How are you, girl?" Austin stood from his position by another calf and gave her a hug. Holly and Natalie both smiled and came to greet her.

"I'm good. Are they okay?" She gestured to the calves.

Luke's extended blinks were telling. He was beyond exhausted. "That one's fine." He pointed to the one Austin and Brock had been checking. "Mama will be okay. She's a little weary after all that, and she won't take this one. Being damned ornery about it, in fact. She took the other, nursed her twice, but don't want this one anywhere near her. And this little girl is bad weak. Looks like we're gonna be bottle feeding and caring for her. I think we already paired up the few that lost their calves earlier in the spring. She was late calving, so we're out of luck."

"Been a long time, Indie. It's good to see you," Brock Camden grinned at her. She returned the gesture.

"You too, Brock." She gave him a quick hug before turning back to Luke. "Her mama doesn't want her?" That thought snared her voice. She slunk down to sit in the pile of hay beside Luke. She understood not being wanted by your own mama all too well. "Poor thing. Can I feed her?"

Giving her his sexy half-grin, Luke nodded for Grant to relinquish the bottle. He stood upright and stretched his arms over his head. "She'll let you mama her, for sure. She's bad off." He shook his head. Regret weighted his voice.

The calf was too weak to stand to be fed, so she did indeed let Indie love on her while she ate hungrily at the bottle. "I didn't get to say hey at Saddleback's last night since Luke up and mauled me. Are you back on the ranch for good?" Indie asked Brock as she continued to rub the calf's side and let her nuzzle against her thigh.

Everyone including Luke laughed.

"You know how stubborn my brothers can be when they want something, but Luke's not the only one glad you're here to visit." Holly managed to hug Indie around the bottle and the calf.

"If that ain't the pot calling the kettle black, I don't know what is." Luke grunted. "You got enough stubborn in your head to take on a bull and win."

Holly stuck her tongue out at her brother, making Indie giggle.

"I missed you, too, Hol. How goes the psych degree? You got plenty of crazy right here in the Glen to treat, I'm assumin'."

"You kidding me? I'm getting out of the Glen as soon as possible. I'm the baby so they have to let me come back and ride my horses whenever I want, but I plan on setting up shop in a city where no one knows my daddy and my brothers. No one knows me as *little* Holly Camden. No one knows me at all," Holly declared.

All of her brothers rolled their eyes simultaneously. Indie nodded her understanding. She remembered thinking those very things, so she certainly couldn't argue with Holly. She'd made her escape as well. Gazing out at the rolling pasture land while she cared for an adorable calf with Luke by her side made that desperate desire to fly away much harder to locate however. She wondered if Holly would regret her decision someday. She could always return to the ranch in the future. It would always be a place Holly could fall, a net that would keep her from harm. Not everyone had that.

"Being away from the Glen kind of makes you miss it sometimes, though," she admitted.

Luke couldn't hide the broad grin that spread across his face. Indie rolled her eyes. "I never said I was moving back, just that I miss it sometimes."

"I'll take whatever I can get." He winked at her.

"Trust me, I lived away from the Glen for damn near a decade, and I'll admit it's got its quirks. Took Hope a few months to get settled in, but there ain't no place like it. Nowhere else on the planet where I know Hope and Nathan are safe and cared for constantly. There's just no place like home," Brock vowed.

"Hope and Nathan are ...?" Indie had a guess but wanted to confirm.

"My wife and my little boy."

"Wow." Indie shook her head. "I guess I still think of you as the kid who could catch anything Luke threw, but you're all grown up." If she wasn't mistaken, she would say Brock Camden blushed at her declaration.

"Well, I guess I did finally get my shit together. Once we're sure the calves are getting fed and settled, I'll get Hope to bring the baby out here so you can meet them."

"We all grew up, sugar," Luke's reminder was barely a whisper. "Everything may look the same around here, but it ain't all the way you remember it."

The calf let the bottle slip from his lips and lolled in Indie's lap, still weak and tired. She reviewed Luke's plans for the next two weeks. He was right. Things had changed, specifically him.

As she watched him stand and gently check the calf that the mama had nursed, she caught sight of his broad shoulders and his more-than-capable hands, the way his muscles contracted with the effort of making certain the calf was healthy, and the firm set of his jaw. He'd certainly changed, all for the better.

Regret that she hadn't taken more time to really study him every time they'd been together in the past fifteen years ate at her. She used to try her best to visit her daddy and sisters, endure a little time with her mother, while pretending away her own needs and desperate desires to be back in his arms if only for a few hours. Her stubborn will would dissolve completely, and she would fly to his front door and right into his bed under the cover of darkness. Now, she had the next two weeks to indulge herself in him. It was high time she figured out just what brand of kink Luke Camden wanted to bring to her bedroom, and she was more than interested in discovering what else might've changed about him.

Eventually, the rest of the Camdens headed out to check the other herds. She and Luke stayed behind to watch the ailing calf. Another deep yawn contorted his face as he rubbed his eyes. "I can stay with her if you want to go back to bed," Indie offered.

"Nah, I'm okay. Just beat. I want to see her stand and walk around a little 'fore I leave her. She needs another bottle here in a few minutes anyway."

"Been a long time since we bottle fed a calf." Indie recognized the longing in her own tone.

"We've always been a hell of a team, darlin', and don't be sitting there thinkin' I'm gonna be putting the two of us off another night just 'cause I'm tired. I'll come up with the energy to show you exactly how the next two weeks are gonna work."

Unable to help herself, Indie leaned and brushed her lips across his. A hungry grunt accompanied his fingers tunneling in her hair.

"Give me some more of that," he commanded.

She turned her head and lost herself in rough abrasion of his stubbled chin against her face, the hungry masculinity of his breaths, and the flavor of wild abandon that always came when she tasted his lips. With the calf still lying across their laps, she dragged her palms down the chiseled planes of his chest. He caught her right hand and pressed it to the steel bulge behind his zipper. She gasped at his forceful nature and the fierce rigidity of his denim-covered cock.

"Feel me, sugar. Rub me. You still owe me for gettin' you off last night. Came home alone with the scent of you on my fingertips. Made me crazy wantin' you, needin' you." He turned his head and captured her breath with another panty-melting kiss before he continued. "Mmm, darlin', I dreamed about you, and you made me wait. I'm fucking tired of waitin'. Then you call me up this mornin', tell me you didn't follow my instructions. Seems to me you need to be reminded who's running this portion of our reunion."

Her mind raced faster than her frantic pulse. Her clit throbbed against her panties. "Yes," she managed as she traced along either side of his wide cock, taunting him instead of touching him. Danger flashed in his eyes. Desire darkened them to a deep indigo. His hand landed on hers once more, pressing it to his cock.

"I said *rub* me. Up and down, just like that. You keep your hand on me, feel what you do to me, what you've always done to me. Feel how bad I need you." His body jerked as she stroked with more vigor. Heat from his crotch poured into her hands. His musk, saddle leather, and a fresh mountain stream filled her lungs. Her entire body required his. Patience had never been her forte, and she'd never had any at all when it came to him.

"Luke, can't we just go to your house for a few minutes? God, I need you. Please."

"I've a good mind to stand up right here in the barn, tie your hands behind your back, and feed you my cock 'til I come hard and fast between your lips, make you swallow everything I give you. You suck me like a fucking dream, sugar. I need some of that pretty mouth."

"Yes. Do it. Now!" She whimpered from the thought alone.

"Now you know precisely how I've been feelin'. Damned infuriating, isn't it? Gotta feed the calf first, but then, honey, we're gon' do a whole lot of that." He pulled away and stood to prepare another bottle of colostrum. She panted for breath. Irritated gall swam in her veins. So, that's how he was gonna play, making her beg and then wait for him.

"So, *this* is my punishment for wearing socks to bed?"

His dark chuckle did nothing to calm her raging libido. "Oh honey, you'll know when you've been scolded for not following my orders."

Cocking her jaw to the side, she tried to mean mug him, but his answering smirk said she hadn't hit the mark. "You're so damn cute when you're curious and being impatient, and you already know that temper drives me wild with wantin' you. Don't worry, sugar. I ain't forgettin' the socks. I'll take care of you as soon as I get you home."

At that moment, Holly entered the barn. Her smirk said she'd heard at least some of their spat. Her mouth twisted to the side as she eyed her brother, mischievously. "Hey, Indie, did Luke tell you he broke the engine on the tractor?" She stuck the tip of her tongue between her teeth and giggled as Luke turned to glare at her.

Indie laughed at him outright. "Uh, no, he didn't. What'd you do, honey? You know you oughta leave the wrenching to those of us that know what we're doing."

He rolled his eyes and handed her the next bottle. "Yeah, I know. There's yet another reason why you should come back home. I may can deliver twin calves, but I suck at motors. It kept starting and then it'd die. I decided to rebuild the engine."

Nodding, Indie almost felt sorry for him. She appreciated that he'd readily admit when he wasn't good at something. He, unlike every other man she'd dated briefly in the last few years, never had a problem with the fact that she was a mechanic. He honestly admired her work and was proud of her. Another round of desire worked through her. "You have leftover parts, don't you?"

"Yeah," he sighed. "You can harass me about it all you want if you'll just fix the damn thing."

"Would it quit all of a sudden or did it die a slow death every time?"

"It'd make it a round pulling the bailer, then it'd just quit."

"Sounds like it's a fuel tank issue. May not be the engine itself at all."

"See, this is yet another reason why I love you."

He kept saying that. She knew it was true. She also knew that love wasn't enough to keep them together forever. Nothing lasted forever.

"Well, what does it mean if it's a slow-death thing?" Holly inquired. Indie recognized the intrigue in her eyes. Holly had been like that since she was a little girl. She loved learning things. Holly was only six when Indie and Luke had begun dating at fourteen. Back then she used to announce to everyone that she was going to be an astronaut that lived in space so her brothers would leave her alone, and she wouldn't have to muck horse stalls. Now, Holly Camden was all grown up as well. Indie's mind continued to spin over the years she'd missed.

She finally forced a grin. "Electrical problem. Fuel-pump is a much easier fix. I'll look at it when we get the calf fed, and I'll put the engine back together using *all* the parts."

"You can look at it tomorrow. We have plans this afternoon," Luke insisted.

Holly laughed at him outright. "I'll just leave you two to your plans then."

"Actually, tomorrow afternoon I have to go play good big sister at the mayor's house and endure my little sister's bridal shower." She stuck her finger in her open mouth pretending to gag herself.

Chuckling, Luke handed the bottle back to Indie, and the calf took it readily. "Damn, a whole afternoon with your mama showing off, the mayor, and other girly shit you hate. I'll have to come up with some way to spoil you up good when you get here tomorrow night after enduring all of that."

"You better. If I make it through the whole damn afternoon without choking either my mama or one of my aunts, it'll be a miracle."

Luke grinned. "It ain't like they don't all deserve to go a few rounds, but I'm guessing Tuck and Melony would appreciate you keeping that fiery temper in check. You can bring it all over here afterwards tomorrow, and we'll find some way to work all that heat out of ya."

"I'm guessing you have several suggestions of how I might do that." Indie couldn't hide her delighted grin over his plans.

"Have no doubt, darlin'. I'll always take care of my girl. Don't matter what you need."

Indie directed her attention to the calf who was attempting to stand.

"There she goes." Relief perforated Luke's tired tone. He guided the calf onto her hooves. Indie stood to keep the bottle at her mouth.

"Keep feeding her. I'm gonna fix up a stall for her. She can't be outside for a while."

While Indie continued to feed the adorable little Hereford, Luke loaded in several bales of hay into one of the horse stalls. He added an old blanket and declared it perfect for the unwanted calf. It still broke Indie's heart that the sweet thing's mama didn't want to have anything to do with her. That wasn't how life was supposed to work.

"I think we should name her," Indie announced when Luke performed another quick check of the calf while she ate.

70

"Honey, you know that isn't a good idea." Sympathy softened his eyes as he gazed at her.

"I know, but I won't be here when she gets sold off, so it'll be okay. Please."

That declaration dampened his gaze. "Thought you were gonna give me a chance, a real chance."

"You just want me back for my wrenching skills." She tried for a joke that fell flatter than a deflated tire. An irritated eye roll was his answer to her teasing. "How about Cassie? She looks like a Cassie to me. Please, Luke." She knew he wouldn't deny her anything. He never had.

"All right, sweetheart, fine. But you and Cassie will both be here a year from now when we're breeding her and a year after that when we're selling her off if I have anything to say about it."

Another yawn overtook Luke. He blinked his eyes repeatedly. Exhaustion weighted their lids.

"I think you need a nap before we go on with your afternoon plans."

"Tell you God's truth, I'm exhausted and half-starved. I'll do my best, but I may collapse on top of you when we're finished and sleep."

"I like the idea of you being on top of me, but why don't I make you some lunch and you get some sleep before we do anything else."

"Thought you didn't want to cook for me." Luke guided the calf into the makeshift pen and settled her in the hay.

"I don't want to be *told* to cook for you," she corrected. "I don't mind cooking on my own terms."

"You don't wanna be *told* to do nothin', darlin'. Too bad too, 'cause I would sure as hell not mind watching you standing at my stove buckass nekkid with a spatula in your hands, or maybe wearing nothing but a little apron for me."

Indie snorted at the very idea of such a thing ever actually occurring. The teasing grin he was sporting painted an identical smirk on her lips. "Ain't happenin', cowboy, but I might fix your tractor engine disaster in the buff. Depends on how long you keep putting me off. You keep playin' me I might beat your ass with that spatula."

Luke's answering growl echoed off the barn walls. "You wrenching in the buff'll do, too, and trust me, I'll make your waiting worth it, darlin'. Have no doubt."

When Cassie finished her next bottle, Brock ordered Luke to get some sleep. He and Hope took over the feedings for a while so Indie drove them back to Luke's house centered on a raised hill in his section of the expansive family ranch.

When they entered, Luke headed directly for the soft leather sofa in the center of his living room, collapsed, and then settled his cowboy hat over his eyes. "Make yourself at home, sugar. Just give me like ten minutes." His voice was pleading. Indie's heart pricked.

"You sleep. I'll make lunch."

Having always gotten up before the sun to do chores, Luke possessed the ability to fall asleep at a moment's notice. As soon as that hat went over his eyes, he was out. Something's about him would never change. That realization brought a grin to her face as she quietly explored Luke's two-story stone and siding home.

Her eyes scanned over the massive stone fireplace in the living room that dominated most of a wall. Everything else inside was wood. The paneled walls, the flooring, and kitchen cabinets were mismatched hues of polished oak that somehow all fit together.

Inhaling deeply, she allowed the scents of him and of the ranch to fill her lungs as she headed towards the kitchen. The breeze from an open window in the kitchen whispered through her hair.

She passed his bedroom on her way and noted her red panties tossed on his dresser. Part of her was disappointed. Images of him jacking off with them had intrigued her all morning. Realizing he hadn't, she considered feeling bad for him. Clearly he really was hard up, but she'd been more than willing the night before and he'd left. She desperately tried to believe it was his loss, but currently, she was the one feeling a little lost.

In years past when she'd come to him, he'd take her like a man possessed, like he'd been just as desperate for her as she'd been for him. She didn't know where all of his newfound stubborn patience had come from, but she intended to put an end to it. After his nap, she'd find a way to get him in bed.

Satisfied with that idea, she tried to quietly explore his kitchen until she figured out what to cook. She grinned at the ancient Maxwell House coffee tin with Dale Earnhardt's number three Goodwrench car emblazoned across it stored in the cabinets above the stove. If she'd popped the plastic top, she knew she'd locate several thousand dollars in cash he always kept there just in case. Very few cowboys ever really trusted anyone outside their own families, especially if their job title included the words banker, lawyer, or government official. Her father had a similar coffee can in his kitchen cabinets. Only difference, his coffee can rarely had twenty bucks inside.

Thoughts of her father's comment that he couldn't afford to take a day off brought another round of worry to her stomach. He never had been very good at saving, something her parents used to argue about constantly. Her daddy would give away his last dollar to help his neighbor. Indie loved that about him, but it worried her.

Opening the fridge, she located all of the ingredients she'd need to make grilled cheese sandwiches, one of Luke's favorites.

Chapter Eight

Luke roused when the scent of grilled onions permeated the air. Lifting his hat from his face, he rubbed his eyes and sat up, still exhausted. His eyes landed on Indie expertly grilling onions at his stove. The long silken fall of her hair swaying down her back made him desperate to end his self-imposed determination to take his time torturing her with making her wait for his pleasure. Damn, but if her cooking in his house contentedly wasn't a beautiful sight he didn't know what was.

He summoned another round of stubbornness and joined her in the kitchen. Circling his arms around her waist, he drew her back to his chest and nuzzled her neck. She swayed her hips, brushing his cock with the ample curves of her ass.

A low growl formed readily in his chest. He loosed it rapidly as she continued to taunt him.

"That wasn't a very long nap." The smirk on her face said she planned to drive him insane with need until he finally threw her in his bed and took her with the wild abandon she was clearly craving. Little minx thought she was winning in the battle of wills.

"Gorgeous woman is standing at my stove cooking me lunch. I intend to eat it. I may beg off for another nap later. I'm still whupped, and I'm bettin' my girl is, too. You were up late. Let's eat then crawl in my bed. I promise we'll stay there all damn afternoon, and evening if you're willin'."

"Think I've already proven I'm willin'. Little offended you'd rather sleep first. We still playing your stupid 'make Indie wait 'cause she wore socks to bed game?"

"Who the hell said we were napping first, sugar? I'd planned on taking care of your punishment before my nap." Okay, so maybe she was winning. He wasn't a fucking saint. He could still draw it out after their lunch. He ordered himself to keep it under control, but damn those beautiful curves, the way she smelled, the lush softness she tried so hard to cover with her temper-driven armor — it all made him frantic to show her how much he loved her. "Jesus, Indie Jane, I want you so fuckin' bad. You test a man's patience something fierce."

She said nothing, but the smile that had at one time belonged only to him returned to her pretty face. Dammit, two weeks from the next day, it was gonna be his smile again. He was determined. She added the onions to the sandwiches she'd prepared, buttered the bread, and tossed it in the pan she'd used to grill the onions, just the way he liked it.

They ate in amicable silence. She'd made him three sandwiches. His appetite had lessened slightly since his old football days, but giving that he'd had nothing to eat since the night before, he didn't bother to comment. He devoured the sandwiches, fortifying himself to devour her. Still irked over her comment about not playing his wife, he did the dishes.

Leaning back against the kitchen counter opposite the sink, she crossed her arms under her breasts. The slight lift of those luscious curves made his mouth water. "You about done with that, cowboy?" She gestured to the dishes.

"Mmm, mmm, mmm, my baby doll does *not* like to wait. Impatient little thing." He stared her down, drying his hands on a rag. Letting his eyes run the length of her body, he licked his lips. So many things he longed to do with her. No part of her would be left wanting. Every single soft patch of her skin would know his touch, his taste, his needs. "Bed. Now," he ordered.

A flash fire ignited in her pale green eyes. "I do so like this dominant side of Luke Camden. Bring it on, cowboy."

With that she headed towards his bedroom. He sure as hell planned to bring it. If she'd let him, for the rest of their lives he'd drive her far more than crazy each and every night.

His boot collided with the bedroom door slamming it shut. She startled at the noise but the fire in her eyes continued to rage uncontained. "You're all mine, Indie, baby. All mine. You'll do as I say. You understand that?"

Her tongue darted between her lips. "Oh, hell yeah."

A hungry grunt he couldn't halt escaped him. "You didn't seem to understand that last night. Let's see if you can't do it better this afternoon. Take them clothes off for me. Show me your gorgeous body. All of it. It's mine. I want to see it right now."

A hint of nerves played in her eyes as she toed off her boots.

"Someday, honey, I'm gonna finally show you how fucking beautiful you are." Breaking from his original plans to stay fully dressed while she writhed naked in his bed, he popped the snap on his Wranglers and lowered the zipper. His raging erection was more than apparent in his briefs. "That's what you do to me. Just thinking about you bare in my bed makes me harder than a damned railroad spike. It's all you. You're the only woman in the world that makes me this hard, makes me hurt with it."

The slight tremble of her hands and the soft moan from her lips as she eased her t-shirt upwards said maybe he was getting through to her.

"Keep going, sugar. God, I need to see you." Unable to help himself, he kept his eyes trained on the red satin bra attempting to contain her generous cleavage.

"I usually backhand guys that stare at them like that." She tried to sound threatening, but was far too turned-on. Her voice was low and breathy, laced with need.

"Good," Luke grunted. "They're mine, too. Nobody else gets to stare at them, but I'll look 'til my fill. Get used to it. You're so damned beautiful. Take that bra off. Right now. Show me, honey, 'fore I lose my mind, rip it off myself, and unload my cock all over those pretty pink nipples."

A shuddered moan accompanied the pop of the clasp on her bra. Her breasts spilled forward, anxious to escape their enclosure. Luke growled out his adamant approval. She slipped it down her arms and tossed it in the floor.

"Keep going," he ordered.

Her jeans joined the bra and t-shirt on the floor. He edged closer to her with magnetized force he had no hope of denying. "Take your panties off for me, honey. I know you're already wet. Show me."

Her breaths quickened, short and shallow, swaying her breasts in a mesmerizing dance that kept him entranced by her beauty. Helpless to resist touching her, he caressed her cheek while she slipped the panties down her long legs. His fingertips tracked from her neck to her breasts making her quake.

So many questions played in her darkened eyes. He'd answer every single one of them.

"So damn pretty, Indie. God, baby, I need you every single day." His fingers continued to explore down her abdomen, following the luscious curves of her body. She tensed as he encountered the deep auburn curls covering her mound. He dipped lower to find her drenched with arousal. A hungry growl thundered from his chest. "So wet for me. So damn perfect. Turns my girl on when I tell her what to do, doesn't it?"

A rushed moan and a whispered, "Yes," was her only response. Her mouth parted and her eyes closed in ecstasy as he traced back and forth along her slit. Leaning in, he devoured her lips, ravaging her like a parched man finally brought to a cool spring ripe with water. His tongue demanded her taste. Drawing her body to his, he gentled the kiss, memorizing the feeling of having her like this again. Grasping her ample backside, he indulged himself in the heavenly feel of her curves as he kneaded her flesh. Ordering himself to remain solidly in control, he stepped back, cradled her face in his hands, and gently stroked her cheekbones. Her kiss-swollen lips beckoned his mouth once more.

"Now, go lay down in my bed, relax, and spread your legs for me."

She complied readily, making him have to hide his smirk as he settled in the armchair in the corner of his room.

"What are you doing?" she huffed once she was reclined against his pillows.

"Watching, and you don't get to ask questions, sugar. We're in my bedroom. You do as you're told."

She narrowed her eyes spitefully and considered arguing. He could read her like a book. When she thought better of it, he went on with his next commands. "Spread out more. I want to see your pussy drip for me." With a half-huff of annoyance, she opened her legs further, giving him a front row view to her pouty, pink slit. His cock jerked, desperate to be consumed by her greedy little pussy.

"Now, show me. Show me how you bring yourself, darlin'. Touch yourself. Pretend it's my hands and my cock doing whatever the hell you want. Make yourself nice and juicy so I can taste that sweet honey, 'cause next time you come it'll be on my tongue."

"Oh my God," she moaned. Contemplation and a hint of fear were penned in her eyes.

"Look at me, Indie," he ordered. "Keep your eyes on mine while you touch yourself. Show me."

With a quick lick of her lips, she hesitantly raced her hands across her breasts.

"Slow down, sugar. We ain't got nothing but time. Pinch those pretty nipples for me. Show me exactly what you would do if I weren't sittin' here."

"But you are sitting there."

"Now." He hadn't meant to be quite so demanding, but he knew that's precisely what she required. Her soul needed to feel the raw power that came from her submission. Her demons needed to be damned. He'd conquer every single one of them and silence them thoroughly. His eyes flared as she obeyed. Her fingertips spun around her nipples, drawing them to stiff peaks at the height of her breasts.

"Damn, sugar, so pretty. I can't wait to watch you come for me."

Indie trembled against his mattress. The low rasp of his voice spurned her on. The piercing gaze of his ice blue eyes kept her pinned her to his mattress. Never in all of her life had she ever envisioned actually masturbating in front of Luke, but his demands melted her every inhibition. The carnality she could see burning in those gorgeous eyes coupled with the obvious need tensed in every muscle of his body. She inhaled deeply, drawing in his musk from the soft, rumpled sheets surrounding her.

Letting her eyes close, she skated her fingertips down from her breasts to her thighs and tried to hone in on the raw eroticism thrumming between them. He was five feet away from her, but Luke Camden held a power over her. He always had. Physical contact wasn't required. With one quick glance her way, her entire body responded. His desire heated the blood coursing rapidly through her veins, making her desperate to be in his arms. She'd always needed him to kindle the flames into a raging fire and then his steady calm to cool its burn.

"Show me, Indie. When you're thinking of me in your bed at night, show me how you touch yourself." His low rumbled tone strained with wanton greed.

Unable to locate her typical stubborn refusal to do anything anyone ordered her to do, she focused on his labored breathing and let it carry her towards ecstasy. With her fingertips, she gently traced circles along her inner thighs, imagining him making the same move, hyping her anticipation as she moved closer and closer to her pussy.

A low moan sounded from him as she traced her swollen lips. Liquid need seeped from her slit. Her pussy flexed anxiously so desperate to be filled.

"Lord Almighty, you are so damn sexy. I can't take it. You make me burn."

She opened her eyes, curious to discover why she suddenly heard movement from the corner where he was still seated. The metal snap of his belt buckle hit the wooden chair. Luke slid his jeans and briefs down enough to reveal his massive cock, but he didn't come to her. She kept her fingers working up and down her slit as he wrapped his own fist around himself. The murmured slap of skin on skin drew a frantic groan from Indie. He primed himself with long, slow drags up from his root, keeping his molten gaze locked on hers. "I said show me."

Shock worked through her system. She was drenched, and he'd yet to touch her. Slick, and hot, and aching. Knowledge that he was watching her, ordering her every move, and getting off from the show sent heady euphoria whipping through soul. How had he known? Like he'd read the book of erotic fantasies that so often played out in her mind, he knew precisely what she longed to explore. Just as he'd promised the night before, he did in fact intend to push them beyond any vanilla-flavored sex parameters they'd shared over the last few years. Judging from the look of undiluted sin chiseled in his features, he intended to have her six ways from Sunday just for an appetizer.

Thoughts of what he might order up next had her pulse pounding. She circled her fingertips around her clit and writhed in his bed, mostly for show. The tender bundle of nerves throbbed with every frantic beat of her heart, though, and she lost more of her fear.

"Luke, please," she begged. She needed more. She needed him.

"No, sugar. You do as you were told." He remained in the chair pumping his cock, keeping his hardened gaze locked between her thighs.

It occurred to her that perhaps this was her punishment for the sock incident. That thought had her rubbing with more vigor. Voyeurism as her scolding was definitely not something she'd secretly played out in her head. Truthfully, she wasn't that creative. The effect it was having on her was intoxicating, however.

"I usually have a vibrator when I do this." She was mildly concerned her fingers weren't going to bring about the desired effect.

Another hungry grunt came from her admission. "Oh, honey, we'll have to play with that next time. Keep going. I want to watch you come."

Slipping her fingers just slightly to the right, she located her own magic spot, the one that always drove her over in seconds. Her body lifted and rolled against his sheets. Another groan of approval echoed off the walls. She trembled as the tightening sensation began behind her mound. A soft moan escaped her lips as she imagined Luke's body restraining her own as he belly-crawled up her and drove his cock deep inside of her.

"Look at you dripping in my bed. So sweet and so damn sexy. Make my sheets sloppy wet with your cum, darlin'. Finish for me." His low baritone rumbled across her flesh. Every command loosened her grip on all she'd understood about herself before. Raw abandon consumed her. Never before with him or any of the other men she'd ever been with had she been more aroused. She longed to obey him, but couldn't explain to herself how that fact equated to the pure sexual power surging through her soul. She felt desired and beautiful. With one more stroke of her own fingers, she shook and came on a wispy cry of his name.

"Watchin' you come for me was so pretty, sugar. God, you drive me wild." Luke was on his knees by the side of the bed a half second later as the weak orgasm left her desperate for more. Gripping her waist, he jerked her body towards his face. "Beautiful little snatch, swollen pink and soaking wet for me." He ran three fingers down her pussy, centering his middle finger along her slit. Her entire body shivered.

"It's tender, isn't it, baby? Just relax. I'm about to clean up all of that honey you made for me." With that, Indie whimpered and writhed as he flattened his tongue and ran it softly between her slit, bathing her thoroughly. He granted her clit one gentle suck before he located the overly-sensitive patch of skin between her ass cheeks. She gasped and clenched. A wicked chuckle breathed over her folds. "We'll work on you staying relaxed for me later. Pretty little rosebud." He spun one finger around the puckered opening of her backside. "It's all mine, baby. Get used to it."

Indie had no time to process any other thoughts on Luke Camden rimming her ass or any of his other plans. Her entire body honed in on the longing to beg him to do whatever he'd like. She was his willing companion in every way. He continued his feast of her, and she gave herself over to the persuasion of his expert tongue. When he licked back up her slit, he dipped and spun his tongue in her opening. Her thighs locked tighter around his stubble. He hadn't shaved that morning, and the friction left whisker burns on her skin. The slight chaffing mixed in a seductive cocktail with the soft strokes of his tongue. Her hips undulated and her pussy moved against his mouth.

"You like fucking my tongue don't you, sugar? You taste so damn sweet. I could stay here for hours. Letting you mark my face with your scent. It's so good." His tongue danced higher, spun around her clit, and then drew it in with another soft suckle.

"Oh God, Luke, please, please."

"Please what? What's my girl need?"

"Fuck me!" She barely recognized her own voice, harsh, breathy, and woven with desperation.

Another suck, faster this time. *So close. So close.* She rocked faster against him. It was right there. But he lifted his head and gave her a wicked grin as she whimpered from the unwanted vacancy.

"I would, sugar. I'd sure as hell planned to, but you up and decided to wear socks and then to call me up and tell me about it.

Ornery, don't you think? Drives me crazy wanting you when you get stubborn like that, but I'm not gonna give you anything right now to fill that ache deep inside I know you have. I'm not gonna give you my fingers or my cock, as fucking bad as I want to fill you so full you can barely walk and all you want is more. Now be still." He locked his hands around her hips, pinned her to the mattress, and spun her clit into the fiery heat of his mouth.

Rapid lashes of his tongue brought her to the apex of ecstasy before she could process that he wasn't going fuck her. The empty hollowness of coming around nothing made her long to beg him. She could get him to fuck her. She knew she could. Maybe.

Luke Camden would never deny her anything she truly wanted, but he seemed pretty damn certain of what he was willing to give. *'I'm taking that as a direct challenge, Indie.'* Her taunting about him not being kinky enough for her fantasies replayed from the single brain cell that still housed the ability to formulate thoughts. She lost the capacity to argue or speak at all when the all-encompassing orgasm he drew from her with his tongue ripped through her like a tidal wave. Heated arousal rose from her mound and crashed through her body, sizzling outward from her core to her fingertips, melting her completely. The intensity of the aftershocks made her weak. She was still trembling a full minute later.

His capable hands slipped under her back as he pulled her into a seated position.

With barely a half-second of realization, she blinked rapidly as his straining erection bounced against his chiseled abs. She was face to face with his cock, leaking for her, throbbing, and desperate. Years of horseback riding, hauling hay, cattle, and equipment made his luscious body appear to have been formed of hardened steel. Quickly, he lifted the t-shirt over his head and kicked off his boots and jeans. She ran her fingers down his abdomen and then, keeping her eyes locked on his, she traced one finger up the throbbing vein that ran from the root of his velvet cock up the purple head. Hot air hissed between his teeth. His eyes closed in an extended blink and then locked onto her with another round of molten heat.

The way he stared at her like she was the most beautiful thing he'd ever seen stripped away the insecurities over her thick curves, the scars under her breasts, and most importantly, the markings on her soul.

Grasping his own cock, he dragged the wet tip along her lips, back and forth, covering her mouth in pre-cum. Desperate to consume his salty, earthy flavors, she licked the essence from her lips. "No, ma'am. I'm gonna give you more than a taste, honey, but you lick it from me."

She immediately complied, spinning her tongue around him and teasing the sensitive fold of skin just below his head. His abdomen contracted as he laced his fingers through her hair, and he fed her his cock in one slow fluid glide. "That's it. Take more for me." He half-strangled on the next order. "Put your hands behind your back. I don't want to see anything but my cock sliding in and out of your beautiful mouth and your gorgeous tits teasing my sac when you take me all in. Hands just get in the way, sugar."

Damn. Damn. Damn. Where had this been the last fifteen years? She supposed showing up unannounced in the middle of the night randomly didn't really lend itself to much more than a quick reconnection. Another round of liquid heat coated her inner thighs from his orders. She placed her hands behind her back and held one in the other as she sucked with more vigor. Magically, her kinky fantasies of him began to blur with her reality, and she wasn't certain she would ever recover.

Keeping one hand gently guiding with her hair, his other traced the hollowing of her cheeks. "So damn beautiful. My God, how the hell did I get you?" He shuddered as she relaxed her throat muscles and took him deeper. A rasping growl echoed from his lungs. The dichotomy of the hard set of his muscles paired with the slack of his jaw and the soft hunger in his eyes. God he was gorgeous. The flavors of Luke, raw and potent, saturated her every sense.

She pulled back, spinning her tongue as she drew him in until she released him and then immediately returned almost to his root. His body jerked as a whispered rasp of her name formed on his lips.

"I'm right there, sugar. God. Suck hard. Finish me." A moment later a hot splash of cum filled her mouth. She swallowed it down. "Keep going," he barely voiced the order, lost in what she'd given him. His body trembled as she cleaned him thoroughly.

When he fell into the bed beside her, he cradled her tenderly in his arms, against his chest, tucking her into the heated masculinity that always made her feel safe.

"That was incredible, baby. Thank you." His low drawl was perforated with satisfaction.

Indie hadn't sorted through everything they'd just shared. All she knew in that moment was she wanted to experience more, much more. "Uh, where exactly has all of that been hiding since we were in high school?"

82

"Liked it, did you?"

"Hell yeah, but I ... kind of feel like ... I'm dreaming again ... maybe."

Luke turned to stare into those gorgeous green eyes that had always held the secrets to the entire universe. He had no idea how to explain to her what had just happened. Tucking a stray strand of her auburn hair behind her ear, he tried to formulate some kind of answer.

"Indie, honey, I just ...."

"What?" her soft whisper and the love he saw glowing in the intensity of her gaze spurned him on.

"If I ever ask you for something you don't want to give me, you know I'd never make you." The thought of forcing something on her made him sick.

She pressed her index finger to his lips while he was lost in contemplation. "I know that. As pissed off as I am that I didn't get your cock this time, I really loved all of that. Here I thought you were just gonna paddle my backside for wearing socks." Her impish grin accompanied an adorable giggle, and intrigue played in her eyes.

"You're so damn beautiful." He couldn't help but tell her. Her lush curves were pressed against him, warm and supple. Her cheeks were flushed pink and her lips swollen red from her work. She was perfection. "Would you like to be spanked, darlin'?" The thought alone swelled his cock despite the fact that she'd just drained him thoroughly.

"What would you think if I said I think I might? I told you, my fantasies of you get pretty darned kinky."

He grasped her right hand and wrapped it around his rapidly stiffening cock. "You just sucked the life right out of me, and I'm beyond exhausted. Do you feel what you're doing to me, laying here in my bed, naked and perfect, telling me you want to explore with me?"

A harsh swallow contracted the long feminine column of her neck. She nodded her head.

"That answer your question?"

Another nod was her only response.

"I've never been this way with other women. I've never wanted this level of intimacy with anyone but you. You understand what I'm telling you? I've never let myself be this open about what I want with anyone else, and I never will."

"Yeah, I've never done any of this with other guys either."

"Good, but I really don't want to hear about you and other guys. You're mine. You understand *that*?"

"I'm pretty sure I'll always be yours, Luke. I always have been, but that don't mean I'm staying here."

Too tired to argue with her and still playing cautiously with so much to lose, he leaned and kissed the contention from her lips. Tasting himself inside her mouth, he groaned as he pulled away. "So many things I want to share with you, Indie. What if two weeks just isn't enough?"

"Let's just see what happens for the next two weeks. No reason I can't come back more often."

With a sigh of irritation, Luke tucked her head under his. "Sleep with me for a little while, then we'll go back out and check Cassie before I spend all damn night making you come for me in every possible way I can think of."

"Mmm, I love the sound of that."

"Good."

Chapter Nine

An hour later, Indie's eyes blinked open. A grin formed immediately on her features. She was tucked up in Luke's fiercely protective embrace with a pillow of firm muscle under her face. *Waking up like this every darn day would be pretty nice* her heart taunted. Clearly, it wasn't going to lay off. Against her will, it had taken up Luke's banner. Her brain, however, still had her back. She mentally ran the lengthy list of reasons she would never and could never stay in Pleasant Glen.

She started with her mother, the mayor, the fact that a town with less than two-hundred people could not possibly need two mechanics, that she would make a piss-poor rancher's wife given that the extent of her cooking knowledge pretty much halted abruptly at sandwiches, and the fact that she did not want to stay home, make babies, and tend cattle.

Then she moved onto the fact that Clarke was the deputy sheriff, that the entire town already knew she and Luke were back together because gossip spread around this place faster than fire spread across a dry field soaked with kerosene. Quickly added in the fact that the mailman, Miles, was approximately four hundred and seventy years old, blind as a bat, and still attempted to read everyone's mail before he delivered it. Then she settled on the final reason — she simply could not deal with a town that for all intents and purposes continually re-elected the man that had destroyed her family. It was a slap in her father's face every single time he was named mayor again, and she would not exist in a town that would do that.

Fortified by what she considered to be perfectly logical reasoning, she leaned up in the bed and stared at the ancient alarm clock on the bedside table. It was just after three.

Clearly still exhausted, Luke slept like a baby beside her. Restless, she eased from the bed and redressed. She needed to *do* something. Even considering staying in town, marrying Luke, and completely changing her life was all too much.

Heading out into the pastures, she let the low murmured bellows of the cattle lead her towards the barns. By the time she reached the barn to check Cassie, she'd repeated the phrase, 'You love Oklahoma City. You'd miss it if you left,' numerous times. Somehow, she knew she already missed the wide open spaces, flying across the fields on her horses, and Luke infinitely more than she would ever miss her tiny apartment, breakfast at Jimmy's Egg, Lake Eufaula, the steep-cliffed Mesas, and Route 66. There were an infinite number of things she would never miss about Oklahoma City as well. The constant harassment she received from her male coworkers for one, but she fought valiantly to keep those thoughts at bay.

When she entered the barn, Holly was pulling another empty bottle from Cassie's mouth. Much to Indie's delight, Cassie stood and walked with shaky legs back to the nest Luke had created for her out of hay and blankets.

"She's getting stronger with each bottle," Holly assured. "Still not out of the woods yet, though."

Indie followed the calf into the horse stall and grinned when Cassie nuzzled her head against her thigh. She loved on her for several long minutes before she thought of what would be the perfect remedy for her nerves over the experience she'd just shared with Luke. "So, where's the tractor Luke tried to fix?"

Holly giggled. "It's out in the shed. Come on, I'll show you. We've been making do with the old one. Sure be nice to be able to run them both, though. My big brother is good at a lot of things. Engines are not one of them."

"He most certainly is." The words slipped from Indie's lips in a half moan before she remembered whom she was talking to.

Holly cringed and then laughed at her outright. "That would definitely be too much info for me. I must say you do look mighty happy, and I'm sure he looks like the cat that caught the canary. You two always have that effect on each other."

Indie turned her head to the wind, trying to keep Holly from noticing the fevered blush on her cheeks.

"Oh, come on. I'm not a little kid anymore. I'm majoring in Sexual Psychology, for crying out loud. You don't have to be embarrassed with me."

"What?" Indie gasped. "Do your brothers know that?"

"No," Holly sighed. "No one here knows. I haven't even told mom or Natalie. I don't know how to look Daddy in the eye and tell him I plan to become a sex therapist. I mean, I doubt he's ever even heard of one. To most cowboys the only possible problem that could come from sex is not having enough."

Laughing, Indie's mind quickly conjured Luke's commanding thrum while he guided them deeper into a sexual relationship they hadn't yet explored and how skillfully he'd always orchestrated her orgasms. Even in high school, after the first few times, he always made certain she was satisfied first. "Not all of them, but yeah, your dad's gonna freak."

"Right? And he's been paying for my classes, so I don't know what to do. Thankfully, he's never really looked at my class lists when he pays the bill. Please don't say anything to Luke."

"I won't, but you better figure out how to tell them. They're all gonna be sitting there when you graduate. Be a hell of a thing to discover then."

"Believe me, I know." Holly sighed as they entered the old shed. The metal walls shuddered and creaked with the wind. The tractor hood cover stood open on the beast of a machine. Indie couldn't help but grin. The large diesel engine beckoned her, and the smell of oil mixed with a hint of exhaust soothed her soul.

"All right, where are the *extra* parts?" she chuckled.

"I think he stuck them over here." Holly moved some old buckets, oil cans, and several wrenches off of a metal tool bench. Lifting a half dilapidated box lid, she rolled her eyes and handed it to Indie. "I would've harassed him more if I had a clue what any of this is."

Three washers, a locknut from the gear assembly, two screws, an exhaust stud, several bearings, and bushings from the transmission, what she suspected had caused the problem in the first place, lay in the box. "He took the whole damn thing apart, didn't he?"

"Luke is nothing if not thorough." Holly rolled her eyes.

Shaking her head, Indie refused to embarrass herself again by heartily agreeing, so she set to work.

"No doubt you'll have it working in no time, so I'm gonna leave you to it." Holly offered her a slight wave as she headed back to the horse barn.

Determination drove Indie as she reworked the transmission and corrected Luke's mistakes on the overhaul. When the transmission proved to work correctly, she smiled. Finding engine problems, no matter how obscure, was her specialty. She loved the hunt and accomplishment that came from her work. Her happiest childhood memories were listening intently to her father's teachings while peering under the hood of most any kind of vehicle. For her tenth birthday, he'd splurged and gotten her a diesel engine model and helped her build it. They used to drive her mother and sisters crazy at the dinner table each night. He'd list off several symptoms or diagnostic readings and she'd guess the problem. It was a game she'd always reveled in.

"Gotta be the fuel system," she commented to herself and began inspecting the lines and valves. She dragged the back of her hand across her sweaty brow and cranked the tractor, studying the diameter and timing of the bubbles in the fuel. "Bingo." The engine didn't need to be overhauled at all. The tractor needed a second fuel flow tube at the inlet. She located one on the tool bench and began reworking the fuel system.

Luke's grin expanded the width of his face as he watched her. God, she was adorable. He quickened his steps towards the shed. Her hair was done up in a messy topknot with what looked like a thin metal connecting rod she must've located in the shed sticking through it to secure it to her head. Grease was smeared across her forehead and right cheek, and oil was splattered on her jeans. That light he loved was glowing in her eyes as she worked.

"So, how bad did I screw it up?"

Smirking at him, she set down the wrench. "Raise your right hand."

Laughing, Luke held up his right hand, knowing where this was likely going.

"Repeat after me," she giggled. "I, Luke Camden, will never, ever take apart another engine because I have no fucking clue what I am doing."

He cocked his left eyebrow upwards and narrowed his eyes. "See, I will gladly take that vow, darlin', once my sexy little mechanic agrees never to leave me high and dry with a tractor that won't run and her not here to fix it."

An audible huff accompanied her eye roll. "It wasn't the engine, cowboy. You were pulling too much air into the fuel lines. I added another flow tube and flushed your system. I also pressurized the tank for you and primed everything. Should run like new now."

"You're gorgeous, you know that?"

"Aww, I bet you say that to all the wrench-heads that fix the stuff you took apart and couldn't get back together."

Laughing with her, he shook his head. "Nope, only you. Never had the urge to tell your daddy that, and I suspect he'd rethink us dating if I did." He helped her gently lower the hood cover.

Scoffing at that, Indie rolled her eyes. "You kidding me? You could probably commit murder and my father would still adore you. Pretty sure he thinks of you as the son he never had."

A dozen taunts Luke knew Indie had endured growing up immediately played in his head without his permission. Everyone, including her own mother, used to refer to Indie as the son her father had always wanted. Luke knew Ben never thought that way.

Indie had come into the world mechanically inclined just like her father. Ben adored all three of his daughters, but the bond between him and Indie was special. Despite the fact that he'd named her after the Indianapolis Speedway, after a concession from her mother that she be called Anna, he'd never wanted her to be anything but his little girl.

At the ripe old age of four, Indie had informed her parents that she hated being called Anna and would hence forth be referred to as Indieanna. The shortened version had come sometime around first grade. She'd quickly figured out that her nickname irritated her mother, and therefore she'd made certain it stuck.

"I'm real good with just becoming his son-in-law."

"And people say *I'm* stubborn," she huffed. "Let's go check on Cassie. I want to give her another bottle."

"All right, but then I think I should give you a nice hot bath." He licked his thumb and ran it across the grease smudge on her cheek, wiping her clean. "Although, you look so damn cute covered in grease, kinda makes me wanna leave you filthy. 'Course, ain't nothing sad at'all about having you wet and nekkid in my arms, either. I'm torn."

The purse of her beautiful lips spoke directly to his groin. "Hmm, I could think of a few other ways I could be filthy."

That was it. His fuse of rampant desire short circuited with the thought of his cum all over her body. He pinned her against the metal wall behind her, taking her mouth with fervor and greed. The softness of her lips, the sway of her lush body against his chiseled form, the way her right hand tunneled in his hair. The urgency of her tongue coupled with the wet heat of her mouth. The potent, intoxicating taste of her. It all fed the frantic need swamping his blood.

His hands parted at her delicate neck, one travelling to her ass to pull her closer, the other cupping her left breast, feeling the heavy weight. Longing to keep her locked in the strength of his arms took firm hold of him. Sweet Jesus, she was just too tempting. How the hell had he ever survived without her?

Guiding her with the hand on her ass, he circled her pelvis around his erection. Only problem with having her back in his life, he was constantly stiff and aching. His only relief came when she was naked in his bed nursing his cock either with her mouth or her pussy, and he was damn tired of waiting to have her fully.

She circled his nipples with her thumbs, drawing a strained grunt from his lips. When her hands slipped to his belt buckle, he lifted his head and watched her reaction as she encountered the fierce bulge behind his zipper line.

"I need more than what happened in your bed, Luke. God, I need everything. Take me; fast, hard, furiously, slow, gentle, tied to your bed, up against the wall, in the bed of your truck, whatever. I don't give a damn how, just put your cock in me, fill me so full I ache come mornin'." Her eyes closed as she traced lower, spinning her fingertips over his sac and then grasping his cock again. Luke's breath stalled as he shuddered from the heavenly sensation and the imagery her words painted in his mind.

"Oh, darlin', I plan on taking you every single one of those ways over and over again. I woke up and you were gone." He spun his tongue over the purple brand he'd left on her neck the night before. "Left my bed smelling like you and wet from your juices, honey. Drove me mad. Thought about jacking off all over my sheets, inhaling your sexy scent and thinking about you touching yourself in my bed, begging me to fuck you. That's what I used to do, Indie. Every single time you came to me, spent all night making love with me and then left for Oklahoma, I'd wake up and relive it until I came all over the sheets right where you'd been laying. Then I remembered you were still here, and that you'd given me a chance to make you stay. I ain't quittin' this time. I ain't giving up, so be ready. You still hurtin', sugar? You still feel empty from coming around nothing at all?"

"Yes, damn you. So, why don't you do something about it?"

Before Luke could order her to his truck, "Unka Wuke," pealed through the air followed by Luke's father Ev's customary whistle.

"Shit." Luke spun and caught J.J. when he barreled into the shed with his arms extended. Indie clutched the work bench, trying to steady her frantic breaths. Luke did a quick inventory. A storm of fire in her eyes, lips kiss-swollen and ripe red, her breasts swelled until they were spilling over the top of her bra, raw heat darkened her normally pale cheeks, and the hickey on her neck was a deep purple. Absolutely breathtakingly gorgeous, but it sure as hell wouldn't take a genius to figure out what they'd been up to.

Luke's father, entered the shed a few seconds after his grandson. He couldn't quite contain his chuckle as he took in the scene. "Well, if it ain't Indie Harper back on my ranch. Girl, Jess and I have missed you." He gave Indie a sweet hug, making her grin and further darkening the flush of her cheeks. "Luke's complete horse manure when you ain't here. You ever think about stickin' around?" He winked at her.

"Subtle, Dad. Real subtle," Luke sighed, but he of all people knew his daddy always said precisely what was on his mind.

Indie shot Luke an eye roll. "Oh yeah, because you've been so subtle yourself." She returned her gaze to his father. "So, he's got you in on this too, huh?"

"Hey, I call 'em like I see 'em, sweetheart. You belong here. Always have, always will. Little man here is 'bout to drive Summer up four walls and over a hay bale. Baby Hank was up all night. Austin finally got him to sleep, but they're exhausted. Your mama's got the tiny one, and I was given strict instructions from my daughter-in-law to wear J.J. out. He wanted to come find Uncle Luke, which worked out well, seeing as Tuck and Melony are up at the house lookin' for you two. They went by your place, but obviously you ain't there."

"Big twuck!" J.J. bounced in Luke's arms, making Indie laugh.

Luke turned so Indie could see his nephew fully. "J, this is Uncle Luke's girlfriend, Indie." *Aunt Indie,* he corrected in his mind.

"No," J.J. shook his head at her. "Twuck."

Ev chuckled. "Twice as stubborn as his daddy when he wants some'um." It still struck Luke occasionally how much J.J. reminded them all of Austin, even though he was not Austin's biological child. Some things were meant to be, just like him and Indie.

"Aww, I like Uncle Luke's new truck, too. Does he take you for rides in it?" Indie's soft intonation with J.J. as she tickled his belly touched the deepest wells of Luke's soul, the ones he'd shut up tight when she'd left, and never allowed himself to feel. The pain was occasionally more than he could handle.

J.J. gave her an enthusiastic nod before he reached for her. Panic widened her eyes as he nearly leapt from Luke's embrace to hers.

"I don't know how to ...." She shook her head while simultaneously cradling J.J. in her arms.

"You're fine. He thinks he's found someone that'll get him in my truck faster." Luke couldn't hide his broad grin as J.J. nuzzled his head against Indie's shoulder. When his little hand landed on her ample breast, he cringed however.

"Unka Wuke's twuck!" J.J. commanded again.

"All right, come here, little man. We'll ride in Uncle Luke's truck back to Granddaddy's house, okay?" Luke reached for J.J., but he shook his head and continued to love up on Indie.

"No! All awound!" J.J. lifted his head and shook it back and forth in an odd circle in what Luke assumed was an attempt to explain that he wanted ride all over the ranch.

"Boy, you are about to get yourself in a mess of trouble." Ev carefully lifted J.J. out of Indie's arms. "Uncle Luke said he'd take you back to the house. Granddaddy'll drive you on the tractor or in his truck after that, but you have to behave."

"Truthfully, I need to go back and check our new calf. What are Tuck and Melony here for?" Luke asked his father.

"No idea, son. Just wanted the two of you. Grant and Natalie just fed the calf, and she walked around a little. She's getting there. Tuck said you were up all night with one of Indie's horses, and I know Brock got you out of bed long before sunrise, so I kinda thought you two might want a nap, too."

"How did Tucker know about Juliet?" Indie wondered.

"Oh, sweetheart, you know how the Glen is. I 'spect he and Melony went by your daddy's place and he told 'em. Don't take long for news to spread around here."

Luke fought not to order his own father to shut it. He didn't need anyone reminding Indie of the less than ideal parts of living in Pleasant Glen. He also had precious little patience left. His plan of punishing her for being ornery by not burying his cock balls deep in her pussy was supposed to be over as soon as they woke up from their nap. He was already treading water on borrowed time. He'd been on a knife's edge of arousal for the past week just anticipating their reunion. Horses, calves, his nephew, his best friend, and her sister needed to take a number and get in line. They'd come up for air eventually. Sometime next winter if he had his druthers.

"I still can't get used to the idea that Mel is marrying Tucker," Indie admitted.

"He's grown up too, sugar. Ain't the player he used to be. He's all about Melony all the time," Luke assured her.

"He better be."

"You think I'd let him mess around on your little sister? I would'a beat his ass." Truthfully, Luke was mildly offended.

She considered for a moment. "No, but remember this is the first time I've really seen them together."

"Twuck, peese!" J.J. huffed impatiently.

"All right, go get in." Luke gestured to his truck parked nearby. Ev set J.J. on his feet, and he took off. Everyone followed after him.

"All babies I've ever been around look at 'em and want desperately to touch them like that. I mean, to them I look like the freaking dairy truck just pulled in." Indie shrugged. With gall driven impatience already surging through his veins, Luke drew his hand back and smacked her ass rather hard.

"Luke," she spat as she stumbled forward. "Your daddy is right there," hissed through her teeth as she stabbed her finger Ev's direction.

"Do I look like that concerns me in some way?"

"What the hell is wrong with you?"

"You sayin' shit like that about the woman I love is what's wrong with me. You're gorgeous, Indie. Fucking beautiful. Somebody else said shit about you that way I wouldn't stop swinging 'til they were flat on the ground and beggin' for mercy. What the hell makes you think I won't have something to say about you talking about yourself like that?"

Halting abruptly, she spun and glared at him. "When I said I'd like to be spanked, that ain't exactly what I had in mind." She kept her voice to an infuriated whisper.

"And what exactly did you have in mind, sugar?" he matched her tone as Ev loaded J.J.'s carseat into Luke's truck and pretended to ignore them.

"You know perfectly well what I had in mind." Another round of seductive heat pooled in her cheeks. She discreetly glanced his father's way to make certain he couldn't hear.

Luke couldn't help but chuckle despite the irritation over her insistence that she was somehow unattractive. "I do. I was just kinda hoping you'd say it out loud." He pulled her into his arms and gently rubbed the spot he'd just swatted, soothing the burn. "Look at me."

She complied with a nasty glare. "You are the most beautiful woman in the world to me. Please, stop saying shit like that. For me."

"See you at the house." Ev waved as he climbed in his own truck.

"Fine, but you can't deny that my tits are still huge, even if I did have them reduced," she continued after Luke's father had driven away.

Luke bit back a greedy growl of approval. "Your tits are gorgeous, just like the rest of you. Now, let's go see what Tucker and your sister want, because *I* want to be alone with you for the next several days, and since that isn't an option, I plan on taking you hostage until that stupid shower tomorrow."

"That another kinky fantasy, cowboy?"

"If that's what you want to call it, sure."

J.J. was making a decent attempt at diesel engine noises with his mouth from his car seat in the open truck.

Indie giggled. "I think he might like your truck more than I do. Kid's after my own heart."

"Yeah, I noticed that you stare at my truck the very same way I stare at your ass. I'm a little jealous."

Her laughter sped his heart. The beautiful sound soothed a little of Luke's impatience. If he could just keep her laughing and show her that he could be everything she'd ever want or need, this would work.

"Aww, don't be jealous. I stare at your package *almost* as much as I stare at your truck." With the tip of her tongue between her teeth, she continued giggling and waggled her eyebrows.

"I could make your whole damn night, sugar. Give you full access to my package in the back of my new truck."

"Mmm, gettin' hot in here now. Always did love it when you and I went out with nothing but your old truck, a few blankets, and an all access pass to your junk."

"You have always had an all-access pass to what's in my Wranglers, darlin', and you know it." He held the keys to his new F-450 in front of her face. "You drive. When I get rid of Tuck, I want you all turned on. Driving a dually diesel should work almost as good as wine and roses for boring women I got no time for."

"Aww, don't I feel special? You're lettin' me drive your truck."

"Got the 6.7 liter Powerstroke."

Another round of laughter brought her beautiful smile to her face. "Do you have any idea what that actually means?"

"Not a damn clue. I just know it'll haul anything, and it makes you smile. That's all I care about. Worth every penny I spent if it makes you grin."

"The 6.7 liter Powerstroke is a Ford thing," she explained as he helped her climb up in the driver's seat.

"I'm built Ford tough too, ya know?" God he'd missed flirting with her. His determination doubled down with every moment they spent together.

"Oh, I know you're a stud, Luke Camden. Kinda likin' that you're mine again for a little while, too."

"Not just a little while, Indie Jane Harper. I figure if I say it enough at some point I'll get it through that stubborn head of yours."

Indie rolled her eyes as she released the brake and put the truck in gear. She was almost as excited as J.J. who was applauding and raring back in his seat pulling against the restraints.

"I can't believe Brock and Austin both have kids. It's so weird. I kinda keep thinking of both of them as teenagers."

"Well, you weren't here to see 'em grow up, honey. Truthfully, none of us saw Brock grow up, and Austin's wife grew him up not too long ago so ...." he shrugged. "Hey, you know Austin's married to Summer Sanchez."

"The barrel racer?" Shock colored Indie's features.

"Yep."

"Wow. Guess their kids are rodeo bound, then."

Luke considered that. "Maybe. Summer threatens Austin's life every time he jokes about teaching either J.J. or Hank to ride bulls though. They barely leave the ranch. Both love it here. I think all that living on the road for half their lives makes 'em not want to go again."

"She ain't still ridin', I take it?"

"Well, he knocked her up long before the actual wedding. Come to think of it she's been pregnant as long as I've known her. She stays off the horses while she's carrying, but she's itching to get back. Austin has to get creative to keep her off 'til the doctors give her the go ahead. Hank's only a few weeks old." Luke pointed to a gravel road leading towards the back fields. "Take the long way back. It'll only take an extra few minutes, and he'll love it." He gestured to J.J., who was waving to the cattle they were passing.

Eventually she parked the truck near his parents' home, and they released J.J. from his seat.

"Dan tu," he wrapped his arms around Indie's right leg when Luke prompted him to thank her for the truck ride.

"Indie Jane Harper, you get up in this house and give me some love, girl," sang loudly from Luke's mama. Baby Hank was in one arm and she had the other extended to Indie.

Beaming, Indie raced up the front porch into her arms. "Hey, Mrs. Camden. It's so good to see you."

"You too, honey. Been way too long. Don't you let my son keep you tucked up at his house the whole time you're in town. You come down here any time you want. We'll catch up and have coffee."

"Don't tell her that, Mama. I'll never see her," Luke teased as he accepted Tucker's half handshake, half slap on the back.

Chapter Ten

Indie inhaled deeply. The tidings of being back in the Camden's home, the place that had been her refuge for so many years, washed over her like a healing balm. The scents of lemon Pledge, chicken roasting in the oven, and fresh coffee baptized her and welcomed her home.

"Mel's wanting Runzas. I thought the four of us could all go to Ogallala and get dinner. Hit up Underpass afterwards," Tucker explained.

"Oh, I haven't had a Runza in so long." Longing perforated Indie's tone, but the pleading look in Luke's eyes had her clamping her mouth shut quickly. He clearly did not want to spend the evening with her little sister and Tucker. Thoughts of what he did want made her mouth water more than any thoughts of Nebraska's delicacies in the sandwich department anyway.

Ogallala was the closest city to the Glen, but it was still almost an hour away. They'd be in the truck longer than their meal would take, which was precisely why residents of the Glen rarely journeyed to the small city nearby. "Uh, but I'd have to go home to clean up first. You probably don't want to wait on that."

"We don't mind waiting. I want to hang out with you before the wedding. Please, Indie," Melony all but begged. Guilt churned in Indie's stomach. When Luke had proposed spending every possible moment together, she'd promptly forgotten her sisters.

Luke worked his jaw fiercely for several long seconds before he managed to unhinge it. "We can go if you want, sugar." He made no effort to hide the disappointment in his voice. "Just dinner though." The look in his darkening blue eyes dared either Indie or Tuck to argue with him.

Delighted that he wanted her badly enough to make no bones about cutting out of dinner with his best friend early, Indie bit her lips together to keep from giving him a naughty smirk in front of his mama.

Tucker laughed at him outright. "You got plans afterwards or some'um?"

"Damn straight."

While Indie was reveling in the male posturing Luke was doing unnecessarily since Tuck was clearly teasing him, Melony edged closer to her with her eyes narrowed. "Indie," she huffed quietly.

"What?" Indie turned on her little sister, annoyed at her distraction. Intensity and raw need rolled off of Luke in heady waves. Was she the only one that noticed how gorgeous he was? She glanced around the room. Ev had taken J.J. back out for another truck ride. Jessie was fussing over the baby. No one seemed to care too much about their evening plans.

"You are wearing a strapless dress in my wedding one week from today." Melony tried desperately to sound threatening. Indie almost laughed. Her little sister still sounded like the soft-spoken first grade teacher that she was even when she was furious.

"Don't remind me."

"Indie!"

"What?"

"That mark on your neck is huge. How are you gonna cover that up?"

"Mel, it'll be gone by next week."

"Yeah, but I'm doubting that's the last one you'll have, and what about the shower tomorrow?"

"What about it?"

With a dramatic eye roll, Melony huffed, "Mama's gonna wet her panties when she sees that."

That did it. Indie doubled over laughing. "Oh, I would pay *good* money to see that."

Luke and Tucker both turned to study them. Luke grinned at Indie's hysterical laughter.

Tucker eased closer to Melony, looking concerned. "You okay, baby?"

"Yes." Melony kept up her perturbed glares at Indie. "Let's just go." She turned to Mrs. Camden. "Thanks for letting us play with the baby. You're coming to the shower tomorrow, right?"

"I'll be there, sweetheart. You all have fun."

"See you, Mrs. Camden." Tuck brushed a kiss on Mrs. Camden's cheek before he took Melony's hand and guided her out.

Indie gave Luke's sweet mama another hug before she followed everyone back out of the house. She rolled her eyes at the Skoal can ring worn in the back pocket of Tucker's jeans. Clearly Tuck Kilroy hadn't changed too much. There'd been rings in the back of all of his jeans long before he was old enough to purchase tobacco. When they were in school, he'd fuck anything that would lay still for him. Another round of irritation over her little sister's engagement irked her blood as she let Luke help her up into his truck.

She took a quick shower at her father's house and changed clothes while Luke and Tucker chatted with Ben, and Melony endured one of their mother's lectures via her cell phone on why she'd decided to hang out with Tucker when she should be there helping to set up for the shower the next day. According to Mel, their mother had ended the call with a, "You're marrying him next weekend. You can spend time with him then. Right now you're to be over here working on the wedding that the entire town will be seeing." At that point Tucker had taken the phone, politely told her to back the hell off, and had stowed Melony's cell in his glove box on silent.

"I shouldn't have said anything about getting Runzas. Sorry." Indie climbed up in Luke's truck to head to Ogallala. He still looked pissed.

"It's fine, sugar. I'm just bein' ornery is all. I want you so bad I can't see straight."

Sheer bliss warmed her entire body. She felt a tiny piece of the armor she tried so hard to keep guarded around her heart slip away. "It's nice to be wanted like that."

"I've always wanted you like that. My God, I half-mauled you in the fucking gym at that stupid ninth grade dance your mama made us go to, and back then I didn't have any idea how incredible making love with you was gonna be."

Shaking her head at him as he cranked the truck, memories slowly brushed themselves on the canvas of her mind. He had been overly-anxious and a touch forceful when he'd finally worked up the courage to kiss her under the bleachers that night so long ago.

If she concentrated, she could still see the soft glow of light spilling from the full moon over the back entrance to the gym. It had illuminated the hard set of his adolescent jawline as he stared intently at her, barely blinking, and nervously running his thumbs back and forth over her hands clasped in his own. Their friends were out at the lake having fun, and they were stuck at the ninth grade dance because her mother insisted they go.

"You gonna kiss me or not, Luke Camden?" she'd finally dared.

That was it. He'd gone in like a beast attacking its prey, taking her for everything she was worth. She'd loved him from that moment on. Loved that she could bring out his wild. Loved that he was never afraid to show her how desperately he wanted her. Loved that he'd jump into something and figure it out as he went. And then she loved that he'd gentled the kiss and settled into her and let his sweeter side show.

98

The bumping lurch of the truck as he turned onto the long gravel drive that would ultimately take them to the paved roads brought Indie back to the present. She grinned. "You gonna kiss me or not, Luke Camden?"

He turned to stare at her. His left eyebrow cocked upwards with that sexy-as-sin smirk on his face. "Damn near came in my pants under them bleachers. If you'd brushed up against me, I swear I would've."

"That still the case?" She snaked her hand over his zipper line just to see what he'd do. My God, he was well on his way to a full blown erection. His heat and rigidity filled her hand. No wonder he was so irritated about Tuck and Melony showing up.

Her caress drew a low, desperate grunt from his lungs. The heavenly scent of new leather car seats was drowned in his musk, thick, raw, and potent. Frenzied need was etched in every rugged plane of his body. "Indie, baby, please don't."

"Pull over." She eased her hand away. "Tell Tuck we'll meet them there in a little while."

"No. I ain't doin' you in my truck on the motherfuckin' road out of the Glen. God only knows what Clarke would do with that. We'll go eat, but then, sugar, I'm taking you to bed, and we ain't leaving for a long damn time. Be ready for me. I'm gonna have you all night long over and over. I *need* you, and I ain't too sure I'm gonna manage gentle the first time. I'm too far gone."

"I sure as hell don't want gentle the first time, but please Luke, just let me take the pressure off. I need to feel your hands on me again. God, I was the dumbass that agreed to this. Let me make up for it."

"You're not a dumbass. Don't say shit like that, especially in my truck when I can't paddle your sweet ass for it."

A rushed breath escaped her lungs from the thought of him doing just that. "I'm not gonna make it through dinner. I want you too bad."

"Christ, darlin' you have no clue. All I can think about is ripping them jeans and panties down your legs, straddling you over my lap, holding your hands behind your back, and watching your soakin' wet snatch swallow up my cock as I slide you down it over and over again. Hard and fast. 'Til you're screaming for me. No condom. Comin' deep inside of you. Bathin' you in my cum and not givin' a damn what you think about it. Then watching it drip out of your pussy down your thighs when I let you up." Regret ate at his words. He slid a shameful glance her way before returning his eyes to the road. "Fully aware that makes me an asshole. I'll get it together here in a minute."

"Fantasies don't make you an asshole, Luke, and I was thinkin' basically the same thing."

"I don't have any condoms with me, honey. You come over that seat, I ain't gonna be able to stop myself. Just hold my hand." He clasped her hand in the strength of his own and held her tight.

"Doesn't this make it worse?" She held up their joined hands. "It's like I get to touch the candy but not eat it."

"Makes it a little easier for me." His breaths did steady. "Reminds me how lucky I am that I'm the guy gettin' to have you in my truck, calling you mine again, and honestly, it reminds me how much I have to lose if I fuck this up again."

"Luke," she shook her head. Dammit. When she left it wasn't going to be because he fucked something up. He never could. Why didn't he get that?

"Sorry," he swallowed down what sounded like raw need and biting regret. "Let's talk about something else."

"K, how about when did Tucker and Melony get together? I'd ask her, but to Mel that qualifies as girl talk, and then I'll be inundated with makeup tips, how I should wear skirts more because they're cute, and there's a decent chance I'll have to hear about how Tuck is in bed." She gagged. "No thanks."

Luke's sexy chuckle lightened the entire atmosphere. Being in the truck with him, listening to him laugh, confessions over his hot as hell desires, it was like the sun setting in a thousand shades of rusty orange and deep sangria put on a show simply because they were there together again.

"You don't need makeup, ever, and your ass is so damn hot in them Wranglers I'm about to lose my mind. If you had on a skirt, I wouldn't get to appreciate your curves as easy, and if there weren't two layers of clothes between me and your crotch, it would already have all been over with. Don't listen to your sister. I'll tell you what I know about how they got together, but you ain't gonna like it, so just promise me you won't scalp him as soon as we get to Ogallala."

"I knew it. Was he cheating on somebody else when they met, and she bought his 'I swear, baby, I'd never do that to you' shit or something?"

"Nah, nothing like that, and I told you if he ever stepped out on Melony I'd have plenty to say about it."

Another grin formed on Indie's lips. She couldn't remember the last time she smiled like this. "Thanks for always lookin' out for my baby sisters when I wasn't here to do it."

100

"I'd rather you be here so I can be lookin' out for you, but you know I'll watch out for them, too."

"I know." Indie tightened her hold of his hand.

"I honestly don't remember the chick's name that was getting married, but she was a friend of Mel and Miranda's. This was about a year ago. Anyway, girl went to Pleasant Glen, but we'd graduated before she got there. She was throwing a bachelorette party and wanted to hire strippers. Naturally, men that'll put on a show taking their clothes off for money aren't easy to come by in a ranching town out in the middle of nowhere. So, Ryder Lewis dared Tuck into playing stripper with him for the party. It was good money, according to Tuck, and Ryder owed some on a bet he lost. I couldn't believe Tucker did it, but he thought it was hilarious. According to him, he and Mel hung out before the festivities. A few hours later, he was about to give her a private show and realized she'd had way too much to drink."

"I'll kill him." Indie glared at Tucker's truck just ahead of them.

"Listen to me. He and Melony both swear he just took her home. He stayed with her to make sure she was okay, but he slept on the couch. They've been an item ever since."

"That don't sound like the Tucker Kilroy I knew."

"Like I said, he grew up, too. He even puts up with all of your mama's crazy for her. He's in love."

"If he didn't take advantage of her, why would I not like the story?"

Luke shrugged. "I just didn't know how you'd be about them meeting while he was playing stripper at a party for a gaggle of other women."

Indie considered that. "Honestly, it makes me kind of proud of Mel. She was always the one that worried about what Mama would think of everything. She was always so desperate to please everyone. I'll just bet Carolyn doesn't know how her favorite daughter met her farmer."

"I'd dare say not. Carolyn's not too thrilled with Tucker anyway. Thinks he ain't good enough for Mel. Don't make enough money growing corn."

"No, she thinks he don't make enough money to marry the *mayor's* daughter." Indie convulsed. "I know precisely what she's thinkin'. She actually tried to get Mel to ask Daddy to let the mayor walk her down the aisle. Makes me want to remove my mother's vocal cords via her ass."

Luke's laughter filled the truck cab once again. "I ain't gonna try to stop you. Melony might even hold her down for you. Tuck's so sick of it all he's thinking of asking Melony to move away from the Glen with him. Trying to talk his brothers into selling the farm here and buying ranch land in Wyoming somewhere. His daddy would probably have a stroke. I haven't pointed that out to him yet. Tuck's willing to trade in corn for cattle just to get Mel away from your mama so they can have a life without interference. Don't mention I said any of this though."

"I'm not surprised. Carolyn Harper Jenkins ran me off. Can't blame my sisters for doing the same. Mel loves the Glen though, and Tuck's family has owned that farm for generations. He shouldn't have to give it up just because my mother is a pain. She needs to remember that at one time she was a Harper, married to my daddy, and making babies with him. Drives me crazy she'd prefer to pretend that away. Loves people to think we all belong to Mayor Asshat."

Indie lowered the windows in the truck. With the wind tied up in her hair and his beautiful smile on her features, Luke found himself envious of Tucker. At least Tuck had options. Luke would not only be letting down his entire family if he left their ranch, but every farmer or rancher a hundred miles in every direction. There weren't any other vets in the area willing to take care of anything from ornery bulls to the family pets. Luke had never backed away from any responsibility. After Indie had left, he'd even come home every single weekend of college to help his family work the ranch. Steadfast and reliable were words that had been etched in his soul. That's who the Camden men were, who they'd always been. Trying to separate himself from his responsibilities was akin to trying to rip his soul from his body.

A half-second into his considerations, Indie located one of his Cornhuskers baseball caps in the backseat and used it to contain her long hair. The longing that had already set up residence in his balls increased tenfold in that moment. Damn, he was never going to return them to any color other than blue.

Chapter Eleven

Luke guided Indie into Runza as soon as he'd located a parking place.

"I swear it has been way too long since I've been here," Indie sighed contentedly when the scent of fresh baked bread and sautéing onions filled their lungs. In the mental tally his mind had created on its own, Luke put a mark in the staying column. Runzas were definitely a benefit of staying in Nebraska. You couldn't get one anywhere else.

"Wait. What the hell is a Philly Style Runza? Who came up with that?" she huffed as they studied the menu boards over the registers.

Luke put his arm around her and chuckled. "They fancied shit up a while back. Based on your reaction, I'm guessing my girl still wants her cheese Runza with extra onions and an order of Frings."

"The only way one should ever order here." She beamed at him.

"You still gonna steal all of the onion rings out of my order of Frings?"

"Hey, you're the one that's so convinced you want me back for good. You knew the risks going into this."

Laughing, Luke jerked the bill of the baseball hat she'd borrowed down over her face as he stepped up to order. Yeah, he sure as hell knew the risks, and he was still playing to win. She could have every one of his onion rings. He was after a much, much bigger prize—her.

When she righted the cap and her hair, she sidled up beside him and discreetly pinched his ass rather hard while he was trying to order. Luke clenched both his jaw and his ass while trying to appear unaffected to everyone around them.

"Pop with that, sir?" the cashier asked.

Luke narrowed his eyes in on Indie. God, she was adorable. That naughty smirk on her face, the seductive heat warming her cheeks, it was all he could do not to lay her out across the counter and give the patrons a show to go with their supper. "Yeah, two large, please." He turned to Indie while he reached for his wallet.

"Turnabout's fair play, sugar. You looking to get your ass marked tonight?" he spoke through his teeth.

"Mmm, maybe."

"Okay, you two get a room." Tuck rolled his eyes as he placed he and Melony's orders.

They settled into a booth in the back corner of the restaurant. Indie's contented moan and the way she closed her eyes in ecstasy when she bit into her Runza made Luke certain his cock was being choked to death by his own Wranglers. He studied his watch, mentally calculating how long it would take them to eat and get back to his house.

Tuck glanced from Luke to Indie and back again. He laughed out loud. "You know you're killin' him, right?"

Melony blushed violently before she started giggling.

"Oh, don't worry. I'll take care of him later." Indie waggled her eyebrows keeping her gaze locked on Luke.

An involuntary grunt vaulted from Luke's mouth. Still laughing, Tucker slapped Luke on the back. "Hang in there, buddy."

"Fuck off," Luke huffed, bringing on more laughter.

Indie had stolen half of the onion rings from Luke's Fring box when Melony sat down her Runza and fidgeted with her napkin. "I wish you'd just tell me what she said."

"Babe, let it go, okay? It's no big deal. Mama's fine. I talked to her. Let it go. Indie hasn't been back in town in forever, and trust me, Luke ain't gonna let you see her much over the next two weeks. Relax and enjoy your sister being here. How's Oklahoma, Indie?" Tucker dodged like a pro.

"Oklahoma's not too bad. My job sucks, but it pays the bills. Now, tell us what Carolyn did."

That was the first Luke had heard of her not liking her job. Last he knew, she was wrenching for a big shop in the city that got tons of business.

"Why does your job suck, Indie?" Melony sounded almost as concerned as Luke.

"I thought you wanted him to tell you what our mother did."

"I do, but now I want to know about your work."

"How the hell did you know all of that was about Carolyn?" Tucker asked.

"Mel asked you to tell her what *she* said. Whatever happened sounds like it must've hurt your mama's feelings, which is the only thing talking could soothe. And Mel gets that pained look whenever Mama's being herself. She used to pretend it away, but something's eatin' at her. I can always tell."

"Yeah, so can I," Tucker assured her, "but this is no big thing."

"You tell us why your job sucks, sugar, and I'll get Tuck to tell you what Carolyn did," Luke negotiated.

Tucker glared at him, but he didn't particularly care.

Indie rolled her eyes. "Fine. Same old shit as always. I'm the only female mechanic. All the assholes with inverted half inch dicks crawling up their ass are out to prove they're better than me. They've gone as far as to break something I fixed to make me look bad. Manager knows they do that, but he still gives me all the shit hours because I'm not a member of the shop penis brigade. No girls allowed kind of crap. No biggie. It's not like this is the only job I've had where this happens."

"You know Daddy would *love* for you to come back and work with him," Melony spoke the words before Luke could.

"And you know there ain't enough work in the Glen for two mechanics. We turn around more than eighty cars on any given day. There aren't even that many cars in town. Hell, you could throw in all of the tractors and there still wouldn't be enough work for both of us."

"Yeah, but you aren't turning out eighty a day by yourself, and maybe your dad would like a break," Tuck pointed out. Luke noted Melony's eyes widen and her very slight headshake. Indie did not.

"Moving on. What did our mother do?" Indie demanded.

Tuck sighed and tossed his napkin on the table. "Thanks for throwing me under the bus in your gambling, fucker." He huffed to Luke half-jokingly.

"You said you wanted to help me," Luke reminded under his breath. "And remember the time I pretended to be your old man when the school called because you kept skippin' Geometry? You still owe me for that."

"Yeah, okay, fine." Tucker returned to his normal volume and tenor. "Your mom keeps calling with some ideas about the rehearsal dinner thing. Mom's been really excited about it. She wanted it to be like the barbecues we used to throw for the football team back in the day, and she's so excited Mel agreed to marry me in the first place she can't see straight."

Melony's entire being beamed with excitement. Luke and Indie couldn't help but grin.

"Well, I'm so excited you asked I can't see straight either, but I want the barbecue thing, too. I told Mama that."

"I know, darlin'. I told Mama we wanted the barbecue just like we'd planned. Your mom didn't care for that idea, but I took care of everything. The barbecue is on. Dad's grilling. Footballs will be flyin'. Everything just like we wanted. Don't worry about it."

"And Carolyn strikes again." Indie rolled her eyes.

"She really has been such a bitch about the whole thing. Keeps going on and on about Ernie walking me down the aisle which is the craziest thing I've ever heard. Part of me wishes the wedding part was over so we could get on with the marriage part. That's all I really want anyway," Melony admitted.

Pain and disappointment tensed Tucker's face. "I am definitely looking forward to the honeymoon and the marriage portion, but I want to do the whole watch you walkin' down the aisle thing, too. We can elope if you really want to, though."

"Are you kidding me? After both our mamas have spent all this money and invited people we don't even know from five counties over, we are not eloping. Don't even tempt me with that. Mama would never speak to me again."

"If that's the prize, you should elope now," Indie huffed.

Luke shook his head. He felt terrible for both Tuck and Melony, but he had no idea how to help.

"I'll talk to Carolyn tomorrow when I'm there. Tell her to back the hell off," Indie tried to assure everyone.

"No, Indie. Don't. I can't deal with you two tryin' to maim each other all week before the wedding," Melony pled. "Just let her do her thing. It'll be fine."

Luke knew Indie wouldn't let it go. Melony's bridal shower was likely to be the scene of yet another vicious argument between Carolyn and her oldest daughter. He immediately made plans to deal with the aftermath. What was coming was inevitable, but he'd always been the only man capable of calming Indie. No doubt his skills would be needed the next day. Tonight, however, there were so many other skills he longed to put to work.

Unable to keep his eyes off of her, he involuntarily licked his lips while she slipped the straw from her pop into her mouth.

Finally, mercifully, Melony, who Luke was certain had to be the slowest damn eater on the planet, consumed the last of her Runza and they could leave.

"Let's just go get a few beers at The Underpass. Come on, it's still early," Tuck urged.

Luke wrapped his arm over Indie's shoulders and pulled her closer. "No."

A seductive smirk formed on those beautiful lips, and he almost groaned aloud. "Anxious?" she purred in his ear.

Turning his head as they treaded carefully back to his truck under the cover of moonlight, he brushed a kiss on the sensitive skin in front of her ear. "Aching, honey. So much more than anxious. Damn near dyin' to be inside of you."

"Me too." Her words whispered away on the wind. He tried with all of his might to swallow down the desperation yet again. For the hundredth time that night alone, it just wasn't working. His hands itched to feel her satin skin fevered with desire. His tongue thirsted for her juices. He longed to gorge himself on her sweet cream. His cock burned for her, ached with a pain only she could soothe.

The fuse of patience that was lit and gone when he'd awoken from a nap to find her absent from his bed ignited his entire body. They pulled out onto the two-lane that led from Ogallala back to the Glen, and his patience hit a brick wall. "Pull them jeans down for me. Leave your panties where they are. I want my hand down them."

"What?" She stared at him in shock. The few street lights along the road glowed in her darkened eyes reflecting the storm of need emanating from their depths. "I thought you didn't want ...."

"Dammit, right now, Indie."

"Oh God, yes!" She shimmied her jeans down to her ankles.

Luke's raspy growl echoed off of the windshield. "Spread your legs for me, baby. Right fucking now."

She trembled in the seat as he rubbed the soft satin of her panties against her mound. The scent of her heat-ripened sex spiked his blood. Tensing her glutes, she rocked against his hand as he slipped it inside her panties. "My God you're already soaked. So damn tempting."

"All I can think about is being with you. I need you. I need more. Please Luke."

His mind spun rapidly. She needed him. That admittance was one he could never deny. "I'm gonna give you more, honey. I'm gonna make it feel better." He traced her swollen slit, loving the soaking wet curls he encountered. She shivered. Her body rolled against the seat.

Gently he stroked his middle finger to the apex of her slit and circled that sweet, tiny bundle of nerve endings that would have her flying in moments.

"Yes, yes," she whimpered. "Please."

"When I get you home, sugar, I'm gonna fuck you all night long. Hard. Just like you like. I know exactly what my girl needs. Always." He increased the friction. A strangled moan overtook him as another round of slippery wet heat coated his fingertips.

"Yes," she gasped as she dug her fingernails into his forearm. He reveled in the sensation of her coming in fast pulses against his fingers. His heart flew with the perfection of her and the fiery passion between them. It sizzled through his veins. This was precisely how he wanted her: scratching, and hissing, and begging for more, writhing for him with that wild look in her eyes that dared him to keep going.

Finally, mercifully, they made it back to the ranch. When he was somewhere in the general vicinity of his house, he stomped the emergency brake and they flew out of the truck. He kicked his front door open, slammed it shut, and jerked her into his arms. Frantic, his hands raced over her body, desperate to locate her silky skin, fevered with a hunger he was going to fulfill. He inhaled her lips, burning her chin with the stubble of his slight beard.

Her fingers nimbly worked through the buttons on his shirt while he pulled her t-shirt over her head. Moving in a straight line downward, she went from the buttons to his belt buckle. When her hands landed on his briefs, his cock jerked eagerly to meet her caress. He growled our his pleasure. His head fell back and he tried desperately to summon some semblance of patience. Failing miserably, he half shoved her down on his couch so he could rid her of her boots and jeans.

Repeating the phrase *foreplay* in his head constantly, he couldn't seem to get the message to take. His body required hers. All sense of control vanished staring at her naked, gorgeous curves wiggling against his leather sofa in anticipation.

Clenching his jaw, he rid himself of the rest of his clothes, fell to his knees, and pinned her back against the cushions. He took her lips like a man possessed. Hard and hungry. Ferocious in his intent. His entire life depended on the flavors of her mouth. Their teeth collided, and he turned his head, trying desperately to push away the desire to turn her around and shove his cock balls-deep inside of her, not caring if she was ready or not.

Her hands tunneled in his hair. She sure as hell wasn't gentle. No, she fisted two handfuls and shoved his mouth to her tits.

He lapped at her nipple, sucking, marking, nipping until he'd thoroughly branded her. Sucking harder, he groaned from the delectable flavors of her.

"Dammit, Luke, now!" she demanded.

"Jesus Christ," he moaned. "No. Foreplay first." His body shuddered from being made to wait, even if it was his own doing.

"We've had two entire days of foreplay. Hell, we've had years of it. Now, fuck me like you mean it, Luke Camden. Show me what you're really made of. Let's see this dark side you're only gonna show to me. Right. Fucking. Now." Her hand snaked around his cock. She squeezed and tugged. Hot breath hissed between his teeth from the pleasure. "Come on, cowboy," she cooed. "Show me."

He roared like a beast released from a cage as he leapt to his feet. The wild fire in his own eyes reflected in hers. She slowly ran her tongue over her lips, daring him.

"I ain't in the mood to be gentle or very nice, Indie. I'm too far gone. I've needed this for so damn long. If you didn't mean what you just said, you need to cool it so I can clear my head."

"I don't want gentle, and I don't want nice. I meant every single word."

Something inside of him snapped. The chains that bound him shattered with her words. Every single thing ever heaped upon him, every responsibility, every assumption made about him, every expectation, they all dissolved. *Oldest Camden child, ever-reliable, honorable, good, caring, moral, never complaining, hard-working.* The things he was. The things he would always be. The outer reflection that occasionally didn't match the man inside. Not when he was with her. She made him more himself and accepted his flaws with love, whether she wanted to admit that or not.

"You're sure? Dammit, Indie, tell me now. Once I get started, I ain't gonna stop. I'll have you over and over again, rough, however the hell I want, until I've had my fill of your gorgeous body, until you're raw. Do you understand what I'm saying to you?"

"I'm sure." Intrigue and unadulterated lust stormed in her eyes. Her quick breaths swayed her breasts. Craving need was penned in every curve of her beautiful body from her kiss-swollen lips, to her gorgeous tits, down the inward slope of her abdomen, to the rise of her mound, clinging to the ample curves of her hips and over the swells of her ass.

"In my bed right fucking now. Ass up. Pussy open and ready for me with your head down. If you ain't already hot and wet get that way. Only thing I want to hear from you are your screams of pleasure and my name. Don't make me tell you again. Understood?"

"Oh, hell yeah," she panted. She was on her feet and in his room before he allowed himself to realize just what she was giving him. Racing after her, he groaned at the beautiful image of her gorgeous ass, plump and perfect, rolling with desperation as she swayed her hips.

"So damn beautiful and all fucking mine." Shedding every single thing that would ever have stopped him, he climbed behind her. His thighs slapped the back of hers as he jerked her over his cock, burying himself deep inside with one hard thrust.

"Yes," she groaned. "Harder."

"Remember you said that in the morning." He jerked her hips back faster and pistoned his cock inside of her over and over, furiously. She loved it. Her juices dripped down his groin every time he pulled away. Ripened heat flooded his lungs. Gasping moans filled his ears. Her nails dug into his sheets, clawing out her pleasure. Her swollen pussy muscles milked at his bare cock constantly. "So damn tight, honey. So damn perfect. You like it rough don't you?" he managed to grunt. Nothing had ever felt so good. Nothing ever would.

"Oh fuck, yes," Indie gasped. My God, where had this been for the last decade? Nothing had ever felt so insanely good. Luke Camden was fucking her senseless, and according to his warning this was only one of many times he planned to have her that night. Maybe at some point she'd died and gone to heaven and hadn't even realized it.

Feeling her body shudder from his force and his friction, the familiar tight knot of pure bliss throbbed behind her mound. On his next ravenous thrust, it began to loosen its constraint, unleashing her thoroughly. Pleasure erupted from her core, rocketing upward along her spine. His heated musk was potent with reckless carnality. He took her with raw abandon, and the knowledge that she was the only woman that had the power to make him lose control like this spiked her blood.

She trembled against his force and his girth. How could she have forgotten how massive he was when he was aroused? He groaned out his approval. "It's right there isn't it, sugar? Jesus Christ, I feel it coming. Come on my cock, Indie. Come hard for me, baby. Screaming my name. Let me feel those sweet pussy muscles squeezing around me."

His heat and the satin steel of his cock felt like nothing she could ever have fathomed. Nothing would ever feel this amazing. No one could ever make her feel this desired. No one but him.

"Luke," groaned from her as she collapsed against the mattress. Fevered heat and pure, unadulterated satisfaction radiated from the top of her scalp to the tips of her toes. She shook with release as she came in rapid pulses that quaked throughout her body.

He seized, and she panicked when it finally occurred to her one of the reasons it felt so insanely good. "Luke, the condom," she managed in a breathless gasp.

"I didn't want to wear a condom. I wanted to do this." He jerked out of her pussy and with one stroke of his hand came in hot splashes

110

all over her ass. An involuntary moan spilled from her lips. "All mine," he growled.

For a moment he slumped over her, but before she quite knew what had happened, he'd located a hand towel that must've been on the floor and cleaned her up.

If any other man had unloaded all over her, she probably would have beaten the shit out of them. For some reason that thought continually played on the fringes of her consciousness, but she refused to accept it. She longed for him to mark her in every possible way. She needed to be owned, wanted desperately to fulfill his every dominating desire, but only because it was Luke.

Rolling over when he'd rid her of most of his cum, she stared up at him. A hint of fear played in the unquenched thirst in his eyes. He chased his breath. Her eyes tracked rivulets of sweat streaming from his temple to his collarbone. She longed to lick it away, to taste his salty musk.

"You okay? I'm sorry. I didn't mean to lose control like that," he managed in a pained whisper. Shame radiated from every chiseled plane of his body. Since she'd loved every minute of it, she needed to rid him of any guilt as soon as possible.

"I'm much better than okay, and don't you dare apologize. I sure as hell hope you aren't done, cowboy. I need more of you just like that. Let me see more of this side you'd never show anyone else. I'm a very willing participant, Luke. Stop beating yourself up and show me what else you had in mind."

He closed his eyes and worked his jaw frantically. Indie studied him. Was he attempting to summon more calm, more control over himself so he could attempt to recreate the way they'd had sex for the last fifteen years? She rolled her eyes as she assumed that was precisely what he was doing.

"Don't," she ordered.

When he opened his eyes, they were the precise shade of a scalding blue flame, and she intended to stoke the fire.

"Don't what?"

"Don't try to stop yourself from taking whatever you want. I want to do it. Say it, whatever it is, Luke. This is me. This is us. Show me the part you've kept hidden for way too damn long."

His pecs tensed and a harsh swallow contracted his neck. He was still on his knees over her. Sitting up, she ran her hands down his chest, stopping to spin her index fingers over the disks of his nipples. He loved that. She knew. A staccato series of grunts sounded from him.

His jaw flexed again, but he wouldn't give in. With a smirk, she leaned and spun her tongue around the sensitive flesh. When she nipped at the stiff solid tip of his nipples, a low greedy growl tore from his lungs. His hands clasped around her waist.

"I'm going to keep kissing you and sucking from here," she let her fingernails scrape down his chest, "to here," parting her fingers at his half-flaccid cock, ignoring it altogether, she ran them down his thighs. "And I'm not gonna touch anything else until you tell me exactly what you really wish I would do. Pretty sure you already know I'm damned stubborn when I need to be."

His body jerked, just as voracious for more as she was. Certain Luke Camden was the only man she'd ever have to encourage to get his mind out of his head and into his briefs, she continued to taunt him with suckling kisses and the gentle scrape of her fingernails.

His dark penetrating gaze never left her eyes. His breaths came in quickening pants.

"Tell me."

"Fucking hell, woman," he groaned when she neared his package with her kisses but refused it any attention.

"I'm still waiting."

"Fine. Dammit you wanna know what I want? I'll sure as hell show you, but if this isn't the version of me you need …."

"It is. It always has been. Pretty sure I've made that more than clear."

His fingers laced through her hair with more force than she quite expected. The slight pull amped the arousal blistering through her veins. He pushed her head lower. "Suck me. Taste your juices off of my cock. Taste how good we are together, and let me hear how much you're enjoying it."

Delighted she'd won again, she'd drawn the beast out of the man, she moaned as she ran her tongue up and down his stiffening cock.

"I said *suck* me." His order was demanding and graveled. If she hadn't been able to feel the slight rubbed sensation between her thighs from round one, she would have been certain she was caught up in one of her fantasies of him and had lost all comprehension of reality.

The scent of their releases mixed together and the tang of his sweat saturated her senses. She longed to give him more, and the command to do so tapped into the well of wild she would always require.

Drawing him fully into her mouth, since he was still recovering from his first orgasm, she sucked with fervor, loving the way he lengthened and filled her mouth. The heady sensation of power consumed her once again.

Keeping his hand in her hair, he thrust his hips, pushing more of his cock in her mouth and groaning out his pleasure. When she could no longer contain him in her mouth she focused on the crown, spinning her tongue around his head as she sucked and letting her hungry moans vibrate down his shaft.

Guiding her head with his hand, he drew himself out of her mouth. Pouting at that, she stared at the blazing fire she'd ignited in his eyes waiting to see what might be coming next.

"Suck my balls. Open wide and get me wet."

Another moan of approval rang from her lips as she lowered her head once again. Now they were getting somewhere. His groans turned to rasping growls as she complied, drawing on his sac with gentle suckles and teasing licks. His intoxicating scent was more potent here. She indulged herself with his flavors, flattening her tongue to absorb while she sucked. His body swayed above her.

"Enough," he grunted. "Clean that up." He pointed to the beads of pre-cum now coating the tip of his cock. Spinning her tongue over him she sucked away the salty essence. Tipping her chin upwards a moment later, she stared into the raging fire in his eyes. He grasped her hands, hoisted her up on her knees, and crushed his lips to hers in a brutal showing of male possession. His tongue dove between her lips, stealing her breath and tangling with her own. The raw abandon consumed her like a drug.

"Lord almighty, I love the taste of me in your mouth. I love the taste of me everywhere. Lay back and spread your legs. I want more."

Easing back on the mattress, Indie panted in anticipation as Luke settled between her legs, using the broad width of his shoulders to brace them apart. The slow, sinuous glide of his tongue up her slit made her writhe wildly, desperate for more.

His rope-roughened hands clamped around her waist and pinned her to the mattress with force. "Be still, sugar. Let me enjoy you. I dream about how sweet you taste. I'll never get enough." Somehow, the pressure and strength of his hands keeping her anchored to the mattress juxtaposed with the tender caresses of his tongue freed her soul. She'd never felt more desired, more fulfilled, more accepted, or more loved. His willingness to show her a side of himself she'd never known existed added another dimensionality to their entire past.

Another slow back-and-forth rasp of his tongue from her ass along the curve of her body up to her clit had her considering their future.

When he finally honed in on her clitoris with a thorough bath from his velvet tongue and began to suckle gently, she lost all ability to contemplate anything beyond how insanely good that felt.

He nuzzled his face against her inner thigh as he gently opened her lips with his thumbs. The abrasion of his stubbled beard mixed with the thorough care of his tongue sent another rush of wetness down her slit. A low growl of approval reverberated against her tissues, making her long to move. Giving in, she began to grind her pussy in his face.

"I said be still, sugar." Tension tightened and then frayed his vocal cords. Impatience flashed in his eyes.

"I don't want to be still. I want to be fucked," she defied. "What are you gonna do about it?"

The hot sting of his massive right hand smacking the side of her ass jolted through her body. "Oh, yes," she panted. One single cell of her brain wondered if she should be ashamed that she'd nearly come with the strike of his hand and that she desperately craved more. That one brain cell shut up quickly, however, when he gorged himself on the juices her body readily supplied.

His tongue speared deep between her slit. Another strike of his hand accompanied him sucking at her clit, and she came again with a choked gasp of his name. Euphoria sated her as she trembled against the mattress, riding the aftershocks of the orgasm he'd orchestrated perfectly.

"Like that don't you, doll baby? You like just a little pain with your pleasure. Made you so fucking wet for me. Made you come for me, didn't it? Not a damn thing wrong with that, so stop gnawing on that lip. I ain't finished yet."

Still lost in a post-orgasmic sea of bliss and confusion, she hadn't realized she was chewing on her bottom lip. Deciding to just believe that he was right, there was nothing wrong with it, she closed her eyes and inhaled deeply in the scent of his musk and his heat.

She heard the condom wrapper tear, and a moment later he surged inside of her. Covering her body with his own, he became her sheltering harbor, shielding her from everything that had no business being in her mind when she was safe in his arms. Accepting her and somehow bringing her every fantasy to life.

"Look at me, Indie," he whispered as he gently eased back and then took her with another slow thrust.

Her eyes blinked open, and she stared into the exhilaration and love that darkened his from ice blue to indigo.

114

"So, damn beautiful. My sweet baby. I've got you." Another thrust so thorough she shook with his tender care. "I know what you need, sugar. I know how to take care of you. Please, just trust me. I love you." His words melted into a low groan of pleasure on his next pass.

"I do trust you." She rocked against him, losing herself in the thrumming sounds of his voice and their slick heat connecting deep inside of her.

Lowering his head, he took her lips with the same decadent greed his cock was currently using to possess her pussy. Slow and steady, he built her again. She seized around him, swollen so tight he could barely move. Her body flexed, constantly begging to be filled.

"Sweet Jesus, you feel good." He forced one more thrust and they both lost it all. The ecstasy that always came from being in his arms washed over her like a healing balm. She collapsed as the waves overtook her, and he wrapped her up in his arms as he filled the condom with another potent round of semen.

Unable to guard her own thoughts, he'd removed every armament she'd always clung to. In that moment she wished he'd left the condom off again. She wanted his heat fully inside of her.

When he eased away and disposed of the condom, she managed to shut that thought down. She'd think about it later. Back in Oklahoma City, alone in her apartment, when she was reviewing the past two weeks and adding them to the lengthy list of fantasies she had of him. She'd think about it then.

Turning off the lamps in the room, he drew her up onto his chest and cradled her against him. He brushed a kiss on her head, against her dampened hair. "I didn't mean to be so rough with you the first time back. God, the things you do to me, sugar. I lose it all. You can yell at me if you want."

Indie smiled against his chest. Her blinks extended in length as he rubbed his right hand over her ass, tending the sting that was already almost gone.

"I don't want to yell at you," she yawned.

Chuckling, he traced his hand up from her ass and tilted her head until she was staring at him in the moonlit room. "You sure? You always want to yell at me."

"I told you, this is precisely what I want. I love that you finally showed me this side of yourself. Makes me a little upset you kept it from me all of these years, actually. I guess I could yell at you about that if it'd make you feel better. I'd rather hear about where that's been all of these years, though."

Luke stared down at the only thing he'd ever really wanted in his entire life. In that moment he knew he'd give up everything for her. What he didn't know was how to explain that it had taken him a few years after college to be able to analyze their somewhat bizarre fuck buddy relationship and to understand that what she craved was that feeling of being out of control.

She'd always had that need, a wild child from the very beginning. The image permanently branded in his mind of her pure glee as his truck spun recklessly over mud in the spring and ice in the winter flared against his skull. Right up until the moment the CV joint snapped, she'd been completely out of control and happier than he'd ever seen her. He was driving. She could do nothing but hang on to him as they rode, and she trusted him and no one else. He could still hear her begging for more. That feeling was what he had to recreate for her constantly for the next two weeks. This time he wouldn't let her down.

She'd loved every demand he'd made every time they'd shared anything sexual for the last two days. She desperately needed him to restore her wild soul by taking away her stubborn determination to do everything her own way. The complexities of that hadn't cemented in his mind until he was nearing 30. It was then he'd finally allowed himself to picture her as the star of his most carnal fantasies.

He'd been an idiotic college freshman when he'd pushed her away by all but insisting she marry him. In the long list of regrets he had over Indie, that was right at the very top. He should have given her some space and some time to process everything that had happened. He should have stayed in the Glen with her instead of dragging her to Lincoln with him. He should have sat her down and just listened as she talked through everything. And if running away was the only thing that would've helped her heal, then he should have run away *with* her.

"What we just shared, I can't give you twice a year when you show up at my house after midnight, sugar. That just isn't how this works. Trust and passion like that, they don't come from a one-night stand. They come from a relationship. I'm not gonna paddle your sweet sexy ass if I don't get to be the one that rubs and kisses it until it feels better afterwards. Also not gonna leave rope marks on you if I don't get to tend them 'til they don't hurt any more. You understand that, don't you?"

"Yeah, I get it." She didn't sound overly thrilled with that explanation however. "Rope marks, huh?"

"Only if you want to try that." Thankful for the cover of darkness as it provided a safe haven for her deepest desires, he pretended not to notice the fevered embarrassment he could feel against his chest.

With a quick clench of her jaw, her determination came back to her in full force. Luke grinned. He knew it would if he gave her just a minute.

"I ain't had anything but sissy city-boys making plays for me for the last decade, except when I came home to you. Now you're laying here after the best sex we've ever had telling me you're gonna tie me up and give me more of that. I'm not sure my body can take it. I may die of happiness. Not too sure I like the sound of ropes though. Isn't there something else we could use?"

Luke forced a half-chuckled grunt. The thought of her with any other man made fury erupt in his soul. "I just came up with at least five things that ain't ropes and I'm beat. We'll do whatever you want, but I ain't ever gonna fuck you like a pretty city-boy, Indie Jane. That sure as hell ain't me. I don't do anything half way. You know that. Every time I take you to bed I'll make damn sure you understand who you belong to, and I'll show you precisely what your gorgeous body was made for. From the most mundane to the raunchiest things you might want to try, I plan to explore every single one of your fantasies in-depth and repeatedly. I'll tell you this, too, there won't be any more pansy-ass pussies after *my* girl. Mine. You got that?"

No answer. Moonlight glinted in her eyes revealing her desire to agree, however.

"I know what you need, and I'll give it to you when I want you to have it. Think I just proved I'll also take whatever the hell I want, too. And I'm assuming everything you just said means you'd like to be tied to my bed while I drive you wild out of your mind. You just don't want anything that leaves marks. That is what you're saying, right?"

"Hell, yeah, cowboy. How many times do I need to repeat myself?"

"I won't ask again. I'll just start takin'."

"Good."

Unable to help himself, he kissed the sides of her impish grin and then centered his lips over hers and sank his tongue inside her mouth with a slow sinful glide. His hands traced gently along her back and down to her ass. Keeping her in the protective sanctuary of his body he lingered in the kiss, never wanting it to end.

When she pulled away with a panted breath, he trailed his tongue down her neck and left another love bite near her collarbone, smaller than the other but every bit as dogged.

"More," she sighed. "Please."

"Don't need your permission, honey. Remember?" he sank his lips between her breasts, leaving another one of his brands there as well.

He continued his path down her body, leaving his mark on the hipbone he could access and then another on her plump ass cheek. When she was a quivering mass of desire, he swirled his tongue over each of her nipples, reveling in the sweet tang of her sweat gathered there from their love making.

Returning his lips to hers, he gentled one more lengthy kiss and then tucked her softly to his body. "Go to sleep, darlin'. I'm gonna want to keep goin' as soon as I wake up in the mornin'."

"Give me more, now."

Keeping her head under his chin, he tried to conceal his grin. Sated and begging for more. Just the way he'd planned it. "You're tired, sugar. You're already gonna hurt tomorrow from all we just did. Just sleep for me. Let me make it feel better in the mornin'."

"I can't stay here, Luke."

You can't tie her down. Caging her will only make her run again. He clenched his jaw to keep from demanding that she stay, but he finally managed, "Why not?"

"I have to see Daddy sometime, and be over at Mama's in time for this stupid brunch thing. Make it feel better now."

"No, ma'am. I know you're raw, baby. Just relax for me. If you can't stay all night, stay for a little while." Recognizing his own determination in his half-commanded request, he wasn't certain how she might respond.

"Just for a little while," she conceded. Indieanna Jane Harper gave in. It was in those five simple words of agreement he knew he was on the right path to getting her to stay forever.

Chapter Twelve

Trying her damnedest to be galled, Indie stared in the mirror of the particle board dresser her daddy had built from a kit when she was a teenager. She tugged the button down shirt she was wearing to the other side. It was no use. The hickeys Luke had branded along her neck and chest couldn't all be covered at once, not that she really cared. Secretly, she hoped her mother had the audacity to call her out. It was her daddy she was a little bit worried the marks might offend. He'd never say a word, but she didn't want to disappoint him.

Letting that thought flip through her head, she quickly decided whatever reaction the marks brought on they were worth it. She loved wearing his brand just as much as she'd loved wearing his cum the night before.

It had taken every ounce of fortitude she possessed to crawl out of Luke's bed last night and drive back home. She could've stayed tucked up warm and safe in his sanctuary of muscle, listening to his steady heartbeat forever and been perfectly happy. That knowledge is how she finally forced herself to move.

If she'd stayed there much longer, she might've woken him up and agreed to stay in Pleasant Glen playing the part of rancher's wife. *Nope.* It didn't matter how amazing the sex was or how much she adored Luke, she wasn't ever going to be okay in this town. Besides, if her own mother couldn't make it work with her daddy, no one ever could. Luke's parents immediately sprang to mind. Dammit, he even had her own head arguing with her in his absence. She needed to get out of that room.

Bunching up a wad of duct tape she'd located in the kitchen junk drawer while her father was out feeding the horses, she affixed the half-crushed ribbon to the 200-Piece Kobalt Standard and Metric tool set she'd purchased for Tuck and Melony's shower present. Grinning at her work, she ran her hands over the quick-release ratchets. She was beyond certain Mel would be inundated with dumbass presents that would largely go unused, but a quality set of Kobalt in the high-end blow-molded case, they could use that forever.

Trucking out of the bedroom, she set the tool case on the sofa and went to pour a mug of coffee. Her daddy was standing at the oven scrambling eggs. "What time did you get home last night, baby girl? I didn't hear you come in."

"Oh." Indie told herself she had no reason to feel guilty. "Uh, it was late. Luke and I went to Ogallala with Tuck and Mel for supper."

A smirk formed on her father's face as he turned to study her. When his eyes landed on the rather large hickeys on her neck, he shook his head. "Uh huh, I'm just betting you weren't out getting Runzas 'til three in the mornin'. You want some eggs?"

"Thought you didn't hear me come in, and no, Mel's thing is a brunch. I'll eat there."

"That was a lucky guess, but you just told me what I wanted to know." He chuckled.

Indie ground her teeth for a moment, but finally grinned. She loved to hear her daddy laugh. The warm melodic sound always delighted her. "You don't have to leave Luke's bed to be home for breakfast with your old man, Indie Jane. You two've been like magnets since you met in ninth grade. I don't want to get between ya."

"I like having breakfast with you, Daddy. Besides, I have to be over at Mama's all damn day. I wanted to see you this mornin'."

"Well, you know I love having you here whenever you want to be here, but seems to me if you conceded to moving home you wouldn't have to try and juggle us all constantly. Save yourself a lot of unnecessary guilt."

"I don't have guilt. I have coffee." She lifted her mug as she settled at the table.

"Uh huh." Ben rolled his eyes as he settled across from her at the table with his plate of eggs. "You sure you don't want anything to eat?"

"No, I'm sure Mama has some fancy food person in from Lincoln cooking up shit I've never heard of. I intend to tell her to leave Tucker and Melony the hell alone, but I'll make nice and eat whatever they're having."

"Indie Jane, you ever think maybe Melony ought to be the one talkin' if Carolyn's doing something that's getting on her nerves?"

"You know how Mel is, Daddy. She doesn't even know *how* to stand up for herself. I'll talk to Carolyn."

Her father's only response was to shove a forkful of eggs in his mouth.

An hour later, Indie repeated the mantra, '*Do not strangle your mother*' repeatedly in her head while she slowly drove over the railroad tracks headed to the other end of Pleasant Glen. This time she needed Carolyn Harper *Jenkins* to listen to her. She would not let her mother

120

run Tuck and Melony out of the Glen any more than she would let her mother ruin their wedding. Indie just needed to keep it together long enough to get through her mother's stubborn insistence that she was always right.

Another round of memories played in perfect detail in her mind as she slowly guided her Camaro up the gravel driveway that led to Pleasant Glen's version of a mansion. About three months after the mayor and her mother had wed, Miranda and Melony had begged Indie to come to the mayor's and spend the night with them. Ben had urged Indie to just spend one night to appease her sisters. He'd insisted her mother wanted her there, too, but even then, Indie knew that wasn't the case.

She'd made it through dinner and no less than four arguments with her mother when Ernie had informed Indie that she was an embarrassment to him and that she'd never lose any weight if she kept eating. After that, she'd snuck upstairs to the master bathroom, poured out the entire bottle of Aqua Bond toupee glue, and had adhered her newly minted stepfather's hair piece to the Formica countertop. Five minutes later, she'd climbed out a bedroom window and headed for Camden Ranch.

A slight giggle escaped her lips from the memory. She hadn't lost any of her spitfire in the last two decades, and just then, that fact made her proud.

"Well, here goes nothing." She grabbed her bag and death-marched to her doom. Her brow furrowed when Tucker answered the door. "She already got you playing doorman, Kilroy?"

He rolled his eyes before checking behind him, presumably to make certain Carolyn wasn't nearby. "She up and ordered Mel outta my bed at six fucking AM. I brought her over here because I'm sick to death of Carolyn pushing her around, and I knew she'd be laying on the guilt about the wedding hot and heavy today."

Indie nodded her understanding as she stepped inside the stately foyer. "Unless you really want to hang out for a bridal shower, you go on. I know you got chores this mornin'. I'll take care of Mel."

"Thanks, but I'm gonna stick around here. I talked my brothers into picking up my slack. I'll hear about it later, but that's better than another night of holding her while she cries over whatever your mom comes up with next."

Before Indie could respond, her mother appeared. She was still in her long, ridiculously overstated, satin dressing robe. Her long, bleached-blonde hair was done up in some kind of fancy twist, and she'd made it through the first steps of her intricate makeup routine. Her face was entirely one pale color with no contrast, making her lips and eyes appear to be almost invisible.

"Well, shut the door, Indieanna. You may prefer to *be* in a barn, but you were not born in one. Your sisters are in the kitchen helping the caterer. Go give them a hand then you can change."

"I'm not changing, Mother." Not her clothes, not her makeup, not one single thing about herself, not for her mother or anyone else.

"This is a formal affair. Friends of Ernie's from Lincoln will be attending as will your stepfather's staff. You will not embarrass him. Surely you have something more appropriate than jeans and boots to wear for your sister's bridal shower."

Grinding her teeth just long enough to keep from lunging at her mother, Indie narrowed her eyes. "I really don't give a rat's ass who's going to be here, Mother. I *am* here and this is what I'm wearing. Deal with it."

Tucker cringed, but Indie held her ground. Her mother really ought to know that the quickest way to get Indie to do something was to tell her not to. Turning on her heels, Carolyn stormed up the stairs, not in the mood to take her on, it seemed.

Shaking her head, Indie located her little sisters standing in the kitchen, whispering heatedly.

"What now?" she sighed.

"This," Miranda jerked a slip of paper out of Melony's hands. "The mayor just gave this to Mel before he left."

Indie studied what appeared to be a bill of sale from Tastefully Yours Catering, Lincoln's premiere catering company. "Why did he give this to you?"

Tucker pulled the paper from Indie's hands.

Already red-faced and blinking back tears, Melony drew a deep breath. "Mama got upset about the rehearsal dinner thing, and me not letting Ernie walk me down the aisle. That pissed Ernie off, and now he says Tuck and I have to pay for this because I haven't shown any appreciation for all of Mama's work on the wedding."

"Mel, baby, we cannot afford this." Pain riffed in Tucker's declaration as he stared in horror at the total on the bottom of the bill.

"I know. I didn't even want to have this stupid shower. This was all her doing, and now ...." Melony's pleading gaze speared through Indie. It hadn't changed in the last twenty years. Anytime Mel and Miranda were terrified they'd done something to gall their mother,

Indie came up with some way to save the day. She wouldn't let them down now.

"Give me that." She jerked the receipt from Tucker's hands and marched up to her mother's dressing room. "What the actual hell, Mother?!" She flung the receipt on the countertop.

In true Carolyn Jenkins form, she viewed Indie as one of her staff. "Clasp this for me." She turned with two ends of her strands of pearls in her hands, waiting on Indie's aid. Rolling her eyes, Indie attached the necklace. After all, one couldn't be the Pleasant Glen pearl-clutcher-in-chief without the pearls.

"I asked you a question. You and the *mayor*," she all but gagged, "know good and well that Tuck and Melony cannot pay for this shindig you decided to throw. They didn't even want it. I swear, you get off on making all of us miserable. Why is that?"

Her mother's haughty glare narrowed in on Indie's neck. "What in heaven's name is that?" She stabbed one of her perfectly manicured fingernails into one of the hickeys.

Indie jerked back. Her fists knotted by her side as she attempted to count to ten in her head. She'd made it to four when she gave up trying. "That is none of your damn business, Mother. Tucker and Melony are not paying for this ridiculous shower, and if you continue to operate under the ridiculous delusion that they are, they'll leave and you can eat all of the petit fours and finger sandwiches with the mayor's staff yourself, which is really what you want anyway. Always preferred for the three of us to be seen and never heard. Nothing ever changes, most certainly not you."

"If Luke Camden is leaving marks on you, I'll just have to have a talk with Everett and Jessie about his behavior."

"Oh my God, Mother! He's thirty-three years old. None of us are children anymore. You cannot order us around. You cannot make Tuck and Melony do what you want them to do any more than you can tell Luke and me what to do."

Fishing around in her mind for a way to get through her mother's stubborn refusal to accept anything she didn't care for, she landed on the one way to get Carolyn Jenkins to back down. "Listen and listen good, Mom, because I'm only saying this once. You go downstairs and apologize to Tucker for what you said to his mother, then you apologize to Mel for this insanity," she shook the bill in front of her mother's face, "or I will drive myself down to the courthouse tomorrow morning, after everyone is at work, of course, and I will loudly let the mayor of this ridiculous town know precisely what I think of him, and of you, and of this," she shook the bill again. "Then I'll elaborate on just how Daddy found out about the two of you. I'll happily remind everyone of the past you'd so like to pretend away."

Fury flared in her mother's eyes, accentuated by the heavy black liner she'd applied. Indie smirked. If Carolyn wanted to play hardball, she'd bring out the metal bats.

"Did it ever occur to you or your sisters, Indieanna, that perhaps Ernie is a wonderful, supportive husband and father that is upset about the way Melony has been acting over what should be a beautiful, joyous day? Did you ever stop to think about how I might feel about being rejected by my daughter, or having all of my desires and hopes for her dashed away because she believes she's in love with a corn farmer that will never be good enough for her? Ernie is trying to teach Melony a lesson she desperately needs. *Your* father lets the three of you get away with murder. He always did, and I won't stand for it. Ernie and I never intended for Melony to pay for this shower I've worked tooth and nail to plan. We are trying to teach her to show a little appreciation, something I failed to ever teach you."

"You know, Mom, none of that ever did occur to me because all of it is complete and total bullshit. You're in it so deep you need waders and a paddle to get out. Now, go apologize or let the mayor know he'll need to clear his schedule because I'll be in for our meeting first thing tomorrow morning."

Luke glanced at his watch again, bored with checking the new calves who all seemed to be handling life well. He'd already fed the bottle calf — Cassie, he recalled Indie's name for it — and had checked the fields they'd burned back last month. Be time to hay soon. That thought did nothing to bolster his mood. Biding his time until he headed for the mayor's mansion irritated him almost as much as waking up cold and alone in his bed had.

The warmth of Indie's curves and her sweet breaths whispering over his chest had disappeared around three. The absence still stung.

Worry over what Indie might encounter at her mother's swirled in his empty gut. It rumbled its disagreement. His mama was making everyone on the ranch breakfast. He'd head that way as soon as he checked the back fields, but truthfully, he wasn't going to make for good company. Far too worried over Indie's inevitable misery at the hands of her mother, all he wanted was to ride in on his pick-up and play the part of knight-in-dirty-cowboy-boots. The brunch thing was supposed to be over around 2:00. He planned to be there early.

124

Scanning the fields and creek in the farthest fields on his land, he narrowed his eyes. "Shit." Heavy footing the gas pedal, he sped towards the water's edge and leapt out. Wading out into the water, his heart thundered out his panic as he pulled a half-drowned calf up into his arms.

Heaving him onto the creek bank, Luke laid him on his sternum hoping to drain some of the water from his lungs. The calf didn't move. Racing back to the truck, he grabbed his kit and a pack of syringes. Opening the calf's mouth, he used a bulb syringe to clear the mucus that had gathered on his snout before he created a makeshift breathing tube and blew air into his lungs.

A moment later, a low gurgled cough sounded from the little fellow, followed by a rush of water out of his mouth, and Luke seated himself on the damp grass, gasping for breath. Working quickly, he drew up a syringe of steroids that would continue to clear his lungs. When the steer finally stood and shook off the water, relief welled in Luke's soul. "You ain't quite big enough for that swim, little fella. Where's your mama, anyway?"

The nearest herd was out in the field chewing cud. One of the heifers was bellowing anxiously. Luke loaded the calf in the back of his truck, drove him to the herd, and dropped him off with the gathered calves resting in the sun. He circled the field, slowly checking to make certain the calf was eating and hadn't suffered any permanent injuries from his attempt at cooling off. When he was certain the steer was going to be fine, he turned and headed towards his parents' house, hoping that he was going to be two for two in the savior department that day.

Guests began arriving at a quarter to eleven. Indie was biting holes in her tongue to keep from commenting on the passive aggressive shit storm her mother stirred constantly. Carolyn had offered Melony a half-hearted apology about the catering bill and explained that the mayor was teaching Melony a lesson. With that comment, it seemed Tucker Kilroy's line of patience snapped in two, and he'd unloaded on Carolyn with both barrels. Currently, both Melony and her mother were sniffling and taking turns shooting vexing glares at one another.

Indie checked the time on her cell phone again. Dear God, how had she only been there one hour?

"Indie." Miranda grabbed her blouse and jerked her into the butler's pantry.

"What?"

"Listen, Mel really wants to have a bachelorette party. Nothing crazy. No strippers or anything, but I completely forgot to plan anything until I heard her talking to Tuck when I got here. Help, please."

"Miranda, I'm really not the party planning kind of girl. You know that. Does she just want to go get drunk or what?"

"This is Mel we're talking about. She wants a stupid rhinestone bride crown, feather boas, body glitter, a sash, gifts that vibrate, fuzzy handcuffs, and pink girly drinks with umbrellas in them. Where the hell are we gonna find all of that in the Glen?"

Indie couldn't help but grin. Though she was only seventeen minutes older than Melony, Miranda had always been more serious and determined than her twin. She was Pleasant Glen High School's power hitter on the softball team and took most things in stride. She didn't have Indie's temper, but she never let anyone push her around either. After years of allowing Carolyn to paint her face with Avon's newest products, she'd followed in Indie's footsteps of not caring for makeup, much to her mother's chagrin. She and Indie had never really understood Melony's affinity for all things girly, but if their little sister wanted to go full-on princess just before becoming a farmer's wife, they'd do their very best.

Another thought occurred to her while she was explaining that they'd have no choice but to make a trip into Lincoln for supplies and that she'd check with Eliza about using the semi-private back room at Saddleback's one night that week.

"Is Tucker having a bachelor party?" Thoughts of some gorgeous stripper shaking her tits in Luke's face made Indie want to vomit and then tie up the fictional stripper with her g-string.

"Not really. Tuck informed Luke and all of his brothers that the last decade of his life had been one long bachelor's party and that he was done with it all. Swears he wants Mel and only her for the rest of his life. He agreed to drinks and burgers with all of them at Luke's house, but that's it. He threatened bodily harm to anyone that tries to pull something."

Still shocked at the new and improved Tucker Kilroy, Indie shrugged. "Guess some things do change."

Miranda nodded. "Yeah, he's got it bad for our baby sister."

"Makes you wonder if baby sis has whips and thigh-high black leather boots hidden somewhere, doesn't it?"

When they emerged giggling from their hide out, their aunts were being escorted into the house. Indie's stomach lurched and she fought the desire to slip out the back door, jump in her car, and fly away.

Apparently, Miranda had been gifted the talent of mind reading since Indie's last visit because she grasped her hand. "Just stay with me. If we have to jump them, I'll take out Aunt Linda, you get Aunt Lori."

"Deal." Indie ground her teeth. Twins were very common on her mother's side of the family. Her aunts were two years older than her mother and were also twice as bitchy.

"Well, Anna." Linda's mouth pursed in indignation and Indie braced for impact. "I was unaware you'd been invited to Melony's brunch. I see you're still not making enough with your little car hobby to afford appropriate clothing, however."

"Linda, dear, do remember things in the *Women's* sections of the store cost a good deal more. At least she didn't show up in coveralls. That's something," Lori sneered.

Miranda's grip on Indie's arm increased as unmitigated fury incensed Indie's blood.

"Just smile and move on. They're trying to get a rile out of you. They always are," Miranda spoke through clenched teeth.

She was right. Ever since her mother had up and married Ernie Perkins, her aunts had gone from bad to worse. Neither had ever married nor had children of their own. They'd taken to mothering Indie's sisters from their birth, but had never wanted to have anything to do with Indie.

When she was ten, her Aunt Linda had tried to talk Carolyn into selling Indie's horse in an effort to make her more lady-like. Indie had overheard their scheming while they sat at the kitchen table trying out a variety of wrinkle creams, and had promptly informed her aunt that it wouldn't matter how much of the cream she used, she'd still be an ugly bitch, and that if anyone sold her horse, she'd make certain her aunt's Cadillac never ran again. That had been the final nail in the coffin for Indie, but the ridiculous jealousy over their little sister becoming the Glen's first lady and moving into a fancy ass house had been more than they could stand. Now, they generally stayed hunkered together anytime they were at the house, making bitchy remarks about most anything and taking pot shot insults at all three of their nieces.

Indie screwed up her face until she managed something she hoped resembled an arrogant smile. "Aunt Lori, Aunt Linda," she sidled closer, narrowing her eyes, "you know, if you really try, you might could grab each other's ears and pull hard enough to actually be able to get your heads out of each other's asses. Good luck with that. Let me know if you need some help. I'm sure I've got some heavy duty jacks that might just work."

Miranda's hand slapped over her own mouth to keep her hysterical laughter from being heard three states away. Indie took a champagne spritzer from one of the waiter's trays and lifted the glass to her aunts before she turned and almost bumped into Jessie Camden. Her eyes goggled. *Shit.* There was no way Luke's mother hadn't overheard her retort. To her relief, Jessie was doing her best to keep from joining Miranda's laughter. Indie adored Luke's mama. She just doubted that Jessie Camden would really want one of her sons to be with someone as unrefined as Indie.

When Indie followed Jessie and Miranda through the buffet line, her aunts' comments were audible to the entire party. "Anna, dear, does someone your size really feel it's wise to have two finger sandwiches. Carbs aren't your friend, you know," Lori tsked.

"Yes, I'm sure Melony would be pleased if you'd show some restraint since you will be in the wedding Saturday. After that you can go back to eating like a hog."

"Oh God. Indie please, please don't hit them," Melony whispered frantically.

Melony had nothing to worry about in that department. She wouldn't give her aunts the satisfaction. The insult pierced through her skin and levied its blow to her soul. It racked its heavy weight on top of every other hateful comment she'd endured her entire life. Pretending to be unaffected was something she'd mastered in high school. The invisible scars were far worse than the kind people could actually see. She knew. She had both.

Keeping a baleful glare on her aunts, she added two more sandwiches to her plate, flipped them off, and joined Jessie at one of the tables.

Jessie looked almost as sickened by her aunts as Indie felt. "Honey, why do you even come here? No one would blame you for never setting foot in this ridiculous house ever again," she whispered as Indie took her seat.

"I'm here for my sisters. It's always like this, Mrs. Camden. I'm fine."

"You are not fine, sweetheart. You are beautiful, and sweet, and smart, and a wonderful woman, but right now, you are not fine. If you

128

want to walk out right now, I'll go with you, put you in my truck, and take you to my ranch where I know my son would love for you to be. This entire thing is ridiculous."

"I'm very sorry, Jessie, what was that?" Carolyn sneered.

Shit. Indie and Jessie both whipped around to discover Indie's mother standing directly behind them carrying a tray of chocolate dipped strawberries to the buffet table.

"Nothing, Mama," Indie whispered.

"It was most certainly *something*," Carolyn demanded with her nose high enough in the air if it rained she'd drown.

"I was just saying that the way you and your sisters treat Indie is ridiculous, Carolyn." Jessie Camden narrowed her eyes. Indie's heart pounded out its shock. No one but Luke had ever come to her defense when it came to her mother. Challenge lit through the stuffy air vacuuming the room of the pleasant chatter that had been present a moment earlier. The silence pounded in time with Indie's frantic heartbeat.

Carolyn glanced around nervously. Every eye was on her. Offering a haughty glare to the onlookers, she leaned in for the kill. "You know, Jessie, Ernie and I are very weary of the Camden's lording your land and your status over this entire town," she hissed like the snake she was, "and I think it's high time something was done about it." With that, she leaned back and daggered the silent room with fabricated laughter as if she'd just told Mrs. Camden a joke. Setting the tray of strawberries on the buffet table, she whisked quickly back to the head table.

"Mrs. Camden, I'm so sorry," Indie offered pathetically.

"Oh honey," she chuckled, "this has been coming to a head for the last several years, and it has nothing to do with you. Don't you worry. Only thing you have to be sorry about is that you let her keep you from Luke. That's the only thing that breaks my heart, Indie Jane. Only thing that breaks his, too." She squeezed Indie's thigh reassuringly. "Ev has a sayin'. If we tried to run cattle with other people's opinions, we'd be up shit creek without a paddle. He's right, too, you know. Letting anybody else's thoughts about your life be your guiding force is the quickest way to be miserable. If our lame-duck mayor and your mama want to take on the Camdens, have no doubt, we won't be the ones that go down."

A hundred different thoughts rampaged Indie's mind. Why would Jessie think her mama and the mayor would want to take on the

Camdens, and over what? The knowing look in Jessie's eyes said she knew much more than she was saying.

Tension continued to whisper through the air as the party bled seamlessly from the food to the gifts. No one spoke of the incident between Jessie and Indie's mother, but everyone kept a keen eye on the two of them and on Indie. The weight of everyone's curiosity was getting to her. She longed to tell everyone in attendance, minus Luke's sweet mama, to fuck off as she bolted out the door.

Melony politely oohed and ahhed over some ridiculous silver serving tray and matching tea set from their aunts.

"Yeah, I'm sure Tuck will relish having tea parties every night after he comes in from tasseling two thousand pounds of corn before shipping it to market," Indie huffed under her breath.

Miranda and Jessie both chuckled their agreement.

"When Tucker and Luke were about eight years old, they used one of Sandy Kilroy's sugar bowls to collect cutworms they pulled off the corn stalks. Now he has one of his own and can leave his mama's alone," Jessie chided, bringing on more laughter from Indie and Miranda.

The gifts from the Lincoln elite were equally as comical when one tried to apply them to Tucker and Melony's farm life together. Bone china, crystal vases, and some bizarre rendition of the Greek pottery housed at the Joslyn Museum in Omaha, hand-picked by Ernie's airheaded secretary, Tiffany. It was the ugliest urn-like item Indie had ever laid eyes on, and when Melony turned it around so everyone could see the image, Indie and Miranda cracked up loudly. The image on the massive urn was of Hades and Persephone, if Indie remembered correctly. Whoever it was, the dude was fingering the girl on the urn, and she didn't look too happy about it. Melony was the approximate shade of the burnt umber urn in question. Her mouth gaped open for a full minute.

"Uh, thank you so much, Tiffany. You *really* shouldn't have," she finally managed.

"Oh, as soon as I saw it, I knew you would love it," Tiffany babbled stupidly. "Ernie always talks about how much you love Greek pottery."

"He does?" Melony shot her *help me* glare at her sisters. "I don't really know anything about Greek pottery."

"Certainly you do, Melony." Panic tensed in Carolyn's tone. "Remember, you went on and on to your father and I all about taking your class to the museum to see Greek pottery."

130

"No, I didn't. We took them to the Children's Museum to play in an exhibit of Rome under Caesar's rule."

"Yes, well, same thing. Open the next gift," Carolyn demanded.

Indie spent the next five minutes trying to figure out how the hell either Ernie or Tiffany had gotten Greek Pottery out of Caesar and Rome to keep from correcting her mother on exactly whom Melony's father was.

Melony grinned as she lifted Indie's gift from the pile. "I don't even have to look at the tag. Thanks, Indie. Tuck'll love this!" A few shocked chuckles made their way through the crowd of people who'd never been so far outside of the city of Lincoln.

"You got your sister *tools* for a bridal shower?" Aunt Linda disdained.

"Yeah, I did. Nice set. I've had the same one for years. I use them all the time," Indie came right back.

Carolyn was making her way over, livid fury aglow in her eyes. "Can I speak to you in the kitchen, Indieanna?!"

Seeing the potential for either a fight or a flight opportunity, Indie followed after her mother.

"Are you happy with yourself?" her mother spat.

"Generally."

"You just love making a mockery of your stepfather, even using your little sister as a pawn in your game."

"What the hell are you talking about, Mother? That's a really expensive set. I worked overtime for a week to be able to afford it on top of paying my rent. How is that making a mockery of anyone? I'm not the one that gave her Greek sex pots. Why don't you go yell at Tiffany?"

"Tiffany's gift was thoughtful. She obviously just got confused. She went all the way to the museum in Omaha for that. *She* put effort into the gift, unlike you. Did you just grab the last thing you saw on your way out of Ben's shop? Is that really how little you care?"

"I just said I worked overtime to get that set, Mother, but you know what, it won't ever matter. Nothing I ever do will be good enough for you. I honestly don't know why I even try."

"Well, you certainly didn't try very hard. Showing up here dressed for horseback riding, looking like you spent the night working a brothel." She gestured to the hickeys on Indie's neck. "And then giving your sister a ridiculous gift like that at a formal brunch with half of the governing officials from the state in attendance."

Stabbing pain ricocheted from her heart to her head, igniting the fury burning in her gut. "You know what, Mom, you can go straight to hell. Trust me, no one will care." With that, she turned and sprinted out of the house, directly into ... Luke's arms.

Chapter Thirteen

"Hey there, baby doll. I've gotcha." Luke caught Indie in her obvious escape. Knowing his baby better than anyone ever had, he'd been waiting on the wrap around porch of the mayor's house right outside the kitchen door. She never would have run out the front because that would have upset Melony.

She buried her head in his chest, clinging to him fiercely. He strengthened his hold and cradled the back of her head with one hand while he steadied her with the other.

"What are you doing here?" hummed against his chest.

Smiling, he kissed the top of her head. "Been out here about an hour. Gets me all turned on when I make myself believe that you need me to save you, and I kinda thought you might like to get away for a little while after this thing. Come on. I packed blankets, firewood, and the cooler in the truck. Got nowhere to be but wherever you wanna go."

"I *did* need you to save me," she admitted much to his shock.

Wrapping his arm over her shoulders, he gently eased her down the porch steps headed towards his truck. "Careful there, darlin'. You keep saying stuff like that I'm real likely to march back in that house and give your mama what-for while sporting the hard-on you just gave me."

"Be my guest." Indie sank her teeth into her bottom lip to keep it from trembling.

Luke fought the desperate desire to tell off her mother and her aunts based on Tucker's description of the beginning of the party. He'd been ordered away just before everyone ate and hadn't been able to give Luke anymore details.

"Your mom didn't call you?" Indie climbed up in the truck and crossed her arms over her chest. Defeat tugged at Luke's soul. Her customary defensive stance. Something else must've happened beyond her aunts' cruel remarks about her weight.

"No. Should she have?" Gravel and dust spit into the air as Luke backed out of the driveway, quickly putting distance between Indie and her shit-for-brains mother.

"I just thought that's why you really showed up."

"Wasn't lying to you, sugar. Never have. Never will. I came because I knew someone would be a bitch to my beautiful baby. I was trying to talk myself out of coming in when you came running out. Wanna tell me what happened?"

Indie shook her head. Luke knew the story would come out in fragmented bits of pain and anger over the next several hours when he made her feel safe enough to talk. He just had to be patient and let her stew on it for a little while, constantly reassuring her that he would always be there no matter what. Convincing her of that was always the hard part. If your own mother didn't want you, why would anyone else? Nausea roiled through his gut at that realization.

Keeping her fingers linked with his, he drew an audible breath and went on with the rest of his plan. "All right then, how about we drive far enough out we lose all hope of a cell signal and spend the rest of the day pretending we're the only two people left on this ridiculous planet?"

That earned him a smile. "Are we also going to pretend it's our job to repopulate it?"

Laughing, Luke nodded. "Sounds like a heck of a plan to me, but all I want is my girl tucked up safe in my arms in the bed of my truck. Everyone else can fuck the hell off."

He reveled in the sweet heat of the kiss she leaned across his truck to whisper on his jaw. "I will never deserve you, Luke Camden, but thanks for always knowing exactly what I need."

Keeping a steady speed, he tried to think of a way to coax her into telling him about the shower. She stared out the windshield of his truck, but didn't seem to be seeing much of anything.

"Ernie's stupid secretary got Mel this weird urn thing with Greek sex on it," blurted out a moment later.

"What?!" Luke fought not to double over laughing.

"Yeah, you should have seen the look on Mel's face when she opened it. It has some Greek god and goddess going at it."

"Bet your mama loved that."

"You know Mama. Somebody from Ernie's office gave it to her so it's the best shit ever."

"Is Greek sex different from the kind we have?"

Indie giggled. "I doubt it's changed all that much."

"Well, maybe they can keep condoms or sex toys in it or something," Luke offered just to hear Indie laugh again. The sound always soothed his soul.

He turned off on an old dirt road about fifteen minutes outside the city limits of Pleasant Glen and a smile finally spread the width of Indie's beautiful face.

134

"There's my smile. Wish you'd tell me what else made my baby ornery enough to run away from the party."

"Did you know there's some kind of feud thing going on between your parents and Ernie and Carolyn?"

That question brought Luke up short. He knew all about the ongoing argument, a lesson in stupidity at its finest, but had no idea how that had come up at the bridal shower. He'd never lie to her, so he went on with the explanation.

"Yeah, Ernie somehow got the idea in his fat head that my daddy wants to be the mayor of Pleasant Glen, which may be the dumbest thing I've ever heard, since my dad is all cowboy all the time. Dad can't figure out where he got the idea and gave up trying to convince him it wasn't true.

"Couple years ago, Mom and Dad were trying to get Brock to move back up here. For some reason, Ernie was trying to buy up more land in the Glen back then. Got no idea why, since he don't know his ass from a hole in the ground, and wouldn't know what to do with prairie land if it wrote him a manual. Anyway, Dad went to a town hall meetin' and called the mayor out on some shady dealings with the state over inheritance tax on ranch land. Town rallied around Dad, of course, seein' as how Ernie was trying to rake in cash by double taxing land that was handed down from one family member to the next.

"Ernie's asinine comeback was that Dad was only telling everyone about it because he wanted to be mayor. Dad swore up and down he had no intention of being mayor, but ever since then, Ernie's had it in for all of the Camdens. I kinda wonder if there's more to it that Dad ain't telling me, but you know everything I've been told. Not that it matters. No one cares but Ernie. Natalie goaded it on, though. Girl never has backed down from a fight and never will. Said maybe she'd run for mayor, and Lord Almighty if that didn't tie Ernie up in knots. Been givin' us hell ever since."

"Why didn't you tell me this?"

"Sugar, when would I have told you? You ain't been here. And I want you every second of every day, so the few times you've shown up at my door it hadn't really occurred to me to keep you from stripping so we could talk about ranch land tax codes."

"Well, we could've talked about it afterwards."

Shaking his head, Luke slowed the truck as it climbed over the mounds of dirt and tree roots, headed towards the creek. "I oughta truss you up in my bed and then start talking taxes and see just how much you like it. By the time I got you untied, you'd have me scalped bald."

Giving him a dramatic eye roll, she sighed her concession. "All right, fine, different question. How about why does this stupid town keep electing his sorry ass?"

"No one else wants the job. It's a town full of farms and ranches, sugar. You know that. The rest of us are up to our ears in either corn or cattle, and we ain't got neither time nor interest to up and run the city. He's run unopposed every single time for the last twenty-five years. He doesn't do jack shit, which is exactly how most cowboys prefer for the government to be, so why fix it if it ain't broke has always been the logic."

His explanation seemed to surprise her. Surely, she hadn't really believed that the town of Pleasant Glen just overlooked the fact that their mayor was a lying, cheating, greedy son of a bitch, and continued to elect him anyway. If there'd been any other choice, Ernie Perkins would've landed flat on his ass years ago.

It took him the better part of the next hour to reach the far side of King's Creek, a small watering hole off of the North Platte that couldn't be reached unless you have a four-wheel drive truck or walk on four legs. Shallow enough to stay warm if there was sun, but deep enough to swim, kids from the Glen had been sneaking up there for decades to get away from town, school, their parents, or anyone that might be looking for them. An old rope still hung from a low hanging branch off a massive Cottonwood for the purposes of swinging out into the water on a hot summer day. The fire pit scarred with years' worth of ashes was right where Luke had left it the last time he'd been the one to build a fire there.

"This looks oddly familiar," Indie chuckled as she took in their surroundings.

"Thought about taking you to field out behind the football stadium, but that wouldn't get us this." He held up his cell phone displaying the, "*No Signal*" warning.

"Perfect." She opened her door and leapt out.

"Not perfect," Luke disagreed as he lowered the tailgate and spread two of the quilts he'd brought across the bed of the truck.

"Why?" Indie turned from her trek to the edge of the water.

Settling on his side on the makeshift pallet he'd created, he patted the vacant space beside his body. "You ain't up here beside me, and you still haven't told me everything that happened at Mel's party thing."

136

With that grin that he swore could light a thousand distant suns, she crawled up beside him and aligned her body with his own. "Better?"

"Much." Brushing a tender kiss across her perfect lips, pink and plump and anxious for his love, he swept her hair behind her shoulders and secured a section over her ear. "Other than the talking that still needs to happen."

He pulled away to stare at the reflection of the water and rumpled prairie lands in her pine green eyes. The scars he'd never quite been able to erase were always hidden there just behind the glassy imagery. It crushed him, hurt him like no physical fist or bullet ever could. It killed him that he couldn't erase her pain from existence. "You're so damn beautiful, Indie. God ... you just ... take my breath away, baby."

Heat pooled in her cheeks, and she rolled her eyes. "Tucker clearly overheard my aunts this morning before he left and called you to tattle on them."

"That has nothing to do with what you do to me, laying here with me, having you all to myself, staring into your eyes ... wanting you ... needing you. Wishing I could make you forget everything but you and me. Put your hands on me, sugar. Just for a second because we're gonna be out here for hours, but I want you to feel the effect you always have on me."

He watched her slender neck contract with a harsh swallow as she skated her hand down his chest and abs and encountered the rock hard bulge tenting the fly of his Wranglers. His grunt of pleasure sounded against the soft ripple of the water lapping at the grassy shoreline and the soft caw of gulls flying overhead.

"That's all you, darlin'. You make me ache," he breathed over her lips before he mated their mouths and dipped his tongue to hers in a seductive dance of hunger. She melted into him, letting him ease just a little of what she'd endured. Her hand continued to explore his fierce erection. If she kept going he was going to embarrass himself. Helpless to resist her touch, he rocked his hips against her palm, drawing a moan from her mouth.

"Just because you think I'm pretty doesn't mean I do." She pulled away a full minute later with the words that would always infuriate him.

Cocking his jaw to the side and trying to rid himself of his now painful boner, he huffed, "Other than turning you over my knee, which I ain't in the mood to do right now, I don't guess there's anything I can do about you being damned and determined to be wrong."

"Luke, I know what you're trying to do, okay? I know you love me. I love you, too, but none of that changes the fact that my mother is a ginormous bitch, or the fact that my aunts can't stand me, or any of the other shit that came from the aftermath of Ernie and Carolyn's affair. You can't kiss it and make it better … as much as I wish you could."

"I know that, Indie. I know I can't take away all of the hell your family puts you through. It kills me, okay? It infuriates me that you believe all of their crap and all of the lies they tell, because hurting you makes them feel powerful and helps them believe their own web of shit they spin to make themselves look better to people that couldn't care less. I love you. You are the amazing, brilliant, beautiful woman that I have always loved and will always love, no matter what you decide to do in two weeks. But if I can bring you out here and kiss you and hold you and just numb the pain a little, that's what I want to do. I want to try. I always want to *try* to kiss it and make it better. Is that so wrong?"

"No." She shook her head and blinked back the tears his words had welled in her eyes.

"Then come here to me and hush." He leaned in again and tried desperately to burn away the memories of her morning with the heat of his desperate need for her.

He took his time with each kiss, memorizing the sweetness of her lips and her breath. He lingered with each caress of his hands. If he could just keep her right there, in his arms, tucked up in his truck bed, away from everyone else that was set to do her harm, life would be perfect.

Though he tried to drown himself in her, his mind ran a steady line between contention and fury. How dare her mother and her aunts make Indie feel like she was less than? Jealousy was one answer. Carolyn Jenkins was good for nothing more than planning a party and making the world outside her home think she was perfect. She was nothing more than a façade herself. She cared nothing about what happened inside her home or inside her daughters' heads. All that had ever mattered was the exterior. What people saw was infinitely more important than the way she made people feel.

When Tucker had called that morning, he'd asked if Luke would drive out to Wyoming with him to look at a run-down ranch. He'd hinted that maybe Luke could get Indie to stay if they started ranching

138

together in another state. That idea felt like he was running away, and that wasn't something Luke had ever done. He couldn't. He wasn't even sure he was capable. There was far too much riding on his shoulders. More importantly, how dare Carolyn Jenkins push her children far enough to make them run?

Shaking his head as Indie nuzzled against his chest, he refused to commit to anything even in his mind. There had to be a way to stay on his family's land and have Indie. Maybe it was high time he had a talk with Carolyn and Ernie.

"Earth to Luke?" Indie lifted her head. "Where'd you go?"

"Sorry, baby. Just fretting over your day. You ask me something?" He guided her body between his thighs and reclined her back against his chest as they watched a turtle sun herself on a warm boulder on the other side of the creek. Reaching into the cooler behind his head, Luke retrieved two Dr. Peppers and handed one to Indie.

"Yeah, I asked you what you were thinking about," she chuckled.

"How badly I want you to stay, and what I might could do to make sure that happens."

"Would you stop? Please. I told you I'd really consider it. Just shut up about it. Every freaking person in my life wants me to do something differently than the way I did it. I get it. I'm a screw up."

"Dammit, Indie, that ain't at all what I said. I'm sorry I keep bringing it up. When I want something, I go after it with everything I am. That's who I am. I've never wanted anything the way I want you. You know that. I've always been this way. I'll shut up about it. I swear I'm not trying to pressure you again." He mentally lambasted himself for repeating the mistakes he'd made in college.

She stared up at him quizzically long enough to make him anxious. "Don't you ever wonder what's outside the Glen? I mean, don't you want to see something besides ranch land on occasion? Don't you ever want to vacation beyond the drive to Cheyenne for Frontier Days or Yellowstone? There's a whole big world out there, ya know."

Shocked at those questions, he considered for a long moment. "Yeah, I know. I guess the honest answer to all of that is there are a lot of things I'd love to see or do, but I'm really only interested in doing them with you." Certain he'd already broken the decree about not discussing her staying, he sank his teeth in his tongue preventing any more confessions, but she knew him far too well.

"Keep going."

Terrified of saying something that might push her further away, he calculated his words carefully. "Tell me what you want to do and see so much."

"I don't know. I just …. There's just a lot of places outside of Pleasant Glen, Nebraska. Don't you ever want to see the great clichés? You know, the Eiffel Tower at night, the Cali coast, Hawaii, the Statue of Liberty, the whole rest of the world, stuff like that."

Shifting so he could stare into her eyes, he went on with what he was certain she would call a chicken shit response. "You're about to call me a pussy."

"I am not. Talk to me like we used to. You used to tell me everything. You want me to stay so bad, then talk."

Drawing a shaky breath, he gently traced her cheekbone with his thumb. "I'd love to see the entire world with you, sugar. I'll take you anywhere you want to go. I don't always have to be on the ranch. I got a lot of family that'd pick up my slack if you want to go places like that sometimes. And I get that you want to see the world. It's just to me, when I hold you, I feel like I never need anything else because I'm already holding the entire world in my arms."

"Wow." Her chin trembled and tears pricked her eyes. She dammed them back with the fierce clench of her jaw. Luke continued to softly traced the soft angles of her face trying to ease its strain. "I'm such a bitch."

"What?" Of all the things he thought she might say, that wasn't one of them.

"I don't deserve for anyone to love me like that. I really don't. All I ever think of is myself. I keep wishing Camden Ranch sat in any other state, or even any other county. I'm sorry."

"Your family is completely nuts, Indie. No one blames you for not wanting to be around them, most certainly not me. Believe me, if I could leave the Glen, I'd follow you anywhere."

"Luke, that's insane."

"I'm serious."

"Me too. You're not giving up your family's land, and money, and generations of really hard work for me. Plus, the entire town — hell most of the state — depends on you. I'd make a terrible rancher's wife anyway. I'm a mechanic. I always want to be a mechanic. It's the only thing I'm any good at. That's why this will only work for two weeks."

"It's absolutely *not* the only thing you're good at, and you don't have to stop wrenching cars for me. Where'd you even come up with that notion? I'd never want you to quit doing what you love."

140

"This town does not need another mechanic, and even if Dad and I somehow made that work, the ranch is a long way from town and even further from the shop, and that's when there's not two feet of snow on the ground."

"I'd make it work. I'd figure something out. Just please know I'd never want you to quit your job for me."

She worried her lip with her teeth for a moment. "Know what I was thinking about last night after I left your house?"

"I'm hoping it was something along the lines of *if I weren't so damn stubborn, I'd still be curled up nice, and warm, and safe, and most importantly nekkid in Luke's arms, making him the happiest man in Lincoln county.*"

Her laughter was infectious, and the sexy smirk she was sporting sent a flash fire of longing to his groin.

"That is *not* what I was thinking."

"Should'a been."

Reaching over his waist, she pinched his ass again.

"Dammit, woman, you ever think about anything but grabbing a'holt of my sexy ass? I'll let you see it anytime you want. You don't have to pinch me."

"Would you shut up?"

"If your tongue is in my mouth."

"Luke Camden ...."

"Fine, pull down them jeans I'll put something even sweeter in my mouth."

"The next time I give you a blow job I could bite you."

Cringing involuntarily, he huffed, "Fine, tell me what you were thinking about and don't say shit like that. Geez."

Giggling and looking entirely too proud or herself, she went on, "I was thinking about when you first asked me out that afternoon in World History."

Chuckling, Luke recalled the scene, down to the boots he was wearing that day. "I'd been trying to ask you out for weeks. Kept chickening out, afraid you'd say no. I overheard at lunch that Simpson was showing some film that took up the whole class, so I figured that was as good a chance as I was gonna get. Called myself a pussy repeatedly and told myself to either to man up or go cry in the truck alone."

"I almost did say no."

Another round of shock and a hearty dose of rejection worked through his musculature. "Why? We were already really good friends."

"Oh, I definitely wanted to be your girlfriend. I just knew I wasn't the kind of girl the new quarterback of the football team asked out. But you always looked in my eyes instead of at my tits, and you seemed so afraid I wasn't going to say yes so I took a chance. I was sure you were going to break my heart. I had nightmares for weeks about you joking with Tuck, and Cal Hodgson, and your brothers about me thinking you were serious, that you'd really want to date someone like me."

"Why the hell wouldn't I want to date someone as smart and beautiful and feisty as hell as you, Indie? I swear I fell in love with you the first day of school when you were cursing that lock on your locker loud and proud, not caring at all who heard you."

"Yeah, well I got detention the first day of school, but thank you for unlocking it for me."

"You're welcome, and I know you got detention. I was late to football practice that day because I waited on you to get out. I was pissed your dad was there to pick you up. I was planning to ask if I could walk you home."

"I never knew that." She brushed a tender kiss on his lips, stoking the fire ever burning for her. "Bet Coach Chalmers was pissed you were late."

"Had to run the bleachers for an hour after practice, but it was worth it to see your ass in them Wranglers when you walked out to his car."

"Most guys back then wanted to see my boobs shake when I walked."

"That wasn't at all a bad view either, honey. You're gorgeous, head to toe and back again."

Laughing and rolling her eyes, she shook her head at him. "I never knew what to do with them. Kind of felt like two alien spaceships had landed on my chest. I was pissed 'cause it was hard to work under the cars at Dad's shop."

Arching his left eyebrow, Luke traced his fingertips over her breasts, loving the way her breath caught and her eyes darkened at his touch. "Oh, I had several creative ideas of what to do with them, but that had nothing to do with me asking you out. I wanted you to be mine, always. I never gave a damn what size bra you wore. Nothing's changed in that department. But I will say back then I didn't know how much you resented them. I always hoped I could teach you to love them as much as I did."

"Yeah, well your back didn't hurt all the time and you didn't get catcalled constantly."

"I do remember letting my fists fly more than once for what some of those fuckers said to you."

"Not quite as often as I let mine fly."

"Well, you always managed to get to them before I could."

"You were the best boyfriend any girl could ever want … and I left." Regret tensed in the choked vibration of her words.

"That ain't the way I remember it at all." Luke cradled her face in his right hand and lifted until her gaze was fixed on his own.

"How do you remember it?" Her brow creased as she set to argue.

"Indie, honey, if I'd put you in my old truck and had driven you to Oklahoma myself, I couldn't have done a better job of pushing you away. You were hurting and you never wanted to be at the university. I dragged you up there. I got scared when you kept wanting to go home. You seemed so sad you couldn't think straight, and I panicked trying to fix it. I should have listened to you, given you some space. Let you know I'd be anywhere you needed me to be. Instead, I all but soldered a ring to your finger trying to cage you in. I did everything wrong. And I'll never forgive myself for that. I should have fought smarter for you, not harder. I was too much of a dumbass back then to understand that."

"Luke, no. Nothing you did was wrong. I was just … lost."

"And I should have slowed down and taken my time to find you, to help you find yourself again."

Focusing her eyes on the soothing water, she swallowed harshly. "You … uh … still have that ring?"

Having no idea what the right answer might be, he erred on the side of the truth, just as he'd always promised. "Yeah. It's in my bedside table."

"You remember the first time we did it?" Relief eased her eyes, as she changed track abruptly.

He tried to keep up with her. If she didn't want to think about the ring, he wouldn't say another word about it. "I'll never forget that, darlin'. I've never been more afraid of anything I wanted so badly."

Her giggle joined the singing birds overhead. "Still can't believe I let you pop my cherry in the back of a *Dodge*."

"I tried to borrow my dad's Ford that night, but it was full of manure and that didn't seem too romantic to me."

Their joined laughter washed over Luke, the sweetest sound in the entire world, save maybe the breathy gasps and moans she made when he buried himself so deep inside of her neither of them had any hope of knowing where he stopped and she began.

As good as it had felt to ease his cock inside of her, that wasn't what he most remembered about that warm summer night. The infinite trust in her eyes, the coy little grin she gave him when his inexperienced hands fumbled with the snap on her jeans, the way her body trembled when he gently pressed his fingers between her virgin lips and felt her timid heat, the taste of her mouth somehow different than all the times he'd kissed her before. That night her saliva was laced with abandon.

"Does that feel good?" He'd been terrified to move. *"Tell me if I'm doing it wrong. I don't want to hurt you, Indie."*

"It feels really good. Don't stop. Please. I need more. I need you, Luke."

His mind easily recounted her begging that night so long ago, and suddenly, he couldn't help himself. His desire and his confusion over everything vanquished his endless patience. The long fuse of need tangled between them burned away like steam leaving a forest fire in its wake.

Layering his body to hers, he inhaled her mouth. Grasping her ample ass caught up in those blue jeans, he rocked his strain against her mound, yearning to bury himself inside the velvet heat of her pussy. His hands raced to her shirt, working through the buttons furiously, desperately seeking her silky skin.

Breaking away from the kiss, she gasped for breath. "We just gonna do this in the middle of the afternoon out here in front of God and everybody?" The rasping tonality of her question said that's precisely what she longed for, and since they were miles from another human being, he wasn't too concerned.

"God doesn't mind, sugar. He already knows how gorgeous you are. He made you, and He knows a man can only stand so much temptation. He knows how weak I am for you. We talk. He's good with it."

Finally loosening her shirt, he rolled it down her arms, stopping at her elbows effectively pinning them by her side.

"Hey," she laughed.

"Perfect." He smirked as he tore the bra from her and forced himself to slow. "I want to worship every square inch of you, honey. Lay back and let me enjoy you."

"I'd let you do that without the make-shift restraints."

144

"I know, but you look like a walking wet dream in the bed of my truck with your hands behind your back. I'm indulging myself."

Luke's hot breath caressed Indie's left nipple. Her body shivered its appreciation. Why did he slow down? His tongue made a long languid pass around her areola. *Faster. More. Suck me.* Her mind pleaded. Her nipples throbbed out a protest, but there was no use in verbalizing her requests. He wasn't going to be persuaded. She saw the fervent intensity locked in his icy blue eyes. He was going to torture her in the most delectable ways. Her body rolled in anticipation. The sun-drenched metal of the truck bed heated the quilts under her fevered skin as she melted into his hardened body.

He continued his ministrations, spinning his tongue and placing open-mouthed suckling kisses over every centimeter of her breasts. Gently, he lifted them and kissed the scars along the underswells as if the heat of his breath and tender brushes of his tongue could erase anything that had ever caused her pain.

Kissing it and making it better. She understood as she slipped into a younger version of herself, and the restoration of her soul began. Cautiously, her mind settled in on him. Belief and hope threatened to pervade her heart. With the next kiss along the thick white markings under her breasts, she could no longer keep it at bay. She allowed his love to soothe her, to ease her morning. She allowed herself to believe, if only for a moment, that the one place on earth she belonged was in his arms.

The sun set low over the water, existing in two worlds for a moment, hovering somewhere between the light of day and the indigo dark of night. Indie understood its confusion. Not wanting to give up the fight, but fading fast under the persuasion of the moon.

They'd partially redressed. Indie's shirt still hung open, but she had no desire to clasp the buttons, not when Luke's hands gently caressed over her breasts and belly as they snuggled under the quilts he'd packed. His t-shirt was laying in the grass near the truck somewhere. The tan on his shoulders had deepened into a heated bronze from the hours he'd spent shirtless and over her. Neither of them had any real desire to locate it. Both of their jeans were on but unsnapped.

They'd spent the entire afternoon making love, cuddling, talking, making-out, laughing, and talking some more. Too bad they couldn't build themselves a little cabin there on the side of King's Creek and stay forever. That was an idea she could get on board with.

"You tired, sugar?" his graveled voice whispered through the cool evening air. His hands tended her constantly. His fingers eased through her hair and ran a soft path down her back before returning to her head. Everything was easier in that moment. Her lungs filled with his scent, sating her and relaxing her entire body.

"A little. But I don't want to leave."

His soft chuckle vibrated against her chest as he brushed his lips on her temple. "Never said we had to go. I just thought I might see if you'd like for me to take you back to my house, put you to bed, hold you all night long. I'll even talk my brothers into running my cattle in the morning so I can stay with you."

"You still trying to take me hostage?"

"No. I'm trying to take care of you." Apparently he didn't find her teasing humorous.

"I know, Luke. I just wish we never had to leave here. This was the perfect afternoon. Thank you for bringing me up here."

"Look at me, baby." He shifted slightly so he could stare into her eyes. "I will always do whatever it is you need at any given moment. Do you understand that? There is nothing I would ever deny you, nothing I would keep from you. I swear I'd move heaven and earth to take care of you. I need to know that you believe me when I say that."

"I do, Luke. I swear. Real life just isn't as easy as it is up here, okay? It's just not."

"I know that, but it ain't as complicated as you've got yourself convinced it is, either."

"I wish I didn't have to go get my car," she sighed.

"We could pick it up in the mornin'. Or I'll get Grant or Holly to go with me to get it. That way you don't have to show up over there."

"Grant and Holly are not allowed to drive my car."

That brought another one of those sexy-as-sin chuckles to his lips. "I know that, darlin'. I'd drive your car. They can drive my truck."

She watched his chiseled jaw tense with each word, the way his soft lips formed each syllable. "Kiss me," she urged, unable to keep herself from begging.

"Gladly." Caressing her cheek, he angled her face upward and brushed his lips over hers in three quick kisses before he turned his head and mated their mouths. His tongue explored her as she memorized his taste and his heat. Deepening the connection, his arms cradled her closer, holding her in the safety of his embrace.

146

He nipped her bottom lip and then dove back in for more. Thrilled, Indie tried to give him as good as she got. His tongue coaxed hers. There was more to this kiss than the sexual power it held. His tender love was there as well. She couldn't halt the smile that ultimately broke the kiss.

"Just what are you grinning about, Indie Jane?"

"You, and how I still wish I never had to stop kissin' you. I used to count down the minutes in all of those stupid classes we had to endure in school until I could get back to your locker so we could kiss some more."

"Kissing you constantly might make eating or breathing difficult, but if a guy's gotta go, I wouldn't mind dying if I was kissing you."

"I don't want you to die. We'll take snack breaks."

"Good plan, but I think we should head on back before the wind finds its way into these quilts. I don't want you to get cold."

Nightfall had already robbed the air of its warmth. The constant Nebraskan breeze coming off the creek whipped through her hair and threatened their sanctuary.

"Fine," she pouted.

"Just taking you home to my bed, sugar. Just us. No one else. I promise."

"No, you have to take me to get my car, and I have to go back to Daddy's. I know he's worried. Mel surely told him I ran out. He's probably been calling to check up on me."

She could almost hear Luke's wheels spinning. He was trying to formulate an argument. Based on the frustrated furrow of his brow, he was coming up short.

"Call him when we get back into town."

"Luke. Please."

"Fine." He couldn't quite hide the roll of his eyes. When they'd redressed, he slowly guided the truck back down the narrow dirt road towards Pleasant Glen.

Chapter Fourteen

Out of breath and red-faced Thursday night, Indie rolled her eyes as she continued to blow up the dozen Pinky the Inflatable Party Peckers she and Miranda had located at a novelty shop in Lincoln that morning.

Miranda was standing on a chair in the back room of Saddlebacks securing a hot pink banner that declared *He Put a Ring On It* in rhinestones to some old nails in the wall with fuzzy handcuffs.

"Don't let Luke catch you doing that. He might get jealous that you're slobbering all over another pecker," Miranda giggled.

Indie leveled an irritated glare at her little sister. "If Luke Camden ever finds out about any of this, I'm holding you personally responsible. Too bad our mother refused to attend this little shindig. God knows she's full of hot air we coulda put to use."

"True, but Mama's busy blowing her hot air into a paper sack because we're throwing this party for Mel."

"Yeah, well our baby sister better appreciate this. I would not wear a *Party Girl* tiara for anyone but her."

"She's so excited she can't see straight," Miranda assured. "She'd thanked us about four dozen times before she and Tuck got into it, remember?"

"Yeah, yeah I know. I just don't get all of this." Indie gestured to the tables full of dozens of plastic penises, metallic beads, feather boas, sashes, and one hot pink tambourine with a cartoon cock on it for people to *bang*.

A clipboard with Miranda's lists caught her eye. In an effort to be good sisters and good bridesmaids, they'd gone as far as to make lists of everything Melony wanted for her bachelorette party. When Indie finished the last Pinky, she flipped through the lists to see what needed to be done next.

Her brow furrowed as her eyes landed on a list Miranda had added to the clipboard that she hadn't seen before. Bile began doing the back stroke through her stomach. "Please tell me Megan Morgan is not *the* Megan Morgan that I graduated with."

Miranda's sheepish expression said there was only one Megan Morgan in their world. "Indie, I swear she's not like that anymore. We all grew up. She and Mel are good friends. She's really nice now."

"Miranda! People do not change. I thought I taught you this. She once told Luke to give her a call when he got tired of losing his dick in my fat rolls ... right in front of me."

Miranda's mouth hung open in horror. She struggled for a full minute to regain her composure. "Okay ... well ... I didn't know that ... but I swear she isn't like that anymore."

"If she says one word to me ...."

Miranda held up her right hand. "If she's a bitch in any way at all, I will personally help you put an entire pack of Ex-lax in her Kahlua martini. Then we'll jump her outside the Lady's room. You have my word."

Rolling her eyes, Indie continued to study the guest list, trying to decide if the half-dozen sets of fuzzy handcuffs were going to be necessary for restraining the bitches that had been invited without her knowledge.

"Man, I still remember coming to see Luke in college and you wearin' a t-shirt that you'd written *You're in luck you can fuck the Tuck* on in permanent marker." Grant guffawed. "You sure you're ready to settle down?"

Tucker doubled over along with everyone else in the laughter at his own expense. "God, I was such a rat bastard." He shook his head. "I swear I'm ready. I only wear that shirt for Mel now."

Luke shook his head. Tucker, Austin, Grant, all of the Kilroy brothers, a few members of the old Pleasant Glen football team that had stayed in town, Ev, and Tuck's daddy were all on Luke's back deck drinking beer, eating burgers, and reminiscing. Luke had considered inviting Indie's father as well, seeing as Tucker was about to become his son-in-law, but after a few tales of Tucker's most asinine stunts, he was glad he'd decided against that.

When Tucker checked his phone yet again, Luke wondered what was going on. He followed him back in the kitchen for more food and another beer. "Mel sending you pics from their party or something?"

"I wish," Tuck huffed under his breath. "Carolyn pitched another fit this afternoon, all but insisting that Ernie walk Melony down the aisle. When we refused, she called Melony an ungrateful brat. I spoke my mind out loud this time and upset Mel. She stormed out before I got a chance to apologize. Now, she's at this party furious at me. I've texted her a dozen times. She won't answer. You think Indie and Miranda got strippers for this thing?"

"Tuck, come on, this is the Glen. The roof would fall off of Saddlebacks before Ed Olsen would let strippers in there. And even if he did, Mel ain't gonna cheat on you. You just gotta keep your mouth shut about her mama."

"Yeah, well that's easier said than done, and I met Mel at a bachelorette party; those girls get crazy. You think *guys* have filthy minds? You don't know the half of it. You wanna go with me to check on 'em?"

A note of concern twisted up Luke's spine. He didn't want to verbalize what he was thinking, but better now than never he supposed. "If you really think you need to check up on her, I'll go with you, but that doesn't sound like a good footing for a marriage."

Irritation narrowed Tucker's eyes for a brief moment before he shook his head. "I know she wouldn't cheat on me. I'm just freaking out." He lifted his hat and ran his hand through his hair before reaching for his Skoal can.

Understanding brought a smirk to Luke's mouth. "We freaking out about the wedding, the marriage, or the potential move?"

"All of it. None of it. I don't know. You heard all of those ridiculous stories of the boneheaded crap I've pulled. And Dad overheard me talking to Wes about moving. I swear for a minute there I thought he was gonna cry. I've never seen my old man cry. I'm complete chicken shit. Why the hell does somebody like Melony Harper want to marry me anyway? I was actually thinking about turning my back on my family and our land. She's sweet and … perfect and …." Tucker bit off the end of his declarations, clearly afraid he'd admitted far too much.

Chuckling, Luke nodded his understanding. "I'll give you a pass for tonight and won't even call you a pussy for all of that."

"Thanks."

"It's pretty obvious to everyone that Melony thinks you hung the damned moon just for her. You were thinking about moving for her, and we all did stupid shit coming up. She ain't marrying who you were. She's marrying who you are."

Tuck seemed to consider that. "Well, I ain't moving. That's Kilroy land and I'll go to war with Carolyn again if I have to. I'll just try to keep Mel out of it. And you're getting mighty good at giving advice. Maybe we are grown up."

"He gets that from me." Ev entered the kitchen just then carrying a stack of used paper plates.

Luke couldn't deny that. His father had been dispensing with solid advice for his entire life. Maybe not quite as good as his mama's, but almost. His mother had, after all, tried desperately to talk him out of proposing when he was nineteen. Of course, he hadn't listened. Before he could agree with his father's declaration, his cell phone buzzed in his pocket.

"Hey, sugar, you okay?" He hadn't expected to hear from Indie during Melony's party.

"Yeah. Kinda."

Luke's heart sank along with the sip of beer he swallowed down. "What's wrong?"

"Mel's all sad because she and Tucker got into an argument. Everyone's running late so no one's really here yet. She's worried no one's coming. And ..."

"And?"

"And the fact that this still bothers me just pisses me off, but Miranda invited Megan Morgan and a few of her old groupies. You remember what bitches they always were in school. And Melony wants everyone to wear these ridiculous tiaras. I don't know. I just ... wish I was with you."

"I'm on my way." His heart had roared back to life somewhere in the vicinity of his gut and then had returned to his chest in one leaped bound.

"Luke, no. Thank you, but I'm just being a big baby. I need to be here tonight for Mel. You can't come." The panic in her tone did nothing to change his mind. If she needed him, he'd be there come hell or high water.

Truthfully, he didn't really remember much about Megan Morgan other than her name. Clearly, Indie didn't care for her. That was enough proof for him to despise most anyone. Now wasn't the time to explain that the reason whatever had happened with this Megan person still got to her was that she'd let the wound fester instead of opening it up, talking about it with him, and letting it heal. As most infections go when they're left untreated, they only get worse.

"I know Holly and Nat left a little while ago headed that way. They should be pulling up anytime now. How 'bout Tuck and I come down there. We won't crash the party. We can just kick back a few outside of that room. That way if you need me I'm right there."

What in the world did I ever do to deserve someone like Luke Camden, and how in the hell did I ever leave him? Another round of self-disgust racked in the irritation already storming through Indie's stomach. She shook her head.

"Thanks for being so great, but really, don't do that. If I'm gonna get Mel to loosen up and actually enjoy her own party, Tucker can't be here. It'll be fine. I swear. Maybe I'll come over there after the party." *And stay?* She knew beyond any shadow of a doubt what was coming out of his mouth next.

"And stay the night finally?"

Why couldn't he understand that if she stayed an entire night wrapped up in warm sanctuary of his arms, she may never be able to leave? She just couldn't take that chance. "Maybe," she lied, too terrified to admit the truth.

"Mmm hmm," he knew she was placating. He always did.

"Oh, here come Nat and Holly. Let me go. I'll come over when this stupid thing is over with, I swear."

"I love you, Indie."

"I know."

Shoving her phone back in her pocket, Indie turned to greet Luke's little sisters, thankful they were there. At least she wouldn't be stuck with whatever the adult versions of *Mean Girls* looked like in Pleasant Glen all night long.

Anxious to get the party started, Miranda stuck tiaras on Holly and Natalie's heads and ordered them to start drinking.

"What's wrong with the bride?" Holly gestured to a sullen Melony, slowly sipping wine, running her fingers along the feather boa around her neck and staring off into space.

"Got into a spat with Tucker before this. Something Mama said. I don't know what, but help us cheer her up," Miranda pled.

"That I can do," Holly beamed.

A few teachers from the elementary school that taught with Mel showed up next and things took a turn for the better. Indie recalled one of them from back in the day, but the rest had married ranchers in the area or had been transplanted into the Pleasant Glen corn fields via their farmer husbands or some kind of *Close Encounter of the Third Kind*, she supposed. They seemed nice, and Melony was thrilled they'd arrived.

"Blow jobs, blue balls, or cock sucking cowboys?" Holly called from the doorway that led back to bar.

Indie shook her head. This was going to be a long night if they were already doing shots.

"Let's do a round of blow jobs. Whoever gets all of theirs down gets a prize." Miranda leapt on the bandwagon. Melony started giggling and her smile had returned, so Indie decided to play along.

152

She was thankful Ed and Eliza weren't there that evening and had left Saddlebacks in the care of their tattooed, tongue- and brow-pierced bartender, Aaron, who looked about as out of place in the Glen as Indie felt. He lived in the garage apartment on the Wilson's old property just outside of town and had worked the bar at Saddlebacks for several years.

Indie suspected his rippling muscles, bad boy vibe, and edgy attitude was why Eliza had hired him without Ed's knowledge. According to Miranda, when Aaron got the job, Ed and Eliza had gotten in an argument that lasted a full week and took place all over town. It finally ended at their house when Sheriff Wilheim was called out because Eliza had smacked Ed over his head with her favorite umbrella. After that, Aaron had proven himself to be a highly-capable, responsible bartender, and things had settled down. Why he wanted to stay in the Glen no one seemed to know, however.

"Can we get … uh … shots for everyone?" Miranda lost just a little of her bravado when Aaron gave her an overtly flirtatious smirk.

Indie rolled her eyes. "He probably needs to know what kind of shots to make, Randa."

"Oh yeah," she giggled. Dear God, her sister actually giggled at this dude, who was admittedly good looking, but was obviously either running from the cops or somehow involved in the witness protection program to even be in this town. Besides, Aaron didn't hold a candle to the rugged masculinity and protectiveness that was Luke Camden. You just couldn't beat a cowboy.

"What am I pouring up for you, sweetness?" Aaron winked at Miranda.

Indie fought not to gag. Her sister, however, was all but swooning. "Oh good God, the chicks for the bachelorette gig in the back room thought it would be fun to do blow job shots. Just send them back when you get them made."

Aaron chuckled. "Aren't you one of those chicks?"

Simpering, Indie supposed he had her there. "Technically, but not happily."

"I see. Well, you two hang tight right here. I can't leave the bar to make a delivery to the back room, and Myrna's been talking to table five for a half hour now and still hasn't gotten their order." He gestured to one of the waitresses nearby. "Been a long while since I poured up BJ's. Don't get a lot of requests for those in the Glen."

"Yeah, well, maybe you can send them to the Lady's Aid Society meeting at the church next month. I'm sure they'd appreciate that." Indie rolled her eyes at Aaron's snorted laughter.

"You know these shots are basically to get guys to buy you more drinks, right?"

"I'm not the one that decided on what we were drinking."

When Aaron began pouring up the Kuhlua, Saddleback's front door gave its customary creaked whoosh. Bile singed Indie's throat when Megan Morgan waltzed inside, followed by none other than Cindy Beltz and Heather James. They'd been attached at the hip, usually via some kind of deranged cheerleading pyramid scheme, since high school. Long live the Pleasant Glen bitch brigade. Clearly nothing had changed. Nothing ever did, she quickly reminded herself before narrowing her eyes. Her molars were likely to turn to dust if she ground her teeth any harder.

"Indie! Oh my gosh, it's been ages. It's so nice to see you," Megan declared rather loudly, but the shock echoing in Indie's mind was so deafening she barely heard her. Miranda elbowed her and grinned.

"I'm so glad you're here. We're just waiting on blowjobs." She gestured to Aaron, who was now laughing at her outright.

"Aren't we all," he commented to himself.

The wicked trio all giggled and then offered Indie sheepish grins. They were almost ... kind. Indie's brain glitched. She blinked repeatedly. Something was clearly wrong. She was dreaming or having a stroke or something. While she tried to remember if strokes were common in her family, Megan stepped closer. Indie instinctively stepped back.

"Listen." Megan leaned in. Her cheeks filled with a heated flush. She glanced at Cindy, who nodded her head. "I've tried to work up the courage to find you every time I heard you were back in town and I didn't. God knows I should have, but maybe I'm still an epic bitch somewhere deep inside or something. I want to apologize for the way we treated you in high school. I know it was ages ago, but that doesn't matter. My AA counselor used to say all the time that we should clear up any past regrets whenever the opportunity arose. I deeply regret the things we used to say to you. You certainly don't owe me your forgiveness, but I wanted you to know I'm sorry."

"We all want to apologize, Indie," Cindy vowed.

"I told you," Miranda spoke through her teeth.

"Hey, I heard you and Luke were back together. That's so great. You two were always so good together. I think that's why we were so awful to you and everyone else. We were jealous," Heather added sheepishly. "Luke came by to check on our dog, Rufus, yesterday. Matt said it'd been a long time since he'd seen Luke so happy."

The mechanics of rejoining her lower jaw with her upper swam around in Indie's mind for a full minute. "Uh," she finally managed. "Okay. Thanks. I guess."

Heather grabbed her forearm and gave it a squeeze. Indie ordered herself not to smack her hand away.

"Aaron, can I just have a 7-UP?" Megan asked. "We'll take these gifts back and check on the party."

"You got it." Aaron added a full tumbler of the fizzy drink to the tray full of shots.

"Megan Morgan is an alcoholic?" Indie finally formulated a full sentence.

"Apparently so." Miranda shrugged. "Feel kind of bad we're having this in a bar. I bet that's hard for her."

"Yeah," Indie had to agree, and yet Megan had come anyway. She'd come to celebrate with Melony and obviously to apologize to her. *Wow.* Either hell had officially frozen over or some things *had* changed.

Carefully lifting the tray full of glasses, Indie followed Miranda back to the party. While they'd been gone, Cheyenne Miller and Makayla Harris, two of Holly's best friends, had shown up.

With her cohorts by her side, Holly Camden took over. She lined the shots up along the edge of the food table. "Okay, hands behind your back, lips over glass, and drink. Since there are no guys here to impress into buying us more drinks just before we turn him down for the inevitably offered dick, we'll change the rules. For every one of us that gets it down without spilling a drop and keeping your tiara on your head, that means Tuck has to go *down* on Mel without her returning the favor."

Laughter erupted from the group of women in the back room.

"Here I'll show you," Holly went on when no one stepped up to the line. Indie watched in amazement as she locked her hands behind her back, arched her back to accentuate her relatively insubstantial cleavage, wiggled her butt like there were a dozen college-guys watching, and wrapped her lips over the shot glass. When she'd downed the whole thing, she set the glass back on the table via her mouth, stood, and bowed.

"If Luke Camden saw her doing that, he'd shit an entire cow," Indie commented to no one in particular.

Cindy and Megan laughed heartily, however. "There is no doubt about that. I imagine Brock, Grant and Austin would have the same reaction," Megan agreed.

"And Mr. Camden," Cindy agreed.

"They could shit themselves a whole new ranch," Heather giggled.

Taking in the room around her filled with feathers, inflatable penises, and hand cuffs, watching *little* Holly Camden do shots, and laughing with those formally known as the bitch brigade made Indie all the more certain she'd gotten off at the *Twilight Zone* bus stop in the recent past.

"Well, come on everyone. Megan can be the judge," Holly graciously included Megan without encouraging her to drink. Indie wondered if it bothered Megan to watch everyone else down shots.

"Given what we're trying to win for Melony, I'm not likely to say any of you spilled any." Megan's entire body was strained though she'd tried for a joke.

"True, but still it'll be fun." Holly directed everyone to the line of shot glasses.

Cindy followed Indie up to the table. "I tell myself all the time I can still party like I did in my twenties, then I get around kids actually in their twenties, and I'm like nope, can't do it anymore."

Indie couldn't help but agree. Heated remembrances sizzled in her cheeks as she clasped her hands behind her back the very same way Luke ordered her to every single time she gave him a blow job of the non-alcoholic variety, not that sucking on his cock was any less intoxicating. It was an activity she rather enjoyed a great deal more than doing shots with old classmates and her little sisters. She loved his thickened heat, the husky groans he made that sounded like they were wrenched up from his soul, and the flavors of his salty musk. Stifling a moan from the thought alone, she studied the milky shot she was about to take and tried to remember what Aaron had added beyond the Kahlua.

Cindy gave Indie a quick grin. "Hey, you know, I could skip this whole deal and record you doing it on your phone. You could send it to Luke and we could see how fast he got up here. Bet he'd plow right through half of the cattle guards on Camden Ranch."

Okay, so the overt attempt at female bonding was a little over the top, but it was also kind of nice. Indie forced a smile. "For the sake of the cattle and the fences on the ranch, let's not get him up here." They both laughed. "Plus, I really do *not* want him to see all of the Pinky Party Peckers."

156

That did it. Cindy doubled over laughing.

"Okay, everyone ready?" Megan called. Indie noted the edge of anxiety in her tone. This stupid game was hard for her. Clearly Megan Morgan had demons Indie had known nothing about. Demons that most certainly played too close to the surface in a bar.

In that moment, as Indie leaned over the table, the girls who were so cruel to her in high school became three dimensional. They hadn't only inflicted pain — they'd also endured it.

As she wrapped her lips over the shot glass and fought not to drool like an idiot, she lost just a little of the wrath she'd always clung to like armor. They were grown women, and every single time she came home she'd played judge, jury, and executioner in a mental trial of memories she lorded over them in her head that no one else attended. Maybe it was time to let bygones be bygones. Maybe.

Performing the shot, Indie swallowed down the drink, set the glass back on the table, and wiped the residual alcohol from her chin. Dirty innuendoes and laughter filled the air. Indie found herself genuinely smiling and enjoying herself. She shook her head as Melony laughed through the shot, bubbling the contents and effectively covering her mouth and shirt in liquor.

"I'm not thinking Tuck would appreciate you laughing with him in your mouth," Holly taunted.

"I couldn't. He fills up my whole mouth." Melony turned seven shades of red at her own joke.

When Myrna showed up with pitchers of margaritas and platters of food, everyone dug in.

Two shots and two margaritas was apparently Cindy Beltz's limit. "Do you know who called me yesterday?" she asked far too loudly.

Indie bit her lips together when Cindy hiccupped. Since she was probably the most sober of anyone there, besides Megan, she decided to see if maybe Aaron could fix them up with some coffee.

"Mama. She needs rent money again. Like I ain't been paying it for a year now."

Freezing at the door, Indie tried to recall what she knew about the Beltz family.

"She hadn't been around for two decades, Cin, why the hell do you still pay her rent?" Heather spoke in between long draws of her drink.

"I know, but if she gets thrown out of another place she'll come stay with Rich and me, and he'll lose it and leave again."

Wow. Had Cindy's mother left when she was in school? How had Indie never known that? And her husband had clearly left her at some point. Shaking her head, she rushed back to the bar. She didn't want Cindy to embarrass herself with anymore drunken confessions. At one time, she'd hated her, but now … she felt sorry for her. Cursing the empathy that took up residence in her heart without her permission, she asked Myrna if they could get some coffees.

When she returned with a dozen mugs of coffee, her eyes goggled. Holly and Cheyenne were standing on chairs, singing and swaying to the beat of the terrible cover band that had started playing. Ah, to be twenty-three again.

Melony opened a few of the gifts while the buzz of the alcohol was in full effect, meaning every vibrating sex toy she received was passed around twice. The women laughed like they were the funniest things on the face of the planet. Miranda and Indie were pleased Melony was having fun and that was all that mattered.

When Holly and Cheyenne started lamenting the lack of men, however, Indie grew concerned. As it stood, she and Megan were going to need to hotwire the Pleasant Glen school bus to drive all of these women to their respective houses at the end of the night.

A moment later the party erupted from the back room and spilled into the bar. Blow up genitalia and vibrators were left in puddles of margarita mix. Before Indie knew what was happening, Holly was hitting on Aaron and he looked highly intrigued by her offers.

"You sure the Harper girls won't mind you two crashing their party?" Ev asked Luke and Tucker as they climbed out of the truck in the parking lot of Saddlebacks.

"She can yell at me if she wants to. 'Least then she'll be talking to me," Tucker sighed.

Luke slapped him on the back. "I bet she hadn't thought about your spat in hours. And we ain't crashing. They rented the back room. We're just here to make sure everyone gets home all right and that no one's being a bitch to Indie."

The cover band Ed Olsen had hired recently assaulted the air with their attempt at country music. Luke cringed at the squall of the speakers.

"Dude, did they just rhyme Texas with Lexus?" Tucker laughed.

"See, the girls may be more than ready to call it a night if they've been listening to … wait what do they call themselves?"

"Come on, you remember, Pleasant Glen's own Pleasant Pheasants."

The men heaved open the door to the bar laughing.

158

Saddlebacks was packed between the Bachelorette Party, the Pheasants' friends and family who were clearly too kind to tell the band how badly they sucked, and the crowd that had been at the rodeo over in Kempton that night.

Luke's eyes immediately zeroed in on Indie. Her luscious curves and long auburn hair and the most beautiful smile he'd ever seen. His visual inventory halted at those gorgeous lips. His baby was here with girls she used to despise and she was smiling. His heart tripped over its next several beats.

"That boy better be able to run ... fast," Luke's father growled.

Furrowing his brow, Luke's eyes landed on his little sister sitting in the lap of Aaron, the tattooed bartender of Saddlebacks. Luke and Aaron were good friends, but he didn't care for the fact that his baby sister was sucking on his tongue ring.

Indie lifted her head just then. Her sweet grin at Luke faded quickly when she saw where he was heading. She beat him to Aaron and Holly by two quick steps.

"Uh, Holly," she spoke frantically.

A half moan was Holly's only response. Luke was certain he was going to vomit. His fists clenched repeatedly by his sides while he tried to remind himself how much he liked Aaron and all that Aaron had been through in the last few years.

"Holl, now!"

"What?!" Holly lifted her head. Aaron blinked repeatedly, then wrapped his hand through Holly's hair and guided her mouth back to his.

Indie gave Luke a pleading gaze before loudly announcing, "Hey, Luke."

That did it. Holly jerked away from Aaron. "Is it just Luke?"

"I'm fucking standing right here," Luke growled from behind her. Indie shook her head.

"Grant?"

Another head shake.

"Austin?"

And another.

"Brock?"

"No," Luke spat.

"Oh shit ... Daddy?"

Indie nodded frantically as Holly bolted out of the Aaron's lap. Aaron spun to meet Luke's infuriated glare.

"Sorry," he offered.

"S'ok, I guess. Holl's a little young for you, man."

"Really? She looks plenty old enough."

"Definitely not the thing to say." Indie rolled her eyes.

"Aren't you supposed to be *behind* the bar, Aaron?" Fury dripped from Ev's tone as he glared at Holly. "Not hanging all over my little girl."

"We stop serving drinks at eleven. I'm off, sir. I'm sorry. I didn't mean to offend. Just blowing off a little steam."

"Not with her," Ev declared.

"Not sure if you two have noticed this or not, but she ain't so little anymore."

Indie rushed into Luke's arms, presumably to keep him from dragging Aaron out into the parking lot, hooking that ring in his eyebrow up to his hitch, and pulling his ass through the gravel, not that he would ever do something like that.

"You two are both ridiculous," Holly huffed. "Someday you'll figure out that I'm not a baby." With that she headed back into the party room.

Galled at the interaction, Luke marched after her, towing Indie by his side. "I really don't give a damn how old you think you are, I don't want my sister choking on some bartender's tongue ring."

"You got something against bartenders, Luke, or is it just that nobody's good enough for me if they're not a cowboy?" his sister sneered.

"Drop it now, Luke, or she's gonna blow," Indie spoke through her teeth. "Believe me, I would know. I recognize the signs."

Ordering himself to calm, he drew a deep breath. "You've been drinking, and Aaron isn't a guy you need to get involved with."

"And how would you know that?"

"I know because he's a good friend of mine. You stop licking his spit long enough to notice the seven nautical stars tattooed down his right arm? He's seen things you can't even fathom, and quite frankly you aren't mature enough — and you sure as hell aren't committed enough — to deal with even half of the shit he's been through."

This brought Holly up short. Luke knew it would. His little sister needed to stop thinking she was smarter than everyone else. It was high time she learned a lesson.

"What do the star tattoos mean?" Indie asked instead of Holly.

"Means he took a platoon into battle in Afghanistan, and seven men that were brothers to him didn't make it back home."

"How do you know that?" Holly demanded.

"I come in here several times a week. I struck up a conversation when Eliza hired him. Sure as hell had to be a reason he settled in the Glen, and he looked like he could use a friend. Turned out I was right. He's got a Black Lab and a Border Collie mix he actually rescued in the field, fed with his own rations, and talked his superior officer into letting him bring home. I take care of them and of him when things get ugly. Right now, I'm trying to take care of you, too."

"Fine. You're right. I'm not really looking for the kind of relationship he probably needs, but maybe we were just blowing off a little steam."

"The last thing he needs is to get attached to you, Holly. You're going back to Lincoln in a few weeks. Give the guy a break. God knows life hasn't given him many. Now, how many of the party guests need a ride home?"

"Megan's the designated driver for most everyone. We're fine."

Chapter Fifteen

Indie was astonished. She knew she shouldn't be, but Luke Camden never ceased to amaze her. Somehow he was always able to see below the surface of people, past the parts they put on display, past the bravado and the anger, past the masks.

More than all of that was the fact that he saw the realism so carefully concealed under the surface, but never judged. He accepted them and tried to help them if he could. Precisely the way he saw through the volatility and the anger she'd carried since childhood. He saw through everything heaped on her by her mother. Through it all he not only saw her, he loved who she was underneath the constraining masks she showed the corroding world around her.

The shift Indie felt in that moment, staring into his eyes, seeing the love he felt for her and the lust she had the power to ignite there in the depths was violent. It was somehow not only a mental or emotional change. It was physical. Her eager feet edged closer to him. She had no power with which to resist. Wrapping her arms around his chest, she prayed he saw the difference within her at that moment.

She felt his throat contract against her head and the smile that formed on his solid features. "What's my girl needin'?"

"You," she whispered.

"Right here. Always. Let's get this disaster cleaned up and I'll take you *home*."

Home was in his arms. Did he know that? It always had been. It always would be. His tightening hold of her said he did. He understood, just like he always had. Now, she just had to figure out if there was any way possible to make this work. Could she really come back to the Glen and stay? The complications she'd clung to for so long evaporated in the heat passing between them. Didn't she owe it to them to try?

Luke's smoky chuckle warmed her soul. "My God, what did you all *do* to this room?"

"Had a bachelorette party," Melony laughed. She and Tucker appeared just then, holding hands and grinning like nothing at all was wrong. It appeared their argument was over.

"I told you chicks were way dirtier than us." Tucker handed out garbage bags and they all began cleaning up food, drinks, sex toys, inflatable penises, and other décor.

The sexy-as-sin smirk formed on Luke's face as he glanced around the room, presumably making sure no one was paying him too much attention. He winked at Indie as he quickly folded a black pair of fuzzy-handcuffs and shoved them in his back pocket.

Indie's heart performed a high-flying kick routine. Her nipples tightened painfully against the lace of her bra and a rush of wet heat coated her panties. She'd been a touch nervous about the rope marks, but fuzzy cuffs, well no one would see any evidence of those now, would they? Images of her cuffed to his bed whipped through her mind. In an effort to speed the clean-up, she gathered everything on the food table into the paper table cloth and deposited the entire thing into one of the trash cans.

Luke laughed at her outright. "Anxious, sugar?"

"Those cuffs in your pocket, cowboy, or are you just happy to see me?"

"Both." He whispered a kiss in her hair and went back to work.

When he held up his right arm and wound a feather boa around his hand and bicep like he was winding a lariat she laughed, but her humor was cut short when he stuck the boa in her purse.

Sweet Lord in Heaven, they needed to leave. Now. Whatever he had planned for their evening was far more interesting than anything happening at Saddleback's Honky-Tonk, or in the entire Midwest for that matter.

Mercifully, a few minutes later they'd cleaned up the back room, threw all of Mel's gifts into a few gift bags, and thanked Aaron for everything. All Indie wanted was to leave. Luke Camden, the one and only guy who'd ever held her heart, had pure unadulterated greed etched in every muscle of his gorgeous body. The lust in his eyes had darkened to an indigo fire and there was a pair of handcuffs in his pocket. The craving need resonated between them like a flash fire of electricity capable of setting the entire town ablaze.

She held up the keys to her Camaro, smirked at his shock, and tugged him towards the parking lot.

"You letting me drive because you're still buzzing?" Disappointment weighted his tone. Always a gentleman, even with cuffs in his pocket, or maybe because there were cuffs in his pocket. He wouldn't tie her to his bed if she was drunk.

"No. I only had one shot. I hate girly drinks, you know that. I'm letting you drive because ...." she faltered. She didn't know how to explain what was happening between them, what had happened that evening. "Because I trust you. I always have." *And because I want to tell you how much I love you. That I've always loved you. That I want to stay. But I don't know how to say any of that out loud.*

Confusion knitted his brow as he studied her.

"You're the only guy I've ever let drive her." She prayed he understood what that meant.

The dark carnality in his eyes softened and warmed. The variant blue fire turned to pools of heated love all for her.

"Go get in, sugar. So much I want to do to you tonight. I hope you're ready for me. I'm needin' you, all of you. And I ain't asking your permission anymore."

"God, yes." She all but sprinted to her car and threw open the passenger door.

He winced when he settled in the driver's seat. Removing the handcuffs from his pocket, he handed them to Indie. "Don't lose those."

"Don't worry."

Luke took a moment to rev the engine and smoke the tires, making her laugh.

"What? You've never let me drive it before. It's a damned vintage Camaro, and I know my girl made it fly. I intend to enjoy this."

"I was hoping you were gonna enjoy me."

"Oh honey, have no doubt. You're gonna be enjoyed over and over again all damn night if I have my say."

"You have your say." She'd needed this for far too long to be argumentative. Her rebellious side needed a night off, or perhaps the indulgences he offered her restlessness were just too good to ever oppose.

He turned to stare at her as he kicked up gravel behind the old tires on her car. "Driving me wild, sweetheart. Making me hurt with it. You're the only woman who's ever eased the pain. You know that?"

"I know." Her lungs seemed to have forgotten how to draw air. They seized with longing. Her mouth was drier than the Sahara. She willed the miles of dirt road between the bar and his house away. Every fence he had to key his way through made her burn, until she was certain if he didn't take her to bed soon she would combust. "Kiss me," she finally begged.

"God, I love you beggin' for me." He shoved the car in park in the middle of one of the Camden fields. "So fucking sexy."

All in one quick breath-stealing move, he cradled her body over the gearshift, mated his mouth with hers, and rasped his right hand over her breasts.

164

Her hands made quick work of locating his denim-trapped cock in the relative darkness. She could feel the fevered need through the thick fabric. He rocked the strain against her palm.

"Let me take you home, darlin'." He spoke in the breaths between their tongue-tangling kiss. "I'm gonna make it feel so good." Their mouths moved with magnetized force they had no hope of fighting. "Cuff you to my bed and spend all damn night having my way with you. Touch every inch of your gorgeous body with my fingers, my tongue, and my cock."

"Now," she whimpered. "I need you."

"Oh, honey, I know precisely what you need."

Somehow they made it to his house, groping each other like teenagers in heat. He tore her shirt over her head and tossed it somewhere in the general vicinity of the front porch. They stumbled through the front door, tripping over each other's feet. Frustrated with that, Luke lifted her into his arms like she weighed nothing at all.

Natural instincts took over. "Luke, I'm too ...."

"If you're about to say some shit about your weight, stop now. You're talking about the woman I love, remember? The most beautiful woman in the entire world to me, so shut your mouth or I'll fill it full before we ever get to using them handcuffs." His gruff tone was laced with danger.

She sealed her lips shut and allowed herself to believe for the moment that she wasn't too heavy for him to carry. He certainly didn't seem to be struggling. Burying her face against his neck, she tucked herself into his protective embrace and relaxed. "That's it. There's my sweet girl."

He seated her on the bed and dispensed with her boots and jeans. Time slowed around them. His gaze sizzled over her skin. Dark fire burned in his heavy-lidded eyes.

"Thought you were gonna cuff me to the bed?" She gnawed on her lip. The intense study of her body made her overly-aware of being exposed.

"Plenty of time for that, darlin'. Right now, I just want to look at you. I swear, Indie, you're my every fantasy come to life. I've dreamed about having you like this, lookin' up at me like that, wantin' me, needing me, so damn many times, half the time I can't figure out if I'm still just dreaming. I just can't possibly deserve to be the man you give this to. I *don't* deserve this."

"Luke," emotion strangled her throat. "You do. You're the only man that ever has,"

"God, baby, the dirty things I want to do to you. The things I want to show you. The things you shouldn't know. And I'm about to take them from you. I don't deserve that."

"You wouldn't be taking if I weren't offering, so shut up and start teaching me. I *need* to learn."

His low growl sluiced through her veins and sizzled across her skin.

"Stand up and let me look at you." He grasped her hands and pulled her to her feet. "My God, you are perfection." His hands followed a path forged with his eyes. Over her shoulders, along the thick straps of her favorite red bra. He tongued the lace abrading her nipples, melting her thoroughly with the rough friction.

"Yes," she hissed as she attempted to work through the buttons of his shirt.

"Stop." He jerked back, startling her. "Where are we, Indie?"

She couldn't help but grin. Speaking of fantasies come to life. The appearance of his dominant side stirred her very soul. "The bedroom."

"Right. So, you do as I say. Leave my clothes be. We got all night."

A part of her longed to argue. Heat radiated from his entire body, and she needed more. Her body rolled in anticipation as her hands slipped from his half-opened shirt.

"Good girl." He continued his ministrations on the wet lace of her bra. Her nipples throbbed in sweet agony. Anxious and raw. He sucked the lace into the heat of his mouth and she whimpered for more.

"Please," finally escaped her lips and whispered over his shoulder.

"Please what, sugar?"

"Please take me."

"Oh honey, I ain't near had my fill of just looking and touching you. Be patient for me."

Patience had never been her forte, especially when it came to Luke, but he wasn't giving in this time.

He worked his lips from one lace-captured nipple to the other until finally, he loosed her bra. Her breasts spilled forward anxiously into his capable hands, but he didn't stay there long. Tossing the bra away, he stepped back. "Just watch me lookin' at you, Indie Jane. So fucking hot in them naughty red panties it oughta be illegal."

Following his texted request that afternoon that she wear something naughty for him, she'd gone all out and picked up a pair of cage-back red-silk panties from the mall in Lincoln. Tiny straps of fabric exposed more than covered her backside. She'd almost chickened out of wearing them, afraid her ass was too big to pull them off. Judging by the flush settling high on his cheekbones, his darkening eyes, and the more than obvious arousal, she shouldn't have worried.

Luke took his sweet time dragging his gaze up and down her body. It was thrilling and empowering to see the effect she had over him. His erection visibly throbbed against his zipper line. He licked his lips repeatedly, working his jaw like he couldn't quite decide which part of her he wanted to devour first. She was good with anywhere, just so long as he got started.

Quickly, he finished the buttons she'd started on his shirt and let it drop to the floor. Her eyes tracked to the smattering of dark hair covering his chest and then down the trail of hair along his hardened abdomen that ultimately led right where she so desperately wanted to be.

"Turn around nice and slow for me. Show me them curves and the rest of those panties. I'm loving what I see so far."

Swallowing down a sudden case of nerves, she performed the turn. His hungry growl echoed against the recesses of her skull silencing every doubt she'd ever harbored over her curves. She heard his belt buckle hit the floor, the soft swish of his jeans, and clunk of his boots. Suddenly, he was on her, pressing his erection to her ass cheeks between the two slight straps of fabric straddling her crack. It burned like a hot brand against her skin.

"You feel what you do to me when you're naughty for me, darlin'?"

"Yes!"

He rocked against her, taunting the overly-sensitized nerve endings at the puckered opening of her backside.

"You have the sweetest ass I've ever seen. Ripe and swollen. Perfect. Anxious for me." He gripped the globes of her ass cheeks, kneading her flesh like he loved that she was far more than a handful. His heated whisper over her shoulder was her only warning. His teeth sank into that spot near her collar bone that made her weak. He sucked, drawing a strained groan from her. His hands wrapped around her waist, pressing his cock deeper between her cheeks. "So many things I want from you."

"Take them." Her voice was so low and craving she barely recognized it as her own.

"Intend to." He fell to his knees and his teeth grazed along her right cheek, sucking and nibbling as he traveled inward. "Lean forward. Put your hands on the footboard."

Complying, she felt him part the straps of the panties, such as they were, and gasped from the sensation as his tongue painted her taint. Some sense of unnecessary warning or panic always floated just out of her reach when he did that. Instead of protesting she rocked her hips, urging him onward. Her body wanted more. Her brain readily waved the white flag. Nothing that felt that good could possibly be bad.

Suddenly, he pulled away. Her entire body protested the unwanted vacancy. She stung with the abandonment.

"Turn around." His voice soothed her pain. She turned back to face him, and he was face to face with her soaking wet pussy. Grabbing her hands, he placed them on her mound. "Do as I say. Take them naughty little panties off nice and slow for me. I want to watch them work down your sexy legs. Then hold your lips apart. Offer your sweet little snatch to me."

"Oh, hell yeah," she groaned, lost once again in his commands. When she'd shed her panties, she opened herself for him and his wicked tongue worked up and down her slit and teased at the hood of her clitoris until she was certain she'd lose her mind. He suckled at her swollen pink folds until his moans of pleasure reverberated through her entire body.

"Please, please," she begged with every taunting lick. His teeth scraped slowly along her inner-lips making her pussy weep for more. When she could barely hold herself upright any longer due to the tremors rocking through her, he placed his hands over hers and used his thumbs to ease back the hood. "Yes," she sang as he drew her throbbing pearl into his mouth and suckled gently.

The orgasm ricocheted up from her mound, zinging through every nerve-ending of her body, leaving her weak. She slumped forward. He stood and cradled her head on his shoulder. Her bones were the consistency of Jell-O. Her heart thundered and sweat dewed at the nape of her neck. The room spun, so she squeezed her eyes closed and buried her face against the tensed warmth of his chest.

"See, good things happen when you offer yourself up to me. Let me put my baby to bed. There's so much more I want." With that, she was back in his arms and being settled gently into the soft sanctuary of his bed. Her lungs re-engaged and drew in the scent of his musk from the sheets and the heat from his body. In that one moment, she existed entirely inside his perfected masculinity.

Sensing Indie's need for constant contact, Luke kept her body locked to his as he climbed into bed on top of her. He settled back on

168

his knees between her thighs and tried to convince himself that he was really getting to live out just a few of his dirtiest fantasies. Since she was laid out before him primed and ready, he decided to contemplate his good fortune later.

Smoothing his hands up her soft belly and wondering if she'd ever give him a week or two to do nothing more than run his hands over every inch of her silky skin, his eyes landed on her tits. Her release still flavored the hot air. The scent of her ripened sex filled his lungs, driving him onward.

"Now, offer them beautiful titties to me, sweetness, just like you did your pussy." Well aware that he was treading on dangerous ground, he had to prove to her that there was no part of her entire body that he didn't find stunningly attractive. The scars marring her breasts were part of the story that made her who she was, and there could never be anything more beautiful than his Indie.

Apprehension tensed in her eyes. She worried her bottom lip with her teeth.

"Come on, honey. Give me what I want." There was something different about her that night. An abandon, or perhaps a concurrence glowed in the fire in her eyes. She was there, and for once she wasn't plotting her escape. She was right there with him this time. And leaving seemed the furthest thing from her mind. His very soul rejoiced as she scooped the heft of her ample breasts upward with her hands, an offering indeed.

His heart roared in his chest. His cock throbbed against her belly, marking her with pre-cum, as he lowered his head to her left breast and spun his tongue around its turgid peak. Her back arched in invitation.

"That's it," he hummed against her as he took her nipple captive with his mouth. Anticipation thundered through his blood. He'd always been of the opinion that her smile was the most beautiful curve on her entire body, but her drool-worthy tits and her sweet ass, lush, full, and feminine were very close seconds. If only she didn't dislike them so much. If only he could show her how she embodied his definition of perfected female. He timed the drawing pulls of his mouth to the squeezes of her hands on her breasts, working with her, pushing her closer to the edge of surrender. "God, you're so damn pretty. You gonna come like this for me, honey? Gonna give me what I'm after?"

He switched breasts and unleashed unrelenting devastation with every draw. She writhed under him, wild and needy. Loud moans crashed through her. Luke swore every sound she made wrapped around his cock and squeezed. He ordered himself to calm. There was still so much left to do. Raking his teeth over her nipple with a possessive growl, he loved the shiver that overwhelmed her. With one more fervent suck that was sure to leave a mark she came with a wispy sigh of his name. She ground against him. The weak orgasm slicked against his thigh.

He cradled her in his arms, neither of them wanting to break the connection they were building. When her breathing steadied, he lifted his head. "See what happens when you obey, darlin'? Such good things. And I'm all done asking." Forcing himself up, he sped across the floor, retrieving the cuffs and boa from her bag.

Her eyes danced with reckless abandon. Fevered heat glowed in her cheeks. She watched his every move. Anticipation and desire broadcast from every luscious curve of her body.

"Yes." She rolled against his mattress as he grasped her hands. He settled pillows behind her head and back, then along each of her shoulders before he looped the chain of the cuffs around a spindle on his headboard.

"Are we supposed to have a safe word or something?" She looked like the very idea annoyed her. Rules were never Indie's thing. He chuckled to himself.

"How about if I do something you don't like you just tell me to stop, sugar. I'd never hurt you. The words 'no' or 'stop' leave your pretty mouth, I sure as hell will listen. Doesn't matter what I'm doing."

"I know you will." The absolute trust displayed in her eyes spoke directly to his heart. This was what she'd needed all along. If only it hadn't taken him a decade to figure it out. The right cuff snapped on her wrist.

"That feel okay?"

She nodded.

"Too tight?"

"It's fine. It's hot as hell, actually. Just do the other one."

Luke tried to hide his smirk as he joined her wrists over her head and bound them. He settled back on his knees to stare down at her beautiful body on display all for him, a buffet of delectable femininity vulnerable only to him.

His cock throbbed and bounced against this abs. "My God, Indie, baby, I love you. I love you like this. Bound for me. At my mercy."

Her body writhed at his declaration. She shuddered in need.

170

Grasping himself, he squeezed his cockhead, tamping his rampant need for the time being.

"Damn, you ever think about entering that thing in the County Fair? You'd win, you know." She gestured her head to his erection.

"Only blue ribbons I want are from you, but I'm clearly going to have to fill that sassy mouth with something just to get you to hush. Keep your mouth closed." Threading his fingers through her hair, he crushed the silky strands in his hand, giving himself an unobstructed view of her mouth taking him in when he decided to allow that. He dragged the head of his cock over her lips, back and forth, and then pulled back. "Now taste me on your lips."

Her eyes glazed with lust as she obeyed. Then he took her succulent mouth with a deep kiss, indulging in the taste of his seed on her tongue before he repeated the process over and over, giving her samplings of his pre-cum, ordering her to lick her lips, then devouring it off of her tongue.

"Now all the way in, baby. Suck it like a good girl."

"Oh God," she panted as he baptized his cock in her mouth. Her hungry moans reverberated through his shaft. Her hot, wet mouth surrounded him. His entire body shook with each heavenly drag. Pure lust sizzled in his balls. My God, how had he ever existed without this? The unfathomable power she held over him. She was the one in cuffs. He was the one begging for more.

"Milk it, honey. Just like that," he grunted as she sucked him in deeper. He was set to detonate. He had to stop her. Pulling away from her mouth, he allowed himself one more taste before he snapped a small section of the boa and pulled it away from the rest.

The metallic clink of the handcuffs against the headboard with every writhe of her body sounded against her moans. He dragged the clump of faux-feathers over her breasts, watching her nipples throb from the sensations. Centering them between her luscious tits, moving slowly back and forth along the sensitive skin, he kept his eyes locked on hers.

"Tell me how wet sucking my cock made you, darlin'."

"So wet," she whimpered as he circled her adorable navel with the boa. Slowly, he traced it over her mound, watching her entire body jerk back and forth desperate for his touch.

"Good. Now, spread your legs for me."

Her ready compliance was intoxicating. He wasn't certain he was going to survive this night. She was simply too much, too perfect, too gorgeous bound to his bed, writhing and begging for more.

"You are wet aren't you, baby?" He slipped the boa along her soaking wet curls, teasing the most sensitive parts of her inner thighs and taunting her pussy with his own version of delectable torture. Back and forth. Over and over again until she made ragged thrusts into the air. Her body pled for her when her mouth was no longer able to do anything more than cry out her own pleasure.

Certain her body could not sustain this level of heavenly pleasure, Indie gave herself over to his every wish. He ran that damned boa up and down her body setting her on fire. She had no control over where he taunted her body next, and she'd never been more turned on. The clink of the cuffs on the bed amped her need to come as it surged through her veins. But the look of dark, undiluted sin in his indigo eyes said he had no intention of giving in yet.

"That feel good, sugar?"

"You know it does, damn you. I need more."

"Who's in control, Indie?"

"You are." And that fact alone was almost enough to drive her right over the edge.

"That's right. And what happens when you get sassy?"

"Mmm, I get to suck your cock," she taunted.

"You like that don't you?"

"Oh, hell yeah."

"Have to come up with a better punishment then." He winked at her and tossed the boa away finally.

Settling between her legs, he spread her wider using the width of his broad shoulders to brace her apart. His thumbs gently stroked along her pussy lips. She swore the erotic touch tugged just behind her mound, tightening the need until it bordered on pain. He gave her nothing more.

"Now, since you think you need more, I'm gonna ravage this beautiful pussy with my fingers and my mouth, but you're not gonna come until I tell you. You understand me?"

A part of Indie longed to ask what happened if she couldn't follow that particular command, but his response would take precious time away from his mouth being between her folds and his tongue stabbing deep inside of her. She nodded and thrust in his face, feeling the stubble of his five o'clock shadow prick at her slit.

"Anxious, darlin'?" His chuckle was laced with raw sexual prowess and sent a rush of fresh desire over her flesh. "High time I teach you some patience."

172

A slow drag of his tongue between her lips drew a frantic whimper from her lungs. Every gasped breath brought another dose of his musk to her lungs. Heated sex and raw power filled her. His teeth grazed her drenched tissues, back and forth. She loved that. He knew.

His tongue flicked across her clit and her hips shot up off of the mattress. That earned her a sharp smack on the ass while it was raised in the air. "Be still, Indie."

Sweet Jesus, when she'd dared him to be kinky she had no idea he'd so thoroughly fulfill her every secret fantasy. How the hell had he known? How the hell would she ever recover from this? She was certain that she wouldn't, and suddenly she was fine with that. This was worth every risk she might have to take to get it and keep him.

He returned to his work. His wickedly eager tongue kept her hovering just above ecstasy. Suddenly, two of his fingers circled her clit and explored her innerfolds.

"Please, please, Luke."

"Want me to touch you here, baby?" He circled her opening, taunting but never satisfying.

"Deeper."

"Mmm, I love you beggin' for it. Love you grinding your sweet little snatch in my face. I'm gonna give you what you're wantin', sugar, but remember the rules." His fingers entered her fully, and she felt her muscles begin their tell-tale rhythmic spasms. Clenching her jaw, she managed to push away the orgasm she craved.

When his tongue centered in on her clit, she knew she was going to break this latest rule. She couldn't hold it back. It wasn't even a possibility. He orchestrated her far too perfectly for her to stand a chance. She shook with the effort. Begging in broken syllables of ecstasy, she cried out for him.

"Need to come, sugar?" His rasping tone sizzled over her skin. She walked a fraying tight-wire of sanity, and she was going to fall.

"Please," she managed.

"Mmm, not yet." He continued his delectable torture.

Her strained moans became savage in their need, echoing against the walls. Sweat dewed on her breasts. Her abdomen quaked constantly. She couldn't hold it back. "Please, Luke."

"It's right there isn't it, sweetheart? You need to let it go, don't you?"

Unintelligible pleading is all she could manage as his fingers strummed against her g-spot. Her body writhed and rolled. She couldn't remain still.

"All right. You've been a good girl. Say my name when you come. All I want you thinking about is what I'm giving you, how I got you there, and who's in charge." He set her free, pushing her over the edge and catching her simultaneously. He fulfilled her darkest desires. With her hands bound over her head, he unshackled every constraint of her heart. He set her free. He let her fly, and when she finally floated back to earth, he caught her safely in his arms because she was his.

"Most beautiful thing I've ever seen, honey. When you let go for me, I swear … you're just so damn gorgeous."

"Luke, please, no more taunting. I need to be with you."

"I was just thinking the same thing." He opened the bedside table drawer, presumably to locate a condom. She shouldn't ask this. She shouldn't even think it. The internal shift she'd felt at the party took over her brain. The desperate desire took wing from the fissures of her heart and soared out of her mouth.

"Don't wear that. Please, I don't want anything between us."

A parade of emotions flickered through his eyes. Desire, concern, love, excitement, lust, possession. They were all there.

"Indie, honey, are you sure?"

"Yes." She knew a spoken assurance was the only fitting response. A simple nod would never convince him that she wanted this.

He settled his hips between her thighs. His blood-engorged cock rested at the apex. Another rush of wetness coated her lips. He rocked against her, shuddering at the point of contact.

"Do you want me to pull out?" His question burned with urgency.

"No. I want everything you are inside of me." Acutely aware of him, her every sense filled with Luke, she watched his pulse hammer in the hollow of his throat and felt his seed leak on her abdomen.

"Look at me," he commanded. Her eyes were already focused on his. She kept them locked there. "Are you certain you're ready for whatever might come of this?"

"Yes." She'd never been more certain of anything as insane as she knew that might be.

She was going to stay. Luke's soul rang with the certainty. If she didn't want him to use a condom, she'd decided to stay, to be his forever. Had he not been so racked with need he might have cried in relief. As it was, the woman he'd been in love with for half his life was asking to be fucked with nothing between them. He'd save the emotions for later.

Bracing himself on the mattress, he slowly eased his head between her lips, reveling in the silky cream that guided him in. "God, I've wanted to watch my cock sink into your pussy my whole damn life. Watch me, baby. Watch me own you. I'm gonna make it hurt so good for you." And he would. He knew precisely what she longed for, and he would never fail her.

"Yes," she gasped as he thrust fully. Luke lost himself in the incredible feeling of having her skin on skin, of being inhaled by her body so deeply he had no hopes of ever recovering from this, from her.

He made three frantic thrusts. In and out, connecting in a rush of heavenly oblivion. But then he slowed, calling himself an idiot. This wasn't right. The commitment she'd offered him, what she was allowing him. What the hell was he doing with her cuffed to his bed, fucking her like a kinky one-night stand? No. This was so much more than they'd ever shared before.

"Shh, baby, just relax for a minute." He managed to work the safety catch loose on each of the cheap fuzzy handcuffs, freeing her. He took her wrists in his hands and soothed them with the soft heat of his mouth. Kissing his way along the line of her pulse, he settled them by her sides and made another slow, languorous thrust, memorizing every silk-imbued ripple of her pussy against the fevered steel of his cock.

A moment later, her hands wound around his back holding him closer, not letting him go. "I'm right here, Indie. Forever. Just let me get you there. I've got you." He sank his lips to hers, rocking his hips against hers, filling her and easing away in slow, steady perfection.

"Look at me." In and out to the rhythm of her soul. Warm tears trickled from the sides of her eyes. His heart shattered and mended simultaneously. His love finally eased the pain she kept hidden in the beautiful depths of her eyes.

"I love you," she shuddered through an orgasm that held far more love than lust this time. And it wasn't the rhythmic pulls and ripples of her pussy that nursed him dry. It was the all-encompassing emotion of what they'd just shared that shattered him thoroughly. His body jerked and shook. His jaw clenched on a low groan of ecstasy as he spilled everything he was, everything he'd ever hoped to be, deep inside of her.

An uninhibited moan of satisfaction thundered from his lungs when he eased away from her and watched his seed trickle out of her swollen pussy. Wrapping her up in his arms, he held her, praying she'd never even want to leave his bed.

He felt her sweet grin form against his chest and he cradled her tighter to him. "I love you too, baby. You know that. We're gonna figure everything out, okay? I'll do whatever you want. I'll do anything, Indie. Just trust me."

"I do."

Brushing kisses in her mussed hair and wiping away the salty tears that had to come from both confusion and connection, he inhaled her scent and allowed himself to imagine never having to let her go.

Chapter Sixteen

Indie was quite certain of only one thing- she'd never been more confused in her entire life. *Dammit, Indie. You knew this would happen. You knew you'd fall right back in love with him. You should never have agreed to this.*

She buried her face against his chest, hating herself for crying. Who the hell cried after the best sex of their entire life? Clearly, she needed psychological help. *You don't have to leave.* Her heart made the timid reminder. The knot in her throat enlarged. She could barely breathe. *You could stop torturing him and yourself.* They'd just had completely unprotected sex. The ramifications of that were too much to consider just then. She was capable of nothing but existing moment to moment. The future had to remain at bay.

"You okay?" Fear tensed in his thrumming intonation. He tended her with his arms and soft warm kisses he constantly brushed over her skin.

She managed a nod. *Please don't make me talk yet.* He seemed to understand her unspoken plea.

"I've got you, sugar. I'm right here," he constantly reassured. "I know you're scared."

The certainty of his statement didn't seem to require her agreement, though she made another nod.

The silence wrapped around them, tucking them in amidst every uncertainty she'd clung to since the night he'd dragged her out of Saddlebacks and kissed her by his truck.

Her hands explored the rugged muscle of his back, over the strength of his hips and then up the firm lines of his six-pack to his broad chest. The outer armor of her sanctuary, capable, steady, and strong. Ever-ready for whatever might happen. Nothing about that had changed in the last decade. She knew it would be far too easy to declare her intention to stay. She also knew nothing lasted forever. What she didn't know was if the incoming debilitating heartbreak that inevitably came from the end of every relationship would be worth the years they remained together.

She couldn't hurt him. No one — not even Luke Camden — could possibly love her forever. Her own mother didn't love her. She'd just asked him to have unprotected sex with her. What was she thinking? She could've just ruined his life. The perfection of what they'd shared and the terror over what might come next went to war in her mind.

The fear won. It always did. She understood it. Knew what to do with it. It made sense to her when nothing else ever would.

"I should probably go on. Daddy'll be worried," she managed. *Run. Just leave now before you do something else horrible to him.*

Shock broadcast from every firm square-inch of his entire body, followed by pain. If she'd buried a knife in his chest she couldn't imagine that his face would display·a more terrifying picture.

"What?"

"Luke ...." she tried desperately to steady her racing heart. "I ... know this was different. I know ... something happened. I just have a lot to think about. I need some time. And Daddy's expecting me back after the party."

"No." The one word evulsed from his soul. "No. You're not leaving tonight. We can think and talk together. You need time. You take it here. Don't run from me again."

"I'm not." *But you are.* Her heart wasn't having it this time, it seemed. "I promise." She lied to both of them, and he knew it. "I just have to understand, and Daddy's probably already worried."

"Indie ... please," his tone was ragged, desperate.

"Luke, even if I stay here I have to go get my stuff." There, that was a legitimate reason for returning to her father's house. "I don't have any clothes."

"Stop lying to me." His eyes clouded with fury. She'd never been frightened of Luke, but she was terrified of hurting him.

"I'll be back."

Before he could make any more demands, she scooted from the bed and threw on the clothes she'd worn to the shower. She just needed to breathe away from those arms that made her feel like she really could exist with him forever, away from that intoxicating way he smelled like hay and leather and home, away from him. Then she could figure out what was supposed to happen next.

He followed her out of bed, working his jaw like he was biting back a violent eruption of words with the strength of his teeth. When she picked up her bag, his teeth apparently lost their damming ability. "Dammit, Indie, do you understand what we just shared? You understand that you just asked me to make a commitment to you forever? And you understand that I would never have done that if I'd thought you were fucking leaving me ... again?"

"I'm not leaving!" shouted from her. Yes. This she understood. This she could do. Keep arguing. Just keep fighting. Fear and anger. Those made sense to her. They'd accompanied her entire life. She

178

could tap into the ready will of her temper and shut out everything else. This was how she'd always survived.

"Bullshit."

"You're being an asshole."

"You are not leaving."

"You cannot keep me here," she came right back, twisting the knife further.

He edged closer, narrowing his eyes. The anguish in them cut her to the quick, but she refused to feel the pain. "Why do you do this to me, Indie? Why do you kill me like this?"

Because if I don't show you how horrible I can be, when you figure it out on your own you'll hate me, too.

"I'm going." With that she flew out of his house. She made it to her car before she broke down completely.

Luke paced and rubbed the fist he'd put through the wall in his bedroom just moments before. Damn it all to fucking hell. He was a bigger idiot than he'd ever thought possible. Demanding that she stay. Dumbest thing he would ever and could ever have done. Dumber than letting her leave that God-awful day back in college. Engage Indieanna Harper in an argument and expect to get anywhere worth being. He was a fucking moron.

Shaking his head, he ordered himself not to go after her. A showdown in her daddy's driveway at two in the morning. Not a good move. He'd fucked up enough for one night.

You know why she does this, Camden. You've always known. Running his left hand over his face since his right was still throbbing from his self-abuse, he tried to figure out how to dig his way out of the shit hole he'd just created. Probably be a real good idea to stop digging. A woman who's been told her whole life that she was unlovable will go well out of her way to prove it.

What he wouldn't give to tear Carolyn Harper Jenkins limb from limb, and he was the first man that'd beat a fucker stupid for laying a hand on a woman. He had to go with what he felt from Indie, not what came out of that ornery mouth of hers. And fuck it all to hell, he'd bound her to his bed, had her at his mercy, forced deep all-consuming orgasms and tearful emotions from her, and instead of dealing with the space she wanted to process all of that, he'd demanded she stay, again. Every time he held her down, she ran. Why couldn't he remember that?

His jaw and his wrist ached. He didn't care. There had to be some way to erase the damage he'd just inflicted in their near perfect night. He should have held her close for as long as she would've allowed it, told her how much he wished she'd stay, offered to drive her home, and gone to bed. She would've been back by morning. She'd been closer to agreeing to stay forever not one hour ago than she'd ever been before, and he'd blown it being a dumbass.

He'd felt her giving in. He'd gotten ahead of himself. And goading her into an argument was a rookie mistake. She was the strongest, bravest human being he'd ever known, but she was also broken, and he'd done nothing but tear her further apart instead of helping her find the strength to mend her own soul. He knew he couldn't do it for her, but dammit he wanted to be the one that stood beside her for every step she made towards recovery.

Indie stumbled up the carport steps at her father's house. She had no idea why she was even there, other than the fact that she was a bitch of epic proportion for doing this to Luke. Her wrists still felt odd from being in fuzzy handcuffs for the last hour.

Dammit, why couldn't she just for once stop fighting about everything? Why couldn't she just be in love and deal with life from there? Why did she just keep running? *"One way or another, sweetheart, you gonna figure out that what you're running from is what you should be running to. If that weren't the case, why is my girl still running?"* Her father's words throbbed in her skull.

Shaking her head, she eased the door open and stepped inside, certain her father was asleep. She'd come up with a plan in the car. She would get her stuff to prove to Luke that she was really going to try this time, and she would apologize to him.

He was right. They had to figure out things together, even if what they figured out was that she simply couldn't stay in the Glen. At some point surely he would realize that he deserved someone so much better than her, but she owed it to him to see, didn't she? At the very least she owed him the two weeks they both wanted and to come see him more often, assuming he ever wanted to see her again at all after she'd asked him to have sex with her without a condom, then ran away after calling him an asshole. Her stomach roiled with self-disgust. Regret-loaded bile singed her throat.

Wait, was someone … giggling? Her brow furrowed. An oddly strained moan reached her ears, but she wasn't paying enough attention to contemplate it. She had to apologize to Luke. Heading to her bedroom to execute her plan, she froze in the kitchen. She fought not to gag. No. No. No! What the hell? Ugh! Turning around, she fled the scene, trying desperately to bleach her mind of the image of her father's bare ass on the sofa pounding into some … woman. She shuddered.

Blinking repeatedly, she tried to figure out what the hell was happening. Remembrances of the day she'd walked in on her mother and the mayor hammered in her head. The past and the present whipped into an odd frenzy of confusion. She couldn't breathe. She couldn't think.

A late-model Oldsmobile was parked by her father's truck. Her father had … a girlfriend? No — a lady-friend? Wait, what the hell did people his age call this? Did her daddy bar hop? Who was this chick? Did he know her? Why hadn't he mentioned her? And … dear God in heaven … her father was fucking a woman who owned an Oldsmobile.

Throwing herself back in her car, she floored it out of the driveway. Running back to Luke's house was the only thing that made sense. If he didn't want to see her, she'd apologize for everything that happened and drive out to Miranda's and stay with her. Tomorrow she could just go back to Oklahoma City. Everything was easier there. Pleasant Glen held far too much of the past, and yet somehow not enough to anchor her there. The changes were more than she could work through.

She made it back to his front door in record time. *Please let him forgive me.* She wasn't a girl that prayed for herself too often. There were people that needed help far more than she did, but not having Luke hate her was all that mattered.

He jerked the front door open before her fist made the connection and hauled her into his arms, hugging her so tightly the air evacuated her lungs.

"I'm so sorry," he gasped.

When he eased his grip enough for her to speak, she stared up at him, fairly certain he must've hit his head after she left. "What on earth do you have to be sorry about? I'm the one who's here to apologize."

His red-rimmed eyes levied another round of guilt on her heart. She wasn't certain how it was still beating under the current insanity of her life. Drawing a deep breath, she went on with her speech. "I'm so sorry I did all of that. I should never have asked you not to use a condom, and I freaked out and ran away, just like I always do. Then I was a total bitch to you. I'm just …."

"Scared. I know. It's okay to be scared, sugar. I said I'd give you two damn weeks, which isn't enough time anyway, then I acted like a douchebag and tried to argue you into staying. It hasn't even been one week. Fuck it all. I don't know what the hell I was thinkin'."

When Luke Camden's vocabulary reduced to that many curse words, that wasn't a good sign. He spoke like every other cowboy on the planet with a vocabulary that would make sailors blush, but it wasn't like him to let them fly with such ease. He usually had a little more finesse. So they were both clearly freaking out. Somehow that made her feel a little better.

"Maybe the two-week thing is a lot of pressure."

His harsh swallow and half-nod said he didn't like where this was going. "I'm sorry I pressured you. I swore to myself I wouldn't do that again."

"I'm not asking for an apology. I'm asking for your forgiveness. Maybe we could just take it sort of day by day. I won't necessarily leave after the reunion, but even if we decide to try this ... permanently, I do have to go back to Oklahoma at some point. I have to go back to work at least long enough to quit my job or whatever. I just think it's a lot to consider. I'm sorry I freaked out." There. That was what she was supposed to say, what she was supposed to feel, if only the crippling fear left room for any other feelings.

He dragged her back into his arms, layering her against his chest. "Stop apologizing. You had every right to freak out. I was being an asshole. You want day by day. You got it."

"Um, I can't go home ... I mean ... I can't go back to Daddy's."

"Most of me wants to thank my lucky stars for whatever made that so, but I have enough brain cells awake to want to know why."

"Well," she convulsed against his chest. He stepped back and cradled her face in his right hand.

"What the hell happened, sweetheart?" Genuine concern etched his features.

"Well, Daddy ... and noises ... naked noises," she shuddered. "And ... the couch ... just right there ... in the living room ... I saw ... and an Oldsmobile ... and gross."

Humor played in his eyes, and a half second later he was laughing at her outright. Irritated, she shoved him back. This only made him laugh harder however.

"Stop laughing at me."

He caught her hands before she could push him again. "I take it Diana was over at your dad's?"

182

"Who the hell is Diana?" Another round of gall inched up her spine. Why had no one mentioned Diana to her?

"According to Eliza, your Daddy's friend with benefits."

"Oh my dear God! What? He's too old for a friend with ... ew!"

"Okay," Luke planted a kiss on top of her head that she did not find particularly soothing. "Deep breath for me. They've dated off and on for maybe a year now. I'm guessing they're back on. She's a waitress at the Open Range in Ogallala, and she fills in at Saddlebacks when they need a hand. She still owns a little portion of the corn farm she and her husband had back in the day. He passed a while back, from what I've heard. And your daddy is far from too old to have needs, sugar, even if you don't want to think about it."

"Why didn't he ever tell me this?"

"Maybe because he had a pretty good idea this was how you would react." He winked at her. He was playing with fire and he knew it.

"I wouldn't have reacted this way if I'd known she was coming over and therefore would not have had to walk in on ... that."

"I suspect he thought you'd be staying over here."

"Can I?"

Luke's brow knitted. "Indie, honey, I've been beggin' you to stay with me for damn near a week now. We just got into an argument because you wanted to leave. Of course you can stay."

"I was asking because of the argument. How is this so difficult to understand?"

"But the argument was my fault."

"No, it wasn't! It was my fault."

"You needin' to fight badly enough to argue about arguing?"

Dammit. He always managed to douse her fire. How was one man so good at stoking it to all new heights of passion when that's what he wanted, and turning it off like a knob on a stove when she wanted to be mad?

"I ain't sayin' we can't keep going, darlin'. I'm just making sure you were aware that's what was happening."

"No." She sank against him. She was exhausted and this night was more than she could deal with anymore. "She owns an Oldsmobile," she fussed into his chest.

His chuckle shook through her, warming her soul. "Maybe don't hold that against her. She makes do with what she has."

"Great. Now I have more guilt."

"Why don't I take my baby to bed, and let's forget everything that happened from about five minutes after the most amazing sex we've ever had until right now?"

"You don't want to hash the whole thing out?" Somehow Indie didn't quite believe he was going to be that good to her.

"Later. Maybe. Thought we were taking this day by day." The concession in his voice bordered on defeat. Indie just didn't have the strength to call him on it.

"That sounds good."

She could be pregnant. She probably isn't. You hoping she is? Luke tossed and turned in the bed, trying his best not to disturb Indie. At least she was sleeping soundly. *If you're hoping she is so you can get her to stay, you really are an asshole.* His mind wasn't playing fairly. Didn't matter. He had no more control over his thoughts currently than he had his temper earlier when she'd run.

Okay, no more bare-backing until she's really ready for the commitment you want. A ring or something. He stalled his motions and his thoughts momentarily on that decree. The head on his cock, however, played the part of the devil on his shoulder. *She asks, we give. I've never felt anything so amazing. Like you'd ever be able to deny her that anyway. You're still a weak motherfucker when it comes to her. Always have been. Always will be.*

Luke sank his fist into his pillow and ordered both his heads to shut it. For now, she was right beside him. Her easy breaths said she'd let their tumultuous night go for the moment. He needed to do the same.

What does day by day mean, exactly? He huffed audibly. Indie scooted closer to him, attempting to soothe him even in her sleep. Grinning to himself, he guided her sleeping form up on his chest and cradled her closely. Her responding sigh of contentment eased his restless thoughts. *Who cares what it means? Right now she's where she belongs.* If you added enough days together, you'd get a whole damn life. Nothing wrong with that.

Chapter Seventeen

Long before sunrise, he slipped from the bed. He'd put his brothers off on haying for the past week. They had to get it in, but it had several more days in it and he may or may not have that much time left to convince Indie to stay. Hell would freeze over before he spent the next week on a tractor instead of on her. Some things in life just couldn't be put off.

He perked a cup of coffee into one of his many travel mugs, left her a note on his pillow, and headed out into the cool damp air of morning.

Stopping by the barn, he thanked Grant for bringing in the horses and gave Atlas, his personal copper quarter horse, a rub down before he saddled him.

He'd been out to check on Juliet twice since he'd taken the bandages off of her hoof. She was healed up, but not quite ready for riding. Indie loved to ride her horses more than she loved working on cars, and that was saying something. He eyed Whirlwind, a feisty mare that now belonged to Summer, Austin's wife. Whirlwind was a beautiful horse that had no time for going slow.

Austin was saddling Lusty, his gelding. "Hey, you think Summer would mind Indie ridin' Whirlwind this afternoon if I can talk her into going on a quick trail ride with me?"

"Hell no. Well, she might mind, but she'll get over it. Save me a day of trying to keep her off of the damn horse anyway. She birthed my nine-pound kid not six weeks ago. I watched the whole damn thing. Getting back in a saddle's gonna hurt like hell. I don't know what she's thinking, and Doc says she needs to give it another week or two because of the stiches. She keeps thinking Whirlwind's not getting rode, and it's making her antsy. So, Indie'd be doing all of us a favor."

"She gonna give you shit about it though?" Luke inquired.

Austin smirked. "She gives me shit about everything. Why the hell do you think I married her? Ain't a damn thing better than my girl."

Luke couldn't really deny that part of what made Indie so damned addictive was the fact that she had twice as much sass and fire as she had sweet tenderness. She was sure as hell a fighter when she was fighting, and occasionally when she was loving, too. So, the Camden men liked their women with some spitfire. Nothing wrong with that.

Indie was trying to convince her eyes to open when she heard Luke tiptoe back into the bedroom. Sunlight warmed the room. She inhaled the mix of his salty musk and their lovemaking entrenched in the sheets mixed with the scents of horses and hay. She couldn't quite hide her grin. Chuckling, he brushed a kiss in her hair.

"Good mornin', beautiful."

Peeking her eyes open a half-notch, she watched him toe off his boots and work his t-shirt up to his elbows and then over his head. Sweat glistened on the perfect planes of his broad chest. His solid shoulders contracted as he worked the buckle of his belt and the snap on his Wranglers. They were rubbed and worn at his substantial thighs. Capable, hardened, cowboy perfection all for her. Damn, but a girl could definitely get used to waking up to this.

When he left the room wearing nothing but boxer-briefs, she pouted but still couldn't quite make herself get out of his massive bed. Sleeping in the full-sized from her childhood wasn't working so well. She'd had kinks in her spine and an aching neck all week. Stretching her hands over her head, she reveled in the room his king provided.

Luke returned a moment later, looking like he'd stepped directly out of one of those men's underwear commercials. He was carrying her a steaming mug of coffee, and judging from the bulge in those sexy undies, his cock was pleased she was naked in his bed.

"You gonna keep pretending to be asleep, sugar, or can I coax you up with some coffee?"

Giggling, she worked her way into a seated position and reached for the coffee. He held it just out of her grasp.

"I get a good morning kiss first."

"Coffee," she whimpered.

Chuckling, he leaned in and whispered a gentle kiss on her lips. She pulled away a half-second later and made another grab at the mug.

"Not finished, sweetness."

"You are a sadist, and I hate you."

That brought on more laughter. "Careful, Indie Jane. Be sweet. You have to go through me to get the coffee."

Setting the mug on the bedside table, he proceeded to kiss his way from the sides of her scowl, over the fading hickeys on her neck, to each of her nipples that he tongued and suckled, making her weak with desire. Her body was confused. She desperately wanted him to keep going, but she also really needed caffeine.

186

When he lifted his head, his sinful smirk sent a surge of wet heat to her pussy. "Now, was that so bad?" He handed over the mug full of liquid sanity with cream and sugar, just the way she loved it.

"I'll hate you less when I get to the bottom of this mug."

"I'm well aware. When you decide you love me again, come get in the shower with me." With that, he headed to his master bathroom. She heard the old pipes squeak when the water began its rapid fall.

"I've always loved you. I always will. But I'm finishing this whole damn mug before I set one foot in that bathroom, so there." She called just before she drew another long sip.

"Oh yeah?" He returned to the bedroom just long enough to strip out of his underwear, waggle his eyebrows, and run his right hand up and down his extremely impressive erection. "My cock didn't get near enough lovin' last night, honey, and you are looking so damn fuckable this morning. Don't make haul your sexy ass in there."

Her mouth watered, and she almost dropped the hot coffee in her lap. Damn him, and his fucking gorgeous body, and his remarkably long, thick cock that had her downing the coffee in one extended swallow. How the hell did feeling this weak for him make her feel so powerful? She'd worry on that later. Kicking her way out of the sheets, she all but sprinted into the bathroom.

He was standing by the shower door, still sporting a cocky grin and one hell of a hard-on. "'Bout time."

"I came in here to pee," she sassed.

"Liar." With that, he caged her between the heat that radiated from him and the cool marble countertop. Her back pressed firmly against his chest. She turned to look up at him, a much more appealing picture than staring at herself in the massive bathroom mirror.

"No ma'am." He gently turned her head, fixing her gaze on the reflection of her own thick curves, scars, and other assorted imperfections. "My God, sugar, look at how beautiful you are."

She rolled her eyes. "I have sheet marks on my face." *And huge tits that have no hope of ever facing forward, and scars everywhere, and cellulite, and my stomach is dimpled and not in any way toned, and I haven't seen the inside of a gym since we were in high school ...* she shuddered.

"They're adorable and they came from sleeping so sweet in my arms last night. Watch me and feel what you do to me." He positioned his cock between her ass cheeks and lifted the heft of her breasts in his hands. "Watch me get your gorgeous body ready for me, Indie. My God, you are perfection. So damn pretty. Just the way a woman's 'sposed to look." Her breasts spilled through his fingers. His cock throbbed against her ass and the look on his face said he was so turned on he hurt with it. The carnal fire burning in his eyes doused a little of her self-flagellation. That look he had staring at her body in the mirror said he was about to fuck her senseless.

"Luke ... I ... mmm ... don't want ...." His fingers twisted and taunted her nipples. "Oh God, that feels good ... to do this in a mirror. I look terrible." She watched his hand draw back. The firm slap of her bare ass stung and oddly brought another rush of heat to her pussy.

"Hush. Nothing gets me going the way your body does. I'm damn tired of hearing you put yourself down. You are sexy as hell. You can either watch me take you in the mirror or I can turn you around and make you watch me paddle you in the mirror. My choice, and it all depends on what comes out of your mouth next."

Both scenarios sounded extremely naughty and both turned her on to all new heights, but thoughts of watching her rather large ass jiggle in a mirror had her sealing her lips shut, not that she'd admit that to him.

"Excellent choice. Now watch." He rocked his hips forward, slicking the hollow at the top of her ass with pre-cum while he ran his hands down her waist. His fingers pressed into her hips, and his sac teased at her pussy. "Lean back against me and keep watching."

She settled her head on his chest and followed his orders. Keeping his right hand on her breasts, he placed his left over her mound. Her body arched in a slow roll, and for a moment she forgot to hate herself.

Electricity arced between the primal urgency in his eyes and her body. Her own eyes were bright and fervent. Her lips, anxious to be kissed, looked like they'd been dipped in expensive red wine. Her long hair was in an untamed mane on her shoulders, swishing softly, teasing at her ample breasts. Fevered heat streaked her chest and face. Her nipples peaked and throbbed. Her waist contracted. The arch of her spine and the thick roll of her ass was ... beautiful? Maybe. Sexual? Oh yeah. Graceful? Definitely. She felt alive with the power of her own femininity.

"So fucking pretty, darlin'. So soft. Jesus Christ, you make me hurt. You make me crazy. How can you not see how beautiful you are?"

But maybe she could. If she just believed him enough to convince herself.

"Watch what I'm gonna do to you." His fingers parted the swollen lips of her pussy. Breath tangled in her throat. She saw the tender cream her body supplied for him, for them. It knew precisely what to do. It provided everything they needed. Shouldn't she be thankful?

188

She decided she was as she watched his long fingers rub up over her clit and then dip down to her opening. "See how pretty you are when I get you like this?"

Her hips undulated against his strokes. Another wave of intoxicating femininity washed over her. She couldn't look away now. She wanted to see her body's responses to his.

"That's it. And when I touch you like this," he stroked her g-spot with the fingers deep in her drenched channel and her clit with his other hand, "God, you get so wet for me. Listen."

He stroked harder, whipping her into a frenzy as she heard the slick essence move with his fingers. His thundered moan echoed off the bathroom tile, further amping her arousal. She felt her body clench tightly around his fingers.

"And that's how I know you're getting needy for it. I feel you squeeze my fingers, I know my baby's on fire, and I know I'm gonna get you right where you need to be. I'm gonna get to feel it. Nothing makes me feel more powerful, Indie. Nothing but you. I live for this."

"Oh God." She shuddered against him. She watched her body shiver with need. The beauty of it simultaneously confused and enlivened her. His eyes were an indigo fire. His entire body honed in on hers like he'd never seen anything more stunning.

"Then I do this and I tell you to breathe because I want you to enjoy this as much as I am." He slicked the thumb of the hand inside her through her wet heat and then circled the puckered opening of her backside. "'And 'cause I know my girl likes it naughty sometimes. Likes when I touch her here where no one else ever has. Because you're mine, sugar. All fucking mine. Deep breaths for me."

He pressed his thumb through the tight ring of muscle. Her body relished the pressure and the rampant desire. She came hard with the next stroke. There, in the split second before her eyes shut out the world around them, she saw the feral power of her body, raw and wild with carnality and heat, tensing with undiluted passion, and the victorious look in his eyes. She'd watched her fingernails claw at the marble counter, heard her own wanton cry when he overwhelmed her every sense, and felt his cock give a fierce throb against her back. The picture emblazoned in her mind, and try though she might, she could find nothing in it unappealing.

Luke's body was racked with desperation. The wildfire in Indie's eyes surged through his veins.

"Now watch me fuck you raw, sugar." He turned them to the side. Unable to stop himself, he gripped her hips and sank himself between her pussy lips balls-deep. Her eyes flashed and her back arched, giving him even more. A savage growl of approval ripped from his lungs.

Nothing could ever feel so good. Nothing *should* ever feel this good. He managed to remember why he was able to experience every silky ripple of her pussy and the flood of warm honey drowning him. The condom. Indie's eyes were glazed with lust, locked on the image of his cock thrusting in and out of her in the mirror. Her teeth gripped her bottom lip. Sexy moans constantly sounded from her. God, she was loving this.

He squeezed her ass, trying desperately to show her how incredibly sexy she was. If she wanted a show, he'd sure as hell provide. There were other ways around the awkward condom usage discussion.

He kept his thrusts rhythmic and ravaging. Every pass he made pushed him closer to the edge of abandon. Longing clawed at his skin. The primal urgency of it all sliced through him. The musk of her arousal joined the steaming air filling his lungs. His vision blurred.

Her pussy milked him constantly. Sweet Jesus, another stroke maybe two. He was too close. Tension sizzled in his balls with the familiar need. He was right there. She came again, tensing around him and shaking wildly. Jerking out of her with a guttural cry, he unloaded all over her back and ass. The erotic image had him spurting again and again. Potent and uncontrollable, he bathed her in his cum.

They eventually made it into the shower. Never more than a hand-width apart. As the warm water sluiced over their fevered skin, he washed her, thorough in his care. His lips found hers and they indulged until the warm water ran cold.

Her phone rang while they were half-toweling off half making-out in the bedroom.

"It's Daddy." She cringed. "What do I say to him?"

Luke bit his lips together momentarily to keep from laughing at her very obvious discomfort. "You could tell him how good I just fucked you, or you could try, 'Hey, Dad. How are you?'"

She stuck her tongue out at him just before answering.

Settling on the bed and lamenting the momentary absence of her skin on his, he guided her into his lap. There. That was better. And there was his sweet grin on her face. He just had to stay the course and this was going to be their forever.

She rolled her eyes. "Daddy," she sighed. "I'd be happy to run the shop for you today. Does this *friend* you're spending the day with happen to be female, because you can just say that to me. I'm not a little kid anymore. You and mom have been divorced forever. It's fine. Just tell me."

Luke couldn't quite make out her father's response, but her shudder said he'd done as she asked and she wasn't quite as okay with it as she'd like to be.

"Are you bringing her to the rehearsal dinner tonight?"

She drew another deep breath, and Luke tenderly rubbed her back, trying to soothe her.

"Okay, well, good. We'll meet her then. Uh, yeah, I'll be there in about an hour. Love you." Indie tossed the phone on the bed, and buried her face in his neck.

"You okay, sugar?"

"Yeah, Daddy's taking his chicky-mama to breakfast and spending the day in Ogallala, which doesn't sound like him at all. He never takes a day off. Apparently, *Diana* thought he should ask me if I'd mind running the shop today."

"He might not ever take the day off because he can't. If you're not here, the entire area is without a mechanic. Maybe he's making hay while there's sunshine, so to speak."

"Oh, believe me he was making plenty of hay last night."

Chuckling, Luke brushed another kiss on her cheek. "I was hoping you'd go riding with me today. Guess that'll have to wait."

Disappointment flickered in her eyes. Shit. He shouldn't have said anything. He'd been trying to show her everything available to her on the ranch not make her regret filling in for her dad.

"I'd much rather go riding with you, but I want to show Dad that I'm supportive of him, ya know? I bet Mama doesn't know his girlfriend's coming tonight. *That* should be interesting." A wicked grin formed on her face and Luke shook his head.

"I know that look. Am I gonna need bail money for this barbecue thing tonight?"

"Never put anything past me." She leapt out of his lap, brushed a kiss on his cheek and proceeded to get dressed, much to his chagrin.

There wasn't a single cloud in the Nebraskan sky that morning. Luke kissed Indie once more before watching her drive away. Glancing at his watch, he willed the day to pick up the pace and the night to linger.

They were all excited to take the night off and kick back a few. Beau Riggins and Travis Walker, Pleasant Glen High's Offensive Tackle and Center to Luke's Quarterback and Tucker's Wide Receiver were coming in for the wedding. Trash talking texts had begun the week before about the cornfield football game scheduled for that night.

Not that he'd ever admit it to anyone else, but Luke couldn't wait to play again. He wondered if he still had it, and seeing his old team would be fun. The icing on the cake would be seeing Indie on the sidelines cheering him on again.

Since Indie was busy for the day, Luke decided he might as well head into Ogallala to pick up supplies from Dr. Halverson. He rolled his eyes as he climbed up in his truck. There'd be a solid hour of letting Halverson massage his ego and his degree just to get the meds, but he could pick up Runza's for Indie and take her lunch, so that made the trip worth it in his book.

Chapter Eighteen

"Can I watch you work on my mommy's car?" Hannah, a little girl who'd come in with her mother a few minutes before, wandered in from the tiny waiting area and stood solemnly beside Indie.

Grinning at her, Indie nodded and found the old stool she used to stand on to work beside her father. "Sure. Do you like to work on cars?"

"Yes, and I like to catch lizards, and I can catch more than Houston and Cody, them's my big brothers, and I can run faster than them too, even though they're bigger than me, and I can climb higher in the Cottonwood trees by our creek, and I can ride on the calves real good and not fall off, and I can catch a baseball in a glove even if Houston throws it really hard and it stings my hand, and I can hit a homerun right out of the back fields."

"Wow. I used to love to do all of those things better than all of the boys, too."

"Really?"

"Yep. You want to help me?"

Hannah nodded enthusiastically.

"Okay, do you see that ring right there?" She pointed to the oil dipstick. "Pull that out and let's check the oil. We're gonna wipe it off first and then stick it back in. I think mommy needs a new gasket and filter."

Hannah did as Indie asked, beaming the entire time. "Did your daddy say it was okay for you to work on cars even though it's a boy's job?"

Indie frowned. "Why do you think it's a boy's job?"

"My daddy says there's boy's jobs and girl's jobs, and that I need to stop playing with all the boys and learn to do what Mommy does. But the girls at my school are boring. I want to play baseball on the boy's teams like the Pirates, and be a mechanic that works on big huge trucks, and maybe also be a bull rider in the rodeo, and a firefighter, and an astronaut, and also maybe the President."

"Wow." Indie's heart pricked. "Those would all be amazing jobs."

"I know, but Daddy says I can't, and I need to stop talking about it all the time 'cause it's silly."

"How old are you Hannah?"

"Eight."

What kind of asshole would tell an eight-year-old to stop being silly when they were trying to discuss their career? With a deep breath of oil-laced air, Indie tried to calm her temper.

"I don't think any of those jobs are silly. And I think girls can do anything boys can do … even better. You want to know what my daddy used to tell me?"

Hannah's eyes never left Indie's hands as she disconnected the battery.

"He used to tell me that I could be anything I wanted to be as long as I worked really hard. I always wanted to be a mechanic, so I learned everything I could about cars and trucks and engines. Now, I get to do this every single day, and you know, there is nothing better than making your dreams come true. And I think if you work really hard you can be anything you want to be, too. No matter what your daddy says. Maybe just don't tell him I said that."

"You want me to pinky swear?" Hannah held up her hand with her smallest finger extended.

Chuckling, Indie pulled off her gloves and linked her finger with Hannah's. "You just pinky swear to me that you won't ever let anyone tell you what you can and can't do, especially if they think you can't do it because you're a girl. Deal?"

"Deal!"

"Sounds like excellent advice to me." Luke's low, slow drawl sped Indie's heart. She stood and peeked around the hood of the old Dodge Caravan. "Hey there, beautiful." He popped a quick kiss on her lips. "I brought you lunch."

"Thanks. Luke this is Hannah. Her mommy's van isn't working quite right. She was helping me check the oil. Hannah, this is my boyfriend, Luke."

"Hey, I know you. You're the horse doctor who fixed Biscuit's leg when it gots swolled up. Biscuit was Cody's horse, but he gots to get a new one and now she's mine," she explained to Indie.

Luke leaned down to Hannah's level giving her his kindest smile. Indie couldn't help but love him even more. "That's right, I did. How's Biscuit doing now?"

"She's real good now. Thank you for looking after her."

"That's my job, sweetheart. Girl's gotta have her horse. How else will she show her big brothers who can jump the fences the best?" He winked at her. Indie wanted to hug him, and if she were being quite honest, she never wanted to stop.

Hannah's eyes goggled and her precious smile extended the entire width of her sweet face. "You remembered I can do that?"

"I remembered. And you know what else? I have two little sisters, and don't tell them I said this, but they can both ride better than I can."

"Really?"

"Really. One time my little sister Natalie had to help me up when I got thrown. There's nothing boys can do that girls can't do, too."

"That's what Indie said."

"Well, Indie's almost always right. Hey, I got an extra order of Fring's. Go ask your mom if you can have them." He offered her the box of fries and rings, and Hannah hugged him fiercely.

"Thank you. I'll go ask, but then I have to finish helping Indie work on the van."

Indie and Luke beamed at her as she raced back inside the waiting area.

"You're amazing, you know that?" Indie threw her arms around him.

"Nah. She must've told me a hundred times about how she and Biscuit could clear all the jumps on their property and how her brothers couldn't do it. Then her dad spent the rest of the time I was there complaining that he had to pay for me to treat her horse when, according to him, she refused to learn to cook supper. All I could do not to hold him down and let Hannah beat some sense into him with that baseball bat she swings quite well. Ended up not charging him a damn thing with the understanding that if her horse, and only *her* horse, needed me he'd call. Fuck-whistle's way too anxious to get her off that horse and in an apron. Makes me wanna skin him alive."

"Remember last night when I said I love you?"

"Hell yeah."

"I really, really, really do." She squeezed him tighter and decided then and there to figure out some way to make this work.

"Oh yeah?"

"Yeah."

"You could take your own advice you know."

"What's that mean?" Indie went wipe her hands off on a shop rag so she could share lunch with Luke. The Runza's smelled delicious, even though she was well aware he wasn't missing a chance to show her all that Nebraska had to offer — as if he wasn't enough.

"About not letting anybody decide for you what you can and can't do."

"When have I ever let somebody else decide anything for me?" The memory of being handcuffed to his bed the evening before welled in her soul. Love and lust fought for dominance in her mind. She felt her cheeks heat as her grin expanded. "Except maybe you when you're wielding handcuffs and a boa."

He waggled his eyebrows and gave her a sexy growl. "You do it every damn day, baby doll, but I ain't got time to argue with you about it. Hannah's about to be back out here, and after we eat, I promised I'd go into Lincoln with Tuck to pick up the tuxes for tomorrow. Driven all over the damned state today."

Lifting her Runza just before she sank her teeth into it, she nodded. "Hey, yeah, why'd you go to Ogallala?"

"Needed supplies from Doc Halverson and Carrion's office. Lucked out. Their morning was full of surgeries, so I didn't have to listen to them drone on about how if I weren't a dumbfuck I'd trade in my cowboy hat for a white coat and have a *real* degree."

Before Indie could ask just who Dr. Halverson thought he was and if Luke would like for her to *adjust* whatever fancy-ass car he probably drove, Hannah burst back into the garage bay.

"Mommy says to say, 'Thank you very much, Mr. Camden' and to apologize for bothering."

"You're not bothering us, Hannah," Indie vowed. She was still trying to figure out when she'd ever let anyone decide anything for her. Maybe Luke was pissed about having to go ask for veterinary supplies and therefore cranky, or maybe he really didn't want to get back in his truck to go with Tucker to Lincoln. She knew he vastly preferred to be on horseback.

"Can I go see Romeo and Juliet, please?" Hannah gazed longingly at the horses in the nearby paddock.

"Sure." Indie grinned as Hannah took off.

Just then, a candy apple red Audi coupe pulled up to the bay doors. The distinctive sizzle under the hood said she was in for a long afternoon.

Luke's brow furrowed. Clearly, no one knew the owner around town. Indie wasn't surprised. You didn't see a lot of S5's out in ranch land, and in her experience only dickheads owned Audis. They were like magnets for forty-something year old men with more money than sense, making up for all they lacked in both heads with a fancy-ass car and a young mistress with enough air in her head to fill the tires on all the Camden tractors.

196

A moment later, her suspicions were confirmed. Guy was just a little older than her with hair he probably paid someone to slick for him and dressed in a suit that cost more than three-months rent on her apartment. He sauntered up to Luke, taking care not to get his alligator boots dirty.

"Is this really the only garage between Lexington and Ogallala?" he huffed.

Indie watched Luke's eyes narrow. "Not really sure to tell you the truth, but it's definitely the best."

Whipping the Gucci sunglasses off of his face, he gave Luke an incredulous glare. "I highly doubt that. Does anyone here know how to work on anything but John Deere products?"

Luke's nostrils flared and Indie noted the flex of his biceps in the pressed, button-down shirt he was wearing. She couldn't quite hide her smirk. If this douchebag wasn't careful, his ass was going to get an intimate meeting with Luke's shit-covered work boots, the kind *real* men wore.

Trying to remember that her daddy needed the money, Indie stepped up. She had a policy of adding a minimum $250 charge for being an asshole anyway. "We can take care of your S5. Sounds like you might have a leaky vacuum line. Audi's are notorious for that. Coolant's hitting your manifold. That's the sizzle you're hearin'."

"And whom might you be?"

Making no effort to hide her eye roll, Indie pointed to the sign over the garage. "I'm Indie Harper. This is Harper's Garage."

"I see, dear. And when will the actual mechanic be back?"

Luke huffed audibly. "*She's* the mechanic. Best there is. She just diagnosed your car without even lifting the hood."

"I see." If the man's lips curled anymore they'd block his pointy little nose and keep him from breathing. Indie didn't see this as a loss. "I think I'll just take my chances and find *someone* with some actual experience with luxury automobiles in Ogallala. I'm sure it will be fine."

"You got a fire-extinguisher in there?" Indie ordered her fists to remain by her side.

The man's pompous grin made her want to vomit. "No. Why in God's name would I travel with a fire extinguisher? Is that how you planned to 'work' on my car?" Okay, the finger quotes around the word work were several steps too far.

She bared her teeth, and Luke wrapped his arm around her to keep her from lunging at the asshat. Indie had never actually required her fists for fighting. They worked when necessary, but her tongue was a far more versatile weapon.

"My God, if you were any more of a tool you'd come with a Craftsman warranty. You know what, why don't you take your half-inch dick and your pansy-ass car all the way to Ogallala with no coolant in it. Take a deep breath when it starts smoking. 'Least that'll support your empty skull for a while. Most of the ranches along 80 have some kind of watering hole for the cattle. You could always drive it on in before it catches fire. 'Course, if you hit any of the cattle or the corn stalks out here, I'll guarantee you there'll be at least a dozen cowboys out to whip your sorry ass. But take your chances. Personally, my money's on the stalks and heifers."

She let the man spit and splutter while she returned to the minivan.

"Got no idea why you ain't already back in your fancy car, mister, but if you need some help I'd be happy to escort you," Luke snarled.

"I have never been treated so rudely. Believe me, I won't be back."

"Best news I've heard in a while," Indie called from the bay.

Joining her in front of the Caravan, Luke was chuckling. "How far you figure he'll get before it starts smoking?"

Smirking, Indie listened closely to the car as Mr. Asshat had to make a three-point turn to get out of the gravel driveway. "Worst case, he'll get it to the Kilroy's place, best case the south entrance to the Brady's ranch, but that's being generous."

Luke brushed a kiss on her cheek. "Let's finish eating. Then I've got a few calls to make." He fished his phone out of his pocket and gave her that wink that made her heart vibrate against her ribs.

"Who are you calling?" God, she loved that cool confident grin.

"I'm going to pick up Tucker, so I'll tell his daddy and brothers not to help the douchebag when he pulls up. Gotta call Cash and Sienna Brady and tell them the same."

Luke made no effort to hide his laughter when he leapt out of his truck beside a smoking Audi on the long dirt lane that led to Tucker's small home in the middle of four dozen corn fields. Tucker and his younger brother Wesley were both sporting the signature Kilroy smirk.

"Damn, city-boy, you drove right past the best mechanic this side of the Mississippi," Wesley chuckled. "Why didn't you stop?"

"Oh, he did," Luke chimed in.

Tucker stuck the tip of his tongue between his teeth laughing heartily. "I'd bet my profits on the entire back half of this farm you tried to tangle with Indie Harper and got your pretty boy ass handed right back to ya, didn't you?"

"City slicker didn't think my sexy little cowgirl could fix his over-priced smoke box here."

"Figured that was it. Three things you need to know once you enter Lincoln county. One, cows and corn are everything. If you think they ain't, you're probably a vegetarian, and we got no time for the likes of you anyway. Two, what doesn't kill ya will make ya stronger, everything 'cept cowgirls 'cause they'll just kill ya. And three, never, and I mean never, contend with Indieanna Harper."

"If you think about it, rule two and three both apply when it comes to Indie," Wesley considered. Tucker and Luke both nodded adamantly.

"Fine, whatever. I do so enjoy how idiotic cowboys like to revel in their own blatant stupidity by spewing forth country wisdom like the shit that comes out of all of your precious cows. I'm calling a tow truck."

Tucker, Luke, and Wes all narrowed their eyes as they edged closer, letting their biceps and their egos bulge.

"Come again, asslicker," Tucker snarled.

Seeming to realize that insulting cowboys in the presence of three men who slung hundreds of pounds of hay, heifers, and corn for a living might not have been his best idea, the idiot in question stumbled back until his ass smacked into the hood of his smoking car. He leapt forward when the heat scorched through his three-piece suit.

"Go ahead and call your tow truck, fucker, but Indie ain't fixing that car for you. Hope you make enough to buy another one of them things," Luke gestured to the car, "because it'll cost you at least that much to tow the thing to Ogallala."

"And if it's still sittin' on my property when we get back, we're having a good old-fashioned cowboy bonfire with it. Put your skinny ass on the spit, too. If I was you, I'd get before you get gotten," Tucker spat.

A few minutes later the guy was yelling at someone on his cell phone, and Luke and Tucker were barreling down the road headed to Lincoln.

"Is it bad that I can't wait to get this whole fucking thing over with?" Tucker finally stopped gnawing on the inside of his mouth and spit out what was wrong. Tucker Kilroy had been Luke's best friend for most of his life. They'd teamed up to terrorize their kindergarten teacher when she sent Tuck to the principal's office for bringing a bullfrog to school in his pocket. They'd been a team ever since. They'd worked through everything from learning to ride horses and then women, puberty, and life in general.

"Not as long as it's the wedding you want over with and not the marriage."

"Nah, I never want that to be over with. But this whole damn thing with Carolyn making Mel crazy. I swear I wish she'd been living with me long enough that we were common-law or whatever that is. I don't need her in a white dress. She's beautiful in one of my t-shirts."

"I'd say that's how you know it's right. Tomorrow night it'll all be over with. Things'll calm down after that. I kinda want to see Indie in a white dress, so enjoy it while it lasts."

"You think she's gonna stay this time? She looks mighty happy lately."

Luke grunted at that. "Swear to God, I never know what she's gonna do. Thought I'd convinced her last night, but the girl makes her mind up just to change it." That wasn't true. Indie was terrified and she let the fear make her decisions for her, but Luke wasn't going to voice that even to Tucker.

"Don't they all."

Luke chuckled. Maybe they did.

"I'm pulling out all the stops trying to get her to stay. Carolyn sure as hell ain't helping. Every time they're in fifty feet of each other Indie's right back to running."

"You expect Queen Carolyn to help you with anything you're dumber than I thought."

When Luke finally made it back to the ranch, anxious to be outside a truck for a few hours before the barbecue, Brock and Grant were sitting on his front porch.

Brock spun a football up in the air a few feet and then caught it with ease. "Figured we should practice a little before tonight. See if the Camden brothers still got it."

"We still got it," Grant and Luke answered simultaneously.

"Good, 'cause I got something to prove tonight. First actual game I've ever played in where I was legal. Plus, I want to show off for Hope," Brock readily admitted.

"I'd had something similar in mind," Luke agreed, thinking how much he might enjoy impressing the hell out of Indie on a makeshift football field.

"Then let's do this."

200

Chapter Nineteen

After taking the world's quickest shower, Luke toweled off and threw on a t-shirt and ratty pair of jeans. It was essentially just a backyard get-together with his closest friends and a football game. He'd been to a handful of rehearsal dinners as his brother and friends had married. This was by far the best kind to have to attend.

"I plan on drinking tonight. You're my ride," Holly informed him when she hauled herself up in his truck.

"I'll drive you out there, but I'm driving Indie home … alone … without my little sister."

"Fine." Holly rolled her eyes. "I might could help you with Indie, you know."

Genuinely humored, Luke fought not to roll his eyes. "Help me do *what* with Indie?"

"Help you keep her, dumbass."

"Oh, I have to hear this. What does my baby sister think I should do to get Indie to stay here?"

"It won't be easy."

This time Luke made no effort to halt his eye roll. "How much is Dad paying for your psych degrees, Hol? I haven't made it happen in fifteen years. I didn't figure it'd be easy."

Holly's glare said he should take his last comment back, but he didn't. "You and your smartass-self have to convince her that she isn't her mother."

Luke spit out the sip of Dr. Pepper he'd just taken as he headed through the first cattle guard between his land and Natalie's. "What? Indie Harper is about as unlike her mother as you and that heifer." He pointed to a grouping of cattle in a nearby field. "No, wait. You both have female reproductive organs. Okay, you and that bull out there."

Holly laughed at him outright. "I know that, and you know that, but we aren't the ones you have to convince. Every single time she does anything that even remotely reminds her of her of Carolyn it terrifies her. She's so afraid she might hurt you the way her mother hurt Ben she won't even give herself the opportunity to hurt you. It's fucked up, but that's what Indie sees as the ultimate love. She's sacrificing herself for you. Here's the real kicker — she doesn't even know that's what she's so afraid of. She projects her fear that she might be like her mother onto her mother, the mayor, and the town. She lumps it all in as one big terrorizing fear and runs away when she gets too close to considering putting herself right back in the middle of it. That is all coupled on top of her knowing she's a kickass human being, but not particularly liking her body. Now, ask me again how much my degrees cost, dipshit."

"How the hell do you figure all that?"

"You already knew about her issues with her perception of her weight, and I already know you're working to prove to her how beautiful she is inside and out. I could run down a lengthy list of psychological terminology and concepts that explain the thing with her mother, or you could just take my word for it. Don't you ever wonder why it seems like the only person you have to fight her for is *her*? She's her own worst enemy, and it's your job to show her that she's nothing like Carolyn without saying that directly."

Fucking hell, she's right. Barbed tension roiled in Luke's gut, slicing him to shreds. Bile singed his throat. His muscles weighted with what seemed like a problem with a dozen possible solutions but only one outcome. She was leaving. How the hell was he supposed to show Indie she wasn't like her mother if she wasn't even aware she thought she might be?

"You may not be able to do this, Luke. She might have to realize it on her own."

"Yeah," Luke swallowed harshly. "I'm aware."

Kilroy Farm was only a few miles from the ranch, so Luke and Holly spilled out of his truck a few minutes later. Natalie parked beside him. Grant had ridden with her. Austin, Summer and the babies followed. Brock had little Nathan's seat in one arm and the other around Hope. He was leading them down the hill towards the party, followed by Ev and Jessie who were balancing several casserole dishes of food from Camden Ranch.

A dozen discussions played out in Luke's mind as to how to go about convincing Indie that she wasn't her mother, but one was just as bad as the next.

"Oh no." Holly stopped in her tracks. Nearly bowling over his baby sister, Luke halted his pace and ordered himself to pay more attention. His entire family had stopped in their tracks.

"What?"

"Look." Holly pointed out into the massive, empty field the Kilroy boys had rotated out for that planting season. Long folding tables they'd borrowed from the church were set up in rows. The smokers had been going all day. The delectable scent of barbecue filled the air. Buns, pickles, and a dozen different side dishes, all provided by ranching and farming families that lived nearby, overflowed from aluminum trays and casserole dishes lined up on the tables near the smokers.

None of that looked out of place. However, Indie was up in her mother's face screeching. Just behind the mayor and Carolyn were at least two dozen people, dressed in white uniforms carrying trays, white linens, and chair covers. Luke took off down the slight hill that led to the field. Holly's rapid footfalls echoed just behind him.

"Mother, how could you do this?!" Indie demanded hatefully.

"What did she do?" Luke panted when he reached the showdown. He glared at Carolyn Harper for good measure.

Pain and volatile fury broadcast from every beautiful inch of Indie's face. It wasn't quite as bad as the blunt-force, horrifying embarrassment that shown on Melony's.

"Tell them," Indie ordered.

If Carolyn had rolled her eyes any harder, they would've lodged themselves in her skull. "I felt certain that I explained to Tucker's parents that the mayor's daughter's rehearsal dinner could not be some kind of after-football-game barbecue. I told Sandy I'd take care of everything."

Indie shook her head. "She decided to up and have Mel's rehearsal dinner catered to her specifications. Hell, they even brought white table cloths and prime rib to the event."

"Carolyn, why do you do this?" This time it wasn't Luke or Indie rebuking her mother. It was Ben. He and Diana made their way over from the parking area hand in hand. "This isn't want they wanted. Why can't you just leave 'em be? Let them be who they are."

A devastated Sandy Kilroy was trying to appease everyone by offering to set up more tables to hold the additional food when, "I am not the mayor's daughter!" erupted from Melony.

Shock colored Tucker's features, but he stood steadfast beside her. "I do not want some fancy dinner, mother! I told you this repeatedly. We're having a party just the way Tucker and I wanted, and you know what, if you want us to go through with the wedding the way *you* planned it, tomorrow, you need to tell everyone that didn't not receive an invitation from me that they need to leave. If you'd like to stay, you're welcome to, but you're not going to make me feel guilty or bully me into anything else. If you can't deal with that, you need to leave as well. We can get married in Lincoln at the courthouse. I'm not negotiating with you anymore. This is my marriage, which is vastly more important than what takes place tomorrow anyway. That wasn't something you ever quite figured out, was it? But guess what, I'm nothing like you. I already know the marriage is more important than the wedding. Seems like you haven't learned one damn thing in the last thirty years."

Even the ever-constant Nebraskan wind that whipped through the cornfields abruptly halted its incessant blowing at that declaration. No one blinked. No one spoke. No one even breathed. Every mouth in the general vicinity hung open in shock.

Red-faced and visibly fighting back tears, Melony grabbed Tucker's hand. His eyes closed for a brief moment before he turned with her to the crowds frozen in place around them. "Thank you all so much for coming," Melony voice caught. Luke noted Tucker's hand squeeze hers. "We're excited you're all here. Thank you for bringing food and helping us celebrate. You all mean the world to us, so let's have a barbecue." She forced a grin and gestured to the awaiting food.

Indie's mouth finally closed and she locked her dumbfounded gaze on Luke. He offered her a grin and opened his arms beckoning her to come hide in him.

Before she raced to him, Holly whispered, "Well, one of the sisters finally figured it out. Here's hoping Indie's next."

"I bet if you'd asked Luke to wear his old uniform, he would've just for you, Indie," Megan and Cindy joined Indie on the sidelines of what the men had declared to be the game field. Indie laughed, still an odd sensation given her current company.

"I should've. Definitely would not mind seeing him in *that* again."

"Tucker has this box with his old uniforms and letterman jacket and everything in it. He acts like it doesn't mean anything to him, but if I move the box, he freaks out," Melony giggled.

"Oh, they're all loving this. They've been talking about it for weeks," Cindy vowed.

"Brock is so excited he can't see straight." Hope, Brock's wife, joined the ladies on the sidelines. Indie didn't really know much about her. She was soft-spoken and kind, and Brock was clearly head over heels for her.

"He never got to play for the Glen, and he always wanted to so badly," Megan agreed.

"Yeah, I know. I can't really say I'm sorry about that, though, because I'm really glad he ended up in school in North Carolina with me. Fate was definitely on my side. He loves it so much here. I hate he didn't get to finish growing up in the Glen, but I don't think either of us would change how it all happened."

Indie considered that. She wasn't certain she really believed in fate. And if fate even existed why did some people end up with a great life and others a shitty one? How had she and her sisters won the loathsome horrible-mother prize in the parental lottery? It just didn't seem fair.

"I didn't realize you and Brock were high school sweethearts, Hope." Cindy gave her a genuine smile. Indie still couldn't quite negotiate the differences between Cindy Beltz in high school and her now. It seemed like she was potentially being punked, and it made her edgy.

"We weren't. It was a long, complicated road to us getting together, but it was worth every bump along the way."

Indie longed to demand that Hope define each and every 'bump' that had occurred, and if she was really sure they were all worth it. She wanted to know what Hope really thought of the Glen. She'd had a choice, it seemed. They could have stayed in North Carolina where they met, right? What had driven Brock home? Did Hope resent being made to live here?

The customary male grunts and trash talk erupted from the field as they lined up for the first play.

Before Indie could probe further, her father was upon them. "Indie, baby, I wanted to officially introduce you to Diana Wagner, my … uh … girlfriend." Ben stumbled over those last few words. He was going to need to work on that.

Ordering herself to breathe, Indie stepped forward and offered Diana her hand. The realization that she desperately wanted Luke by her side for this startled her almost as much as the welcoming warmth of Diana's smile.

"It's so nice to finally meet you, Indie. Your daddy talks about you all the time. He loves you so much." She beamed at Ben. "I'm gushing again, aren't I? I'm so nervous."

Indie couldn't help but grin. "Don't be nervous, and, believe me, I love my daddy more than anything. It's nice to meet you, too."

Her father was entirely too old to blush, but Indie noted the blood pooling in his cheeks.

"Well, she's always been my girl." Ben winked at her.

The wind picked up pace, whipping her long auburn hair across her face. She turned in time to see Luke throw a beautiful pass to Brock on the other end of the field. Her entire body lit with pride and excitement.

Brock reached and picked the ball out of the air with the skill of a fantastic athlete. He tucked it and ran before Beau Riggins could take him down.

The absolute bliss on Luke's face spoke directly to Indie's heart. She wolf-whistled and cheered with Hope.

Luke blew her a kiss just the way he always had when he completed a pass in high school.

The tension and outright fury she'd been clinging to after her mother's stunt and Melony's declarations to the crowd eased their vice grip. She willingly slipped into a younger version of herself yet again, and she welcomed the loss of the anger and confusion that had been her constant companions since she'd returned home.

"And that must be Luke." Diana grinned. "I haven't really been in town enough to be able to tell all of the Camden boys apart. They all look so much alike."

But they didn't. Indie wanted to argue that only Luke had those killer blue eyes and that sexy smirk that made her weak. Only Luke seemed to carry the weight of the entire world on his broad shoulders willingly and without complaint. Couldn't everyone see how his very soul shown in his eyes? Couldn't they tell that the color varied ever so slightly to reflect his emotions? Couldn't they see how capable his hands were no matter what needed to be done? His brothers and cousin were all admittedly good-looking cowboys, but Luke ... Luke was everything.

"Oh, well, they're used to being called by the other's names. Trust me, I birthed them and I swear half the time I called Austin Holly or Brock Luke. I remember being so tired after Holly was born I think I called Grant one of our dogs names that morning." Jessie sidled up beside Indie. Everyone joined her laughter at her own expense.

Indie was only more confused. They really were nothing alike. She knew Luke's mama was only teasing, but it bothered her. Was she really the only person that saw him for all that he was? Everything she'd ever understood about the way she loved and adored Luke Camden sharpened its focus. He wanted her to stay, and she kept running away. Why did she just keep hurting him like that?

Luke came off the field when the rag tag team of defensive players headed on. Grabbing a water bottle from one of the Styrofoam coolers, Indie raced towards him.

"You're amazing." Now she was the one gushing.

"Not bad for an old has-been," he chuckled and downed the water with one compression of the plastic bottle.

"Not bad at all, and you're not a has-been."

She rolled her eyes at his grunt of disagreement. His t-shirt had been discarded before the game began. Sweat glistened on his pecs. The sweet scent of corn and grass coupled with his musk on the cool breeze as it filled her lungs. His jeans rode deliciously low on his hips. Her mouth watered, and her heart played the part of the missing marching band.

"You are really sexy, though," she informed him.

His eyebrows lifted and her favorite half-grin played on the corners of his lips. "And what does that get me, sweetness?"

"Mmm, lots and lots of things." She planted a full, craving kiss on his mouth.

A moment later he took over the kiss, tossing the water bottle aside and wrapping her up in his sweaty embrace instead. He didn't seem to care that most of the residents of Pleasant Glen and at least fifty people from out of town were now watching their display. Or, maybe, he was showing everyone who she belonged to. That thought sent electricity zinging throughout her body. She pulled him closer, and his low rumbled moan slipped down her throat and nestled itself firmly in her heart.

Another round of applause and wolf-whistles broke out from the crowd. Grant jerked his brother back to reality. "We all know how much you love her, man. Save the celebrating for the end of the game. We need our quarterback."

Luke shot a cocky smirk around to his teammates. "You all can wait another minute or two." With that, he settled back in and extended the kiss.

Eventually, Brock and Tucker forcefully dragged Luke back onto the field. Everyone was laughing and having a great time. Sweet, encouraging grins were sent Indie's way from everyone in attendance, everyone except her mother. Carolyn was still pouting with the mayor. She'd refused to eat or socialize with anyone. No one seemed too concerned with this, and the lack of attention her fit was receiving only served to make her more unbearable.

"All right, Miss Indieanna, I know I ain't supposed to do this, but it kills me to see my son miserable, and you know I love you just as much as Luke. What can we do to get you to stay, sweetheart?" Jessie broached carefully, stepping out of her bounds but trying desperately not to offend.

"I really do want to stay, Mrs. Camden. You know I love him. It's just ..." she threw a weary glance at her mother," ... it's a lot to consider. I have to figure out how to be here with her and ... I don't know how to do that."

"I understand. I really do. I came up in Denver with a mama who didn't like me much more than yours seems to like you, but I learned eventually that she did and does love me. She just never really knew how to show me that. I ran here. I let Ev sweep me off my feet and right into a life I'd always wanted. I let him love me until he'd filled the voids my parents left behind. I think that's all Luke wants to be able to do for you. But you have to be here to let him. If that's what you want."

"I know. I think it is what I want, but I'm so scared I'll screw up again and hurt him. That's what I don't want. I can't do that again."

Instead of pointing out that her refusal to stay and marry her son was what was hurt him the most, Jessie Camden just smiled. "You see all of those boys you grew up with out there, trying desperately to hold on to something that's been long gone for well over a decade?" She gestured to the players huddled up on the field. Indie nodded. "What they're trying to recapture is important. It's worth holding onto, even if it's only for tonight. The past makes us who we are and gives us the foundation to become who we're meant to be. The hardest part of living is trying to figure out what to hold onto and what to let go of. And letting go sometimes takes a whole helluva lot more courage than holding on ever will. Holding onto memories that only serve as a reminder of pain, that's like grabbing the wrong end of the branding iron, sweet girl. You think you're gonna make your mark on your enemy, but you're the one that always ends up getting burned."

"Yeah," Indie's glance wandered back to her mother's pout. "I know you're right. Just not always easy to let go of what you should, I guess."

"Not easy at all, but sometimes holding onto the wrong things keeps us from reaching out and grabbing what we know we really need."

"Anna ... your mother isn't feeling well. When will all of this," the mayor gestured dismissively towards the game, "be over?"

Startled by his appearance, Indie leveled a cold glare on her stepfather. Before she could rebuke him, Jessie, Cindy, and Megan stepped up.

"Why did you just call her that?" Cindy huffed. "She hates to be called Anna. That isn't her name."

How did she know that?

"And she has always hated being called that, but you, Mayor Jenkins, seem to enjoy taunting her in any way you can. Is that because of her relationship with my son, or are you really just that asinine?" Jessie spat.

"He calls her that because he wants to hurt her. I would know. I recognize the look. I used to see it on my own face way too often." Megan squeezed Indie's hand. "And he does it because he knows this whole damn town vastly prefers Indie and Ben to him. He's jealous. Same reason he's so awful to all of the Camdens. Grow a pair, mayor. The game will be over when it's over. I seriously doubt anyone cares if you and Mrs. Jenkins leave."

Her would-be saviors circled closer, offering her love and support. No one had ever defended her directly to the mayor. Indie had no idea how to react. Suddenly, Luke's sweaty steadfast arms were around her waist, pulling her closer. He'd left the game. "You okay, sugar?" His glare was fixed on her stepdad. "You need something, mayor?"

"Carolyn expects everyone to be ready and at the mansion early tomorrow morning for photographs. This ridiculous *party* has gone on long enough."

"Says who?" Holly Camden chanted as she approached. "We'll all be there in plenty of time to see Tucker and Mel say I do. Don't mean we can't do whatever the hell we want to tonight."

"Let the kids play, Ernie. My God, they ain't hurting anything," Ev Camden leveled his decree, wielding the respect of everyone in attendance. The fact that the entire town would readily follow his orders visibly infuriated the mayor.

Tucker and Grant fell in at Luke's sides. "Hear, hear, mayor. We got a few more plays and then we're moving the party up to the creek. We'll all be there when we get there tomorrow. Mel can walk down the aisle anytime she damn well feels like it," Tuck informed him.

And as any great politician does when faced with his outraged constituents, Ernie Perkins slithered backwards. He glanced nervously from Ev to Jessie, then to Tucker's parents who'd come to see what the fuss was about. Indie couldn't help but revel in the outcry of support. She'd never asked for any of their help, but they all offered it readily.

Drawing in a deep breath of Luke-scented air, Indie swallowed down raw emotion. Maybe Jessie was right. Maybe she'd clung too long to a set of parents who didn't want her or deserve her instead of reaching out and grabbing on to the people that really did.

"I would think that you all would have enough respect for both Melony and Carolyn to want to be there for all the hard work that's been done for a proper wedding. I'm sorry I clearly misjudged you all. If you want to stay and *play*, be my guest. This seems a bit of an overreaction to me asking when the party would be over."

Ah yes, telling the opposition they're overreacting, classic move. Indie rolled her eyes. "I really don't think this reaction is only in response to your question, *Dad*," she sneered. "I think we've all been pretty pissed off with you in general, and then the stunt you pulled trying to cater a damned barbecue has everyone a little on edge. Take Mama on home. I'm sure you have a full night of her bitching to get to."

"We were only trying to help out. That's how I run this town — helping out our neighbors and caring for other's well-being. Your mother and I are naturally concerned this could get out of hand."

"Oh, that's rich." Natalie Camden rolled her eyes.

"She's right," Ev agreed. "Only person you've ever been interested in helping is yourself, Ernie, and these kids, who aren't really kids anymore, are playing ball in a cornfield. Other than them all being sore tomorrow, what in God's name could be wrong with that?"

The mayor's eyes narrowed in on Ev. Outright gall radiated in the air between them. Indie's stomach tensed as she watched what was about to happen. Her heart leapt to her throat when Ernie's fists clenched by his sides as his face reddened in fury.

Luke eased Indie behind him as he, Grant, Austin, and Brock closed in ranks around the man that had raised them. Tucker, Wesley, and Duke Kilroy Jr. and Sr. joined the line. If Ernie thought he was going to hit Everett Camden, he had several fists anxiously waiting to prove him wrong.

"How like Ev Camden to start a fight he knows he can't lose," Ernie spouted nonsensically.

"I'm not starting anything. I'm telling you to leave my children and all of their friends be. I will fight for my kids. Maybe you should try it sometime." He gestured to Indie and Miranda, who were both trying to see from behind the wall of men in front of them.

Peeking out from behind Luke's massive form, Indie saw what looked oddly like terror freeze in the mayor's eyes. What on earth was going on? How had her baby sister's rehearsal dinner barbecue turned into this?

"And there you have it. Caught in the Camden web once again. We'll see you all in the morning. Don't be late," Ernie huffed as he turned on his heels and stalked off.

"What on earth is he talking about now?" Jessie demanded of her husband who appeared equally dumbfounded. "What web?"

"Darlin', your guess is as good as mine. You know everything I know. I told you what went on in his office that day. I 'spose he's still ornery about the land tax we argued over. Man's more useless than tits on a bull. He's hated us for years. Not a thing I can do about it, and I'm sure as heck not gonna lose sleep over it."

Jessie glanced around the gathered crowd and shook her head. "Come on, this is Tuck and Melony's party. You all go have fun. Don't let him take it from you. It's not worth it."

Turning and pulling Indie back into his arms Luke had a somewhat delusional fantasy about their wedding being something akin to one of the McCoy daughters wanting to marry one of the Hatfield boys.

Mayor Jenkins was dumber than a stump and twice as nervous as a long-tailed cat in a room full of rocking chairs. He always had been. He clearly always would be. Shaking his head, he debated asking Indie if she wanted to head up to the creek with everyone or if she'd rather go home and talk.

Her pine-green eyes were alight with questions. "How does no one know why Ernie hates your daddy so much?" she whispered. "He seemed afraid of him."

"Sugar, if I even had a guess, I'd sure as hell tell ya. He got his panties in a wad when Dad took him to task about the taxes on Brock's half of the ranch when the deeds were changed. That's all any of us know."

Natalie and Holly both nodded their agreement.

"He's mad because he was looking to make a tidy profit off anyone who handed land down to their kids. The Kilroys, the Bradys, the Kennedys, the Pearsons, us, everyone who has multigenerational land," Natalie explained. "Dad called him on the carpet. He lost a lot of money he thought was going to be the county's and would ultimately fatten his paycheck."

The furrow of Indie's brow said she didn't believe that was it.

"Yeah, and just where does our mayor think he's going on my land?" Tucker gestured to a few swaying corn stalks in a nearby field.

Someone was walking through them. Ernie was the only person missing. Was all of that some kind of distraction for something else?

"Stay right here." Luke brushed a kiss on Indie's forehead and took off with Tucker and Wesley Kilroy.

"Shh, shh, I want to see what he's doin'," Tucker hissed as they neared the field.

Moving silently through cornstalks wasn't an easy task, but Luke slowed his pace and made do.

Wesley's boot snapped a stick and the sound announced their arrival. Luke, Tucker, and Wes all stopped to puzzle over the fact that the mayor had dropped what looked to be a sandwich bag full of dirt he'd shoveled from Tucker's field.

"What the actual fuck are you doing, Ernie?" Tucker stepped out from behind the stalks.

Ernie's hand trembled. "Soil sample. It's my right as the mayor of this town to make certain you're using ethical growing practices."

"Uh, no, no it ain't, and if you don't get your ass outta my field, I'll show you precisely where your rights end. Right about the line where the road turns into Kilroy land."

"If I were you, Tucker Kilroy, I'd bear in mind whose daughter you're marrying tomorrow, and on whose land you're marrying her."

"Fine. I marrying Ben Harper's daughter on the county's land. Don't even strain my mind to bear that."

"Carolyn was right. Melony could've done so much better." With that, Ernie stomped out of the field and left Kilroy land.

"What the hell?" Wesley lifted the sack of dirt.

"No idea. It's like Dad said, he's a useless as tits on a bull," Luke scorned.

"Ain't it obvious? He's trying to get me in trouble for something. He's been trying to ever since I started dating Mel. He had the county out here a few months ago checking for something I'd never even heard of. He's an asshole. Never gonna change."

Luke had no reason to think Tucker was wrong, but the whole thing sounded off to him. At that moment, he needed to get back to Indie. He'd worry over Ernie later. She needed to talk, and he was going to prove to her that he was capable of helping her work through anything without pressuring her into something she wasn't ready for.

It took him less than a minute to locate his sweet baby still talking to his mama. "You wanna go up to the creek with everyone, doll baby, or you wanna head back to the ranch? Your dad and Diana left together a little while ago. I'm paying him to keep letting her stay over so you'll have to stay with me."

"Funny."

"Come with us, Indie," Melony begged. "This night has been crazy. I want you to come."

Luke knew she'd never turn down her little sister. Indie Harper was loyal through and through.

Her gaze flickered from Luke to Tucker, to Luke's parents and brothers. Right then, he knew he was in for a long night. He needed to get her to talk even if it was in his bed long after the impromptu bonfire at the creek. Whatever had shaken her, whatever she needed to know, he wanted to show her that he'd be right beside her to figure it all out. Still having no idea how to convince her that she was nothing like her mother, all he knew was she wanted to take things one day at a time. So that was precisely what he was going to do until he figured the rest out.

He stared unabashedly at her luscious ass when he helped her up in his truck. Damn woman drove him insane with need. He'd never get enough. Getting her to stay this time became more dire with every passing moment. His very breath depended on knowing she was his.

She leapt as soon as he cranked the engine. "I want to know what is going on with Ernie and your parents. That was weird, and don't deny it."

"I ain't denying a thing, sugar bee. Your stepdaddy is more than a few bricks shy of a load. He was out in Tuck's cornfield taking some kind of soil sample with his hand and a sandwich bag. Crazy as a loon's what he is. You want to pick everything apart, I'll be right there with ya, but I honestly got no idea what the hell he's thinking. Tuck says he's trying to get him in some kind of trouble with the state. Maybe that's it."

"There's more to it than that. I just know. If that were all he was up to, what would that have to do with your family? I may hate Ernie, but I know him well enough to know there's more to it than him getting caught with his hand in the cookie jar or cornfield or whatever. And what in God's name is wrong with my mother? Catering a party someone else was throwing is extreme even for her. Melony's wedding has driven her right off the cliff of sanity, and she was only hanging on by a thread before."

"Your mama's always wanted to show off for the town, baby," he measured his words carefully. "Nothing new there either."

"The whole thing is just weird. I keep feeling like I'm gonna wake up and the entire last week is gonna be a dream. I don't like this."

A slight sense of panic crawled up Luke's spine. "What's *this* exactly?"

"Not you. I love being with you. But Mama's finally gone off the deep end. Ernie's up to no good. I don't know how I know. I just know. Dad has a girlfriend. Megan Morgan is *nice*. My little sister is marrying Tucker Kilroy. Cue the *Twilight Zone* music."

Chuckling, Luke laced his fingers with hers. "Things do change. This is the first time you've been home for any length of time in years. I know it seems like a lot, probably overwhelming, but I'm right here if you want to talk about any of it." There. That was good. He settled into this conversation, relaxing as he followed the line of pickups headed towards King's Creek.

"Even you've changed … a little."

And just like that tension hardened his muscles yet again. "Thought you liked the changes I'd made?"

"I do. I guess it all just threw me a little more than I was expecting. All the new facets of making love with you. Sometimes, I kind of miss the old way, I think. As much as I get off being fucked in handcuffs." She shrugged. "I'm confused I guess."

"Indie, sugar, look over here at me."

Her eyes found his as he glanced away from the road he could damn near drive blindfolded. "Being with you," he shook his head trying to locate the perfect words, "making love with you is everything to me. Doesn't matter when, where, how, handcuffs, tie-ups, in the bed of my truck, up against my bathroom sink, or staring into your eyes with no accessories while I take you nice and slow in the bed at my house. None of that is as important as giving you all of me, taking care of you, worshipping your beautiful body, and bringing you satisfaction. I told you we can explore anything you want to explore. And if you need a night, a week, or hell an entire lifetime of plain vanilla sex, I'm still in this no matter what. And *that* right there will never change."

"I know." She leaned across the console and brushed a tender kiss on his jawline. "You mean the world to me Luke Camden. I just wish I knew how to be everything you need."

"You are everything I need, sugar. You don't even have to try. That's what I keep trying to tell you. Just be you. That's all I'll ever want."

Chapter Twenty

"Come on, Indie Jane, you know you want to," Luke coaxed again just before sunrise the next morning while he continually kissed her awake.

Incoherent groans were her only response. Staring down at her beautiful lips pursed in protest, the pink heat in her cheeks, and the soft slumber in her closed eyes, he swore he fell in love with her all over again laying there on his chest.

He'd more than proven to her the night before that he required no other accouterment other than his swollen cock to make sweet love to her.

"I made you coffee," he persuaded.

One eye opened to half-mast, and he got a slight grunt of interest.

"And my girl's gonna have to go spend the rest of the mornin' with her sisters, putting on dresses and crap all over their faces, which you know you hate, so have a little fun with me before you go."

"Nooooo," she whimpered.

"Are we no-ing the dress and makeup or getting up?"

"Both!"

"If you get up now, I'll watch the race with you all afternoon tomorrow." He pulled out the big guns.

"Promise?"

"Promise."

"And we can make fun of everyone at the wedding today and do something naughty somewhere in the mayor's house?"

"Oh, honey, you are singing my song. I'm all over that, and I'll be all over you all afternoon."

"And we can go to the hill on the other side of the lake for the sunrise?"

"Not if you don't get your sassy-ass moving, sugar."

"Fine." She sat up and extended her arms up over her head. The sheets she'd buried herself under tumbled down. Luke was instantly mesmerized by the soft sway of her ample breasts and the sweet raspberry heat of her nipples.

"Mmm, maybe we should stay in bed, now that I see you like this." Tracing his fingertips up her waist, he spun them gently around her nipples, awakening them to his touch.

"No. You woke me up for a horseback ride, so we're going riding, cowboy."

"You could ride me instead."

"Should'a thought of that before you woke me up."

Low fog covered their bodies as they made their way to the barn. As soon as the sun rose, it would burn it all away. Luke couldn't wait to watch it with Indie.

When they arrived at the barn, Summer was brushing Whirlwind, and Luke wondered if she planned to ride her without Austin's knowledge.

"She's just loving on her." Austin appeared out of the thick fog settling over the fields. He had baby Hank on his shoulder and was holding J.J.'s hand.

"You sure you don't mind if I ride her?" Indie asked cautiously.

Summer gave her a sweet grin. "I don't mind at all. I just miss her. She needs a good ride. She'll be thrilled."

"I'm sure she'll miss you. I'm definitely not a barrel racer. I saw you ride several years ago in Broken Bow. You were amazing. You won that night, didn't you?"

"I'm honestly not sure. They all blurred together. I loved racing, but it never really got me where I needed to be. That's the thing with a race. The finish line might not be where you're supposed to stop. Austin taught me that."

Austin and Luke joined the girls. Austin brushed a kiss on Summer's cheek. "If you think about it, racing did get you here in a roundabout kind of way."

"I guess," Summer shrugged. "However I got here, I'm never leavin', Austin Camden, so you better love me forever."

"That was always my plan. Now get your sassy self back inside. Hank's grunting and you know I ain't got the equipment to feed him."

"And didn't you luck out in that department, cowboy?"

"Sugar, if I had titties of my own, I'd never get a damn thing done. I'd just play with 'em all the time."

Everyone erupted in laughter as Luke shook his head at his little brother.

"Hey, Summer, can I ask you something really quick before you go?" Indie sounded frantic. Luke's surprise silenced his laughter.

Summer lifted Hank from Austin's shoulder. "Sure."

"How'd you know this was your finish line?" She gestured around the ranch, and Luke's heart stalled. He didn't breathe, terrified he'd somehow miss Summer's response.

Summer considered for a long moment. "I guess I finally got sick and tired of running. I swear, I ran my whole damn life. Ran around barrels, ran from my daddy, from my ex, from everything. A good friend of mine told me that I had to realize I was worth saving. Kind of like I had to figure out what I was running from so I'd know who to run to."

With that, Hank broke out in a pitiful wail of hunger. Indie gave Summer a quick wave before she saddled Whirlwind. Luke longed to ask what Indie had made of all of that, but he decided to let her simmer with it for a while. He'd done enough talking.

When they returned from their ride, Indie cradled little Cassie in her arms and gave her a morning bottle.

"I ain't ever gonna be able to sell that cow, am I?" Brock quizzed Luke quietly.

"Hey, if keeping her here will keep Indie here, I'll buy her off of ya."

"You really gonna be that guy? You're gonna be the rancher with a pet cow?"

"Think that shows you just how bad I want her to stay."

"I'd say so. I just wouldn't be telling anybody around town you're gonna have a pet cow."

"Good plan."

Four hours later, Luke was sitting in Tucker's house assuring him, yet again, that he had Melony's ring in his jacket pocket. Fighting not to roll his eyes, he held up the diamond band and shoved Tucker onto one of the kitchen stools. Wesley handed him a bottle of beer from the fridge and Luke ordered him to drink it.

"I still don't know how the hell to be married. What was I thinking?" Tucker took a long drag of the bottle.

"Tuck, bro, you need to chill. She loves you. You love her. There'll be good times and bad times, but you'll get through them together. Life will be great," Wesley sighed. This was the tenth time a similar speech had been made.

"Oh Jesus, what if I get her pregnant?!"

"I'm gonna go with the obvious answer of *then you'll have a baby*," Luke chuckled. "Mel will make a great mom, and if you just do what she says all will be well. You can raise up another wide receiver." He checked his watch again. One more hour and he could shove Tucker in front of the altar on the Mayor's property, Melony would make her appearance, and Tuck would be able to breathe again.

"Oh my God, a kid! I don't know what to do with a baby. He doesn't have to play football if he doesn't wanna either. I mean, I don't want him to get hurt. If he's gonna play, we need to get him on a good team, though." Tucker's eyes spun and Luke and Wes made a concerted effort not to laugh at him outright. He was now concerned about the peewee football career of his child who was not yet conceived. "Hey, if he wants to try for Young Rodeo you think Austin would help him train? The competition's tough."

Biting his lips together and shaking his head, Luke finally managed, "I'm sure Austin would be glad to help out your kid, Tuck. Let's maybe, you know, get him birthed before we buy him a helmet and chaps though, okay?"

"Yeah, that's a good plan. You're really smart." Tucker vowed like Luke had just single-handedly negotiated the Iranian disarmament.

"I'd highly recommend you knock your wife up before you start signing your kid up for sports, myself," Wesley chimed in.

"Shut the fuck up, Wes," Tucker huffed.

Throwing his arms up in the air, Wesley shuffled down the hallway. "You're acting crazier than a shit house rat, bro. Get it together."

Finally, mercifully, an hour and two minutes later, Luke shoved Tucker Kilroy up in front of the crowd of white folding chairs in the back field of the largest home in Pleasant Glen. "Look at me," he ordered quietly. Tucker complied. "Do not move from this spot until you see Melony come down the aisle. I'm going to go walk Indie down. What are you *not* going to do?"

"Get married."

"Tuck, I swear to God I will whip your ass six ways from Sunday if I have to, and I won't even mess up my tux. Now, what are you *not* going to do?"

"Move."

"Good." Luke slapped him on the shoulder and sighed his relief as he offered a few smiles to the gathered guests. To his knowledge, there hadn't been this many people in Pleasant Glen since … well … ever. Carolyn Jenkins must've invited half the damn state.

Following the sounds of hissed whispers, Luke located the rest of the wedding party gathered behind the tent that had been set up for the reception.

"No," Melony spat. "Daddy is walking me down by himself. You and Ernie go now. Just like the preacher said."

"I firmly believe we should all walk you down, Melony Grace Harper. I saw it in a magazine. It was all very nice, and we all had a hand in raising you," Carolyn smarted.

"Mother, have you been drinking?" Indie demanded hatefully. "What is wrong with you? We've been practicing this all fucking morning. Just go!"

"Carolyn, if you don't mind, I'd like to walk my youngest daughter down the aisle. I think you've done enough." Even Ben looked outraged. Luke had never seen Indie's father lose his temper.

"Let's just go." Ernie took Carolyn's hand and guided her towards the aisle.

"I swear, the peroxide they pour all over her head to turn her that blonde has pickled what was left of her brain," Indie snarled.

Chuckling, Luke brushed a kiss on her cheek. "You look damned pretty all dressed up, baby doll." She did. Dressed in a short, green sleeveless dress that showed off her gorgeous hourglass figure with her hair up in a fancy twist and makeup highlighting her face. He didn't get to see her in dresses often.

According to Indie, her mother had stuffed her into a dress that couldn't handle her rapidly developing cleavage in seventh grade and ordered her to her first middle school dance. When she arrived, she was informed by the principal that she was dressed inappropriately because 'big girls had to cover up.' Her choices had been to change into her P.E. uniform that was stowed in her locker or to return home. In true Indie Harper format, she'd waited on the principal to return to the dance, had pulled the battery cables on her car, deflated all of the tires — complete with taking the valve stem caps — and had raced home and vowed never to wear another dress again as long as she lived.

Luke hadn't attended the seventh grade dance. He hadn't yet figured out why any guy in his right mind would give up a night at the local rodeo to go *dance*. The first time he'd heard Indie recount her reasoning for never wearing dresses, he would have given anything to have been there for her. He would've helped her work over the bitch principal's car and would have run with her wherever she wanted to go. He knew there had to have been tears that night, knew she had to have ached with the rejection of her own body, though she'd never confessed to that.

The gall he still felt dragged him back to the present. He offered her another smile and brushed a kiss just under her earlobe as he whispered, "I think I prefer my girl in them Wrangler Q-babies she wears so well with a smudge of grease on her face, or better yet, nothing but that damned sexy red lingerie you wear that drives me wild." He winked at her.

"And that, Luke Camden, is one of the many reasons I love you." She was bringing the L word in more often than ever before. He couldn't help but hope against hope that it meant something this time.

"Luke, is Tucker okay? He seemed a little ... *weird* ... when he called me this morning," Melony whispered as the music began.

"Just a little nervous. Wants to do right by you. Soon as you walk out there, he'll be fine."

Indie, Miranda, and Melony all beamed at him.

"Any guy that can make all my girls smile is one hell of a man." Ben offered him his hand. After Luke accepted the hand shake, Ben turned to Melony. "You sure ready for this, little one?"

Melony brushed a sweet kiss on her daddy's cheek. "I'm ready, Daddy. I promise."

"Then we better get to it," he choked.

Luke lowered his head. Wesley Kilroy, who was walking Miranda down, did the same. Neither would ever admit to seeing the well of tears Ben Harper was trying to dam back with sheer strength of will.

With every step Luke and Indie progressed down that aisle, he prayed this wouldn't be the last aisle he got to walk her down. They parted at the preacher and watched Tucker and Melony vow to love one another for the rest of their time on earth. Tuck never missed a beat. Just as Luke had predicted, his nerves dissolved immediately as soon as Ben placed Melony's hands in his.

Chapter Twenty-One

There were enough officials from the state capital offices oohing and ahhing over the reception to keep Carolyn happy for the next year and a half.

"Boy, she really thinks she's shitting in high cotton now, doesn't she?" Indie sniped as Luke pulled out a chair for her after they'd gotten a plate of food.

"You been in Oklahoma way too long, sweetness. They only shit in cotton south of the North Platte River. Up here we shit in corn, remember?"

"All I know is she's *full* of shit."

At that moment, Carolyn was laughing ostentatiously with the lieutenant governor's wife.

"Can't really argue with that."

The reception droned on with Luke growing more antsy by the moment. He pulled at his tie for the fourth time in as many minutes and lifted his hat to wipe away a ring of sweat along the band.

Indie had been yanked up for another picture with Melony and Miranda, and he was bored out of his mind. If one more good-for-nothing politician out of Lincoln tried to schmooze him by talking about how much respect and concern they had for the small town ranch owners, he was going to rope several of them, throw them on horseback, and tell them to go pull his bulls off of his heifers in his back two-hundred acres, and move them to the next fields over, which was his task for the next morning. Then he'd be happy to talk with them about how hard he worked and why he didn't much appreciate them taxing his land and his cattle at the time of purchase and then again at the time of sale.

The seductive sway of Indie's dress and the tempting line between her breasts created by the tight fit of the bodice on her gown made his mouth water. She and Miranda were sharing a vexing grin and trying not to laugh at whatever they'd just shared. She looked good enough to eat, and he sure as hell wanted a bite.

He shoved his hand in his tux pocket, searching for the bandana he'd shoved there for the purposes of mopping the sweat off his brow. His heart leapt to a sprint when his hand landed on a slip of elastic. Saliva flooded his mouth as he discreetly glanced downward to confirm that there was a crimson thong constructed of smooth satin and rough lace in his pocket.

Summoning Herculean levels of self-control, he ordered himself not to pull the panties from his jacket, bring them to his face, and inhale the delectable flavors of his Indie. His cock stiffened painfully as their eyes locked one each other with magnetic force. She was thirty feet away from him, and he swore he could feel the heat of her lush curves imprinted on his skin. Sexy little minx knew she was killing him slowly.

When she finally returned to the seat beside him he wrapped his arm around her and leaned in. "You're making me ache, Indie Jane. Knowin' your bare under that dress, open and ready for me." He whispered a kiss just below her jawline. "Naughty girl needin' to be owned, aren't 'cha?"

The mischievous twinkle in her eyes and the purse of her full lips put a stranglehold on his aching cock. She was not longer a craving. She was a requirement.

"Lord Almighty, I need you, sugar. Getting damned ornery with needin' you, honestly." Glancing around to make sure no one was paying them too much attention, he nibbled her earlobe, making her shiver. "They're gonna expect us to dance here in a minute, but after that, whenever you're ready, head inside the house. I'll make nice while you figure out where you'd like to be fucked, then I'll come find you. And then I ain't gonna be so nice."

"Mmm," she breathed. "You're making me wet, cowboy."

"Good, darlin'. I'll gorge myself on your honey before I bury myself inside that greedy little snatch, so sweet for me. Don't make me wait, Indie Jane. I'm flat out of patience. You put your panties in my jacket, you're getting it rough."

"Good. That's precisely how I want it," she defied. "Am I finding a room in the house or a location on my body where I'd like to be fucked?" The teasing coo of her voice, and the fire storm in her eyes damn near fried his brain.

"Oh, sugar, you are treading on dangerous ground."

"I like dangerous. Always have. Always will. Remember our deal? You keep me sane. I'll keep you wild. Right now, I'm needin' a whole lot of sanity, cowboy."

"Indieanna, the wedding party has been asked to dance! Why aren't you moving?" Carolyn's screeching tone stabbed through the palpable need between Luke and Indie at the same moment her garishly red fingernails stabbed into Luke's shoulder. He turned to glare at the woman, equally furious at both what she'd interrupted and the claw marks dug into his arm.

Rolling her eyes, Indie jerked Luke out of his seat. "We're going, Mother. I see no one's thought to Xanax your punch cup yet. Have to remember to do that before big events."

Gnawing on the inside of his lip to keep from unloading all of his murderous thoughts on Indie's mother in front of the entire town, Luke eased Indie into his arms and started to sway.

"I'm sorry she's such a bitch," Indie sighed.

"It's fine, darlin'. Come here and dance with me."

It wasn't fine, but he refused to point out that her mother had always been and would always be a bitch. He kept his eye ever on the prize. She needed precious little justification for leaving the Glen because of her mother. He'd be damned if he was going to give her the ammunition to kill him with.

Some song Luke didn't know played from the band, and she nuzzled her head against his neck. She was in his arms, her breasts teasing his chest with each sway, her ample ass just below his fingertips, and the sweet scent of her hair played in his breath. His left hand seemed to have a mind of its own. It slipped lower, longing to cup her lower curves and squeeze. Self-control be damned. The thong in his pocket burned a hole in his resolve. The entire fucking town was watching them. The savage beast housed in his soul that no one could summon but her shook its cage.

"I ain't gonna make it through this song, Indie. I told you, my patience is gone." Trying to be discreet, he rocked his hips forward ever so slightly, letting her feel what she was doing to him.

A soft moan hummed from her. "Can't really sneak out right now without a distraction." And there it was. That sexy as hell sly grin that always turned him inside out formed on her face. She stepped back and clutched her side.

Trying not to laugh, Luke plastered on a worried expression. "You okay, sugar?"

"Yeah. Damned dress is pinching me. There's a tag or something. It's leaving a mark. Can you help me?" she announced just a little too loudly. Then she took his hand and glided out of the crowd and up the deck stairs. All eyes were on Tuck and Melony. No one seemed concerned about Indie.

Racing into the house, Indie almost toppled over one of the caterers carrying out a tray of those ridiculously tiny sandwiches no one at the party really understood. Indie assumed her mother and her stepfather's cohorts were only pretending to conceptualize why someone would make sandwiches that one needed to consume twelve of to feel full.

"Please watch where you're going, Miss. Guests are supposed to be outside," the caterer scolded.

"This is my house. I'll be wherever the hell I want to be."

Luke's quiet chuckle and her hand tucked safely in his spurned her on. Heady rebelliousness fed her soul. So, there were people downstairs. No problem. Heading into the grand living room that Indie despised, she took the marble steps two at a time with Luke hot on her heels.

She halted abruptly on the upstairs landing. Bile flooded her throat. An enormous portrait of her mother stared her down. Their eyes were exact duplicates. Indie fought to keep down the thirty-five finger sandwiches she'd consumed in the last few hours. Eyes were the worst possible thing you could inherent from someone you despised. Malaise roiled in her gut. How could she be certain that she didn't somehow see the world the same way her mother did? She had her eyes. How could she be sure she wouldn't do to Luke what her mother had done to her daddy? It was all right there in the spite penned in her mother's pine green eyes.

Brazen defiance lit through her veins. She turned the corner into what had once been Miranda's room. Pulling open one of the bedside drawers she located a bottle of lube and handed it to Luke.

He stared at it like she'd just gifted him gold bricks. "This mean what I think it means?"

"I'm certainly hoping so. Come on." Racing to the end of the long hallway, she didn't stop until they were in her stepfather's home office.

Luke eased the door closed. The click of the lock spiked her blood.

"Had a feelin' you'd pick here." His cool blue eyes ate her up with a hunger that bordered on possession. He caged her up against a wall and branded her lips with a drugging kiss. His tongue took ownership of her mouth, punishing and forgiving in a rush of carnal heat.

He spun her around and backed her towards the massive oak wood desk in the center of the room. In a brutal showing of male intention, he shoved a newspaper, a few files, a ridiculous marble name plate, and an acrylic desk set off the desk and into the wide leather chair. She'd obliterated his endless control. The ultimate aphrodisiac. His raw power drew her in like a drug she required to exist. Her entire body honed in on his. She needed to be devoured, needed to be fucked so hard she forgot who she was, and far more importantly, who she came from. He pulled the pins from her hair and

224

let it cascade down her back. His hands were up her dress a half-second later, gripping her hips, rocking his erection against her mound.

"Lift your dress, sit back on the desk, spread your legs, and be quiet for me, sugar. I'm hungry."

"Oh, fuck yes." Her ass collided with the edge of her stepfather's desk as she complied.

"More. Lean back on your arms. That's it." His commands were laced with greed, and she wanted nothing more than to misbehave with Luke Camden.

He fell to his knees, placed his massive hands on her inner thighs, and spread her out wide. She gripped the far edge of the desk behind her as his tongue traced up and down her slit.

"Already nice and wet for me aren't you? You need it bad don't you, sugar?"

"Now." She shuddered as his lower teeth slide along her drenched folds.

"And my beautiful girl's wanting it dirty. So damned perfect." He leaned her back an inch or two more and his tongue spun anxiously over her taint. Her entire body quaked with need. The hard wood under her ass juxtaposed the tender worship of his tongue.

"Pretty little rosebud. All for me." That was all the warning she received before he moved his ministrations to the puckered opening of her backside, painting it with his tongue.

Her entire body clenched. "Relax for me, sugar. Just relax."

Indie felt the rough calluses on his thumbs gently ease her lips apart. A loud moan flew from her lungs as he drew her clit into the fiery heat of his mouth and suckled.

"Quiet, baby. I ain't near finished." He fucked her opening with his tongue, jamming it inside of her, driving her to the brink of sanity.

She managed to quell her moans to soft needy sighs.

"Please, Luke, I need more."

"I know precisely what you need, Indie. I always know." With that, he took one long draw on her clit and then released her as he stood. He flung off the tux jacket and bowtie then rolled up his sleeves, revealing his powerful forearms. His lips were sheened with her heat.

She sank her teeth into her bottom lip to keep herself from pleading again. Next came the buckle on his belt. His prominent erection protruded and sprang free when he lowered his briefs.

She watched him grip his thickened shaft. Pearly beads of pre-cum glistened on the head of his cock. She licked her lips. Her body rocked

225

anxiously on the desk. Easing her legs apart once more he pressed the side of his shaft against her slit tempting her clit with his crown.

"Oh, yes," she gasped. He pressed harder, back and forth against her. The exquisite friction almost more than she could bear. "Oh, right there," she groaned when he hit the perfect spot. The next second, one hand covered her mouth and the other continued its delectable torture as a guide for his cockhead. Back and forth with unrelenting pressure right where she desperately needed him.

"I said quiet, baby. Be nice and quiet and let me give you what you need."

Her body undulated with the slide of his shaft. Every pulse point timed itself to the strokes of his cock against her. Warmth licked up her spine. Her racing pulse throbbed in her clit. Her pussy wept out its pleasure. She rode the delicious friction until pure, unadulterated bliss erupted from her core. She broke on a muted scream against his hand.

He gave her no time to recover. The aftershocks of her orgasm cinched around his cock as he pounded inside of her, as he gave her precisely what she required.

Okay, she needed to go on the pill. Clearly, condoms were just not going to happen with them. Given the heavenly feeling of his satin-covered steel member thrusting inside of her, she couldn't find it in herself to care.

Her body inhaled his. His hands lifted her ass, giving himself the perfect angle to hit every single one of her hotspots. The question was no longer could she stand to move back to the Glen. It was how on earth would she ever give this up if she couldn't.

"So. Fucking. Tight," he grunted. She watched his jaw flex as he took her fast and furiously. He slowed only long enough to lube up his fingers. "Lay all the way back for me."

She'd never been more compliant with anyone in her entire life. She laid out on the desk letting the skirt portion of her dress fall over her stomach. His slick fingers rubbed at the opening of her backside and then gently eased inside the tight ring of muscle.

Her breath caught on a slight moan of incoming pleasure. "Feels so good when I touch you here, doesn't it, sugar?"

"Yes," she managed as her body drew him in further.

A greedy growl thundered from his lungs. "God, I can feel myself, Indie. I can feel my cock inside of you. Drives me fucking wild."

All the times they'd been together, all of the kinky things they'd shared in the last week, she'd never seen him quite like this. His eyes shimmered with lust, open in half-slits of pleasure. His expression

226

loaded with undiluted sin. Every muscle in his body tensed. All sense of the man she loved burned away into primal savage beast. All because of her. The heady cocktail of lust, love, and power made her believe in that moment that she could love him forever.

"You don't want me to come in your pussy though, do you? If I pull out, I'm gonna unload all over your pretty little dress. So, tell me. Tell me where you want my cum, darlin'. You want it right here?" He twisted two of his fingers together, added more lube, and pressed fully inside of her ass. "Sweet little rosebud. I'm gonna open it wide." He did indeed spread his fingers wider, readying her.

"*YesOhGodYes*," bled together into one long plea.

He granted her one more thrust in her pussy before he withdrew. Her body shook with the unwanted vacancy. He quickly edged her ass to the very end of the desk, applied more lube, and then eased just his cockhead inside her opening.

"That feel good?"

"Oh, hell yeah," she writhed against the desk. It wasn't lost on her that he was fucking her ass in her stepfather's office. She exulted in what her mother would surely call heresy. Always her perfect partner in crime. Her perfect lover. Her best friend. She really couldn't ask for anything more than Luke.

"Breathe for me, baby. Just breathe. That's it." Tension was visibly locked in his agonized expression. Sweat glistened on his temples. "God, sugar. I've got to move."

"Yes. It feels amazing. I need more." She relaxed her body and pressed outward against him.

He surged inside of her, still trying desperately to go easy.

"I'm fine. Just take me."

That did it. He pulled away, added another round of lube, and pressed in, quickening the pace with each pass. His fingers moved back to her clit, strumming her like an instrument only he knew how to play.

She shook. Her body rolled in exquisite desperation. Another orgasm throbbed behind her mound. Every nerve ending in her body sizzled with need.

"Every single part of you is mine, Indie. All of you. You understand that? All mine."

His words shattered her thoroughly. The quick flexes of her orgasm against his cock milked his climax from him as well. They came together, gasping for breath and groaning out their mutual pleasure.

"Just relax." He soothed when he'd caught her breath as he steadied her body carefully. "Everything feel okay?" She gave him a quick nod, since she'd never felt better in her entire life. Gently, he eased out of her and grabbed tissues from the box now on the floor to clean her up.

"Come here to me." He helped her up and then before she quite got her footing, he scooped her into his arms and settled them in an oversized leather chair in the corner. Tucking herself against him, she wished for several long moments that she could stay right there curled up in his arms forever.

"That was amazing," she whispered.

"You're telling me. Making love with you is always incredible, but that … that was something else."

She brushed a tender kiss on his neck, tasting the tang of his sweaty musk. His pants were still undone. She could feel the cool metal of his belt buckle against her ass and the elastic of his briefs along her thigh. The sensations of being completely absorbed by him soothed her soul.

"Guess we have to get dressed and go back out there." Regret weighted her words.

"Just sit with me for a few more minutes. I need to hold you." He cradled her closer. She certainly didn't mind until the sound of footfalls echoed down the hallway.

"Shit!" She leapt out of his lap, ignoring the twinge of discomfort in her backside.

Luke quickly buttoned up and attempted to restore the desk. "There's lube on this desk pad thing. Pretty sure we're had."

"Who cares? Just come on." As soon as Indie righted her dress, they flew to the door. Pressing her ear against it, she tried to discern who was talking on the other side.

She leapt backwards when whoever it was jangled the doorknob. "What are we going to do?!"

Luke's quick gaze flitted around the room. There was nowhere to hide. A few filing cabinets stood along one wall. They could hide on the side of them for a moment, but as soon as whoever was out there fully entered the room they would be seen.

"Easy, sweetness" Luke soothed. "Just play cool. I got this. We were in here talking. I was helping you with your dress."

The commanding thrum of his voice, sure and steady, eased her slight panic. She reminded herself that she didn't really care who knew she'd been in there. An inopportune memory played in the periphery of her mind.

228

"Easy, baby doll. I got this." An overly-confident, seventeen-year-old Luke Camden had escorted her hand in hand to the student parking lot right after first period. They hadn't gone out the gym doors or snuck out the back door near the Science labs. Nope, he'd marched her right past the front office and the lunchroom. Her daddy had gone to Lincoln for parts and they were going to skip a crappy lunch, an English quiz, and Mr. Dunlop's unending droned-lecture on the rise and fall of the Roman Empire to ride her horses all day.

Her heart had raced the same way it was currently. She heard a key slide into the lock on the office door, but the memory kept playing out in her mind.

They'd been stopped by the Vice-Principal. *"Going somewhere, Mr. Camden?"*

Luke had nodded as if walking out of the school was a perfectly normal thing to do. Always quick on his feet and smart as a whip, he supplied, *"Yes, sir. Mrs. Bowen asked us to get some ropes out of my truck. She's using them for the levers and pulleys assignment today. Indie's daddy sent in some old wheels and axels. We're getting those as well."* Miraculously, his is cocky smirk hadn't given them away.

"Oh. Well, don't be long."

"We won't. Gotta get everything back to class … sir."

And that had been that. They'd slipped into his truck and had driven away without anyone ever finding out.

The office door pushed open and Ernie and his secretary Tiffany stepped inside. Luke scooped something off the desk and shoved it in his pocket. He crossed his arms over his chest. "All I'm saying, Indie Jane, is that maybe my daddy doesn't know what he's talking about."

Indie spun on her stepfather. "We're in the middle of a discussion. Do you mind?" Pretending the other person was in the wrong. Always the way to go when you're caught.

"This is my office!" Ernie huffed. Finally, it occurred to Indie that perhaps her stepfather *was* in the wrong.

"Yes, it is. And why exactly are you and *Tiffany* up here during the reception?" Her mind spun. Guilt taunted Tiffany's chocolate brown eyes. Another memory overwhelmed Indie. The moment she'd walked in on Ernie and her mother in her parent's bedroom caught red-handed. *Oh my God. Oh my God he's doing it again!* The hair on her arms and the back of her neck stood straight. Her heart pounded somewhere in the vicinity of her throat.

Luke was behind her a half-second later. "I've got you. Breathe for me," he whispered. "That is an excellent question, Mayor. What *are* you doing up here?"

"I do not have to answer to the likes of you, Luke Camden! Just what are you two doing in my office? As if your daddy isn't bad enough, keeping tabs on everyone in town. Policing everything the way he sees fit."

"Mmm, mmm, mmm, Mayor. You know, my daddy has a sayin', 'Man who's always cryin' wolf usually has a steak in the trap.' Seems to me maybe you ought to stop worrying about my old man and start worrying about whatever's making you slither like a snake right in front of my eyes."

Indie's stomach turned. Even her cool hand Luke looked shocked. His words were calm. His threat substantial enough to make the mayor squirm, but his eyes said there was an incoming storm, one he wasn't certain he could stop.

"Whatever you think you saw in here, you didn't. Leave. Tiffany and I have some work to discuss for tomorrow. This blessed wedding cost me a fortune. Some of us have to work for our keep."

"And just what the hell is that supposed to mean?" Indie's nerves bled quickly to gall-driven fury. Was he actually insinuating that Luke didn't work for his money?

"Come on, doll baby. A man hell bent on being right won't ever believe he's wrong." Luke took her hand and guided her back outside.

"Luke! He's … they're …well … and my God, what is it with him and his secretaries? Ugh!" evulsed from her mouth as soon as they reached the living room.

"Indie, baby, are you okay?" His arms were around her again, steadying her, but she couldn't process what she'd just seen. He couldn't be doing this again. Could he?

"No. Yes. I don't know. What the hell does he think he's doing? We should go back up there. Catch them in the act."

"We don't have any proof that he's up to no good … yet. And you will under no circumstances go up there right now. I won't stand by and watch you dance with your demons. When trouble comes calling you don't have to give it a seat. Let's get back to the party." Indie was torn between vengeful longing to stick it to the mayor and terror to relive the moments that had torn her entire world apart so many years ago. Maybe Luke was right. She should just let sleeping dogs lie. And Ernie Perkins was a dog if she'd ever seen one.

Chapter Twenty-Two

Luke guided Indie back out to the reception, forcing himself to appear unaffected by all that had just taken place. He didn't want to scare her. If their illustrious mayor made his baby run yet again because he couldn't keep his half-inch dick in one woman, he swore he'd draw and quarter the bastard alive.

And what the hell did he mean by whatever they'd seen in his office? What was in there he was so afraid they'd found? Luke needed to talk to his daddy, and somehow he needed to get back in that office to look around.

The best offense was always a good defense. Coach Chalmers had beaten that into him. Luke had to know what he was dealing with. He wouldn't let the fallout of yet another mayoral extramarital affair hurt Indie. Not this time. He wasn't a dumbass kid anymore. If the mayor wanted to play with fire, Luke would make certain Indie wasn't the one who got burned.

Before he could stop her, Indie dropped his hand and jerked Miranda from the dance floor. The hissed whispers started as soon as they were out of the crowds.

Glancing back at the house, Luke let his mind wonder over all of the things he'd seen on the desk before he'd cleared it with one quick swipe of his hand.

"You, bro, look like you've been thoroughly fucked, and I'd dare say Indie Jane's hair was up in one of them fancy twist things women do, and now it's down. Gettin' laid in the mayor's mansion. Nice job. Even I'm impressed." Grant handed Luke one of the cold bottles of beer in his hand and then immediately clinked them together in an awkward toast.

Rolling his eyes, Luke refused to respond. He sure as hell didn't kiss and tell, even with his brothers.

Never needing any encouragement to keep going, Grant studied him. "Gotta say, though, it don't really seem like you. You ain't ever been the sneaking around type. You used to do whatever the hell you were gonna do right out in the open. Anybody had a problem with it they could be damned. That had to all be Indie's idea." He gestured with his beer back towards the house.

"Have I ever made your dumbass-self think that I would carry on a conversation of this sort with you?" Luke snarled. His brother was wrong. It was precisely who Luke was when he was with Indie.

231

Together, the way they were meant to exist. That hadn't all been Indie. The perfection they'd just shared was a function of them together. Only problem was, their tryst had just effectively launched them from the skillet to the fire.

A low whistle slid between Grant's teeth. "Damn. Some'um got up your craw. Figured you'd be in a better mood since you just got your rocks off."

"You figured wrong. Hey," Luke changed course, "You know anything about Dad and Mayor Jenkins' feud that I don't know?"

"What? I just spent the better part of the last half hour with some sonuvabitch from the Governor's office jawin' me ta death, and now you want to talk about taxes, too? Jeezus, I'm glad I ain't gotta get fixed up for this kind of thing too often."

Out of patience, Luke jerked Grant away from two elderly women near the food table pouring booze from airline bottles into their punch. "Indie and I got busy in the mayor's office. We were interrupted by Ernie and his *secretary* coming in. They both looked as guilty as sin. Ernie said some shit about what I'd seen in the office. Like there's something in there he'd be in trouble over if I found."

"So, that's why you're madder than a wet cat. You *didn't* get your rocks off."

"Don't make me whup your ass, Grant. You know I will."

"All right, all right. Simmer down. Geez. What on God's green earth was Ernie doing with … wait his *secretary*? Are you shittin' me? Boy don't ever branch out does he?"

"Hell if I know. I'm far more interested in what it was he don't want me seeing in that office."

"If I know you, and I do, I'd say what you're interested in is keeping Indie out of the fray if this all blows up bad enough to make a freight train take a dirt road."

"Yeah, that too."

"Well, if you wanna know what's up in that office there's only one way to find out. You are new to the sneaking around game. I, on the other hand, invented it. Let's give Ernie and his hoochie-mama a minute. Guy can't take longer than that. Ain't got the cahones for it. Then we'll go take a look-see."

Grant was right about one thing. Luke had always gotten away with shit, relying on his confidence and his mind to get him out of sticky situations. Calm, cool, and confident was always the name of his game. Grant, on the other hand, got whatever he was after by never getting caught with it in the first place.

232

"Let's get." Luke urged. "There's Tiffany now. Mayor can't be far behind her."

Grant chuckled. "I take it there's no pun intended."

"Just shut up and come on, 'fore Indie figures out I went back up there."

"All right, ease up. There's the mayor now."

"He's heading this way. You know nothing," Luke reminded his brother.

Grant gave a single nod before the mayor was upon them, dragging Clarke, the deputy sheriff, behind him. "Arrest this man for trespassing. Now. And Anna as well."

Clarke's eyes goggled to the size of horseshoes a half second before a ridiculous grin crawled across his face. Clarke had always hated Luke. He looked like the mayor had just named him king of Pleasant Glen.

Luke laughed at them outright. "Trespassing, huh? I'm thinking you're gonna have to come up with something else seeing as I'm an invited guest to this shindig, your stepdaughter's boyfriend, and your son-in-law's best man. Seems to me Indie's got more blood right to be here than you do. It's *her* sister's wedding."

"And just what is that supposed to mean?" the mayor bellowed.

"You hard 'a hearing or just dumber than a hill of beans?" Grant chuckled. "Means we ain't going anywhere."

"What's going on?" Luke's father sauntered up, looking none too pleased. Luke kept his eyes on Indie. She hadn't yet noticed the mayor's reappearance. She and Miranda had Tiffany backed up to one of the buffet tables, conducting an interrogation of their own.

"Your son and Anna were up in my office, uninvited. Like father, like son, I suppose."

Humor played in Ev's eyes as he slid a slight eye roll to Luke. "Can't imagine what was going on up there." He chuckled before returning his glare to the mayor. "That don't really seem like an offense worthy of bothering our good deputy here, so why don't you leave my son be. Melony and Tucker are getting ready to leave. I imagine you'll want to see that. And I do not take too kindly to my kids being threatened. Never have. Never will."

"Of course, the Camdens are free to come and go as they please in any man's home in the entire county. What's it gonna be this time, Everett? The founding family excuse or the largest ranch in Western Nebraska drivel you love to rub in everyone's face?"

"You know, Ernie, I got no clue what crawled up your sorry butt and died, but the Camdens got no problem with you or anyone else. We sure as hell don't go around blabbing about how much land we own. We ain't got time nor desire. Nobody but you seems to give two hoots about the fact that my great-granddaddy's great-granddaddy founded this town, or who owns the most land. You're the only crowbait horse in this pissin' contest. Go on and give yourself a blue ribbon 'cause nobody else gives a half-holler. And quite frankly, I'm sick to death of hearing' about it."

Luke and Grant duplicated their father's stern expression.

Ernie narrowed his beady eyes. "Someday, Ev, I'm gonna figure out a way to show this entire town that we don't need the likes of the Camdens to survive."

"See, that's just it, Ernie. You stupidly seem to believe the town cares what you think. Our land sits where it sits whether the town's here or not. It was there for generations before you and I ever came to be, and it'll be there when my great-great-grandbabies are running it. One ain't got nothing to do with the other. What is your deal with wanting to own everybody's land anyway? Pick another fight. Seein' as you're the only one climbing in the ring, you've already lost."

Ernie's entire being was scalded red and puffed up like a tick about to burst. His toupee had shifted oddly, covering more of his right ear than his left. Refusing to meet Ev's eyes, he scanned the crowds until he located Tiffany. Miranda and Indie still had her trapped in a conversation she surely didn't want to be a part of.

"You and your sons can go straight to hell, Ev Camden. You've gone too far this time." With that, he slithered away, presumably to rescue Tiffany.

"Dad, what the hell? He's crazier than a Junebug in Ju-ly." Grant leapt as soon as Clarke walked away, obviously disappointed.

Ev rolled his eyes. "I wish I knew what exactly started all of this." They watched Ernie's path be intersected by Carolyn, who was fit to be tied over something, naturally. "You remember your granddaddy used to say biggest thing in a small town are the secrets it holds?"

"Yeah." Grant lowered his voice. "Luke thinks Ernie's stepping out on Carolyn with his new secretary. You think that's what this is all about?"

Disgust hardened Ev's chiseled features. "No. It's more than that."

"What did he mean when he said 'like father like son' when he was talking about me and Indie bein' in his office? And what was all that about land? You know more than you're saying, Dad. Spill it." Luke honed in on the pieces of the conversation that might hold a clue as to what the hell Ernie Perkins was so terrified the Camdens knew.

Guilt tensed in his father's kind eyes. "Couple years ago, your mama and I decided to try anything to get Brock back up here. She knew there was some reason he wouldn't come back to visit. We'd been worried sick about him for years. I thought he was ashamed my good for nothing brother was his daddy and about what had happened when he was a kid. She knew it was something more.

"I started trying to figure out if I got the opportunity how I could give Brock back the land that was rightfully his. That's when I discovered that Ernie was trying to fix it so generational land was taxed to both parties twice. I wasn't having my kids being robbed blind like that. You know this. Natalie started researching. I talked with a lawyer friend of mine. Ended up at the courthouse. His secretary let me in his office. I just wanted to talk to him before I made a big stink about everything. See if I could reason with him. He wasn't in the office when she let me in, but there was a land map of the county spread out on his desk and a bunch of papers from a lawyer's office. He'd gone in and drawn up a few changes I assumed he'd like to make. Namely, to own half of Ben Harper's property, a good hundred acres of the Kilroy's place, and to cut 'bout ten thousand acres off of ours under imminent domain."

"What?!" Grant and Luke bellowed at the same moment.

"I put a stop to it. He'da never gotten it through the state anyway. Whole thing was crazy. Imminent domain on ranch land that borders nothing but more ranch land. Twenty miles from the closest road. But I *was* in his office, snooping, I 'spose. I imagine that's what he was talking about."

"So, that's what this whole thing has been about?" Luke demanded. Gall scorched through his veins. If Ernie Perkins thought he was gonna take Camden land or rob Indie's daddy of his farm, Luke would make sure he understood fully what a no-good piece of chicken shit he really was. Hell, he'd taken the man's wife. Wasn't that enough?

"I'm sorry I didn't tell you kids. I saw no reason to get you all up in arms over it. Not long after that, Brock showed up here with his sweet Hope, and I got him his land. That was all that mattered to me. I did warn Ben and Duke that he was after a portion of their farms, but Indie and Tuck don't know nothing about it, and you need to keep it that way. Ben talked to a surveyor who assured him the land was his unless he sold it." Ev shrugged. "Duke Kilroy let Ernie know he'd get Kilroy land over his dead body. I thought Ernie had dropped it."

Luke and Grant shared a quick glance. That was all it took. They were thinking the very same thing. They had to get back up to that office and figure out just exactly what it was Ernie was hiding now.

Conveniently, Sal Cartwright and one of his sons sought Ev out, giving Luke and Grant a chance to disappear. The DJ was calling for Tucker and Melony's last dance of the evening. They had to hurry. Luke didn't want Indie coming to look for him. If she found out Ernie was after her daddy's land, he'd be bailing her out of the state pen that night.

"Let's get while the gettin's good." Grant urged. With a few quick steps, they disappeared to the side of the house and entered through the front doors this time.

Luke's heart hammered against his rib cage. Cold sweat dewed on the back of his neck as they slunk through the grand entrance hall headed towards the back steps. Terror and wrath fought for dominance in his mind. He couldn't recall another time he'd felt so frantic. Foreboding doom echoed with the footfalls of his boots on the marble stairs. Cowboy boots weren't the greatest shoes for moving anywhere quietly.

Grant stepped behind him. Their gazes swept the perimeter of the house constantly to make certain they weren't being followed. When they reached the landing, Luke eased to the large picture window that overlooked the grounds. Ernie was standing with Carolyn. His simper still laced with righteous indignation, but he was making conversation with a few of the guests from the governor's office.

One of the caterers stalked through the living room. Luke and Grant tucked themselves tightly against the wall. She never glanced up the steps. When she disappeared back into the kitchen, they flew to the office door at the end of the hall.

"It's locked," Grant whispered.

With a deep breath, Luke summoned his usual calm. He'd figure it out. He always did. Digging his hand in his pants pocket, he extracted one of Indie's hair pins he'd dispensed with during their foreplay. He'd scooped it up off of the desk just a moment before Ernie and Tiffany had made their appearance in the office.

It took him less than a minute to pop the standard knob lock. They eased inside and shut the door.

"What are we looking for exactly?" Grant quizzed as he scooted to another window to spy on the reception.

"There was a newspaper and some file folders on the desk right here. They're gone."

"Ernie's dancing with Carolyn. Indie's lookin' for something. I 'spect it's you. We better get a move on." Grant glanced around the office. "There's a newspaper right here." He stalked across the room and lifted a paper from the top of a filing cabinet. "Why the hell is Ernie reading the Elk Creek Tribune?"

Forcing himself to remain calm, Luke took another detailed inventory of the office. Nothing else seemed to have been moved but the file folders.

"Elk Creek?" He'd heard something about the tiny town three hundred miles due east of the Glen. It occurred to him that if the paper was on top of the filing cabinet maybe the files were nearby. Using Indie's hairpin once more, he popped the lock on the top file drawer. "Wasn't that the town that they're mining for rare earth minerals or something?"

"No idea. You want me to keep reading this or start going through drawers?"

"No need to go through any more. I just found the files."

"Was in a hurry to shove 'em somewhere, wasn't he? Dumbass." Grant shook his head while Luke extracted a stack of file folders haphazardly stowed in the drawer and handed half of the stack to Grant. "Hey, look here." There was a letter-sized county land map in the top of one of the folders. A red box was drawn around the east side of Ben Harper's farm and around approximately ten thousand acres of Camden Ranch right where Luke's land met Grant's on the southern border.

"What are you up to, Ernie?" Luke murmured as he continued to dig through the file folder. Grant started in on another one. Under the map was a lengthy letter from the Mineral Resources Data System. Luke's brow furrowed as he continued to dig. Surely, Ernie wasn't dumb enough to think Pleasant Glen could become Elk Creek.

"Uh, Luke …" Grant's normally deep, steady voice shook violently.

"Shh." Luke continued to study. He spread out the papers and maps on the desk, certain that what he thought he was seeing couldn't be true.

"Luke, man … uh … you need to see this."

"In a minute. Holy shit. He thinks there's oil on Ben's land. Some surveyor convinced him that there might be lines down flowing from Buffalo Gap."

"Luke, you have to see this! Now!" Grant shoved the file folder in his hands.

"Wait, what the hell does he think is on my land?"

"Bro, it doesn't fucking matter. Read this!" His finger landed on a printed email from what appeared to be a lawyer's office in Rapid City, South Dakota, probably working with the surveyor who was claiming the possibility of oil in Pleasant Glen if he had to guess.

Annoyed, Luke took the stack of papers from his brother. A notary-sealed document was under the stack of emails. Starting with the email, Luke's heart sank rapidly to his feet.

"This can't be real," he choked as his eyes landed on the words, *'This will need to be handled carefully. The paternity test you requested from the blood work done on Miss Melony Grace Harper when she applied for her marriage license proves that she and obviously her identical twin sister Miranda Carolyn are your daughters. As we discussed on the phone Thursday, keeping this under wraps might become difficult if you pressure their presumed father, Benjamin James Harper, for the land you wish to acquire in exchange for your silence on the women's parentage. I have included a notarized copy of a petition to change legal name and lineage to be shown to Mr. Harper, if you decide to go forward with this.'*

Vomit and bile flooded Luke's mouth. The words on the page blurred. His head spun. Blinking rapidly, he willed the words to say something, anything different. He was going to be sick.

Grant looked up from the mineral plat Luke had been studying. "So, he wants to trade his daughters for oil, assuming there is any, which there ain't. Real piece of work, our mayor. What are you gonna do?"

For the first time in his entire life, Luke's mind went absolutely utterly blank. He had no clue how to handle this, who to ask for help, and the most terrifying complication of all … what to tell Indie.

"Ben would give him the land." His voice was distanced and tunneled. He barely recognized it as his own. "He'd go along with this just to keep his girls from knowing, and that motherfucking asslicker knows that."

"Yeah, nobody'd ever deny that Ben Harper is the salt of this earth, man, but you have to tell Indie. You can't keep this from her."

"I can't. I just … can't." She would leave. He knew. She would run again, certain she was alone in the world. She would never stay if she found out that her precious baby sisters, the girls she'd give her life over for, weren't really her sisters.

Grant's hand cuffed his shoulder stabilizing him. "I know you want her to stay, marry her, the whole deal, and I know you're terrified this'll make her run again. I do. But you can't keep this to yourself. If she ever does find out …" he bit off the inevitable conclusion. If Luke told her, she would leave and never return. If he didn't and she found out some other way, the outcome would be the same.

His heart refused him the next beat as he tried to envision her reaction. He wasn't certain she would ever recover from this. His sweet baby. He just didn't know how much more she could endure at the hands of her mother and Ernie Perkins. All he knew was there was nothing he could say or do that would get her to become his permanently after this. Staring at the file folders like they contained a viper's den, he watched his entire life dissolve before his very eyes.

The click of boot heels echoed through the door. "Someone's coming," Grant hissed. He gathered up the folders and quickly shoved them back in the filing cabinet.

"Luke, are you in there?" Indie's voice rang through the thick suffocating air. His entire body shook.

"Okay, deep breath. I'm gonna let her in. Don't have to tell her anything just yet," Grant eased.

Somehow, the only ridiculous thoughts he could manage were that he still didn't know why Ernie wanted his land or Tuck's land, and that his Granddaddy Camden was right. At that moment, he would've given every acre he'd ever hoped to have, every head of cattle grazing in his pastures, every single thing that made him a cowboy; he would sell his soul to make certain Indie never knew any of this.

A cool rush of air accompanied Indie's appearance when the door opened. "What are you doing up here?"

"Uh …" His lungs refused him air. He couldn't speak.

"Just snooping around. Seeing what was up here Ernie was thinking you might'a found when you were making use of the office." Grant tried for a teasing tenor but didn't quite make the mark. She was onto him. A storm of suspicion gathered in her eyes.

"Well, did you find anything?"

"No," Luke's voice returned to him just in time to pound the first nail in the coffin. He lied to her.

"Tucker's looking for you. Says you need to get everyone's tuxedos before they leave."

Luke managed a nod. The knowledge that he'd promised to return the tuxes to the rental place the next day filed itself in a domino of fracturable thoughts. *Ben. Miranda. Tuck and Mel. Oil. Money. What an absolute douchebag Ernie Perkins really was. The undeniable knowledge that he'd refused to ever even consider—Miranda and Melony Harper looked nothing like their older sister. Did Carolyn know who her children's father really was? Had Ernie done this on his own or with her knowledge? Wait. That was why she was so insistent Ernie walk Melony down the aisle. It had to be. Did Ben ever suspect? And … Indie.*

"Okay," he managed as he dragged Indie into his arms. The scent of her hair steadied his breaths. If he could just freeze time in that moment, he might survive this. His arms strengthened their hold.

"Luke, what's wrong?" she demanded.

"He's worried about you." Grant certainly wasn't lying. "Uh, he told me about Ernie and the secretary chick. You know how much he loves you. He don't want you to go through all this again, darlin'."

"Oh." Indie pulled out of his grasp and offered him her sweetest smile. "I'll be fine. I always am. I cornered *Tiffany*, but I couldn't get anything out of her. It ain't like I didn't know Ernie is nothing but a piece of shit. If he's screwin' around again, maybe this stupid town will finally get rid of him. I mean," she faltered momentarily, "I feel bad for Mom. Kind of. I don't know. Can we just go? I don't want to think about it all right now."

Chapter Twenty-Three

Luke sat on the back porch of his parents' house, mentally damming the universe to hell. Indie was still in the kitchen with his mama having coffee and a second helping of dessert. At least she was eating. If he was going to have to watch her walk away again, maybe he'd finally convinced her that she was the most beautiful thing to ever grace his earth or anyone else's.

Half of him wanted to return to his mother's table and demand that she come home with him. Their moments together were inevitably numbered now. The other half was afraid to be alone with her. She knew him like no one else ever could. She'd already asked him twice what was wrong. With every lie, he hated himself more.

He'd been through every scenario he could come up with. If he confronted the mayor with what they'd found, it would only push him to go through with his plan more quickly. Ernie, technically hadn't done anything illegal. Blackmail would be tough to pin on him, since it hadn't yet occurred. Far worse, if Luke took any action at all, Indie would know he'd kept it from her and that would be the end of everything he'd ever lived for in the first place. Of course, even if he marched in there and told her now, she'd still run away. He was nothing more than a sitting duck waiting on the rat-bastard to make his move.

If there was an affair and it was revealed, Ernie Perkins would most surely be run out of town on a rail, making his desire for money all the more. Luke momentarily wondered if it had yet occurred to Indie that her family would become the laughing stock of the town yet again. Seeing as she was sitting in his mama's kitchen being loved up on instead of flying back to Oklahoma, he doubted she'd considered that as of yet.

Ev and Grant sauntered to the back deck, both eyeing him cautiously.

"Let's take a walk," Ev urged. Luke was well aware it was not really a request. He rolled his eyes.

"Not really in the mood to talk, Dad."

"Well, I am in the mood to know what's got my oldest son looking like he's either been ordered to hang at sunrise or he's lost his best friend, so walk with me."

"Pretty sure he's on his way to that last one, Dad. Ease up, okay," Grant sighed.

A single nod of understanding accompanied the shuffle of Ev's boots away from the porch. Luke and Grant begrudgingly followed.

"A week ago, I told you your mama and I would do anything in our power to help you convince your sweet Indie to stay. Looked to us like things were going just the way you wanted them to. My offer still stands, son, but I need to know what happened between this morning when you were putting her up on Summer's horse and having the time of your life and tonight."

"Grant and I snuck back up to Ernie's office after we talked to you."

"That's always a bad way for a story to start, but keep going."

"Indie and I had … uh … been up there earlier, and there were some files on the desk I saw, but when I went back they were gone, so Grant and I got to looking for 'em."

"I take it you found them."

"Yeah, we found 'em, all right." A clot of Nebraskan dirt from the worn path they were walking met the toe of Grant's boot and rolled away.

"And …?" Ev urged.

"Ernie wants Ben's land because he thinks there might be oil there, and we found a letter from his lawyer. It's kind of a long insane story, but basically …" Luke glanced back towards the house, terrified to say this aloud, "Miranda and Melony are Ernie's daughters, not Ben's."

"What?!" Ev stopped in his tracks.

"Yeah, that's what we said, too, only a lot more colorfully," Grant added.

"Dear merciful Lord in heaven. Ben and Carolyn didn't even move to the Glen until the twins were toddlers. How the hell long was she having an affair before Indie walked in on them?"

"No idea." Luke longed to drive his fist into something, anything that might turn the horrendous emotional toil into a physical pain that could be dealt with.

Ev shook his head. "And now you know and Indie Jane don't know and when she does know …."

"Luke's afraid she'll run away again."

"She will." Luke saw no reason to hold onto some ridiculous hope that she wouldn't. The outcome was inevitable. Time was the only variability. There was no way out of his only life, and time slowed for no one.

His father cuffed his shoulder and gave it a consolatory squeeze. There really was nothing he could say that would make this different, and he knew it.

"You know, Holly was near 'bout four years old when she grabbed the wrong end of the branding iron on my watch. She still has a scar on her palm, and I still have a scar on my heart. I'll never forgive myself for not catching that little hand before it got to that iron.

"Took me 'til Austin was fourteen and damned and determined to kill himself on a bull to understand that I couldn't keep my kids from getting hurt in this life. He shattered his ankle and shin that summer, and I would'a given anything to be the one trying so hard not to cry laying on that gurney in the emergency room. But I couldn't be. He had to hurt, and I had to watch and that just never did seem right to me. If I can hurt so you and Indie don't have to, son, I will. If you need to leave our land to have her, then that may be what you have to do."

Luke was too far gone to even feel the shock of his father's words, but he tried to absorb the love and the sacrifice he was being offered. "Thanks, Dad, but it won't matter. Soon as she finds out I knew and didn't tell her even for a second, she'll never trust me again. She's been hurt too many times. She doesn't trust anyone. Never really has."

"Never say never, Luke. A woman who opens her heart to you while it's still broken is braver than any person you'll ever meet. Indie did that for you, and you have no idea what else she's capable of. Maybe you should go tell her now. If you knowing and not talking is gonna be her undoing, go talk."

"I got no earthly idea how to tell her Mel and Miranda aren't her full sisters. They've always been her anchors. She took care of them and … hell, I got no idea how to tell Tuck he married Melony Jenkins, not Melony Harper, but somehow I gotta figure that out, too."

"I'll tell ya God's truth, their *mama* ought to be the one telling all of 'em."

Grant and Luke made grunts of agreement.

"I'll tell ya this, too, Indieanna's always been a wild hurricane of a girl. Powerful, beautiful in her might, with a few weak spots that she's always tried so hard to protect. Problem with all of that is she needs someone … no, she needs *you* … to remind her to breathe, son. She gets whipped up in her own winds and ends up drowning in her own storm."

"She don't need me. It's me who needs her. 'Sides, she wasn't ever looking for a hero. She was always looking for a weapon." Luke turned back towards the house like he was being beckoned by a siren's song.

His body ached with what he should do and what he somehow knew he wouldn't. Weakness pervaded his soul. Helpless to resist, his traitorous boots led him back to his parent's porch, back to her.

Time was now fractured, marked, and measured, from this moment on. It fell in two distinctive pieces. Before she left and after. It might've worked as an analogy for his heart, but he'd existed without her often enough to know that his heart always remained intact — it just wouldn't exist within its rightful cage. It abandoned his body to run with her each and every time she left. His chest remained hollow and void until the next time she returned to him. This time there wouldn't be a return. He doubted she'd ever even fly over the Lincoln County line again. It would be far too painful. He'd never ask that of her.

"You ever gonna tell me what's wrong?" Her soft voice speared through him. There she was, waiting on him.

"Yeah. I will. But not tonight, okay? Please. I don't want to think about it anymore. Can I just have tonight?"

"You can have whatever you want Luke Camden, but you can't hide things from me. I know something fucked you up bad."

Yeah. Life itself. "Didn't you used to tell me all the time that the whole damn world's fucked up, sugar?"

"Yeah, I did, but I'm not so sure that's the case anymore?"

"Oh yeah?" He held his hands out as she jumped from the porch railing into his waiting arms.

"Well, maybe. I mean I endured a whole crazy, Carolyn-filled day, and I survived without hitting anyone. And I did it because I was with you. Maybe Pleasant Glen isn't all that fucked up. Maybe just the mayor is, and maybe I could survive back here as long as I'm in your arms."

His breath vaulted from his gut like he'd been sucker punched. She'd just twisted the knife in his chest and she had no clue. All he was capable of in that moment was holding her to him and praying that somehow her body pressed to his chest would ease the stab wound.

She lifted her head to study him. "Bet I can make you smile. Let's go back to your house."

Cradling her precious face in the strength of his palm his lips sought hers, the only drug that could ever erase the pain. When he kissed her, he swore he could somehow taste the rest of his life. Every single thing he'd ever wanted, every single thing he'd ever hoped to be, the only life he ever wanted to live was penned in the delectable flavors of her mouth.

244

He *was* a man slated to hang at dawn. His tongue sought hers. This might be their last kiss. She wanted to be taken to his bed. The last time he'd have the honor of worshipping her.

They stumbled up his front steps. He tried to memorize that intoxicating grin on her beautiful lips, when he lifted her into his arms, and the scent of her hair. Memories would be all he got to keep. He had to tell her. And this would be the last time he held her this way, the last time he would exist within her, the only way he'd ever wanted to be.

Standing her by his bed, he wished for the millionth time that he could freeze time right here, right now. Her hands sought the hem of his shirt in a rush of need. He caught them.

"Slow down, sugar. We got all night, okay?" His voice shattered. They had *all* of only one night.

"Luke, what's wrong? Just tell me."

Gently, he laid his index finger across her lips. "Not now. Just be with me. Just be right here with me tonight."

He lost himself in a whirlwind of their past and their present. The future no longer belonged to him. His future existed only with her.

Lacing his fingers through her soft hair, he forced himself to remember the way it felt when he crushed it in his hands. The sweet sighs she made. The way her curves melded against his body as he laid over her.

His heart hammered rapidly against her chest as he buried the pain deep inside of her. He longed to make it disappear entirely.

"I love you, Indie. God, I love you so much," he managed on his first full thrust.

Out and in. Desperate to delay the inevitable ending. He slowed and relished the feeling of fitting her to him. God, it was so unfair. Why, why couldn't he have her? He swore on his next thrust he'd give up anything to have this forever.

Chapter Twenty-Four

Luke slowed his death march to the barn the next morning, angry and raw from leaving Indie sound asleep in his bed so he could go do chores.

"Hey, man, we moved your bulls already, and we'll work your calves today. You go on back and get in bed with Indie," Grant offered him a kind smile. Brock and Austin nodded their agreement.

"For what it's worth, Hope says to tell you everything will work out," Brock offered tentatively. His wife had Gypsy heritage and frequently made predictions of this nature. Luke had never thought too much about them. He wasn't certain if they ever came true, and just then he couldn't find it in himself to care. What did *working out* even look like? Certainly not a wedding, babies, and a life on his ranch. That wasn't even a fathomable option anymore.

"Thanks," he managed. But he had no real desire to return home. That would only hasten the confession, only expedite his own end.

A few minutes later, he stood in his bedroom staring at her beautiful curves cocooned in his sheets. Her long auburn hair painted across his pillows. Her bare ass exposed where she'd kicked the covers off of one leg, and her cleavage tempting him in an image of perfected feminine seduction.

A rock-like enclosure cinched around his throat. God, he'd always hated Carolyn Jenkins for the way she treated his baby, but he'd never hated anyone the way he despised her good-for-nothing, piece of shit husband. Vengeance stirred temptingly through his veins. When you were fighting a battle you'd already lost you might as well go out in a blaze of glory. There was nothing keeping him from beating out his fury in the mayor's face. Clarke could arrest him. At least someone would be happy.

Before he could execute his plan, the shrill ring of his cell phone shattered the relative peace of his room.

Indie rubbed her eyes and sat up as Luke quickly answered just to shut the damn thing up.

"Luke!" Aaron Andrews, the bartender from Saddleback's, voice pled.

"Hey, man. You okay?" Luke had received numerous phone calls from Aaron since he'd taken up residence in the Glen. Most of the time it was to come check on the dogs, but sometimes the meds and the counseling just couldn't erase what the guy had been through.

"No. Something's wrong. I heard ... I don't know ... gunshots. I freaked and returned fire. I don't know what happened until a few seconds ago. I blacked out or something. And now ... Lulu she's not ... she's not okay. I don't know. Help me."

Lulu was Aaron's Black Lab. For months, she'd been all he lived for. He'd blacked out after hearing gun shots, probably from hunters near his property despite the posted signs that there was a veteran suffering from PTSD living nearby.

"Okay, Aaron, deep breath for me. Can you count for me?"

Aaron complied. "One, two, three ...."

"That's it. Just keep counting for me. I'm on my way. I'll take care of Lulu. Okay? I promise. That's it. Keep counting."

"Who was that? Why did you tell them to count?" Indie was already pulling on her jeans.

"It was Aaron, from Saddlebacks. He's not okay. Every time he hears gunshots he has flashbacks. I've got to go check on him. I'm sorry, baby, you can't come with me. I never know what I might be walking into over there. Just stay right here. I'll be right back."

Panic surged through Indie. She couldn't recall any time in her entire life that she'd ever seen Luke come unglued. He was on the verge of losing it. Something had been wrong last night and now Aaron.

"He took a platoon into battle in Afghanistan and seven men that were brothers to him didn't make it back home."

Her mind quickly recounted Aaron's story. Tears pricked her eyes. Poor guy. Luke flew out the door. Racing to the front windows of the house, she watched the dust stirred from the truck tires settle back on the ground.

Glancing skyward, she stared at the sunrise over the low prairie lands until she could see orange light every time she blinked. "Hey God, it's me Indie. I know we don't chat all that often or whatever, but uh, if you can do something that might make Luke smile today, I'd really appreciate it. I swear, no one deserves it more than he does. Oh, wait. Sorry for swearing in a prayer. Uh. Thanks." There. If Aaron and whatever had happened was okay, Luke would smile and that was really all she'd ever wanted.

Her eyes landed on the stack of tuxedos Luke had thrown on his couch. She needed something to do besides wearing out his floors pacing until he got back.

No reason she couldn't return them to Lincoln. Somehow she knew Luke wouldn't be back for a while, and she felt like going for a drive anyway. She could even stop by her daddy's on the way, maybe have coffee and get to know Diana a little better.

Lifting the hangers, she suddenly remembered that her panties were probably still in his jacket pocket. Mrs. Kilroy had lovingly packed Tucker and Wesley's tuxes back in the cellophane coverings. The other three belonged to her father, Luke, and Ernie. Scowling as she dug her hand in one of the others she came up empty in both pockets and moved to the next. Bingo. As she pulled the satin thong from the pocket, she gagged and threw it to the ground. Her heart leapt from her chest to her throat in a split second as she stared at a slick black pair of extra-small panties. "Oh my God. Oh my God. Oh. My. God."

Holding up the suit jacket, she stared at it in utter disbelief. Her father was nearing six foot five. Luke stood just an inch shorter. The jacket she was holding was for a man much shorter and rounder.

Her mother would no more wear a black thong than she would set herself on fire. White cotton ruled Carolyn Jenkins' extremely conservative world.

"Ew, ew, ew, ew, ew." She rushed into Luke's kitchen and located a pair of grill tongs that she planned to incinerate later. Next came a Ziploc bag. She managed those steps before the realization of what she was about to have to tell her own mother settled like a brick in her stomach.

After everything Carolyn had done or said to her over all of their years on earth together, Indie had never really wanted to hurt her mother. Never like this, anyway. *Someone has to tell her.* "Ernie you are a rat bastard, and I hope you burn for this." By way of the tongs, she slipped the evidence in the bag, ordered herself to woman-up, and headed to her mother's home.

Aaron was on 3,476 by the time Luke eased quietly through his front door. A Colt .45 was on the floor. He'd searched the property and found no one nearby. Despite all of the insanity going on in his own world, he reminded himself that remaining calm and cool were the only way to help Aaron through the panic attacks.

Careful not to speak or touch anything, Luke eased to Aaron's side. He was seated on the floor, dutifully counting. Blood slowly seeped from Lulu's right rear hip, near an entry wound. Buster, Aaron's Border Collie mix, circled Lulu constantly, keeping steady watch. Bile

248

singed Luke's throat. He had to move quickly to remove the bullet without sending Aaron spiraling into another horrendous episode that would surely land him back in the VA hospital in Omaha.

"Something's wrong with her," Aaron voice was terrified and childlike.

"She's gonna be okay. Just let me get my bag, and you keep counting."

"No. I'm okay now. I need to help her."

Luke highly doubted that was true, but arguing with him wasn't an option. "Uh, okay, help me get her on the table. Can you do that?"

Aaron managed a nod, ran his dirty hands over his face to wipe away the tears Luke would later swear he never saw, and gently lifted Lulu up onto the old kitchen table.

Indie slowed her car before turning into her mother's home. Old newspaper headlines recounting the previous affair, the one where her mother played the part of the mistress, rolled through her mind. For the first time in well over a decade, they didn't make her want to run. Luke was here. She could do this again. She would survive. As long as he stood by her, she'd make it.

Taking her time engaging the parking brake and climbing out of her beloved Camaro, she wondered how her mother might react. Fits of hysteria were sure to play their part. Wouldn't *that* be fun.

Ernie's car wasn't in the driveway, but Miranda's was. That was something. She wouldn't have to do this completely alone. Garnering determination, she rapped on the front door and prayed this wouldn't come as a complete shock to her mother. Maybe she already suspected or something.

The words *once a cheater always a cheater* beat in repetition against Indie's skull. She knocked again.

Miranda opened the door. "What are you doing here?"

"Where's mom?" Indie whispered.

"She's getting ready. You know that takes like twelve years. What's going on?"

"Come on. We need to talk to her before Ernie gets back from wherever the hell he is." Grabbing her sister's arm, they raced up the stairs.

"Indie, why are you back here this morning? Your stepfather is extremely irritated that you and Luke were in his private office yesterday. You need to leave before he gets back. I don't want you upsetting him again."

Quite accustomed to playing the role of the unwanted, Indie let the disdain roll off her back, this time with a little effort.

"I really could not care less that Ernie is upset, Mama. I honestly couldn't. Do these happen to be yours?" She held up the makeshift panty bag.

"What on earth?" Carolyn and Miranda both stared at Indie like she'd sprouted two additional heads.

"I found these in Ernie's tuxedo jacket. If they're not yours, and I'm pretty sure they aren't, I think you might want to call your lawyer."

Miranda's mouth hung open for a full minute before she slapped her hand over it.

Carolyn, however, rolled her eyes. "That is ridiculous, Indieanna. I suppose this is like the time you glued your stepfather's hairpiece to the counter or backed over his best putter with your father's car, hmm? Still trying to get back at us for ruining your life or whatever it is you're so convinced we did."

Gall flooded Indie's chest. She narrowed her eyes and tried with all of her might to keep her temper in check. There was a first time for everything, she reminded herself. "No, Mother, it is not like those times. I'm not trying to hurt you. I'm telling you that your husband is cheating on you."

"With that Tiffany chick," Miranda vowed.

"Tiffany?" Her mother actually chuckled. Dear God. Indie was going to kill her. "His secretary. Really, Miranda. This is ridiculous."

"Mother!" Indie erupted. "*You* were his freaking secretary and he cheated on his wife then with YOU! My God, would you really rather believe him than us?"

Spite clouded Carolyn's pine green eyes. Indie recognized the look all too well. It was like staring into a mirror. "You know, I have put up with just about enough of you, Indieanna Harper. I'll have you know that I share something with Ernie his first wife, and most certainly *Tiffany*, will never share with him."

"Oh yeah. What's that?" Indie spurned her on.

"Children."

"What happened to her?" Aaron asked this continually. "I don't understand what happened to her."

"Not sure," Luke lied. "But we're gonna get her fixed up, okay? Just keep breathing for me. She's doing great."

"But I don't understand what happened to her."

250

"I know." Opening the wound further to clean it and repair the damaged muscle tissue, Luke searched for the bullet. He prayed it wasn't in her bladder or reproductive organs. If there was internal bleeding, it was highly unlikely he'd be able to save Lulu.

There it was. His heart thundered out its thankfulness and his shock. A bullet had lodged in Lulu's hip bone, but it wasn't from a .45. It had come from a much smaller gun. When he finished here, he'd be going to the sheriff's office. Whoever fired the gun had some explaining to do. For now, the bullet had to come out if he was going to save her leg and her ability to run. She was a hunting dog by breed. Lulu loved to run almost as much as she adored Aaron. She'd survive, but he hated to leave her without a limb.

Two veterinary nurses, a Navy psychologist, and an actual degree would've come in real handy just then. Since none of those were readily available, determination set his jaw. He'd get this done, but it was going to be a couple of hours. He just needed Aaron to hang in there with him.

As if it had been written in some horror movie script, when Indie finally managed to make some sense of what her mother had just confessed, Ernie marched into the master bedroom carrying papers. He was followed by two men in designer suits.

Willing her heart to locate some kind of steady pulse, Indie tried to order the tears burning her eyes away. She lost the fight when her father slunk into the room with red-rimmed, horror-stricken eyes of his own.

"Daddy." She raced into his arms. How could any of this be true? It just couldn't be.

"If you want to cry and blame someone, Anna Harper, you blame that snooping boyfriend of yours. If he hadn't found this yesterday, I might've decided not to go through with all of this. As it stands, he's left me no choice. I'm certain he informed you that your sisters are merely your half-sisters. Your father has willingly agreed to sign over his land to me so I won't be announcing this to the papers. Your work here is done," Ernie sneered viciously.

"What?!" Indie jerked from her father's grasp. This had to all be some kind of horrible nightmare. None of it could actually be true.

Silent tears leaked down Miranda's face. "No. No, you will never ever be anything to me but the asshole who married my mother. You will never, ever call me your daughter. Do you understand that?" She replaced Indie in Ben's arms. "Never!"

"Ernie, why on earth are you prattling on about Ben's land? No one wants that godforsaken piece of property. It's not even in the best part of town," Carolyn disdained.

"Hush up, Carolyn. I have our divorce papers here." He jerked something else out of one of those folders.

Indie's mind was on life support. She couldn't make sense of anything going on around her. "Daddy, you are not giving him your land. What is he even talking about?"

"I don't want to put you all through this, baby girl. I don't need nothing but my girls. All of them." Ben brushed a kiss on the top of Miranda's head. She strengthened her hold as tears continued to shudder violently through her.

"Put us through what? We already know now," Indie shrieked.

"Any of it."

Indie turned on her stepfather, her temper making a rapid recovery though the rest of her was still adrift at sea. "You are nothing more than a coward asslicker of the lowest degree. You aren't even worth the gunpowder it would take to blow your ass to hell, though that is precisely where you belong. Daddy may not want to tell the town about all of your affairs, but I will. I'll tell them all. Every single one of them. Your days in the Glen are numbered, Ernie. Go pack up your precious desk."

"And you have always been a fat-ass brat put on this earth to gall me. Unfortunately, this time, I'm certain you're right. I've no doubt Luke went straight to his father with all of this when he discovered it yesterday. I've phoned Tucker and Melony to inform them that they aren't actually married since her name is incorrect on the license."

"Wait. What? Luke knew about all of this?"

"My word, you're fat, and stupid, too. I've said that repeatedly. Found one of those stupid hair pin things stuck in the file cabinet drawer. I feel certain it was yours since you two were up there snooping yesterday."

Suddenly, everything she never wanted to understand made perfect sense. Her aunts' disdain. Her mother's hatred. Why she looked nothing like Miranda and Melony, the Double Mint twins.

"Daddy, Indie's right. We'll tell everyone. You aren't giving him your land. I won't let you. Why does he even want it anyway? None of this makes any sense, and I don't care what Mama says or what any blood test proves. I'm not his little girl. I'm your little girl," Miranda pled. "We'll tell the whole town, and we don't care what they think."

Indie tried to hear Miranda's voice, but should couldn't make out the words. An incessant hum shrilled constantly in her ear. Luke knew and he'd said nothing. She'd asked repeatedly. He'd said he found nothing in that stupid office. She'd made love with him the night before. He'd sworn for half of her life that he'd never lie to her, but he'd let her go on thinking whatever had gotten to him wasn't that important. He'd lied to her outright.

It was all more than she could bear. Her little sisters weren't even hers, not really. Tears streamed down her father's face, shattering what little remained of her heart. Her mother's constant derision her entire life was because Indie *was* the unwanted child. All of the air in her lungs seized. She couldn't breathe. She could see through the hot tears scalding her eyelids. Acid churned in her stomach. Her head spun. Only one thing made sense. She had to run. Running would make her body breathe again. She had to save herself. She had to survive. It was all she'd ever known how to do.

"Indie, baby, please don't ...." her father's plea closed in around her throat as she flew out of the room. The echo of her own footsteps down the stairs sounded foreign, but at least she could hear them when she was far enough away from that room.

The roar of her engine jolted her back to life. How could he have done this? Maybe she didn't know Luke at all anymore. It had only been a week. And the most important secret there would ever be, he'd kept from her.

An hour later her body jerked spastically when she crossed Kansas state line. She was never going back.

Aaron was having more and more moments of clarity. Luke held his breath and gently wiggled the bullet back and forth to work it out of the bone. His cell phone rang in his pocket, and he almost dropped the bullet.

Cursing under his breath, he forced himself to focus.

"Want me to answer that?" Aaron was desperate to help some way. This work was too precise to let be of much assistance.

"Hey, you know what my brothers do for me sometimes when I'm working on one of our heifers and someone calls?"

Aaron shook his head but was now fully focused on Luke. His eyes and breathing were steady now. This was all going to be fine. Luke told himself this repeatedly.

"They answer the phone and hold it up to my ear for me."

"You got it." Aaron answered. "Hey Tucker, yeah, Luke's working on Lulu for me. I'll hold the phone for him."

Why the hell was Tuck calling him from his honeymoon suite at some fancy-ass hotel in Lincoln? They were supposed to be there all weekend.

With the bullet out, Luke began checking for any bone fragments that needed to be removed, but Lulu was out of the woods.

"Tuck?" he quizzed.

"What the fucking hell is Ernie talking about? Melony's his daughter my left boot. I swear, when I get there I'm gonna kick his ass."

"What?" Panic rocketed up Luke's spine. "How the hell did you hear about that?"

"What do you mean how the hell did I hear about it? Bastard called my cell at five fucking thirty in the fucking morning on my wedding night to inform my wife that she ain't actually my wife since her name's wrong on the wedding certificate or some dumbass shit. I swear, I'm gonna kill him."

Keeping his gloved hands in Lulu, Luke swallowed back vomit and bile. Ernie had gone through with it. Holy shit. He'd done it, and there was no going back. Luke hadn't even kissed Indie goodbye when he left and now …

"Tuck, I gotta go. I'm sorry about all of this. I'll call you later. End the call, Aaron."

Aaron complied.

"Okay, now can you call Indie for me. She's the first one on my favorites list."

"Sure thing."

Luke listened to her cell phone ring endlessly with no answer.

"Hey, Luke, are you okay? You don't look so good. Lulu's gonna be okay, right?"

"She'll be fine. Just let me finish," he managed. His life was over. No reason he couldn't save the dog's. "Uh, could you try to get Ben Harper on the phone for me." For some reason he needed someone to say the words, 'she left' out loud to him. Damn his heart and his hopefulness fully to hell.

He stayed with Aaron until Lulu woke from the anesthesia. When Luke heard her bark and made sure she could hobble around on the bandages, he left to go face whatever hell Ernie Perkins had rained down on everyone's lives.

254

Locating Tucker and a weeping Melony out on Kilroy farm, he got partial bits of the story.

"Clarke arrested Ernie." Tucker cringed and then eased Melony onto Wesley's shoulder. Bewildered but willing, Wes patted Mel's back and let her ruin his shirt. Tucker led Luke out onto the front porch.

"Arrested him for what?"

Tuck's eyes were still spinning. Luke doubted he'd gotten much sleep the night before. "What do you mean *for what*? For attempted extortion, blackmail, abuse of power, a whole bunch of other shit. Apparently, he was under some delusion that Pleasant Glen could be like that little town where they found all that niobium, whatever the hell that is. He was looking to get rich. When nobody would sell him their land he went about trying to find ways to take it. That's what he was doing out in my cornfield — looking for mineral deposits. According to Sheriff Wilheim, his plan was to tell me about Mel being his kid, and he figured I'd keep that from her, so to keep him quiet I'd give him a few of my fields. I didn't get a chance to point out to the dumbass that corn won't grow if there's hard rock under 'em. There's nothing but dirt out there."

Luke attempted to rectify everything he'd just learned. Nothing would compute. All he really wanted to know was if Indie was all right.

"Luke," Melony's timid voice beckoned him.

"Yeah?"

"Miranda said Indie left. She ran away again." A harsh swallow of raw emotion took her breath for a moment. Tuck eased beside his wife, letting her recover in him. "It's none of my business I guess. It's just … Indie needs you. She's always needed you. She wanted you to come after her when she left when you were in college, and … you didn't. I just think you should this time."

"I was thinking the same thing. Just not sure she really wants me anymore. I flat out lied to her over and over again last night." Luke admitted.

"Yeah, I know. When she calms down she'll understand that trying to tell anyone that would be really difficult. She loves you so much. Just try. Please."

"I will." He doubted there was a chance in hell that she'd even speak to him after this, but he had to try. He'd give up everything he was or ever hoped to be to have her, even his home.

Chapter Twenty-Five

Ben Harper was sitting on his front porch when he finally made it to the ranch. He longed to go get J.J. and drive him all over every acre of Camden Ranch so he could memorize it all over again. He never wanted to forget the land that had raised him. But there was no time. He had to go.

"You look about as good as I feel," Ben tried for a joke.

"I'm so sorry, sir. Really."

"I know you are, son. I didn't say this when you called me, but I'm gonna speak my mind now. My little girl needs you."

"I've been calling her all day. She ain't answering. I'm gonna go after her."

"I was hoping you'd say that, but you and I both know keeping something from Indie probably wasn't your best move. I can't say as I blame you. I mean, how the hell do you announce some'um like that? Just gonna take some big talking to get her to listen."

"Can I ask you something, Ben? It's kinda personal." Luke had no idea why he wanted to know, but his nerves were shot and this was by far the worst day of his life.

"Yeah, I suspected all along. Never really mattered to me though. I love 'em all just the same. Carolyn and Ernie dated when we were in high school. I thought she was good lookin' so I asked her out after we graduated. They'd broken up 'cause he was cheating on her even back then. Uh, Indie wasn't ... planned. We weren't married 'til she found out."

A forcible collision of terrorizing thoughts scrambled Luke's mind. Holy hell, she could be pregnant. She might be carrying his child now, and he'd let her run away again because he'd been too chicken to tell her what he'd found in that motherfucker's office. And now he was sitting there talking to her dad. He had to move. Now.

His father was right. Indie had always been a storm, the most beautiful storm in the entire world. But she wasn't the kind of storm you ran from. She was the kind you chase.

"I'm leaving now," he declared startling Ben.

"You mind if I come with ya, son?"

"Get in the truck. We ain't stopping 'til we're in Oklahoma City."

"That's what you should'a done back at the fancy school she followed you to. Right there is that fire she's after, Luke. You just gotta show that to my girl."

Ev Camden watched his son's truck fly up his driveway. His gut clenched. He knew what was coming. Hell, he'd told him to go, but that would never make watching your child leave home any easier. Luke was made to be a cowboy. He'd be miserable in any city anywhere. Ev wanted nothing more than to watch Ernie Perkins burn for all of this.

When Luke leapt from the cab, Ev's stomach churned. A weight settled on his chest he wasn't certain would ever leave.

"Dad, what you said last night about me leaving the ranch. I've got to. I'll try to come back in a few weeks and help you sell off my steers."

Shaking his head, Ev focused on the business to keep the pain at bay. "Don't worry about it, son. We'll take care of it all. Just go get your Indie. That's the way it's meant to be."

Luke's firm jaw trembled, betraying his own horror over leaving. "Would you mind tellin' Mama for me? I don't want to see her cry."

"Uh, yeah, okay. Maybe give her a call when you get there tonight, though."

"I will."

When his oldest son's arms closed around his chest, it was all he could do not to break down. "Take care of yourself, son. You know your mama and I love you more than life itself."

"I know, Dad. I never wanted it to be this way. I thought I could get her to stay this time."

"Life don't always work out just the way we want it. It will work out one way or another though."

Luke managed a single nod before Ev watched him take a visible inventory of the land that had raised him.

With a wave, he headed back to the truck and drove away.

"Well, they up and ran a second edition of the paper. Would ya look at that? Ernie Perkins behind bars. Never thought I'd see the day. I may frame this," Jessie handed the paper to Ev. "Luke goin' after Indie?" She gestured to his truck, just visible down the long dirt road that led off of Camden Ranch.

"Yeah, honey, he is. Said to tell ya he loves you, and he'll call tonight."

"If he hurries, they might make it back by tomorrow morning."

Confused, Ev took his wife's hands. "He ain't coming back, Jess. Not tonight. Not ever."

"What?!"

"I told him he needed to be with Indie. That we understood."

"You told him what?"

"He's planning on settling in Oklahoma City with Indie, assuming she takes him back, which I 'spect she will."

"Everett Camden, I've a good mind to take my fryin' skillet to your head. Why in God's name would you tell him that? They both belong here on this ranch. This is their home. It always has been. Why do the boys always talk to you and not me? Ain't got sense God gave geese the whole lot of ya. Go get your truck."

"Where are *we* going?"

"*We* are going to get my children and to bring them home."

"Can we come too, Mom? We kinda figure Luke's gonna need some help talking Indie into coming back." Holly asked. She was standing with Natalie and Miranda. Tucker Kilroy and Melony came from the other side of the porch.

"I told him to go after her and then realized it wasn't just him that needed to go get Indie. It was all of us," Melony urged.

"Ain't that the truth. Fine, we'll take my Suburban. Let's give 'em a little head start. Let Luke try it on his own 'fore we barge in and save 'em both. Told him we understood. Sweet Jesus, Everett, I swear."

The sinking sun reflected off a billboard advertising for the Colcord Riding Club Rodeo just outside Oklahoma City. The image was of a barrel racer taking a tight turn around the second barrel. "*A good friend of mine told me that I had to realize I was worth saving. Kind of like I had to figure out what I was running from so I'd know who to run to.*" Summer's words quaked through Indie's weary heart.

She'd thought an hour before that she'd asked Luke not to use a condom because she wanted desperately and ridiculously to have some permanent tie to him, but that wasn't it. A baby would've been something worth saving. Indie had never really thought herself valuable enough to save. She was more screwed up than she'd ever realized. Luke deserved better, even if he had lied to her.

Her body was limp with exhaustion after the ten-hour drive. It shouldn't have taken so long, but she'd had a flat and lacked the energy to change it with any speed. Then she'd come up on a thunderstorm that had added an hour to her trip. Now, she was back home and had no more tears to cry, so she'd given herself over to the dry convulsions and hated herself for crying in the first place. Her heart just wouldn't give up the fight. *Oklahoma City will never be your home, not really.*

Luke, her father, Jessie, her *half*-sisters, and even her own mother had phoned dozens of times. Indie wasn't speaking to anyone. Pleasant Glen could just keep all of the pain it housed. She was never going back. No one there needed her anyway. Apparently, her father wasn't even going to have a home for her to go back to.

Another round of ire irked her blood when she pulled into her designated parking space outside her ancient apartment. Blinking through the residual cloud the endless tears had left scarred on her eyes, she could make out the oppressive graying sky settling over the industrial buildings that surrounded her. There were no wide open spaces here. She tried to tell herself it was fine. It always had been.

Half of her belongings were at Luke's. The other half still at her daddy's. She was going to have to at least replace her toiletries at some point, but just then all she wanted was to collapse in her bed and pretend her world hadn't actually ended that morning.

As soon as she stepped into her tiny kitchen, she officially figured out that you never really get just what you want. The rest of Summer's adage tumbled through her head. What she'd been running from was currently sitting at her kitchen table and what she'd always wanted to run to was five hundred miles the opposite direction.

"Mother, what in God's name are you doing here?" She clutched her heart that had been beating sluggishly all damn day, right up until the moment she discovered that she wasn't alone in her apartment. "Better question — how the hell did you get *in* here?"

"Your landlord let me in. I told him I was your mother." Despite everything, it seemed Carolyn hadn't lost the trilling disdain she used when speaking to Indie.

"Got to move somewhere with higher security. Okay, now back to my original question — *why* the hell are you here?"

"Well ... I mean ... isn't it obvious?"

"Uh, no, no it isn't obvious, and I've had a really shitty day, so if you could spill it and then ice it with how the hell you even know where I live, you can leave, and I can get on with enduring the rest of this life I have no choice but to live." Edging her mother to the side, Indie slammed her keys and purse down on the kitchen table. "Still waiting, Mama."

"Obviously I know where you live. I send you Christmas cards. And those horrible people put my Ernie in jail. They made me leave the house. I had nowhere to go. I phoned to tell you my plane would be landing at three. I thought you might actually put forth a little effort and pick me up at the airport. I decided I'd come visit you until Ernie gets this whole mess straightened out and that ridiculous town figures out how much he did for all of them."

Indie lifted her head, and in that moment caught a glimpse of herself in the mirror the tenants before her had left hanging on the wall over the sofa. She'd avoided looking in it the entire time she'd lived there, but hadn't bothered to take it down.

The image reflected back at her caught her off guard. Suddenly, she looked nothing like her mother. Her eyes were swollen and red from crying, but there in the deep green depths she saw something she'd only concisely noticed once before. There was enduring strength and stamina. There was empowered vitality, and with her next blink that cleared a little more of the haze of emotion she saw her own power and her own beauty. The last time she'd been forced to look at herself in a mirror it had been under Luke's urging. Now, she forced herself to really note every single thing penned with indelible ink on her soul. Turning to stare at her mother, she forced herself to notice all of their many differences instead of focusing on their identical eyes.

"Those horrible people?" She shook her head, almost angrier at herself than her mother ... almost. "Those horrible people? That's who you're blaming for all of this? You are standing in my apartment because your husband is in jail and you have no home and blaming Pleasant Glen?"

"I blame Tucker Kilroy most of all. I told your sister she had no business marrying the likes of some lowly farm boy with no prospects at all. And she's such a pretty thing. It's a waste. Anyway, Tucker had that ridiculous sheriff and his lackey deputy in my home charging Ernie with blackmail and extortion or some other nonsense. All over that ridiculous land your father owns."

"Oh, I see. You got scared, and you were embarrassed, and you ran away. We're so much more alike than either of us would ever care to admit, but that stops right here and right now. I have a choice. God, why did I never understand that before? I've always had a choice *not* to be like you. I have the power to be whoever I want to be, and I'm not going to continue to make the same mistakes.

"And, you know what, I don't think you should either. I'm not going to run away anymore. Look at me, Mother. Look me in the eye, because I've been screaming and yelling and raging against you my entire life, and I finally figured out that I was doing nothin' but shouting into my own wind." *'Take a deep breath for me, sugar.'* She heard Luke's calming, reassuring command in her head. The only man who'd ever understood how to make her calm and how to keep her breathing. "I'm going to take a deep breath, and stay calm this time, and you are going to listen to me.

"You are a selfish, ungrateful, bitch, Mother. There I said it. And I'm not finished, so keep your huffing and puffing down. So, you what, you screwed around on Daddy the entire time you were married, or did you give him the nine months it took to get me here? 'Cause I can assure you that as soon as I arrived you wanted to have nothing to do with either of us. Quite frankly, you and Ernie deserve each other.

"I'll tell you this, too — the people of Pleasant Glen are not horrible. They are just *people*. We all have faults, and flaws, and good, and bad, and no amount of makeup, or hair care products, or money changes what's inside of us. We all make mistakes. We all say things we wish we hadn't or don't say things and wish we had. We are all ashamed of things, or have things about us that we wish were different, but that doesn't make them — or even you — horrible.

"And it doesn't matter if you're here or in the Glen if you can't figure out how to appreciate people and how to find something *inside* of yourself that makes you smile, genuinely smile, that makes you proud when you look in the mirror, then you'll be a miserable cow for the rest of your life. And despite everything you've put me through, I don't want that for you. I don't want you to spend the rest of your life with a no-good asshole like Ernie. But I really think you need to figure out who the hell you are before you jump in another man's bed, because other than me, and Mel, and Miranda, that hasn't ever gotten you anything worth having because you were incapable of seeing what you had when you had it.

"I don't really believe deep down in your soul that you blame Tucker any more than I believe you don't understand exactly why Ernie is in jail. You're not stupid, Mom, but denial is a powerful thing. I would know. I've been swimming in it for the last decade or more. So, you want to stay here in my apartment, you got it. You get a job and take over the rent. It would be really good for you. I'll even put in a good word for you at some places around town. But I'm going back to the Glen. I'm going back to fight for the life I've always wanted and somehow stupidly allowed myself to believe that you were right — that I wasn't pretty enough or *small* enough to deserve the life that's been right there waiting on me. Because you know what? I am beautiful inside and out, and I will never, ever be small. I don't want to be small. I want to live and stop worrying about what everyone else thinks about me. I may not be pretty your way, Mama. I'm beautiful my way and that's the only way I ever want to be. I will never ever try to shrink myself to your ridiculous standards ever again.

"Will going back and facing all of this be easy? Hell no. Luke screwed up. I screwed up. I ran away ... again, instead of fighting for myself. We have a lot of work to do, but Luke and I, we're worth fighting for. I am worth fighting for. I've got my flaws. You have yours. But we are nothing alike. The one and only thing we do have in common is the power to go after what we really want, and if we don't quite get it, my God, at least we tried. No one can ask for more than that."

Her mother's mouth was still gaping in abject disbelief. Indie headed to the bedroom to pack up the rest of her stuff. The fire in her soul blazed on. She forced herself to take another inventory of her face in her dresser mirror. This time she saw something in her eyes she'd never seen before—peace. She was going home, for good this time. It wasn't perfect. Nowhere was. But it was hers, and the town had more than proven itself. With the clink of handcuffs, it had chosen her daddy over Ernie this time. All of the years she'd spent toiling in criticism and disdain of herself must've dissolved in all those tears she'd shed on the way back to Oklahoma. She could no longer locate it.

Perhaps it wasn't the future she'd always been so afraid of. Maybe it was the past repeating itself that had frightened her. Well, the past had repeated itself. Another affair involving her own mother and the mayor had taken place. There were sure to be newspaper headlines that would be hard to look at, yet again. But she'd survived. And she was going to keep on surviving. The future was hers to own, and she was going after it with everything she was.

Knuckles wrapped across her front door. Furrowing her brow, she headed back to the kitchen.

"So, you're just leaving me here? Abandoning your own mother?"

Rolling her eyes, Indie jerked open the door.

"Please don't slam that back in my face. I am so, so sorry, baby. Please, can we talk? I swear I meant to tell you I just ... I knew ... I knew you'd leave. I was a coward. I'll never keep anything from you ever again." Luke Camden, in all of his masculine perfection, was standing at her door staring down at his boots, apologizing. His voice was rough, haunted and quick. "I packed my stuff. I left the ranch. We'll move anywhere you want."

This day just continued to stun her. "You can't move off the ranch." She threw her arms around his neck, startling him as he wrapped her up in that heavenly sanctuary of muscle. "I don't want to live there without you."

"What?" He lifted his head and stared at her in rapt disbelief.

"I was just getting my stuff. Mama is apparently staying here, but *we* are going home."

"I told you she just needed to see that fire, son." Indie's father stepped inside from the hallway.

"What are you doing here?"

"Well, I thought if you wouldn't listen to him you might listen to me, and I was worried about you baby girl. Been one hell of a day. 'Sides, somebody had to tell him how to get here."

"You got that right." She exchanged Luke's hug for her daddy's. "Look at me, Luke Camden," she ordered next.

"Nothing else I'd rather look at."

"I promise no more running away. Something bad happens, we stay and we fight together. But you promise no more keeping anything from me, ever."

"You got it. I swear, Indie. Nothing ever again. I know I fucked up, but from here on, we deal with things together."

"Ben Harper, are you actually going to go through with this nonsense with Ernie? You're actually going to press charges," Carolyn made her presence known. She always did.

"You know, enough really is enough, Carolyn, and I've let you drag me and my girls through hell quite long enough. Can't remember if it was Churchill or John Wayne that said some'um 'bout if you're going through hell, keep going. Well, we're all at the end of our trip through. So, yes, I am pressing charges, and I am sorry for whatever that means for you, but there's things worth fighting for. My little girl's coming home. We have a garage to run on that land. Ernie'll have to find his fool's gold somewhere else."

"I never figured out what he thinks is on *our* land." Luke guided Indie back into his arms.

"I like the way that sounds. Our land," she admitted.

"Good."

"It's alunite, which is basically worthless, but might be the reason we couldn't get grass to grow right there beside your house. Ernie heard the word rare and stuck his head further up his ass, I 'spose." Ev Camden stepped into Indie's apartment followed by Jessie, Melony, Tucker, Miranda, Holly, and Natalie.

"Oh my gosh. What are you all doing here?" Every last remnant of fear melted away in the warm embrace she received from the entire crowd.

"We came to tell you we love you," Melony squeezed her tighter.

"And that we want you to be a part of our family," Holly and Natalie took her next hugs.

"That's right, sugar bee. I was just telling all of these youngins who've been forced to listen to Ev snore and me prattle on for the last nine hours that you cannot choose who gives birth to you, or whose bloodline you share, or whose DNA you carry. But you *can* choose your family. Blood don't make a family, Indie Jane. Love does." Jessie brushed a sweet maternal kiss on Luke's cheek and then squeezed Indie for all she was worth.

"That's right. And Jess, and I, and all of the Camdens want you to be a part of our family, sweetheart." Ev winked at her.

"And so do the Kilroys." Tucker wrapped his arm around Melony and beamed at Indie.

"And so do the Harpers." Miranda laid her head on Ben's shoulder making him grin ear to ear.

"Yeah, and Tuck's daddy is gonna be the mayor," Melony announced excitedly.

Carolyn looked as though her youngest daughter had just backhanded her.

"Pops figures Wes, and Duke, and I can manage the corn and that it was high time somebody was lookin' out for the ranchers and the farmers in a town that's nothing but ranchers and farmers," Tucker explained. "He has to run first, though."

Hot tears that Indie had been certain an hour before her body could no longer produce trickled down her cheeks.

Luke kissed them away. "I love you so much. I have always and will always love you. I'm sorry I screwed all of this up. If you want to make this official and become a Camden right now, I'll drive you to Vegas tonight."

"Stop and smell the diesel, cowboy. We ain't getting married in Vegas, and this day has gone on long enough. I do kind of wish we could go home, but let's just camp out here or get everybody hotel rooms or something."

"If you want to go home, darlin', that's where I'm taking you."

"Luke, we've been driving all day."

264

He shook his head. "My girl wants to go home and stay. I ain't stopping 'til I get her there. I told you I'll always give you whatever you need."

"I don't have any more spare tires for my car." She just couldn't help it. Arguing was in her blood. Thankfully she'd found the one and only man it seemed to thrill. His answering smirk and the lift of his left eyebrow said he wasn't too tired to take her on.

"Don't that fancy garage you used to work at stay open late? I'm putting new tires on your car, and you can quit while we're there."

There was a host of eyes all locked on the two of them. Sinking her teeth into her bottom lip to keep her comment locked away for a split second longer, she threw her arms back around his neck. "I do so like your bossy side, Luke Camden," she whispered in his ear.

He didn't conceal his answering growl as well as she'd hidden her response. A mix of groans, laughter, and eww's filled the air around them.

Chapter Twenty-Six

"You really didn't have to hit him." Indie tried desperately not to be thrilled that Jason White, TriStar Automotive's own resident douchebag, currently had the bruised, purple outline of Luke's fist on his face.

Luke was still grinding his teeth as he drove them steadily north. "Asslicker called you *Headlights*, asked if he could adjust your high beams, and then tried to grab your ass. I had every right to hit him. If the pansy-ass city-boy'd ever learned to take a punch, I could've gone several more rounds. What kind of weakling hits the floor on the first hit?"

Leaning across the console, Indie brushed tender kisses along his bruised knuckles. "The asslicking, city-boy variety."

Luke grunted his irritation. "I'm kinda sorry I got you fired … I guess."

That did it. The entire insane, unending day erupted from her heart, and she laughed hysterically in the sudden rush of freedom and the certainty that she'd overcome her own fears. "I'm not. If that was all he said to me, I used to consider it a great day. Jason is the owner's son, so he's never had anyone stand up to him. You just promoted yourself from hero to legend."

His answering grin reminded her of the prayer she'd fumbled through that morning. So she'd been the one to make him smile. Pride welled in her soul. If she got to do that every day for the rest of her life, that was just fine with her. Maybe nothing did last forever, but she was pretty sure *family* did. And she would never know if she didn't try.

The sun warmed the wakening villages along I-80. Luke rolled down the driver's side window of Indie's car, letting the cool whips of wind help keep him awake. Constantly reminding himself to watch the road, his eyes kept sneaking peeks at his precious baby curled up in the seat beside him sound asleep.

He'd blown his plan all to hell several times and still managed to get her to come home. With a nod skyward, he saw no reason not to thank whomever it was up in heaven that had made this all come true. When he'd woken up that morning, he'd been so certain she was gone and never going to return. Now, he felt like his life had just begun. What a difference a day makes.

Rubbing his hands over his face several hours later, he tried to determine what had awoken him. The afternoon sun was sinking low in the sky, and Luke didn't like the feeling that he'd slept the day away. Cowboys didn't do such things, but damn he'd been worn through when he'd finally gotten them back to the ranch. Indie had pulled off all of her clothes, slipped into one of t-shirts, and he would've followed her anywhere. As it was, she took them to bed.

Just then she appeared from the bathroom, looking partly relieved and partly concerned.

"Come here to me, sugar." He took her hand and guided her back in his bed. "What's that look for?"

"What look?"

"Indie, honey, do we need to go over my ability to read your looks again?"

"No. I just like to argue."

"Don't I know it, and don't you know that nothing gets me going like you being stubborn. But you didn't answer my question."

"Nothing really. I just started my period, and I wasn't sure if you'd be disappointed or relieved. I can't decide if I'm disappointed or relieved, honestly."

Brushing a kiss on her forehead, he nodded his understanding. "Maybe a little disappointed, but not really. We were playing with fire, and we both knew it. Might be a better idea to buy the horse 'fore we load up ten carts to pull with it, so to speak."

"I was looking for an excuse to stay. Something that would be more important that just my own happiness. I'm sorry I did that to you and to us."

"You got nothin' to apologize for, sweetness. I was lookin' for a good excuse to get you to stay. And if you study that real close-like, you can't help but figure it looks an awful lot like I was trying to trap you into staying. I'm the one that's sorry. Like I said, we knew we were playing with fire. You realizing that you yourself was the most important reason to stay is the best thing I've ever heard. You just made my whole damn life. We'll get into the baby-making business whenever we both decide we're ready." The shame that had been eating at him for the last few days eased its heavy weight.

She brushed a few kisses on his chest, making him grin, before she settled back. "We both screwed up a bunch of things, but that doesn't scare me like it used to. I feel like I finally grew up. That's weird, right?"

Chuckling, he couldn't seem to keep his lips from every part of her that he could access. "Not weird at all. 'Sides, you'll always be my sassy, foul-mouthed girl with wicked curves that go on for ten country miles, giving her locker what-for, to me. I swear, I fell for you right then, and I'm still gonna be chasing you in my wheelchair when I'm ninety. Get ready."

Her infectious giggle delighted his soul. "You won't have to chase me. I ain't running anymore, remember?"

"My God, every time you say that I swear I come."

They both dissolved together in the melodic symphony of their combined laughter.

Chapter Twenty-Seven

A week later, Luke lightly swung one end of a gathered towel around Indie's backside, caught the other end, and jerked her wet body to his as soon as she stepped out of the shower. His lips sought hers with frantic urgency. Knowing she was his forever had done nothing to quell his unending desperation for her.

"We have to get ready to go. How will Pleasant Glen High have a reunion without their famous quarterback?" she sassed.

As soon as she stopped speaking, he devoured her lips again. Grinning against his mouth, she wiggled her backside along the towel. He tightened his grip pulling her closer.

"Mmm, your bondage fetish is getting out of hand," she laughed.

"You didn't seem to mind last night. Turns me on like nothing else, having you bound at my mercy."

"Yeah, well now I have to wear that stupid bracelet thing Melony loaned me to cover that rope mark on my wrist. I'm thinking of returning the favor."

"You wanna tie me up, sugar, I'll go get the ropes. Let's do that tonight instead of going to this stupid reunion."

"I promised Cindy and Megan we'd be there. Geez, that sounds bizarre coming out of my mouth." She shook her head. "And you know Tucker'll have your hide if he and Mel go and we ain't there."

"Yeah, fine, just promise we don't gotta stay for the whole damn thing."

"We ain't even married yet, Luke Camden, and you already sound like a cranky old man."

"You know that sassy mouth gets you in all kinds of trouble. I'll get you down the aisle soon enough and that still won't stop me from filling your ornery mouth full of my cock or blistering your sexy ass."

"Promises, promises."

An hour later, Luke begrudgingly admitted to himself that it was nice to see everyone they'd gone to school with.

"So, Luke Camden and Indieanna Harper are back together again officially. Took you damn long enough, man, but it's a welcome sight I must say." Beau Riggins joined Tucker and Luke at the punch bowl.

"Well, you know what they say about sleeping with a mechanic," Tucker goaded. Luke rolled his eyes certain he knew what was coming. "They keep you well lubricated."

Shaking his head, Luke joined in the laughter at his own expense.

"I heard Indie's gonna run the shop this summer for Ben. Sasha said some'um about Ben takin' his waitress chick out to the Grand Canyon."

"Yeah, they're gettin' pretty serious. Apparently they both always wanted to camp out there. She has an old camper so they're going for it. I think Indie only agreed to run the shop so she ain't gotta help me hay, though."

"Smart girl," Tucker commented.

"Hey, how's Mel doing? That had to be one hell of a thing to find out when you're an adult?"

Luke had forgotten what a nosy motherfucker Beau always was.

Tucker's goading grin vanished. "Mostly good. Still come in and find her crying now and again. She don't want it to be true. Still won't talk to Carolyn when she calls from Oklahoma. They've added to Ernie's original charges. He's lookin' at doing time, given the fact that he was a public official and used his title to commit crimes. It's a clusterfuck for sure. Now, Ben's leaving for a while. Can't blame him, but Mel worries. We'll all be glad when the shit storm settles down." Tuck supplied way more information than Luke ever would've.

At that moment, the gaggle of women surrounding Indie and her sister broke out in hysterical laughter.

"That can't be a good sign," Beau teased. "If cowgirls are smilin', they're thinking of doing something crazy. If they're laughing, they've already done it."

Eventually Luke managed to extract Indie from the crowd and get her on the dance floor. "You look so damn gorgeous, baby. I just want to take you home." His whispered as he swayed her back and forth on the old gym floor.

"Not yet. We still haven't made out under the bleachers."

"Is that what we're waiting for? I can take care of that right now." With a quick scan of the crowd and not really caring who saw them, he led her off the dance floor and tucked them back behind the home team bleachers to the approximate location of their first kiss. The full-moon glowed through the open doors to his right just like it had that fate-filled night so long ago.

Anxious to get to more than making out, Luke leaned in just the way he'd done back then and the way he'd keep right on doing for the rest of their lives.

"Wait." She stepped back, almost hitting her head on the bleachers above them.

"I don't want to wait."

"Well, you have to." She dug in her Wranglers and pulled out the small, velvet, grey box that he'd had hidden in his bedside table drawer for far too long. His grandmother's large diamond ring shimmered in the moonlight. "You gonna marry me or not, Luke Camden?"

His heart stalled and the air in his lungs seized. "Are you … are you serious? You're ready for this?"

"I told you I'm not running anymore. I should have said yes before, but we both had a lot to learn. So, I was kind of hoping you'd give it to me now."

Wasting no time, he took the box and fell to one knee. For a moment, he lamented not having any time to plan or prepare, but then he understood he'd been preparing for this for half of his life. Swallowing down raw emotion, he reached upwards to wipe away the escaping tears from her cheeks.

"I love you so much, Indie. And I know you used to tell me all the time that nothing lasted forever, but I fell in love with you as soon as I laid eyes on you, and I just fall more and more in love with you every single day, and nothing about that is ever going to change. So, would you please do me the extraordinary honor of being my wife?"

Her chin trembled as she nodded her consent. He slipped the ring on her finger, stood, and swept her up in his arms. Raucous applause and wolf whistles echoed around them.

Startled, they turned to see most of their old classmates trying to see into the concealed space. More than happy to put on a show, he sealed the deal with a forceful kiss that robbed him of breath, of any doubt, of the pain they'd both endured on the other's behalf, and of everything that might go wrong. If she was his, that was all that mattered. The rest they would figure out together.

Epilogue

The cool October breeze whipped through the garage bay glowing orange in the setting sun.

When Indie finished re-installing the ignition switch on the Accord she'd been troubleshooting all afternoon, she rushed to slip her rings back on her finger. She hated taking them off, but working on electrical circuitry made it necessary.

She'd left them on the last time she'd switched out a generator and both Luke and her father had loudly voiced their disapproval. Staring down at her grease stained fingers juxtaposed with the glimmering diamond wedding bands, she couldn't help but grin. Being a rancher's wife wasn't so bad after all. In fact, she couldn't think of anything she loved more.

"You heading home, baby girl?" Her father lifted his head out from under the hood of the Mitsubishi he'd been working on. Indie knew he was anxious to get to Saddlebacks. Diana had been hired there permanently, and as soon as they'd arrived back in the Glen from their trip to the Grand Canyon, Ben had asked her to move in with him.

"Yeah, Daddy, in just a minute. I was gonna get the rest of those bridles if you're sure you don't mind me taking 'em."

"Your horses have been out at the ranch for weeks. Why on earth would I mind you taking the bridles?"

"I know you don't mind, I just thought I should ask. Romeo and Juliet love the ranch. They miss you, though."

"Well, seein' as how they now have thousands upon thousands of acres to roam around on, the entire team of Camden horses to keep 'em company, and my son-in-law to take good care of 'em, I bet they don't miss me too much."

"They do too. You and Diana need to come out there more often."

"Jessie's been after us to come have dinner. I was kinda tryin' to give you and Luke a little time without us bothering. You being newlyweds and all. And it ain't like I don't see you here at work every few days."

"Daddy," Indie shook her head. "Don't be ridiculous. We love having you out there."

Before she could continue to insist that her father come out to Camden Ranch more often, Aaron's ancient Ford truck eased up the gravel drive.

Ben and Indie headed out to meet him.

272

"Truck all right, son?" Ben asked anxiously. Indie knew they were both more worried about Aaron than his truck.

The broad grin on his face when he leapt from the driver's seat set Indie's mind at ease.

"Truck's great, Mr. Harper, and I'm good, too. I promise. Been going to those meetings at the library in Ogallala for veterans. They're helping. Listen, Indie, Luke and Nat invited me to dinner out at the Camdens tonight. I found this on my way over, and I thought if you approved maybe you and I could both give Luke a gift. He's done an awful lot for me. I've wanted to get him something for a while, but couldn't think of what. I think he'd like this."

Indie was more interested in the fact that Natalie had also extended an invitation to Aaron for supper than she was Aaron getting Luke a gift. She knew Luke would never accept anything from Aaron other than his friendship. Her husband gave without any expectations that his generosity be returned. It was one of the many things she loved about him.

But when Aaron pulled a moving bundle of blankets from the front seat her mouth hung open.

"I found 'em dumped on the side of the road. Damn near about broke my heart. Look to be pure bred Beagles. They'd make good ranch dogs. I'd keep 'em, but I'm outta room and budget for dog food. I was just thinkin' Luke needs him a pup or two, even if he don't think he does."

"Oh my gosh," Indie scooped the blanket full of tiny puppies out of Aaron's arms. "I don't care what Luke says, we're keeping them."

Ben and Aaron both chuckled as one of the puppies began licking her chin.

"Maybe now you'll let Luke sell off that calf he's taking heat over you babying and keeping, or maybe you two could get to work on me some grandbabies," Ben chided.

Indie felt her cheeks heat, but she refused to confirm anything at all. "We are keeping Cassie, and the puppies, and you just remember I won't be able to fit under cars with a big belly."

"I'll wrench for you for a few months if it gets me grandbabies."

When Luke saw his beautiful wife bounding across the field with her arms full of a blanket, he knew something was up. He leapt off the tractor and headed her direction.

"Well, here comes trouble if I've ever seen it," he teased when he was close enough for her to hear him.

She stuck her tongue out at him with that same sexy-as-sin smirk that had always and would always do him in.

"You lookin' for something to lick, sugar?"

"Would you hush up and look what Aaron found." She shifted the blanket and revealed two tiny Beagle pups, both whining pitifully. "Please, please, please."

"Indie, honey," Luke's protest strangled in his throat when she placed the bundle in his arms.

"Please. Look how cute they are, and you always wanted dogs."

"Yeah, I know but ... what about what we'd been *discussing* lately." Luke glanced around to locate his brothers and sisters. They weren't near enough to hear him so he went on. "Not sure you're gonna want puppies tearing up the house and a newborn."

"Yes, but I'm not pregnant yet ... I don't think ... and even if I was, they won't be puppies by the time the baby got here. They'll be fine. It'll be perfect."

"I'm gonna remind you of that when they're baying at the moon in the middle of the night and keeping you up."

Just then one of the pups nuzzled Luke's neck and sighed as he absorbed the heat of his body. Poor thing was missing his mama. Luke's heart swelled, and he knew he might as well go ahead and wave the white flag.

"Look at that. They love you." Indie joined the puppies in their pitiful expression.

"Great, now I have three of you giving me the puppy dog eyes."

"Now I just have to train them to use their powers for good," Indie teased.

"I assume by good you mean for whatever *you* want."

"Exactly."

"It's a good thing you're so damn sexy and that I love you so much, Indieanna Camden."

"I was just thinking the very same thing."

From the Author

Coming Autumn 2016 – Holly Camden's story, *Cowgirl Education*. To hear more about Camden Ranch, my upcoming books, and giveaways, sign up for the mailing list to keep up with all the latest news.

Connect with Jillian

Visit my blog http://jillianneal.com to learn more about my writing, my family, and more.

Sign up for my newsletters and emails on my site.

Like my fan page on Facebook:
http://facebook.com/jilliannealauthor

Follow me on Instagram:
@authorjillianneal

Follow me on Twitter:
@jilliannealauth

Follow me on Pinterest:
http://pinterest.com/readjillianneal/

If you loved *Forever Wild*, leave me a review on Amazon, Barnes and Noble, or Goodreads.

About Jillian

National bestselling author, Jillian Neal, was not only born 30 but also came accessorized with loads of books and adorable handbags in which to carry them, at least that's what she tells people. After earning a degree in education, she discovered that her passion could never be housed inside a classroom. A vehement lover of love and having maintained a lifelong affair with the awe-inspiring power of words, she set to turn the romance industry on its head. Her overly-caffeinated, troupe-spinning muse is never happy with the standard formula story. She believes every book should be brimming with passion, loaded with hot sexy scenes, packed with a gut-punch of emotion, and have characters that leap off the page and right into your heart.

Her first series, The Gifted Realm, defines contemporary romance with a fantasy twist. Her Gypsy Beach series will leave you longing to visit the sultry shores of the tiny bohemian beach town, and her erotic romance series, Camden Ranch, will make you certain there is nothing better than a cowboy with a rope and a plan. The sheer amount of coffee required to keep all of those characters dancing in her head would border on lethal, so she unleashes their engaging stories on page after page of spellbinding reads.

Jillian lives outside of Atlanta with her own sexy sweetheart, their teenage sons, and enough stiletto heels, cowgirl boots, and flip-flops to exist in any of the fictional worlds she brings to life.

For more information on the author and her stories, check out her website, at http://jillianneal.com

www.ingramcontent.com/pod-product-compliance
Lightning Source LLC
Chambersburg PA
CBHW020736250626
47155CB00003B/780